SAVING AMY

by

Sarah Natalia Lee

Vanilla Heart Publishing

USA

Saving Amy

Published by: Vanilla Heart Publishing
www.vanillaheartbooksandauthors.com
10121 Evergreen Way, 25-156
Everett, WA 98204 USA

ISBN: 9780981473970

Library of Congress Control Number: 2008925739

10 9 8 7 6 5 4 3 2 1 First Edition

First Printing, April 2008

Printed in the United States of America

SAVING AMY

by

Sarah Natalia Lee

Dedication

For my dearest friends, Maggie, Kelly, and Jessica, who have always been there for me and have never given up on me, even when I let my evil side rear its ugly head.

I love you all so much.

Love bears all things, believes all things, hopes all things, endures all things. Love never fails.. --1 Corinthians 13

Acknowledgements

First and foremost, I would like to thank my darling mother and father for reading to me every day and ensuring my voracity for the written word. Also, big hugs to my stepfather and stepmother, for being so kind and encouraging to me.

I would like to thank Kathi, a dear friend of mine who set aside so much time in her busy schedule to carefully edit my work, and Maggie and Livali, my very first reviewers/editors. And special acknowledgements go out to Jessica and Kelly, two women whom I love very much and without whom this book would probably never have been written.

Thanks also to all my wonderful teachers (who shall remain unnamed for their privacy, but who should know who they are) who have helped me awaken and foster my creativity and love for art: My first through fifth grade teachers, my sixth grade creative writing, literature, and art teachers, my seventh and eighth grade English teachers, my eighth grade science teacher, my two middle school art teachers, my ninth through eleventh grade English teachers (that includes you, creative writing teacher from first semester tenth grade), my drawing/painting teacher, my beadwork/jewelry teacher, and my two wonderful stained glass teachers. Thank you so much for everything you've given me, and I adore every one of you.

A big thanks to my favorite rock group, Evanescence, whose music inspired much of the "vampiric" mood for *Saving Amy.*

A humongous thank you to my Aunt Smoky, for supporting me so much and editing *Saving Amy* so diligently.

And finally, BIG thanks and many hugs to Kimberlee, my publisher, to whom I owe the achievement of my dream.

Love, Sarah

Saving Amy

Prologue

On the eastern outskirts of the expansive city, beyond the lights aglow like a hundred tiny stars in the vortex of blackness, nesting innocently in the comforts of the small, secure neighborhood, a tiny house slept in the middle of a small yard, its white sides glowing in the moonlight. A dog barked from across the street, and a slender figure darted from shadow to shadow, quick as a cat, across the dark lawn and to the sliding glass back door, where it came to a halt and looked in the window.

The young woman was standing in the kitchen, visible in the moonlight seeping through the windows, her legs bare and strong, her curvy torso covered by a lacy satin slip reaching just past her bottom. Her long blonde hair shone as she tipped her head back and let the water pour from the crystal glass into her mouth; her arm lifted to reveal the moderately sized ridge that was her breast line. Desire oozed through the creature's mouth; this one was so perfect, so young, so sexy; he knew he must have her. He waited impatiently until she put her glass on the counter and turned toward the door.

Her crystal blue eyes locked onto his and widened; her beautiful red lips opened in surprise and she slowly lifted her hand to her throat. He smiled satisfactorily; he had her. With three graceful strides she was at the entrance, her slender fingers touching the glass, reaching out for him. She slowly unlocked the door and slid it back, letting him stealthily swoop her into his arms and carry her inside. His eyes focused on the house and dropped to the floor as his mind formed the spell; they were alone now.

She laid her head against his chest as he carried her through the house, searching for a suitable nesting place. He found a bedroom after only moments of looking; she moaned as he carried her inside and laid her tenderly upon the cool fluffy blanket. The sweet scent of mingled lavender and flesh tantalized his senses as he placed himself strategically on top of her; she let out a little gasp as one of his hands found its way inside her nightshirt to her breast. His fingers spread out on her back as his face nestled into the gentle curve of her neck, pressing into the delicate softness of her skin. A faint pulsing was detectable just beneath the dermis, and as he kissed her up and down, he found the spot he knew was his. His lips opened, his teeth dancing on the tender, virgin skin he was about to take. The points marked the spots they were destined to penetrate, the soft area behind her left ear. Unable to contain himself another moment, he rubbed her breast and buried his fangs greedily in her tender, luscious flesh.

Her screams were shrill, ear piercing, but to him they were distant, oceans away. All he knew was the prolific amount of blood gushing into his mouth as they moved, almost too much for him to handle. He wanted more than just the blood; he wanted all of her, he wanted to penetrate her, be inside of her while he drank her precious life, grew stronger from her, make her his. Maybe he would take her as his woman after she turned; it seemed like a high possibility, as he had never fed on anyone so delicious and sexually appeasing as this young woman in his arms now. The hand that was holding her breast slipped between her legs, over her underwear, and she screamed to God, screamed for mercy, as it pulled her nightdress up and began working her panties off.

"No!" she cried, thrashing and kicking as though facing the devil himself. Her strength was depleting rapidly; breathing was becoming more of a desperate plea for life every second that ticked by. Her underpants were under her knees—she felt him taking off his own pants—no, she wouldn't let him do this, she couldn't—but she couldn't stop him. She let out a cry of despair as his bare legs touched hers and his hand caressed her thighs. He was about to do it, and she couldn't stop him...

The beast yelped as a searing pain ripped over his back and through his right side. He turned to face a strong, dark-haired man of about thirty, who wielded a splintered closet rod, trying to save his love. Eyes ablaze, the enemy swooped for the man, bat-like and fast as lightning. The jagged edge of the dowel ripped through clothes and flesh once more and the beast surrendered, swooping out of the room and through the open door in the kitchen.

The woman groaned from the bed and the man approached her, his vision blurring with tears as she looked at him with that innocent, broken face.

"Oh, honey..." he breathed, reaching for her tear-stained cheek and sitting next to her on the bed. "What did he do to you?"

She squeaked in response and he ran his loving hands over her naked body, purifying the temple that had been so viciously deflowered. "Did he manage to do it?" he whispered. "Did he get you?"

"No..." she choked, her voice barely stronger than a breath. "Almost. No-no."

Tears fell from his eyes as he gently wiped the blood from her neck, revealing the punctures the monster had created. "Oh my God..." he whispered. "Could it be? Is it possible?" He ran from the room and dialed 911 before returning with a rag for her to hold over her throat.

"I called the emergency room. They're on their way. Hold this on there...yeah...like that..."

"He hurt me..." she whispered, beginning to cry.

"Oh, darling..." The man lay down and cradled the soft, broken body of his lover in his arms.

"I-I hardly know what happened..." she wept. "Just that it hurt."

"What do we do?"

"He'll come back for me," she whispered. "I know he will. He's not giving up, Rob. He loved it too much."

He looked into her eyes sadly and shook his head as sirens wailed in the distance. "We need to get out of this city."

November

Chapter One

Emma

There was nothing more they could do. It was peaceful, well, peaceful enough, and maybe after all these unbearable years, it was for the best. But her death was still like a two-ton brick of iron falling from the sky and landing on top of me. I loved her more than anything. She gave me so much, and I never gave her enough back. The first few days after her passing were almost unlivable. I wasn't aware of time, mainly because I tried to my ease pain by sleeping the initial shock away. I kept the drapes of my room drawn so I never saw the sun, and I avoided looking at clocks because frankly, I didn't *want* to watch time pass me by. Every second the clock ticked off was another second she wasn't with me, another second away from her life, another second pushing me into the unknown.

I would sleep through most of the day, and at night, when I couldn't sleep anymore, I walked to the bathroom and back in a dead stupor. But no matter how much I slept, I couldn't escape; every time I closed my eyes, nightmares of her illness, her pain, my helplessness, and her death invaded my sleeping mind. I left my lair only to throw up, and I probably lost ten pounds in those four lonely days of nonexistence. I was a zombie at the funeral, not even half aware of my surroundings, unmoved by the corpse in the casket that I was sure was not her. Where was she? I didn't know. But this corpse—this pale, cold little thing—that definitely wasn't Celina Levesque. After the burial, I went back to Aunt Maggie's and barfed before falling asleep once again. I was sure I would die too, simply out of pure grief.

She'd died right before my eyes. I knew it was happening; I knew her beautiful body was shutting down. And all I did—all I really *could* do—was stand there and watch. Listen for that one phone call that would chuck us out of our own lives. Wait for the moment that would change me forever.

That was months ago.

And so the question came up: who would take care of my sisters and me? Kristina was old enough to live on her own, but what about us three? The minors? The ones who still needed to be babied because we weren't ready for full-time work?

My answer: *undefined.*

The court's answer: *Robert J. Levesque.*

And who is Robert J. Levesque? Hell if I know. I heard he lives in Salt Lake City, and he might have some connection to us. I think he was our sperm donor or something. Anyway, Salt Lake City is like two thousand miles from Maine. Which means I'm basically moving to Pluto.

And I'm about to lose everything. Everything I've ever had. Everything I've ever known. I don't know how I'll survive this hellhole. I'll probably end up slitting my wrists in a few months.

My life is over.

I was two years old when he left us. He moved to Denver, though the court now says he lives in Salt Lake, and we never heard from him again. I don't think he ever loved any of us. Not even my mom. And she was his *wife.*

But legal custody was still passed to him in the event that anything happened to Mom disabling her from caring for us four. The very thought makes acid slide over my tongue. I hate him. I hate his guts. He left us. He never came back. He never called or even wrote. Not once. Were we really that dreadful? What a sicko. Giving everything up like that. A wonderful wife and four beautiful daughters. Gone. What a relief.

So now I'm moving in with this freak traitor, this uncaring, insensitive bastard. I want to live with my Aunt Maggie, Mom's older sister, with the flaming red braid falling past her waist and the giant gold hoops like a fortune-teller's. She's really kind, always helping us when we need her. A Ph.D. in astrophysics and medicine, she was always a relief when we were stuck on one of those homework problems that tempts you to use your textbook for target practice. And because she has a high-paying job and no children, she lives in a beautiful big house about an hour from Mom's. Whenever she makes chocolate chip cookies, they're gone in five minutes. And on top of all that, she's pretty hot, even though she's in her forties. We stayed with her during every one of Mama's hospital stays, from one or two nights to four weeks at a time.

Well, tough luck, kid. She's not your legal guardian. The fact that you love her like your second mom, the fact that you even know her, counts for nil. Welcome to reality, Miss Levesque. Here's your ticket. Your plane to nowhere boards in five minutes.

Unlike my grown sister, Kristina, I'm not much of a social butterfly. While she's out partying until one in the morning, I'm sitting in bed reading *The Da Vinci Code*. She's bringing the family reunion to a social orgasm and I'm huddled in the corner with my eyes hidden and Evanescence playing on my iPod. I had a few casual friends at school, but they never really came over. My best friend is probably Jill. Thank God twin sisters are allowed to follow you into the depths of utter despair, because it looks like we're down to our final lifeline: each other. She hasn't opened her mouth for anyone but me since Mama passed away.

It's all over now. *Emma Levesque: The Story of a Prosperous Young Woman* has been canceled, the episodes yanked off the air and the tapes destroyed in a bonfire. I'll never go back to who I used to be. A tears trickles down my cheek as I watch the ground fall away from me as the plane I'm forcibly strapped to lifts from the runway in Augusta and I give Jill's hand a tight squeeze. She kisses me lightly on the cheek and her thumb massages mine comfortingly. The runway and grass stare back at me, another taunting omen to prove I'm not dreaming. I'm leaving my world behind. And there is nothing I can do. Absolutely nothing.

Wake up, Emma. Wake up now.

Chapter Two

October 31, 2007

Amy

I drag my feet on the way back to the graveyard, each step draping another wet blanket of dread over me. I lollygagged as long as possible at the park, but the sky's lightening, so I have no choice but to return. Soon the sun will rise, its early rays piercing the flesh of those unfortunate enough to still be out, although only one vampire in our coven has met with this terrible fate. Ten years ago. Emily Lincoln, tall, beautiful blonde curls falling halfway down her back. One morning she didn't quite make it back in the time. Her chilling screams pierced the early morning, lasting about a minute before ceasing and letting the terrible silence—for even the birds had stopped chirping—close in on the neighborhood. She was gone, her body vaporized by our mortal enemy. An enemy that used to be my best friend.

The mornings at the graveyard are by far the worst. At the beginning of the night, as we all rise from our graves, the others are too filled with the irrepressible thirst for life to pay much attention to me. Their thin, pale forms rise and dart out of the cemetery like rabid ghosts, the promise of warm blood and strong life the only thing they can focus on. After their first feeding, when they can take note of their surroundings because they're filled with the life they ruthlessly stole from the innocent, they all come and go as they please.

Which is when I try to not be around.

Sometimes I go downtown. Sometimes I even lift things like water bottles from gas stations or convenience marts. Not a good exercise for my conscience, but of course I have no money. And having a water bottle with me is a blessing.

But I spent tonight where I usually stay: at the neighborhood park, on the swings. The one place where I really feel at peace with myself, with the world. Swinging up, higher and higher, getting as close to heaven as I possibly can, nearing the place for which I've desperately yearned for two decades now.

I wanted to stay longer, but the sun's coming up. Now I have no choice.

I feel a tear trickle down the cold skin of my face. Tonight is Halloween, the Christmas for everyone in the cemetery, when young children are out in their little fairy and ghoul costumes, wandering from house to house and gathering candy. The first few hours are paradise; in our area, it's so easy for one of us to sneak up on a vulnerable, unsuspecting youth and hide in the bushes and shadows while slowly luring her in. So used to the mediocre taste of young adult blood, the feeling of her young, pure blood sliding down his throat is almost too much for some; a dessert it's usually much more difficult to come by. Everyone goes wild on Halloween night; rules are tossed aside, and dozens of children are hurt, a couple even killed and turned to...no. I can't think about it anymore. I've already puked once tonight.

As I approach, I whisper a silent prayer. *Please, God, keep her away from me tonight. Don't let her get me. Don't let her hurt me.* I feel the tears grow stronger as I continue: *Don't let her do it. It's been four months. Don't let her push for it again.*

I continue dragging my feet as I pass under the ugly iron arch that is the entrance to the graveyard. I survey the scene sulkily. New, menacingly giant headstones and older, crumbling ones from the early twentieth century dot the grass all around the grassy area. It's hard to see—despite the presence of a streetlight near the gate—so I can't really tell if anyone is there. Oh, why did I have to be buried in the center, of all open spots? There's a gate in the front leading onto the street, and one in the back leading into the pine forest. Either way, I have to walk through half the cemetery to get to my grave. And risk coming face-to-face with one of them, or even worse…*her*.

The familiar terror filling my chest, I take a cautious step forward, trying to be as quiet as possible. Mary, a curly-haired blonde with the sleaziest of bell dresses that I'm sure is on the floor nearly all of her feeding time, shoots out of the shadows, causing me to leap out of my skin.

"Oh, *hello*, Amy," she taunts. "Did you remember to eat tonight?"

I shoot a glare that could rip her in two.

"Well, *I* did. *I* got a teenage boy on Fifth Avenue. He must be the *hottest* on the block. And he was *delicious*!" She runs her tongue over her blood-soaked fangs, the crimson liquid glittering in the ugly yellow glow radiating from the streetlight. I feel my throat and mouth moisten, my stomach lurch. "Maybe, if I'm lucky, he'll come with me and we will share our blood like Sarah and Jade have." She pushes forcefully on my shoulder as she prances toward her grave, cackling freakishly.

Cringing in pain as I clutch my arm, I watch her dark form fall upon its headstone and disappear. My eyes close in sadness and pity for the poor young man she's attacking, my mind reviewing every terror of what I know he's facing, the appalling horror of what she's doing to him. Not only is she sucking his blood, but she's such a whore she's probably seducing him into having fast, hard sex with her as she does it. I honestly have no idea why she never becomes pregnant, considering all the men she bangs.

Good Lord, it would be awful if she brought him here and they behaved like Sarah and Jade. Sarah, a mahogany-haired young adult with menacing dark eyes, and Jade, a brunette in an outfit straight out of a Dracula movie, have done things in this graveyard a porno director wouldn't film. And they don't give a damn about who sees.

No one else bugs me as I sprint the remaining yards to my grave and dive to my knees. Just inches from the cool caress of my headstone, I feel cold, merciless hands slither into position on either side of my stomach and my throat swells shut. Madam Noctis.

"Amy," she whispers in my ear, her cold breath raising goose bumps on my neck. I reach out and clutch my stone, but I know it's no use. She needs to let me go before I can enter my coffin.

My tears return, hard, but holding them in only makes the back of my throat sting in protest. She turns me around, forces me against my stone, and then she's on top of me, her knees pressing into mine and causing me to cringe in pain.

"So, my precious little Amy, did you have a successful night?" She runs her long, creepy fingers down my neck. They rest a moment on the two tiny scars toward the base, then move on to caress my shoulders.

My outside remains petrified in silent dread as her cold hands reverse their path and move eerily across my face. I squeeze my eyes shut as one cups my cheek and her lips press onto mine. Cold as ice and still semi-wet with blood, they move from my lips, across my cheeks, and down my neck, sending violent shivers throughout my flesh.

"I remember the night I first discovered you. Sweet, innocent Amy. Cold, alone and scared." She moves closer to that area on my neck with each word. "Your innocent, young blood was about the best I ever tasted. And you just lay there, a sick, helpless baby. You were by far one of my favorites. If only I could taste your thick, warm blood once more..."

She reaches the spot and rests her fangs threateningly on the scars, her breath way too cold, way too creepy. I finally manage to push her away.

"Please," I beg, so softly I'm unsure she hears me. "Please. I've had a really hard night. Just please leave me alone." I close my eyes tightly again as the last few words escape my cold, terrified lips, and I manage to lose contact with her. Consequently, I evaporate from the surface. The next moment, I'm greeted by the appalling feel of twenty-year-old satin in my coffin.

Sickening.

November 1, 2007

Chapter Three

Emma

"You eat enough pretzels, Annie?" Kristina asks grumpily as we de-board the plane in Salt Lake City.

"Shut your face," Annie retorts.

So, who is this guy who is supposed to be our new guardian? Will he greet us at those security lines, or is he so lazy he sent someone else?

As we approach security, I recognize the man I understand to be "the one" from the old photographs Mom put away under her bed after he left, the ones that Jill and I snuck peeks at when we were small. I don't even know why we did it. Was it in the false hope the man we didn't even remember would come back and make Mommy stop crying? I don't know. But we did it.

So he wasn't too lazy after all. He stands erect in the crowd, holding a white sign with big red letters that reads:

LEVESQUE:

EMMA   ANNIE

JILL   CHRISTINA

Although I know he hasn't seen us since we were tiny, I feel a pang of resentment as I see he's misspelled Kristina's name. One would hope if he is who everyone says he is, he should know

Kristina spells her name with a K rather than with a CH. For Christ's sake, his first daughter!

"Girls?" he says as we approach. Annie nods.

"Girls!" He ditches the sign and smothers us in one giant hug, computer bags and everything. I wriggle free almost immediately, having half the mind to blurt out, "If you ever do that again, you're dead."

Robert brings us to his house in a really dirty taxi, saying one car is in the shop and Jaquelina is out with the other.

Who, exactly, is Jaquelina?

The seats are cracked and the floor is covered with ground-in gunk. There is a cigarette butt in the ashtray on the door I sit by. And the worst part isn't the ashtray or the floor gunk. It isn't that Jill, Annie, Kristina, and I are all crammed into the three seats in the back. It's the driver. He yaps like there's no tomorrow.

The ride seems to take an eternity. As we fly down the interstate, I slump sulkily against the left-hand door, staring out the window at the passing city and trying to ignore my disgusting surroundings. I can't help but overhear the driver's idiotic noise— does he call it a voice?

"So, where y'all a-comin' from?" he asks in a gravelly tone that gives the impression his throat needs clearing but can never quite reach it.

Of course, my stupid "guardian" has to tell him everything. "Oh, they're coming from Maine to live with me now. They're my daughters. I haven't seen them in quite a few years."

Hmmm. He doesn't mention the fact that he ditched us fifteen years ago.

"Mmm, really? Well, you kids are gonna like this place. Yup, yup, yup, there be a-plenty a things to be doin' around here."

Like what? Gouging our eyes out for kicks? We're in a city built smack in the middle of nowhere. And I can tell you, the city itself seems about as interesting as a blue TV screen. Business building after business building flies past my window. It all looks very boring.

"Do y'all be a-mindin' if I smoke?"

Yes.

"Oh, no, not at all," Robert replied.

Oh no.

What kind of father does this guy think he is? I've heard in anti-smoke ads that after only a few minutes, you start to have a negative reaction to secondhand smoke. That it can increase your risk of cancer, harm your eyes, make your stomach upset, and give you a headache.

Great. I can already feel the all-too-familiar migraine building deep in my skull. Can't the guy get fired for smoking with passengers in the car? One would hope…maybe I'll get lucky and pass out before long.

Finally, we turn onto a small street in the outskirts of the city. It leads into a very rich-looking neighborhood; fancy white houses with Corinthian columns and four stories line both sides of the street. All the white reflects the sun, half-blinding me. Every mailbox looks exactly the same, and there are no mailbox covers in sight. The city is probably trying to pull off the modern idea of what looks good, the "uniform" trick; in other words, making everything less unique, duller. I've seen it before and was always thankful Mom didn't live in one of those insane asylums.

Apparently now I do.

We drive right through and end up at the bottom of a giant hill. There is a curvy gravel road leading up, at the start of which stands a giant sign that reads *Private Drive No Trespassing.* Huh.

"This be de place?" the driver asks.

"That it is," Robert assures, almost sing-songy. I wish he'd just shut the fuck up already.

The next thing I know, we're winding our way up the hill, the taxi exaggerating each stone enough to give me a headache after what had to have only been a hundred yards. A forest of pine trees stands on both sides. The road winds its way uphill for the better part of a mile, then ends in what's big enough to be a small parking lot of gravel, in front of a big white house with a dark roof and a separate garage. The house looms on the north side of the gravel and the garage stands to the east, creating a sort of giant right angle between the garage door and the front door. Whatever brainiac built this mansion apparently forgot to add a garage.

I scramble from the vehicle as soon as we stop, while the driver takes his time getting out and opening the trunk. I tap my foot impatiently, then, as soon as the trunk is open, grab my computer bag and suitcase and run as fast as I can with the luggage, eager to get away from that idiot.

I clumsily ascend the three stone steps to the semicircular front porch and try the door, which, to my frustration, is locked. I stand there impatiently as I watched Robert root around in his wallet for money to pay the driver. Annie and Kristina, having gotten their stuff, are coming my way. Jill has set her bag at her feet and is busy surveying the scenery. At least she can paint a far-off picture of the giant mountains looming to the west.

"Locked," I explain as Annie and Kristina step onto the porch. Looking beyond them, I see the driver is finally getting back into the cab. Robert turns and starts toward us, flipping for the right key on his key chain.

The cab grinds over the gravel as the driver hits the gas and turns. I watch its retreating trunk bumble over the crest of the hill and out of sight. Even though I really hated it, I feel a surge of panic as it does so, for all remaining traces of the life I know go over with it and disappear.

"Okay. There are four vacant rooms right up those stairs. Your furniture will arrive in a few days, but until then, I've set up beds for you."

I stand with Robert and my sisters in the marble-floored entrance to the house. To our left is the living room, which has a balcony overlooking it from the hallway on the next level, the stairs to which are right in front of us. The dining room is to our right, an arch in the wall providing an entrance. White carpet covers the floors; the walls are covered with swirled white plaster. A living room arrangement sits in the sunken southwest corner; a fan is suspended from the sixteen-foot ceiling over a white couch, a silver flat-screen TV, and two white daybeds to match said couch. There's also a set of glass tables with chrome legs—a coffee table and two end tables—and a chrome floor lamp, an identical table lamp, and a plant potted in a chrome basin to match. Talk about modern living.

I start up the staircase, Annie, Jill, and Kristina following suit. At the top and to the left is the hall that overlooks the living room. To the right is a bathroom, a bedroom, and a closed door. Without even looking at the other three rooms, I turn left and trudge right into the one at the end of the hallway. My toes push the door shut as my stuff falls to the floor in the familiar teenage fashion.

The room that I've claimed is pentagonal, with a diagonal wall on the southwest side. On the west side is a sliding door to a balcony. A walk-in closet with an archway for a door stands solitary on the north side; in the northeast corner, filling the space the closet leaves on the north wall, lies a mattress with pukey-green sheets and a pukey-yellow blanket. Real nice bed, Robert.

I close my eyes for a second, letting the blackness overtake me. I wonder if I can drown in it. Just lose myself and never return, or simply open my eyes to find myself back in Maine, with my mama making pancakes and Annie scanning her calculus text. Maybe, if I keep them closed long enough, that will happen. Oh, how I wish it were so.

Alas, it is not, and I open my eyes to find myself back in that strange room with the ugly "bed" in the corner. I sigh in frustration. I need some air.

The balcony is wooden and has a set of steps leading up from the side yard. A bench sits to the right of the door. Beyond the hill is a good view of the mountains sitting peacefully on the horizon. The city twinkles below the mountains. Maybe I can watch airplanes land.

I return to the "bed" and fall backward onto the pukey blanket. The ceiling is the classic white plaster with that swirled bumpy pattern that's painful to the touch. I miss my home in Maine. I miss my school. I miss Mom. I miss everything I lost when Mom died. I feel my throat clench and my eyes dampen. How am I ever going to get through this?

I haven't lost the sunset. I realize this when I glance out my door and see the brilliant colors filling the sky. The sunset has always been a friend to me. It's always so beautiful, never quite the same, and no matter where I go, it follows. I never have to lose it. The thought is comforting.

I get up and slip outside to get a better look. The radiant shades of pink and orange fill the open sky, painting an extraordinary picture against the cotton candy clouds. For the first time in weeks, I smile. Maybe I haven't lost everything I used to know.

Leaving the deck, I soon find myself at the bottom of the hill, looking into the three-way intersection where Smith Road meets Penny Lane (and ends there—were this a four-way stop, the driveway would have been the continuation of Smith Road). My surroundings must have hypnotized me into a subconscious walk as only cool air and brilliant skies can. I turn west on Penny Lane, which runs along the edge of the neighborhood. As I pass the giant hill Robert lives on, I come across a sight that lifts my spirits even higher.

A vast stretch of grass, trees, and cement pathways. A big, colorful playground in the distance. The corners of my mouth turn somewhat upward; a park at the bottom of Robert's hill. Will it soften the experience for me? I've always loved playgrounds, and I still horse around on them, even though I've outgrown the tunnels and slides.

I make my way across the lawn to the mulched area. There is a huge play structure, probably around five slides, and, best of all, two giant swing sets. I feel happier than I ever have since Mama died. I still have friends with me. I've loved swings all my life. They give me a sense of flying, a sense of heaven. If I still have swings and the sky, with the clouds, the stars, and the sunset, maybe I can get through this without choking on my own sanity.

I swing for about ten minutes, then leap off and head back toward the hill. As the driveway comes into view, I spy a red SUV the size of Michigan cross Penny Lane and start right up. I frown and race after it.

By the time I reach the house, the behemoth is gone and all is still; it must be in that humungous garage. I hear Robert's voice echo from the dining room as I hurry through the front door. Curiosity ushers me through the arch in the wall to the left of the entrance, where I immediately stop short. I've caught Robert in mid-liplock with a skinny blonde woman who I'm sure popped right out of *Sex and the City*. Grocery bags sit unattended on the granite counters and floor. It comes out before I can stop it.

"Who the hell are you?"

Her name is Jaquelina Levesque. She is my stepmother. And she is a perfect example of a human Barbie doll.

She has my last name.

Robert seems very embarrassed with how I greeted her. He immediately starts apologizing.

"I am so sorry, Jackie. I can't believe the nature of that greeting. Emma!" His voice tries to capture a stern tone.

"Oh, it's perfectly all right, Robert," she cuts him short. "She was probably just a little surprised. But haven't you told the girls about me yet?"

"Well, um, actually, no. I've hardly had the chance to talk to them."

"Well, get talking! These are your children!" Her voice echoes an airy high-pitch of ecstasy that an aunt would use upon meeting her four-year-old niece. "So this is Emma! Oh Robert she's so *grown up!*" Jaquelina pulls me into a smothering hug. Her navy blue coat reeks of peppermint and shopping malls.

"What do you mean, *'grown up?'*" I demand, taking my body back. "What were you expecting, a five-year-old?"

Jaquelina just smiles as Robert calls out to Annie, Jill, and Kristina so they too can meet her. He tells me to stay right where I am.

Annie and Kristina enter. Jill follows soon after, a smock tied over her outfit. I smile in spite of myself. Jill is already painting.

After introductions, Robert picks up some wooden things that were lying on the table. He hands one to Annie, one to Kristina, one to Jill, and one to me. I examine it carefully.

It's a crucifix, complete with a tiny dead Jesus hanging from the cross. The whole thing is made of what looks like pinewood. Talk about creepy—a wave of disgust washes over my chest. I run my fingers over it and shiver.

Robert instructs us in a stern voice. "I want all four of you to leave these on your bedside, no matter how much you hate them. Never remove them. Understand?"

Kristina and I don't move. Jill lets out an audible sigh and Annie mumbles in assent.

Robert nods in acknowledgement to Annie's immediate positive answer. Then he continues, "Also, there are a couple of rules we would like to stress to you right now. Never, ever go out after sunset unless either Jaquelina or I are with you. Ever. No exceptions. And, no matter what, *never* let anyone in after dark unless we say you can. If you break either of these rules, it could mean danger to the entire family. Trust us. This neighborhood isn't safe at night."

"But, Dad—" Kristina begins.

"*No.* What we say goes, understood?"

Kristina shoots him a death glare. I know exactly what she was hoping to do; going to parties, movies, the mall, and friends' houses after dark is her area of expertise.

"*Understood?*" Robert repeats.

Annie nods. Robert looks to Kristina and me. "*Understand?* Nobody leaves this room until you all promise Jaquelina and me you'll follow these rules."

"I promise," Annie squeaks immediately, though looking horrified at what she's saying. Jill nods slowly, her head hung. Robert turns to Kristina and me. "Do you two promise?"

We look at each other, and I mumble an assent similar to Annie's. But Kristina argues. "For God's sake, Dad. In case you've forgotten my birth date, I'm a year and a half out of high school. I'm going to need to be out at night because I'm trying to find a good college."

"No exceptions, Kristina."

"I'll be twenty in April and I can take care of myself! If this is about some goddamned criminal—"

"Young lady, I said no. Now promise you won't go out or let anyone else in after dark or you're grounded."

A shock of incredulousness flickers through Kristina's eyes before they lock onto and shoot fire with Robert's. "You can't ground me."

"I can as long as you live in my house under my rules."

She groans in surrender. "Fine." Her voice is curt and sharp as needles.

"Good. Go put those crucifixes beside your beds *now.*"

We all trudge toward the staircase, Kristina making a point of storming out to show Robert what a monster he is.

"Is he loco?" she whispers on our way up. "I'm going to need to be out a *lot* this winter! And *no way* am I putting this stupid thing by my bed! It's *disgusting!* Who wants a figure of Jesus's dead body by her bedside?"

"But Kristina, Dad told us to! We have to!" Annie argues.

"Bullshit! They can't tell me what to do!" Kristina slams her bedroom door. Jill shuts her door a bit more gently.

Annie turns to me before entering her room. "Dad totally freaked when he couldn't find you. We assured him you were fine, that you come and go a lot and are careful. But I think you'd better tell him before you leave again."

"*Phht.*" What's next? Roll call?

I return to the room I occupy and pull out a small photo I have of Mama and me before the sickness overcame her. Whatever cheer the outside gave me has melted and been replaced with a sense of pain and anxiety. I miss her so badly. I miss my old home, my old life. Why did this happen to me? A tear falls from my left eye. I wipe it away and sniff. My life fell to pieces on July 3, 2000, when she was diagnosed, and burned out on April 1, 2005, when she died.

There is a knock at my door. I groan and roll over on the white carpeted floor, refusing to lie on the hideous bed before I absolutely have to. "What?"

"Dinner," Kristina calls dully.

"Ugh!" I stand grudgingly and drag my feet across the white carpet. I'm tired. I'm shaky. I'm melancholy. And I'm *not* hungry.

I get downstairs and sit silently in the chair closest to the staircase. It's cold in the dining room. Oh, how I want to run back upstairs, back to the warm room I'm staying in, and shut the door on the world. I am not hungry, especially for the manufactured chicken and rice that sits on my plate. The dining room is an icebox and a shiver passes through my exhausted body.

"So," Jaquelina begins after everyone's served, "it's wonderful to have you girls here. I must say, I was quite delighted when I heard you were coming to stay with us"—she gives Robert the evil eye—"and that we finally have some children in this house."

Kristina's eyebrows shoot up. "*Excuse* me?"

"Well, three children, and one adult."

"Technically, none of us is a child." Annie corrects. "The dictionary definition states that a child is anyone between birth and puberty in age. Emma is the youngest of us and she left most aspects of puberty behind at thirteen."

"Thank you, Annie, that's enough," I grumble through clenched teeth. I don't need these two strangers knowing the details of my body's plan for life.

"I am still a bit unsure about your ages. Kristina, you made it clear earlier that you're nineteen, but what about you three?"

"Jill and Emma turned seventeen on October twelfth, and I turned eighteen on September twenty-seventh," Annie states bluntly.

"An-nie, shut u-up," I sing warningly, again through clenched teeth.

"So you're a senior?"

"Uh-huh."

"Okay. You three start at Coldwater Central on Monday. I think they've matched your schedules as closely as they could to the ones you had at your old school."

I feel a sort of resentment at the way she says "old school." Yeah. Our *old* school. So that's it. Old school. Old lives. The thought is depressing.

"So, what are your hobbies?" Jaquelina addresses no one in particular.

"Da, um, well, I like reading, and, um, Kristina likes dancing," Annie stutters. I want to turn around and slap her. Perfect Annie. She's way too much of a good girl, especially considering her age. She speaks like she's a thirty-five year-old scientist. She complies like she's five. She's polite to every adult, no matter who he is. It especially annoys me that she's answering this bimbo's questions. Jaquelina has no business in our private lives.

"Really? How much do you read, Anne?" Jaquelina's trying way too hard to keep the conversation going. It's obvious she's the only one who wants to talk. Even Robert keeps his mouth shut. He's staring at us, looking concerned.

"It's Annie. And I read a lot, Jaquelina."

"What area in Maine are you from? Which town? What were your old schools like?"

I groan loudly and slam my knife to my plate. "Finished." I stand furiously and stomp over to the kitchen to set my dishes on the counter.

"Emma, dear, are you sure you're all right?" Jaquelina asks. "You didn't eat much."

"I'm fine, *Jaquelina*." I've been here not six hours, and already I'm sick of her. She's trying far too hard to be our new mom. And she's failing miserably. Even if she did a good job, I would never love her. Never, ever can she replace my mama. And I'm prepared to do what I have to to prove it.

"Where are you going?" Jaquelina calls as I opened the front door the next afternoon.

"Out," I snap.

"Wait. Where are you going? When will you be home?"

"I'm just going out."

"Just around the neighborhood?"

"Yeah."

"Well, be careful."

"Whatever." I pass through the front door.

"Remember to be home before nightfall!"

Slam! is my loving, tender response.

The sun is already setting. I grunt, wishing that this Victoria's Secret model would do us all a favor and go walk off a cliff.

I reach the bottom of the hill and pull my jacket tightly around me. Fast-moving clouds cover the sky, sending distant thunder to my ears. A harsh wind hailing from the west bites at my cheeks, and leaves blow past my feet like bits of paper. I turn left on Penny Lane this time and hike down the road. I'm just past my father's hill when an iron gate appears on my left. Upon closer inspection I see it encircles a cemetery, rather starved for graves considering its size. I amble through the arched entrance and look at some of the headstones, unable to help but notice the many who died very young. *Mary Katherine Bloome, 1960-1983.* Wow. Twenty-three. Near it stands another short-lived: *Elizabeth "Lizzie" Joanne Robertson, 1960-1980.*

As I make my way around the graveyard, I pass quite a few that made it into their eighties and nineties, one even past one hundred, but I also see many who didn't make it past thirty. I can't help but wonder what on earth caused all these premature deaths. I come across a rather large headstone near the center and find the youngest victim. *Amy Leanne Wyle, April 1970-March 1986.* My God. Fifteen. That makes a total of around eight people dead before age thirty, many of whom died in the past thirty years.

Lightning begins to flash across the sky, and the thunder seems to be right above my head. I shiver a little, and, suddenly terrified, turn to head back up the hill. It's getting pretty dark, and the storm's growing very strong.

Chapter Four

Amy

It's a nightmare.
Feels like someone is forcing red-hot iron spikes into your
neck
Then it pierces through your chest
Like a thousand sharp sabers
The harder it sucks
The more widespread the pain
And a tingling feeling as it seems all the love and joy
Is sucked from every cell of your body.
You're barely aware of the thick warm fluid
Seeping over your collarbone, into your shirt and down
between your breasts
Because the pain slashes and jabs and punctures
Until after a century
When you finally pass out
Able to take it no more.

The deadly kiss of a vampire
Is all it takes
To vaporize your soul.

Emma

"You start school on Monday, girls," Jaquelina announces at lunch on Thursday.

"So we've heard," I mumble.

She continues as if I hadn't uttered a word. "Your principal e-mailed me your schedules this morning; I have them printed out." She picks up and leafs through a small stack of papers. "Ah, here they are. Annie, Jill, Emma." I yank mine over and frown as my eyes scan the list. My classes seem to match pretty well, except instead of seven classes, I now have eight, and they stuck me in physical education to fill the eighth spot.

"I'm in gym," I whisper to Jill.

"Me too." She shows me her schedule and my heart sinks. We have only two classes together. It's better than none, I guess.

"Kristina sweetie?" Jaquelina chirps.

"Yes?"

"You're out of high school. What are you planning to do this year?"

Oh God. Is she trying to get small talk going again?

"Ugh. I dunno…" Kristina picks at her macaroni and cheese with her fork. "Maybe get a job."

"You did say you were planning on college, right dear?"

"Yeah, I am," Kristina sighs.

"Are any of you girls planning to get a job?" Now she's addressing Annie, Jill, and me.

"Yeah," I retort. "At a tattoo parlor."

Jaquelina raises her eyebrows for a second, realizes I'm being sarcastic, and returns to pestering Kristina.

"You've been out of high school for a year now, right?"

Kristina sighs again. "Yeah. I would have gone to college directly afterwards, but I took last year to get a job and help Mom during her illness. I'm looking for a good design school now. Okay?" Kristina's voice holds a note of mingled finality and annoyance that tells Jaquelina it's time to back down.

"Um, okay, sweetheart."

Like she cares at all.

I wake at a quarter to six the next morning. Failing to return to sleep, I drag myself out of bed, stand in the shower until the steam seems to suffocate me, and slump down the stairs to satisfy my growling stomach. Jaquelina's cleaning the counters and singing some dumb seventies tune. Figures.

"Em. You're up already."

I groan almost too audibly. "Where's Robert?"

"'Dad,' sweetie."

"He's not my dad," I grumble. She releases a sad sigh.

"He went to work, darlin'."

"Already?"

"Yes. See, he works for a major insurance company downtown, and his hours are six through six."

"Monday through Friday?"

"Monday through Friday."

My mouth drops. Twelve hours a day. Disgusting. Not that I care. What company does he work for, exactly? BusyMen Inc.? I snort at my own stupid humor.

"He was here before," I challenge as Jill slumps into the room.

"Well, he took those three days off because of your arrival. But now he's gone back. It's a busy company, and it's really hard for him to get time off beyond what his contract allows. And, if you don't mind my asking, what are you two doing up so early? You'll have plenty of opportunity to get up at this time of day starting next week. Why don't you take advantage of your last few days to sleep in?"

Under the slim possibility that a dog could figure this out before you could, I feel it would be a great honor for me to inform you that we have spent our lives on Eastern time, Poindexter. That's two hours ahead of Salt Lake City, in case you forgot your calculator. We've only been here for three days and our bodies haven't adjusted yet. Now don't you have a calculus class to get to? I don't say this; I just strut past Barbie and open what I know to be the pantry. We'd eaten waffles for breakfast the last two days, but now it's apparent that our presence no longer calls for constant gourmet meals.

Wheaties, Fiber One, Grape Nuts, Bran 2 Annoy (more stupid humor)...I turn on my heel. "Don't you have any *good* cereals?"

Jaquelina starts at my sudden outburst. "Like what, dearie?"

"Honey-Nut Cheerios, at the *very* least."

"Oh, I'm sorry. I will be shopping later—"

"Well what am I supposed to eat?"

Jaquelina looks from Jill to me, then reaches for the refrigerator door. "Do you like fried eggs? Or scrambled?"

"Fried's fine," I mumble, hoping against hope she can at least prepare eggs without causing us all to suffer food poisoning.

Jill and I sit at the table while she fries the eggs and bacon.

"Are you all right, Emma?" Jill whispers after a little while. "You seem a little angry."

I sigh. "Yeah, I'm fine. I just—I just—"

Jill reaches for my hand. "I love you, Em."

I give her a watery smile as Jaquelina struts toward the table, hips swishing, breasts bouncing. God.

She sets our plates in front of us. "Bring on the salmonella," I mutter.

Jaquelina goes back for her plate and sits at the table. "So, did you girls sleep all right?"

I grunt, poking at my eggs with minimal interest.

"Were the beds okay? I know they aren't exactly royal, but your furniture should be here within a week."

No answer.

"What about your room temperature? Is it too hot up there for you?"

It's fine for me, is it too HOT for you? "Fine," I mumble.

"How do you girls like the place?"

"Whatever."

"Do you like the city?"

I quit answering. After two more futile attempts at breaking solid ice, she gives up and we eat in silence.

After breakfast, with nothing better to do, I zip on my boots and stroll down to the park. Last year, I'd have spent my days in my room drawing and writing. From the night we heard the awful news that the doctors had given up hope, I have been unable to read, write, or do any form of artwork. I've tried a few times, but have only grown frustrated, thinking my work is horrible. At this point, I'd usually throw it out and mope for a while. Eventually I just decided to give up on art and writing. The stories I read meant nothing to me anymore, so eventually I stopped reading as well.

Before all this, at the very beginning, I thought Mama would get better. I thought she'd be all right, that the doctors could save her. I knew hope was dismal, but I thought God would answer my prayers, that he would send a miracle to save our family. Alas, no such luck. God used to exist for me. He used to be there for me. But no longer, because I know better.

The phone's shrill chime pierced my sleep and my eyes shot open, terror pulsing through my veins. It took my a few moments to calm down after realizing it was just the telephone. I heard Mama's tired response from the other room.

"Hello?"

I pulled my comforter around my shoulders and snuggled deeper into my bed. I was just drifting off when I sensed Mama standing above me.

"Are you awake, Emma darling?"

"Yeah."

"Oh, sweetheart." Sadness punctuated her tone, defeating her attempt to hide it.

"What is it, Mommy?"

"Sweetheart...Aunt Maggie was...well...she was in a car accident tonight. She was coming home from the theater, apparently, and a truck hit her."

"What?"

"She was thrown from the car, darling. She's alive, but she broke her neck and has some bruising on her brain. The doctors say it will be a miracle if she doesn't have any permanent damage."

"Oh..."

"Don't worry, honey," she said, choking up a little. "The doctors are taking good care of her. You just go back to sleep, okay?"

"Okay."

Mom leaned down and kissed my head before tucking my blankets around me and slipping away. A few moments later, once silence had settled into my room and mind, I picked up her voice, barely audible, from Kristina's room.

"The doctors may not be able to save her, sweetie."

I didn't hear Kristina's reply. I turned over and try to picture it. Aunt Maggie. Car accident. Dead.

I didn't sleep much for the rest of the night.

Chapter Five

Emma

"Emma! Wake up, Emma!"

Someone opens my door and clicks the overhead lamp on. I groan and turn over.

"I'm sorry, Emma, but we have to go to school." Jill pulls my top cover off and leaves. I look groggily at my watch. Six AM.

It's another thirty minutes before I stumble downstairs. Jaquelina made eggs again; what a surprise. Chicken and eggs. Are gallinaceous birds the only meat she has access to?

She managed to avoid poisoning us before; maybe she can pull it off again. The eggs taste just as weird as last time, but then, everything tastes weird to me.

We're shoved out the door to catch the bus at seven o'clock. No one speaks through the entire hike down the driveway. The bus roars down Penny Lane and stops right in front of us, its stench covering a forty-five foot radius and making me involuntarily stop breathing.

Everyone on the bus looks strange and dark, perhaps even sinister. So many seem to frown at us, the newcomers, as we walk down the aisle, looking for seats. Jill and I sit in a vacant one near the front; I hug her arm and close my eyes.

"Jill," I whisper.

She rubs my arm in acknowledgement. "'S all right, sweetie. It's all right."

The school is huge. It takes me ten minutes simply to find my locker. A806, combination 1-29-27. It's nowhere near Jill's or Annie's. I lost them to the crowd almost immediately.

I am a lone fish in a sea of sharks, or some corny metaphor of the sort. Strangers pass me left and right, and I see a lot more piercings, pink Mohawks, and tattoos than I would have bargained for in such a strictly Mormon city. The rest of the school is just a bunch of students who are so conservatively dressed I'm shocked they aren't tearing everything off in some sort of enraged God-spiteful rebellion.

Behold, the social scene at Coldwater Central High School.

I pretend not to exist as I trudge off toward drawing class.

The art room is big, with a high ceiling and windows, and lots of different materials stacked or stowed all around. Drying racks here, canvases there, paints in an open cupboard above the sink. As we look around, I think I catch Jill smile for the first time since Mama's death. We sit together at a table in the corner.

"Hi, Jill."

She nods her head but doesn't speak so I put my head down.

Once they close, I know my eyes will not open. I involuntarily stayed up until two the night before, and sleep is such a blessing now that it seems criminal to try to push it away. After a few minutes, a woman's voice silences the crowd and Jill jabs me in the arm.

It hurts to open my eyes.

A tall, middle-aged woman now stands at the head of the room. She sets a plastic mug that could probably hold a gallon on her desk, straightens, turns to face us, and crosses her arms. Straight, bleachy-blonde hair that curves at the ends hangs about three inches past her shoulders.

"Good morning, class," she greets, her voice hinted with good-natured spirit. "I hope you all had a lovely weekend." She waits for any indication of response and, seeing none, simply grins and continues.

"I will just get roll call really fast, then you may all get started. Chris."

"Here."

I let my head fall back to the table like a weight dropped off a cliff. Jill has to jab again me when my name is called.

"Wha—?"

"Emma Levesque! Are you here, Emma?"

"Oh. Yeah." Back to dreamland.

"And you're Jill, right?"

I'm guessing Jill nods.

"All right. So you are the two new students I was warned about." It didn't sound like a criticism. I think it was a joke. I forced my head into the air just in time to see a boy in front of me turn in his seat. "Hey. Are you, like, twins or something?"

"Maybe." Why did I have to look up? I'm not in the mood to face these people. I want to sleep.

"Well, it's good to have you in our class, Emma and Jill. Now everyone, you may get started on either your fifteen sketchbook minutes or your insect. I will remind you that Friday is the end of the grading period, and your sketchbooks will be due Friday at four at the very latest. I will be turning in grades on Monday and if you miss the deadline, your grade drops thirty percent. I know you all know that; I'm just reminding you. So if you're behind in your sketchbook, I'd recommend working on that instead of your insect, for which I haven't set a due date."

Lethargic chatter slowly picks up and people stand to retrieve materials and projects. The tall, blonde woman turns away, picks up some papers, and pulls a chair up to our table.

"Hi." She grins ear-to-ear, revealing a row of pearly-white, dazzlingly straight teeth. Although she can't be under forty-five, she is extraordinarily pretty. I can't help smiling back at her a bit as an excited warmth rises in my chest.

"My name is Mrs. Larson, and I'm the drawing and painting teacher. So, were both of you taking a basic drawing course at your old school when you moved?"

Jill nods slowly.

"And what were you learning when you left?"

"Color blending," I groan, resting my head on my hand and pulling that corner of my mouth across my cheek.

"And did you do basic graphite, before that?"

"You mean like pencil blending?"

"Exactly."

"Yes."

"Well that's about what we've covered," she says. "We're not doing color until next semester. Right now we're doing a stippling project." She gives us each a handout. *Stippling Chart* is written at the top in bold text. "All I need for you to do now is follow the directions on this page. Here is the paper you need,"—she hands us each a piece of thick paper slightly larger than letter-sized—"and rulers are over on that table with all those materials. Now. What you're going to do is take one of these fine-point Sharpies and carefully shade the chart using lots of little dots." She pulls out a marker and does a small demonstration on a scrap paper. "The more space between each dot, the lighter your shading gets. Understand?"

"Jill and I did a stippling project in eighth grade," I inform Mrs. Larson.

"Super," she replies. "There are Sharpies in the bin by the rulers. If you need any help, I'll be at my computer." She stands and begins to walk away, then turns.

"By the way, we draw in sketchbooks for fifteen minutes every class period. You just need a spiral-bound thing about like this." She picks up a sketchbook lying on a nearby table. "Okay?"

"Sure." I stare at the blank paper, then look over the instructions. My brain isn't working. I can't process the steps. Something about rulers. I get up to retrieve two, but by now all that are left are crappy bent ones. They're metal, eighteen inches long. Sighing, I return to the table and hand Jill her ruler, then turn reluctantly back to the instructions. I still can't focus. I try, but I know it's useless. Art just isn't my thing anymore. I finally give up with the outline of the chart and put my head in my arms. My body shuts into a sort of half-sleep as images of Mama—her smile, her eyes, her loving glow—play across my eyelids. I can't stop them from coming, but they're only making me more depressed. The end of the ninety-minute period arrives, and I've only managed to make a light half-outline of a stupid stippling chart.

Jill hasn't managed anything.

Neither Jill nor Annie is in my lunch today (there are two schedules, Day A and Day B), so I find myself sitting alone at a table in the corner by the windows. Heavy clouds pass over the sky, bringing an angry humidity in through the open window by my chair. I shudder and shove the damn thing closed.

The cafeteria is noisy. Almost every table seems filled up. There are a few distinct groups: the cheerleaders, all dressed in school colors; the jocks in their football jerseys, and the Goths, easiest to identify because all you have to do is scan the cafeteria for a circle of black. But for the most part, there is no distinct way to identify each friendship group like there is in the stereotypical high school. Who'll be nice? Who won't? There's no way to know. And I'm not about to try to find out.

My chicken sandwich is as dry as cardboard. I spit my food in my napkin and look at what's between the buns; I wasn't paying attention when I took it out of the bag.

It's black, almost too overcooked to be looked at. I feel my nose wrinkle in disgust and I make a mental note to never get the chicken sandwich again.

A boy walks toward my table. I feel my heart speed, and I duck beneath the table to look for a nonexistent pencil I dropped. I wait until I'm sure he isn't planning to sit with me before coming up again.

Later that afternoon, as I sit on the puke bed, angrily punching the keys on my laptop, there's a knock at my door. "Emma sweetie?" Jaquelina opens the door a crack.

I slap the bed in anger. "Do you even know the meaning of 'knock?'"

"But I did knock, Emma."

"But, you see, the whole point is to knock and wait for a reply, not to knock and come barging in," I say, sarcastic sweetness radiating from my vocal cords.

"Well, I know, but—"

"Just tell me what you want," I groan, exasperated.

"Oh, well, moving van is here, darling."

I feel my heart rise. My stuff. No more vomit bed.

I plow past Jaquelina and hurry downstairs and outside. I'm not sure why I'm so excited about the moving vans, other than the fact that I'll be able to sleep in a real bed again. But I pick up some of the lighter boxes labeled "EMMA" and haul them, with some difficulty, upstairs.

It takes the movers a long time to get all my furniture in, as there are only three of them and they're also busy with my sisters. But when our stuff is all out and the van finally rumbles away (its riders probably counting their two thousand bucks), Jaquelina gives us pocketknives and plastic storage containers.

"Now, be careful with these," she cautions as though she thinks she's doing a great job pulling off this whole concerned parent thing. "Call out if you need any help or you cut yourself. And yes, I want you to come directly to me if you do get a cut. Don't just go looking for Band-Aids. I want them washed and disinfected."

Kristina scoffs. I'm thinking the exact same thing. As if we're too small to wash our own cuts and put on Neosporin. Why not bring out the sippy cups and high chairs, save Jaquelina some stress? I take the little green knife into my room and close the door.

There are so many boxes, and my furniture is simply dumped in the room in no particular fashion. Whatever happened to movers asking where you want your furniture? I push some of it into place, not caring what the arrangement ends up looking like. Then I turn to the boxes.

From the moment the blade slices through the tape and I see the pile of books inside the first box, I know I can't do it. Everything in my bedroom represents my past, what once was, but is no more. I try to put some of the books on the shelf, but soon it becomes too hard and I have to switch to a different box.

That one's just as hard. Stuffed animals. School artwork. Dolls. Old photos. I try and try, but it takes me three hours just to get through four boxes and it eventually becomes too much. As I try to open the fifth box, the shining blade of the knife slices into my thumb and a line of bright red blood slithers out. Giving up, I flop on my bed, exhausted, as the throbbing of the reopened wound in my soul pounds inside me.

I cannot do this. It's just too hard. I know I can't push any further or I'll break down.

Chapter Six

Amy

The full moon glares down upon me as I race through the trees, the back of my throat throbbing with blood lust. I can feel that moon watching me, its presence boring into my back like a branding iron. I wish I could shrink to nothing so that it can't even sense me. I'm so embarrassed, so guilty, so alone. The roots pull themselves off the ground and trip me, the pine trees loom above menacingly, and the stars are taunting me and laughing at my misery. I race through it all, trying to find shelter, a place to feel safe.

But there is nowhere for me. I don't belong on this earth, in this universe. I don't belong here, or there, or anywhere. I'm a freak of nature, and even my own soil, my only refuge, knows it.

I sprint farther and farther, only to come back to where I was. It's all a giant circle, like the inside of a ball, and I can't get out of it.

My thirst is moving from my throat and all through my body. It's taking control—I need to satisfy it.

And what luck I have. A little girl is crying softly at the base of a tree; she's out after dark, alone. She's glowing with life, radiating a warmth that I desperately desire, that I desperately need.

She looks up as I approach, fear etched on her small face. I reach out and take her hand. It's hot, swollen with blood.

"Everything will be all right, honey," I breathe, lifting her gently off the ground. "You'll be just fine."

Once I manage to calm her a bit, she lies in my arms, her heat taunting me, beckoning me. I have her.

The moon and the stars are still watching me, looking upon my unspeakable sins sadly. They know I know what I'm doing, and they know I know it's wrong, and it sends guilt and misery through my heart.

But I do not fight. I'm so thirsty, and my body's redemption is lying in my arms. I try not to think about it, try not to listen to her cries, as I lean down and sink my teeth into her neck.

I jerk awake with a slight scream, gasping desperately, my body drenched in a cold sweat. Just a dream. Just another dream. Another version of my terrifying recurring nightmare.

Like most recurring dreams, there are many ever-present elements. I'm always running, terrified and alone, through the forest, knowing I'm being watched. I'm always thirsty, and there's always a child at the base of that tree. Sometimes it's a little boy, sometimes a little girl. I usually wake right as I'm feeding.

I don't know if I'll ever learn what happens after I feed, if anything. But I always wonder what would happen if I don't wake up.

But I haven't done it. It isn't real. I *am* thirsty, though, and it's overpowering. *Oh no.* The longing for the taste of life, oh, sweet life, is always there, always nagging. But I can't give in. If I do, I can do much worse damage to someone than just killing her. I can never give in to the nature of my body.

The nature of my body. My stomach turns over.

I bite down into my wrist and drink my own nectar, praying it'll quench my thirst. Oh, it is sweet. Sweet and full and flowing. I drink and drink until I finally pull my mouth away, licking the blood from my lips. Sometimes it works, but tonight it does not.

The cool night air greets me as I emerge from my grave, settling on my skin but not penetrating. I close my eyes tightly for a second, then make a dash for the back gate. *Maybe I should go to the playground. It may ease this pain a bit.* There is no way I can go downtown. Too many people. I'll lose control.

I pause for a moment outside the gate and take a deep breath. The cool night air circulates in my trachea and lungs, causing my body to relax and the stomachache to subside. Letting out a breath of relief, I race into the forest.

The back way through the woods that slowly takes you over the giant hill looming over the cemetery is rougher and longer than the street, but oh, so much safer. By now the area is pretty much second nature; I know the location of nearly every tree, every root, every leaf, metaphorically speaking. At first, walking through the woods in the darkness was scary, but over twenty years make it more familiar than your own home. I stumble so much less, and trees are pretty easy to miss.

After a little while, the land levels a bit. The thirst still nags in the back of my throat; though I tried to ignore it on the way up, I no longer can. I need blood.

I squeeze my eyes shut in frustration and start in the direction of the house that stands atop the hill. After a little while, the trees give way to a big backyard with a giant building silhouetted against the dark blue sky. I shake my head. Man, these people are *rich*. The hungry ache pulses angrily in the back of my throat and I start across the yard.

I make my way toward the west side, where the water spigot is. Over the years, I have managed to memorize the locations of all the outside water spouts on most of the houses surrounding the cemetery. It wasn't hard; my memory is exceptional. People used to joke that I could look at two identical books and tell which one was mine and which was my friend's. I also had about a billion songs memorized. By now the only one I retain in full is *Eleanor Rigby*.

The faucet is right under an upstairs balcony with steps leading into the yard. "Eleanor Rigby, died in the church and was buried along with her name…nobody ca-ame," I sing softly as I fumble along the brick foundation, trying to find the knob. I hate having to crouch and feel my way around, but, unfortunately, the faucets are usually invisible against the dark buildings. "Father

McKenzie, wiping the death from his hands as he walks from the grave…no one was sa-aved…"

When the rough brick finally gives way to the cool, hard metal, I grasp the handle firmly and ease the water on, squeezing my eyes shut and praying no one will hear it splutter to life. My kind can cast a spell over a house so no one will wake to the screams of their victims, but that only works when we're heavily aroused by the promise of blood. I don't even have a victim.

With a hiss and sputter, a small stream begins to pour out of the wall and into the grass. Perfect.

I run my hands under the water before cupping them to catch it. They always feel so grimy and oily; even though our bodies cleanse themselves all the time to keep us attractive to our victims, sometimes that dirty feeling comes to me.

I cup my hands and let the water fill them. It's really cold, but the ice stays on the surface. I never feel cold past the surface of my skin. I've heard from others, like Elizabeth, that, depending on how much lifeblood you have in your body, it can penetrate you even deeper than it can a human. Apparently it's like I'm saturated with another's blood all the time, because only then can a "normal" vampire feel cold only on the surface.

Once the water overflows, I put my hands to my face and dump the water into my mouth, some of it spilling off my cheeks and down my shirt. It takes about three handfuls of water to finally subdue the thirst. Water, never quite as satisfying, but always worth sparing an innocent soul the unbearable.

I hope against hope no one can hear the screech of the pipes as I close my eyes and gulp more water. I remember having to dart so many times before, sometimes without even being able to turn the water off. I guess I'm lucky there are so many kids in the neighborhood, or else people might get suspicious.

Unfortunately, tonight is one of those bad nights; as I open my eyes, I notice something very different about the atmosphere and quickly realize the outside light on the porch I'm under has blinked on.

For a moment, I'm petrified. I inch to turn off the spigot, then turn slowly.

The light casts a yellow glow off a teenaged girl with short red hair and pale skin. Even through the soul-freezing terror quickly welling in my chest, I can't help but feel a strong, lusting attraction to this beautiful young woman standing before me. We stare at each other for a moment in awe; her eyes grow slowly wider and she eventually utters a little "Uh..." It brakes my paralysis and the next moment I'm hightailing it out of there. It would be a lot scarier for me had I not been caught so many times before.

I race directly back to my grave even though it's exceedingly early; there is no where else I'd rather be. Thankfully, I don't run into anybody, and I fall into my coffin and close my eyes tightly.

The image of that girl rushes through my mind. I try to shun it, but can't. Who was she? I thought just a couple lived there. A man and a woman. I've never seen anyone else.

But here's this girl. She was so adorable; I'd in particular noticed how her eyes glowed bright blue in the light. I'm slightly numb from the experience; I haven't been that close to a human in so many years, ever since—I cringe and furiously, sorrowfully, shove the thought from my mind.

Her heat really turned me on; even though we were quite a few feet from each other, I could feel it radiating heavily from her body. It awakened a hunger in me that still throbs angrily in my throat and chest. Her image swallows me; she was so gentle, so benign. She was a human.

My hands move involuntarily to my legs, and I sigh. Ever since my death, I've never felt good about doing this, but it does work with the water and my blood to help keep my thirst at bay, and I don't have anybody to love so I need some means of achieving sexual release. Otherwise, the mix of desire, not only for blood, but for intercourse, along with the devastating loneliness, could become too much.

I slip my right hand into my skirt, beneath my undies, and gently touch the soft folds of skin between my legs; I work my hands between the two soft lips of skin and my fingers search for the spot. After a few minutes, an intensity begins to grow within my body and I hear my brain screaming out. My fingers move back and forth rhythmically and my legs tense as the feeling becomes more and more amazing. There's no turning back now; I have to keep going until it comes. I squeeze my eyes shut until I reach the zenith, and cry out as my body convulses. It feels so good, so comforting, so wonderful, and I never want it to end.

As I try to come again, uninvited distress brings nausea to my stomach. This is exactly what *she* has done to me, over and over again. The memories of her blood-coated lips on my cheeks, mouth, neck, and elsewhere and her cold, clammy fingers on— *inside*—me makes me shake violently. Her lips have never pulled me into an amazing world of love, passion, and sexuality the way Kelly's did, and her fingers never bring an amazing, intense feeling the way mine do. All they do is hurt me until long after I've cried my last tears. I know I shouldn't let her do it. But I've never really tried very hard to stop her. I just let her do it to me without any attempt at struggle. Why on earth am I so weak?

I keep going, again and again and again, making sure that I've saturated myself with sexual feeling before pulling l my hand from between my legs and folding my arms under my breasts. A contented warmth pulses deep in my vagina. I feel better physically. But emotionally, I'm cold, alone, and betrayed.

Teen Girl Found Dead at Residence

Early last Tuesday morning James and Lacie Wyle woke to a parent's worst nightmare as their nine-year-old son, Nathan, entered their bedroom to tell them that his older sister, Amy, wouldn't wake up. Racing into their daughter's bedroom, the horror-struck parents found their fifteen-year old girl cold in her bed, her sheets and the right side of her neck soaked with blood. Authorities were puzzled by the lack of enough blood outside the body to support the conclusion that the girl had bled to death during the night, though the grieving family never suspected anything other than foul play. "When I kissed her good-night, it was closed," a sobbing Mrs. Wyle told the police questioning the open window in Amy's bedroom. The autopsy revealed only about a quarter of her blood remained in her body.

"The only wound we could locate was a small bite-like pair of punctures that resembles a larger version of the bite of a vampire bat," Dr. Emilee Higgins described, "right at the base of her neck." It has been suggested that blood thieves may have kidnapped the Wyles' daughter and stolen her blood for illegal medical practices, although why they would have returned her to her room no one could provide an answer for, and no one thought they could have pulled it off in her bedroom, with the Wyles sleeping just on the other side of the wall.

"One would think, too, that they would have chosen a more efficient place to extract blood," Deputy Harriett Andrews told investigators. "Her punctures didn't even sever her jugular vein. Such a crime is nearly unheard of; I confess even I had never heard such a theory before tonight."

Funeral services are scheduled for Saturday.

Reading about my own death on my sixteenth birthday, one week after my life was stolen, was like pouring salt water in the hemorrhaging wound ripped through my heart. I saw my picture in the local section of a discarded newspaper as I walked the unforgiving streets of Salt Lake City like a soul lost somewhere between heaven and hell. As I read the article, my body began to numb and my vision tunneled. It was like I was a million miles from my body, which stood there in the cold, bitter wind, looking off into nowhere. Slowly, robotically, I folded the paper, laid it on top of a bench, and walked away. Just walked away.

I never visited that part of the city again.

Chapter Seven

Emma

The first month at Robert's house is not at all pleasant or eventful. Robert goes to work every business day, leaving us with Jaquelina as an afternoon buddy. And all that blonde bimbo of a stepmother can do is swoon over me, asking me all these stupid questions in that Barbie-like tone: "Honey, are you all right?" "Where are you going, Emma?" "When will you be home?" "How do you like the house?" "Is your bedroom comfortable?" "Why are you so pouty all the time?" MY GOD!

School is no better. I can't make any friends. In fact, I don't interact with anyone any more than I have to; so many people seem sinister, and the few that don't I refuse to talk to because I'm too afraid, too shy. A lot of the time I sit at a desk, I don't really do anything; I don't draw, write, take notes, or listen to the teacher. I just lie inside my own mind, trying to hide my face behind a curtain of hair I barely have. I stare into my lap, praying the teacher won't say my name.

Every night, either Jaquelina or Robert invades my privacy to make sure my crucifix is out. They do the same to my sisters; they ran Kristina down the first night because she had disposed of hers. They retrieved it from her trashcan and threatened to ground her if she didn't leave it out. She told us she sets it out at around eight, then tosses it back in the drawer of her bedside table before she goes to sleep. She said it's too ugly to be seen, let alone slept next to. Annie, who keeps hers out constantly, got into a huge argument with Kristina when Kristina told us what she was doing.

But everything changed when I met that strange girl in Robert's yard in the middle of the night. My anger and spite are replaced by terror and about two billion questions. A week passes before I work up the courage to so much as venture onto my balcony after dark. Perhaps seeing another teen in my yard wouldn't be that scary in Maine, but yards were small back there and people cut through them all the time. The town has a population of 10,000; the kind of place where the word "stranger" is simply not in your vocabulary. Even though I'm in Salt Lake City now, I'm emotionally unaware of the true dangers of the area. I know about the crime rates, but in just four weeks' time, they haven't yet had a chance to register in my heart. So why am I so alarmed at this strange girl's appearance?

Perhaps it has something to do with the fact that most people wouldn't venture up a one-lot hill at night unless their business had something to do with the family living there. But I know that really isn't it. It's more about her. She had an eerie look about her, deathly pale skin that caught and reflected light, hair so black it blended with the night, ruby-red lips, and green eyes that glowed like fireflies. Putting all these features together, she resembled nothing short of a zombie from a horror movie. On the scene, I stared for a moment, let out some incoherent utterance, and ran back inside, where I shut and locked the door and drew the curtains.

But she also had a haunting beauty, a beauty so strong, enticing, and arousing that her image haunts me for the next three weeks, gradually fading over time. I tell no one, not even Jill. But she stays in my mind; I can't help but wonder who she is and what she was doing that mysterious night.

I finally decide to venture out again one evening in late November. I find the most relief from my crazy guardians outside. While the day is very relaxing, I'm beginning to yearn for the cool, crisp feel of the fresh nighttime air and the vast, mysterious velvet of the dark. Besides, I wasn't in any *real* danger, was I? That girl didn't hurt me. She just looked scary. And there's actually a tiny part of me that wants to see her again.

At around midnight, I slip into my checkered cloth sneakers and purple down coat. I'm out the door and hurrying down the steps in a matter of moments.

It's a full moon. The sky is a silvery blue and the moonlit grass glitters under my feet. I smile and head for the driveway.

No, I won't settle for lying in the grass. After three weeks, leaping beyond my balcony and deep into the night leaves me daring, and I know exactly where I'm going.

By the time I reach the edge of the park, I'm sprinting. I'm not much of a long-distance runner, and I'm already panting when I step off the sidewalk to cross the grass, but that doesn't stop me. I race right for the swing set, desperate to feel the cool air blow over my face.

I'm about halfway across the grass when my foot falls on something soft. I pull it up too soon and find myself sprawled on the ground, gasping for air as pain rips through my chest and legs.

I quickly pull myself to a semi-sit to see what I tread on. The answer is moaning only two feet from me.

Oh, my God! It's a girl!

"Oh, oh my God, I'm so sorry! Are you all right?" I scramble up and pull her to her feet. Her wrist is as cold as ice.

She just stares at me, horrified, with huge green eyes that seem to glow abnormally in the dark. Chills rush down my spine as I recognize the beautiful, haunting face. Fear shoots throughout my body, but I hold my head high and try to maintain a look of confidence and skepticism as I demand an answer for her trespass outside the room I'm sleeping in. She seems preoccupied, scared, and after uttering a few short answers, she turns and runs like a terrified ghost, disappearing into the night.

Amy

Weeks after the incident in that girl's yard, I see her again. We meet in the park. It brings a whole new wave of feelings to the surface and leaves me practically numb.

One night in late November, I leave my coffin to go to the park. I'm halfway across the lawn between the street and the swings when I trip over my own feet and sprawl to the ground.

And I'm exhausted. It's as though my body has entered sudden fatigue and I don't want to move at all.

Moments later, I feel a quick, heavy pressure on my stomach. A dull thud sounds as I grab my abdomen and moan in pain.

"Oh, oh my God, I'm so sorry! Are you all right?"

I look up. A girl is scrambling to her feet and grabbing my arms to help me up. A severe force shoots through my body as she touches me. I haven't touched a human in over twenty years. The blood lust pounds in my chest and mouth like an angry tiger in a cage. My muscles tense with desire. Her touch, the warmth radiating from her soft hand, is bringing the demon to the surface. I try desperately to fight it back into submission.

"Haven't I—haven't I seen you before?" she asks, sounding a bit frightened.

I look to her feet so that her beautiful face wouldn't entice me anymore. "I dunno."

"Are you the girl that I caught in Robert's yard a few weeks ago?"

I glance up. She does look a lot like the girl I ran into in the backyard of that big house three weeks ago. I sigh heavily. "I guess so."

"What's going on—who the hell are you? And what the fuck were you doing there?"

Nice girl. I realize she hadn't referred to it as *her* house. *Robert's*. The man living there? "What were *you* doing there?"

"I'm staying there," she said defiantly. "Now tell me. Who are you?"

My voice squeaks the truth before I can stop it. "Amy." Damn. Why did I say that?

"Good. And what were you doing at his house, again?"

Trying to survive my undead hell. "I dunno."

"You had the water on."

"I know." I look up, my mouth throbbing with thirst. What a beautiful young woman. I want her blood so badly.

"Well..." She looks me up and down, trying to keep a sarcastic, powerful look on her face, but I can see a waver of fear betray her. The fear that my hauntingly beautiful vampire body instills in anyone who isn't under my spell.

I look to the ground again. I can't stay around her. I'm not sure I can control myself. It only seems like a matter of time before I break. "I'm sorry. I've got to go. B-bye." I turn and run, not daring to look back.

Chapter Eight

Emma

I go out again tonight, only one night after the strange event in the park. I have no clue why I'm doing it; I would think the terrifying effect that girl had on me would keep me inside, but, on the contrary, I find myself wandering out again, that odd hope to see her again stronger now that we've met a second time. I don't understand these feelings; it's like some extraterrestrial force is pulling me outside, away from the safety of the warm house.

She's there, on the swing set, rocking herself slowly back and forth with her toes, her dark hair falling over her face. I can tell it's her; the park lamp shines brightly over the mulched area. It reveals a bluish glow in her hair; it's the first time I've noticed it, not that I've been able to take a good look at her. She's very Goth; I can tell immediately by her outfit that looks like it came right off a Hot Topic sales rack. A long-sleeved purple shirt with a wide stripe of black lace running down the front; a leather corset loosely laced over her breasts and down to her waist; fishnets under a purple-and-black knee-length net skirt; knee-high lace-up black platform boots.

The swings creak as I sit slowly in the one next to her, my hands closing around the cold chains. She doesn't look up.

"I like your hair," I state bluntly. She doesn't respond, instead continuing to stare forlornly into her lap. Her ghost-like fingers hold the chains of the swing gracefully. The unnerving, staggering beauty of her features makes my stomach flutter with a strange mix of anxiety and lust.

"Can't you tell me *anything* about what happened?"

She shudders slightly, but continues ignoring me. I turn my attention from her and push off the mulch. After about fifteen minutes, I drag my feet and, after sitting for a moment in my swing, stand.

"Shouldn't you be home with your mum and dad?" she asks suddenly, bitterly, catching me by surprise.

"My mother's dead," I state just as bitterly. She falls silent again.

"Well...bye." I take a step but am almost yanked to the ground as she reaches and grabs my wrist with a steel-hard grip. Her hand is ice, and I shudder involuntarily.

"Wait," she demands in a voice as hard as her grasp. My gaze flits to her deep green eyes and I can't seem to pull mine away. "Don't come back out here," she demands, her eyes piercing deep into my soul. "Just stay home at night. Don't come back. Understand?"

I stay frozen, shocked and unsure how to reply. Finally I try to twist out of her grip, but she just clenches her hand tighter around my wrist.

"Listen, Emma. I'm not letting you go until you promise me you'll stay home."

The fact that she knows my name frightens me before I remember I'm wearing the jacket with my name sewn on the breast.

"But—"

"It's not safe out here. There are rapists and murderers around here at night. Don't believe me? Try coming out one more time. Just *one*."

Then why is she out here? I am in no position to ask. Right now, I just want to get as far away from her as possible. "Okay, I promise." My wrist is free in half a second and I'm zipping away from the scene, pushing myself as hard as I can until my unfit lungs force me to slow to a fast walk. The street is glowing with the yellow light from the streetlamps and the cold wind nips mercilessly at my cheeks. The houses lining the area are dark save a few bedroom windows glowing with lamplight.

As I move out of the yellow glow and into the as I turn onto Robert's driveway, someone reaches out of the shadows and grabs my wrist. I let out a small scream as whoever it is tries to pull me into him. The cold, clammy skin sends shivers down my spine as its sharp fingernails dig into my arm with shameless force; there is no way this creature is human. I struggle and kick and scream, grabbing the wrist with my free hand and trying to pry myself away. The world melts to nothing as hundreds of scenarios pour through my mind, each more horrific than the last. My feet push the gravel aside as I'm dragged toward the dark; this thing is winning. I look up; two horrible, glowing brown eyes are boring into my soul with a horrendous amount of lust and hunger. It smiles menacingly, revealing a row of blindingly white teeth. Two, the ones that grew next to the four front ones, are an inch longer than the others. My terror doubles. Are they *fangs?*

"No! Help me!" I screech hopelessly as I reach the edge of the shadows; I give a giant tug and loud shriek, but its grip only tightens. Terror threatens my consciousness as I scream for my life. The world seems to spin; I struggle so hard, but it's too strong. What will become of me? The sense that if this creature wins, my very soul will be lost overwhelms me and I wish I would faint. It's just reaching for my midsection when an angel interferes in the form of a far-off scream.

"No! You leave her alone!" A girl jumps from nowhere and bites the thing's arm. Blood gushes from the wound and the creature lets go, howling in pain. I sprawl backwards onto the gravel.

"You!" It smiles.

"Stay away from her! She's my prey, understand?"

My eyes widen as I see the beautiful black hair. *Amy!*

"You don't fool me, Amy," it patronizes menacingly. "You hate hurting people, remember?"

"But I still need to, to survive! You know the rules, and if you don't leave her for me, Madam Noctis will not be happy with you!" Her voice has transformed; no longer is it the timid squeak I know. It's strong, loud, and angry. "Emma! Run!"

"What-wha—"

"I've dealt with this man before! I'm all right! Get out of here!"

I sit, gaping, on the cold gravel, too shocked to move.

"Damn it, Emma, go! *Now!*"

The monster snarls at her, twisting out of her grip.

"Leave her alone, Jason! I found her and I'm going to feed on her! Go find someone else!"

It finally regains human composure, if it ever had any. "You are the weirdest bitch I've ever met," it whispers to Amy. "One moment you're cowering in fear, the next you're all over me because I tried to get some teenage girl. All that and you're still the hottest chick I've ever seen. You're lucky you're already one of us because man, if you weren't I'd make you one." It's moving a hand suggestively over one of her shoulders as it speaks and circles her body; she glares at it, her pain-laden eyes following its every move. It laughs and takes off, the rabid look still blazing in its eyes.

Amy lets out a tiny cry and turns to me. "Emma—"

My legs suddenly return to life, and I stand quickly and run, not bothering to let her finish or even to glance back.

Amy

The redhead who found me in her yard comes to the park that night and sits next to me on the swings. I try not to look at her, try to bite down the lust in my throat as the warmth from her radiant spirit penetrates my skin. My stomach churns with illness; I've been feeling unusually sick since I woke tonight. I even considering killing myself a bit earlier. I've lived two decades like this. Is suicide the only way out?

"I like your hair." Her voice is edgy, blatant, without a single note of kindness, but I still feel my cheeks burn at the compliment. She sits in the swing next to me and asks again what I was doing the night we first met.

Don't say anything. Don't look at her. Don't even think about her.

Finally she gives up and pushes off in her swing. Soon she's high in the sky, soaring up and falling back and soaring up again. A light breeze plays across my face every time she whooshes past. As I sit in silence, a terrifying realization overcomes me. She's perfect. Young, beautiful, innocent, warm, full of life, and out at night…someone is sure to attack her if she keeps coming out like this. And if the one who finds her is Jason or Jade…both tend to rape their victims. She's so beautiful; they'd surely approach her with overpowering desire for her body…from the rush of her blood to the depths of her vagina. If she doesn't get home now, she's a goner. I have to get her out of here.

"Shouldn't you be home with your mum and dad?" I ask as she stops.

"My mother's dead."

Oh. The combination of the way she said it and the unexpectedness caused the news to hit me like a stone wall. I stare intently at my knees, racking my brain for something that will scare her away for good. Something that will keep her from coming out at night for a really long time.

"Well...bye." She starts off, but I reach out almost automatically and grab her wrist, forcing her back toward me.

"Wait," I order, locking eyes with her. "Don't come back out here. Just stay home at night. Don't come back. Understand?"

After a beat of petrified silence, she tries to twist away from me without a word. I barely have to twitch to tighten my unnaturally strong grip enough to stop her. Biting back the horrible pounding touching her warm wrist forces through me, I shoot her my scariest, iciest glare.

"Listen, Emma. I'm not letting you go until you promise me you'll stay home."

She pauses a moment, obviously forgetting that her name is on her jacket. Sewn on in lovely lavender lettering. *Emma.*

"But—"

"It's not safe out here. There are rapists and murderers around here at night. Don't believe me? Try coming out one more time. Just *one.*"

Her face glows ghastly with fear. "Okay, I promise," she chokes, and with that, she tears away from me and across the lawn as though I have the flesh-eating disease. I zoom after her, my strong leg muscles pushing me toward her faster than a tiger runs.

I begin to catch up as we reach the sidewalk, and I follow about five yards behind her. I have to make sure she gets home safely.

Soon, in the light of the ugly streetlamp, her small shock of red hair disappears behind the trees at the bottom of the hill. I continue chasing her as though this run were no more than a casual stroll in the park. Almost immediately, a shriek echoes throughout the neighborhood, and with a jolt of fear, I rip down the sidewalk and find her, struggling vigorously against something that's gripping her wrist. Jason's dark brown eyes gaze menacingly at poor Emma, who is screaming and fighting for her life.

"No! You leave her alone!" I lurch forward and instinctively sink my fangs into Jason's arm just as he's reaching for her small, beautiful body; he pulls back with a howl of pain as blood spurts from the wound. I breathe terrified pants; I haven't bitten anyone, not even defensively, in two decades. The blood, thick in my mouth, is like a spoonful of honey. Cold, but blood nonetheless.

Emma falls to the ground as he lets go. She doesn't move, just stares, shocked, at the two of us.

"You!" Jason grins at me menacingly.

"Stay away from her!" I seethe, clutching Jason's wrist with both hands. "She's my prey, understand?" It's the best threat I can come up with.

Jason almost laughs. "You don't fool me, Amy. You hate hurting people, remember?"

"But I still need to, to survive! You know the rules, and if you don't leave her for me, Madam Noctis will not be happy with you!" I look to Emma. "Run, Emma!"

"What-wha—"

"I've dealt with this man before! I'm all right! Get out of here!"

She doesn't move.

"Damn it, Emma, go! *Now!*"

Jason growls at me, wrenches free of my grasp.

"Leave her alone, Jason! I found her and I'm going to feed on her! Go find someone else!"

Jason slithers his disgusting hand up my shoulder. At his touch, the wretched memory of that morning two decades ago returns full force. I can see the desire in his eyes as he stares longingly into my face. "You are the weirdest bitch I've ever met." His voice is dangerously low as he slowly circles to my back, uncomfortably close. "One moment you're cowering in fear, the next you're all over me because I tried to get some teenage girl. All that and you're still the hottest chick I've ever laid eyes on. You're lucky you're already one of us because man, if you weren't, I'd make you one."

I watch him hurry off down the street, releasing my terror as a distressed cry before turning to Emma, who still lies, paralyzed, on the gravel driveway.

"Emma—"

Before I can continue, she stands suddenly and races up the driveway like a ghost is at her heels. I sigh sadly as I turn back to the street. I don't even know the girl. So why do I feel like I've just lost a friend?

I have no idea why I return to the graveyard so early. My feet just carry me back there sometime in the early morning hours. Jade and Jason are leaning against the fence right by the gate, yapping loudly. I don't care to hear what they're saying, but I manage to catch the words "sex," "blood," and "amazing." They shut their mouths as I come into view and follow me with their wicked smiles.

"Hey baby," Jade taunts. "Want some of this?" He slaps his chest and moves his hips in a way he must believe sexy. I swallow hard and stare straight ahead.

"Or are you too busy with your precious swing set?" Jason adds. "And saving humans?"

"Or maybe she's just busy fucking humans…girl humans!" They both hoot with laughter. Their taunts follow me as I pass them. "Lesbo, lesbo, Amy's a lesbo!"

"Tell me, Amy," Jason asks, "were you really drinking that girl's blood tonight, or did you just say that to save her from me?"

"The demon who thinks she's a human," Jade sniggers and they both honk hysterically.

I try to blink back the tears as I sweep past Sarah, who leaps back, looking horrified. "Ewww! God, stay away from me, freak!"

I fall to my knees and hug my gravestone, wishing that I could disappear forever.

If they aren't nightmares of my devilish existence, they're sad memories of my life, my real one. Mom, Dad, Nathan. My singing, my guitar, the piano. My school, my house, the van. The beaches of Great Salt Lake, the glittering walls of the Grand Canyon, the beautiful cliff dwellings at Mesa Verde on our summer vacations. The sun, the clouds, the lovely blue sky. And Kelly. The love of my life.

After these dreams, I often open my eyes to feel cool tears falling over the bridge of my nose and down my cheek. My old life's absence is drilling a deep hole in my heart, and I want nothing to do with the horror I am now.

I want it all back. I want my family back. I want my life back. But most of all, I want Kelly back. I want to love her, to feel her soft lips press against mine and her cool hands play over my scalp. I want love back. Oh, how I want it back.

Sarah and Jade are in mid-intercourse behind Sarah's headstone when I return one early morning. Sarah's on top, her lips to Jade's throat, and I can just make out a stream of blood running over his neck. I shudder in repugnance and put my hands over my ears to block out the moans and wet smacking. I can't help hoping that they will stay out too long and the sun will kill them.

I see the moon. The full moon, shining through the trees, laughing at my misery. Like it's justice for these crimes I can't control. As if it's funny that I'm such a freak of nature, and maybe it is. Maybe my problems really are trivial and everyone is amused by my suffering.

Everyone but me.

I need comfort, but I have no idea where to get it. The night is cold, and all that surrounds me is barren land with dead trees, trees without leaves. Just long, haunting branches, silhouetted menacingly against the sky, reaching into the open. Reaching for the moon. For me. They loom over my head and I have nowhere to go. Nowhere to hide. I keep running, and running, and running, but nothing ever changes. There's no way out of here.

And there, lying at the base of one of the trees, is the answer. A little boy, all alone, crying and hugging his knees. He's the solution, the savior.

As I draw closer, his cries seem to cease and his face dries as if there were never any tears. He gives me a cold, hard stare as I approach, and even as I sit next to him, he remains stoic and silent. I shudder at the inhumanity of my compulsion, but nevertheless, I need his warmth, his spirit. I bite down on his neck and run my tongue over the area slowly, savoring every drop of his rich, wonderful blood. It flows slowly into my mouth and slides over my tongue and the inside of my cheeks, thick, luscious fluid, teasing my lust as it slithers down my throat.

He does not cry. He does nothing at all. But I can feel his stare boring down on my back, along with that of the moon, the stars, the universe. I'm so ashamed, but the blood is so heavenly. I can't stop. I need more, more.

It's all I have left.

Chapter Nine

Emma

After what happened on the driveway, I don't dare go outside. I get home and lie on my bed, shaking like a leaf, my teeth chattering so loudly I'm afraid someone might hear.

What was that all about? What was that evil creature that had tried to kidnap me? Why did it bleed so profusely when Amy bit its arm? And, the worst question of all, what did Amy mean by "she's my prey"?

Is Amy like him? Her hands were also really cold, though not clammy like his were. Is Amy part of a cult of rapists? Is she a prostitute? Is she planning to hurt me? Am I a target, a future victim? And what would they do? Fear grabs and twists my stomach and I realize I am about to vomit. I launch myself from the bed and manage to make it to the toilet just in time.

Of course, Jill hears me gagging and comes in to see me reaching for the toilet paper, a long line of drool falling into the toilet. Nice.

"Emma! What happened?"

I shake my head. "Cafeteria food," I lie, grabbing a cup from the dispenser and filling it with water. "Maybe we should consider lunch boxes." I put the paper to my lips.

"Are you sure you're all right?"

I nod. *Whish swish whish. P-tooh.* I throw the cup away and flip the light switch as I push her out with me.

I get no sleep that night and can't pay attention in school the next day. I'm lost in a world of horror, and the worst part is, I'm ignorant to what that horror is and how it affects me.

Amy

I sit in the forest the next night, trying to figure out what to do. Jason knows I was lying. He knows I won't bite her. What if he goes after her again? Oh my God, what if he already has? I have to warn her. But she heard me, and she's probably terrified of me.

Why do I even care? She's just one girl. Why do I want so badly to protect her? I want to keep everyone safe, but I know there's no way I can do that. So what makes her so special? The fact that I've spoken to her personally? The fact that I've touched her? Why do I want so badly to warn her, to keep her safe?

I press my palm into my eye as I cry.

Then it dawns on me. I have a tender spot for her. I'm drawn to her in a way I've never been drawn to anyone else. I have a feeling of sensitivity for her, even though I barely know her. Is it because of her mother? Do I feel sorry for her? Or do I feel a connection, like we share similar grief?

Her beauty. Her sugar-sweet, mesmerizing beauty. That cute, childlike face shrouded in innocence, that shimmering orange hair, that small, soft body. All of it, a breathtaking example of Mother Nature's finest art, in such treacherous, deceitful, mind-raping, heart-expunging danger. I want to hold her. I want to pull that poor, childlike innocence into my arms and protect it from the terrors of my own world. I want to keep her safe. I want to protect her. And I barely know who she is. We don't even get along that well. But something tells me her life is an extraordinary treasure, that her survival is vital to the world.

But how can I protect her if she doesn't know the real reason she can never go out after nightfall or the extent of the dangers she'll face if she does? Will the experience with Jason be enough? I don't even know who she is, what she's like, or even how she really reacted to that experience. Sure, she may never go out again, but what if she's the daring type, the kind that goes looking for trouble?

Or what if she, in her sheer disbelief, denies it until it's no longer real to her? No. I can't take that risk. I have to go back to her and make sure she's safe. Even if it means holding her down and forcing her to face the truth. Even if I...even if I have to suck her blood to make her understand.

But I'm afraid to tell her. Afraid of the pressure, of her reaction. Afraid to face the truth that is who I am, to finally speak the words that have controlled my very existence for the last two decades—the words that I have never dared speak aloud. *I am a—*

No! Goddamn it. Can't even think them. How can I ever tell her the truth when I can't even say it to myself?

And I'm afraid of her reaction. Afraid of her face, the look of mingled horror and repulsion that will undoubtedly bear down on me if I even get the courage to tell the world who—*what*—I am. The look that would crush my last bit of confidence, the look I could never face—because it would close the door on my last hope of being anything besides the inhumane demon that has overtaken my body. The demon of blood lust, the demon longing for the taste of innocent flesh, or pure souls...the demon I can never fight away.

I stand at the edge of the forest, my right hand resting on the rough trunk of a pine tree, the dark lawn of her house stretching before me. And suddenly I realize, this is about more than keeping her safe. This is about seeking guidance, reassurance, the light that I have been denied so long. This is a quest for acceptance, for trust, for loyalty, for friendship—for *love*. Love...I barely remember what that is. I know it's something that makes you feel good, something that colors your world and makes everything beautiful, but...I've forgotten what beauty is, what joy is. All I know is this underworld. These Hades' halls. This darkness.

What's the point, anyway? Why would she ever trust you? To her, you are an awful creature that will suck out her life. You'll rape her. You'll kill her. You'll suck on her, then leave her to die. To become another you, without life, without a heart. A tear falls from my right eye. *Anyone would be afraid of you. ANYONE.*

"Why?" I cry. "Why, God? *Why?* Why me? What did I ever do to deserve this? *What?*" I burst into tears and bury my face in my knees.

Oh, God, I must stop. I must regain control and face my fear—the fear of facing the truth.

I stand shakily and head sadly toward Emma's house. I have to get it out. It has to be done, and it will be done. Some way. Somehow.

I am so nervous by the time I reach her house I'm shaking almost too hard to walk. I have no idea how I'm going to get to her without facing the rest of her family, but I don't really care. I go over to the window under the balcony; the room is dark. It's probably pretty late; where does Emma sleep? Probably upstairs somewhere. But I don't dare ascend on the inside, so instead I use balcony steps and peer through the door. The curtains are drawn, but I can see through a tiny crack.

There she is. There's Emma, lying on her bed and staring at the ceiling. The lamp reveals her for the first time in full glory. Her short red hair falls over the edge of the bed, looking soft and wonderful. Her skin is light, yet lacks the pink tint characteristic of most redheads. It's just a very pale peach, like mine...back in my days of life. No skin tone on a living human being can ever match the deathly pallor my skin has become. Her face is twisted with anxiety; poor darling, I'm sure last night left her very messed up. I tap gently on the glass. She sits up immediately, her hair falling messily around her head, and looks about the room nervously. I knock again, and this time she looks right at me, gets up slowly and grabs a book, and cautiously approaches the door and pulls the curtain back slightly. Upon seeing me, her eyes widen in terror and she shuts the curtains again.

"Emma!" I try the door; it's locked. I pound desperately on the glass. "Emma, let me in! I promise I won't hurt you, Emma! Just open it a crack; I need to talk to you!"

No answer comes from her side of the glass. "Please, Emma, please. Just give me a chance to explain myself. I won't harm you; I swear on my soul." Not that I really can swear on my soul.

The curtains pull back enough for her to open the door a bit and peer out at me. "What are you?" she whispers frantically.

"That's what I'm here to tell you, Emma. It's a really long, sad story. Please listen."

Her eyes dart back and forth; she pulls the curtain around her back and grasps the door handle. "All right."

"Okay. Listen. Have you been to that graveyard to the east of this hill?"

She looks behind her for a moment. "Um, once," she whispers.

"Did you notice how many teenagers are buried there? In that one tiny cemetery?"

"Yeah. It kind of scared me."

"Do you have any idea why there are so many?"

"No."

I sigh. "They were murdered, Emma. All of them. By this one woman. Madam Noctis."

"*Murdered?*"

"Yeah."

"So there are murderers around?"

"No. Well, yes. Sort of. God." I shift my position and try to crack my knuckles. Oops. I've already cracked them dead. "Maybe I need to start over. Okay. Just scratch everything I just said. Okay." I shift my position yet again. "Do you believe in what is considered the supernatural? You know, in werewolves and witches and stuff?"

"Um, no."

"Would you believe it if someone told you she was something like that?"`

"Probably not."

"If you saw a creature that you thought was just fantasy, would you believe it?"

"You mean…if I had living proof?" She shifts her weight to her other hip, still clutching the book and handle. I shudder with lust.

"Uh-huh."

"Well, if anyone's given proof, it is obviously true. But it can still be hard to believe. What are you getting at?"

"Emma, I-I'm-I'm a-uh—" I can't do it. My lips won't form the words. Maybe I should show her. But what if it's too much? What if she hurts me?

"I-I'm going to show you this, all right?" I stand back a bit to catch the yellow glow of the porch light on my face. "Okay.

Promise me you won't scream, all right? I promise that I won't hurt you."

"Um, all right." She watches me intensely, terrified and confused.

I give a sad smile, then slowly, reluctantly, open my mouth widely.

She gasps and clasps her hand over her mouth, falling back into her room a little. "Oh, my God."

I close my mouth and give another weak smile. "I-I'm a vampire, Emma."

Chapter Ten

Emma

She is. There's no denying it. The fangs speak for themselves.

I stand by the door, shocked into silence. A vampire? Amy? I can't believe it. Though always a fan of vampire lore—the vast collection of vampire books and DVDs on my bookshelf standing evidence—I never believed vampires existed. But here's the proof, standing on my porch right in front of me. Her pearly white, slightly curved fangs reach half an inch past the rest of her teeth. They grow in place of the top canine teeth, with her four front teeth in between.

"Can I please tell you what happened to me? I've lived like this for twenty years. I really need someone to talk to."

I can't move. I try to speak, but my vocal cords are paralyzed. The water in my mouth has evaporated and my whole body is numb.

"I won't hurt you, Emma. I won't bite you and I won't drink your blood. I don't do that."

I recover enough to manage a few words. "Y-you don't? Why not?"

She looks to her feet. "I don't really know. I've thought about it, and I've managed to come up with a few ideas, but it's really not for sure."

"O-okay," I choke. "I-I'll listen."

She leans against the door. "I was born on April first, 1970. I lived my whole life in this neighborhood with my parents and little brother, Nathan. Do you know my parents?"

"I-I doubt it. I-I really don't know anyone around here."

"Their names are James and Lacie Wyle. They live on Smith Road."

Wyle? That name rings a bell. Wyle...where have I heard that name before? No, wait, I saw it written somewhere...Wyle, Wyle, Wyle...

Then it hits me. "You're Amy Wyle! The girl on that headstone in the middle of the cemetery!"

"You've seen my headstone?" she asks.

I nod. "It's black, right? With engravings of doves and a poem?"

She almost smiles. "My parents were rich. My mother was a police officer and my father was a brain surgeon."

"Yeah. I've seen your grave."

Amy sighs. "Anyway, Madam Noctis —that killer I told you about—is a vampire. I have no idea who turned her. All I know is she's buried in *that* cemetery, and she started this little 'clan' by attacking innocent young humans all over Salt Lake City. I-I was one of her earlier targets. It happened in March of 1986, when I was about halfway through high school. One night, she just came and put me under her spell and..." She shrugs, her arms still crossed. She gazes into the stars, her eyes glistening with a layer of tears. Oh, God. This really is hard for her.

"...I let it happen." She shakes her head and blinks. "Every single night for a week, she came into my room at around midnight and pulled me into her arms. And then...and then..." She starts to choke up and slides slowly down the wall until she rests on the deck, her knees tucked in. A single tear falls from her left eye.

"And then, she'd sink her fangs into my neck and-and-and drink. It was so painful. Because she bit as hard as she could and sucked mercilessly. The pain was searing, and it branched around my neck and tapered off in my chest. The harder she sucked, the farther through my body the pain reached. Each minute seemed like an eternity. I screamed and cried for help but—but no one heard me." She wipes her cheeks, shaking her head. "No one came." She lets out a sob. "And—and I got weaker and weaker with each night. I died on March twenty-fifth—exactly one week before my sixteenth birthday. I was in tenth grade."

And she starts to bawl. She cradles her face in her hands and sobs violently, like a little baby. I stare at her in awe, never having seen anyone in so much pain, not even my own twin sister. I slowly open the door and step out cautiously. "Amy?"

It's as though she doesn't hear me. Her shoulders heave, and she gives audible gasps for air between each heart-wrenching wail. Ten minutes crawl by with me praying all the while that no one can hear her. "Amy?" I'm beginning to think she'll never stop when she finally calms, wipes her tears away, takes a deep breath, and continues.

"After I died, I woke as a vampire. At first, I was really confused. I left my coffin, only to be greeted by Madam Noctis, Sam, Rose, and Elizabeth, the only other members at the time. I mean, since then, Jason, Jade, Sarah, and Mary have arrived. Madam Noctis has crowned herself leader of the clan.

"Anyway, once I saw Madam Noctis, everything came back to me, as if I had woken up from sleep at someone's house and had just remembered where I was. You know the feeling I'm talking about?"

"Mm-hm. I was confused every morning for a week after we came here." Maybe that's a bit of an exaggeration, but it happened several times.

"Well, as I said, I suddenly remembered everything. The long, painful nights in my room, the fear, the helplessness. Every single night came back to me; all the ones Madam Noctis had made me forget the moment they were over. And I immediately knew what must have happened to me.

"I remember the shock and terror that overcame me that night. Reality became clearer and clearer as I sat on the ground and just sort of caught flies for about ten minutes." She gives a heartbroken grin. "I mean, I was *terrified*. I was a vampire. The life I had loved was over. I'd lost my parents and Nathan. I was condemned to the graveyard. The others must have thought it was strange that I was sitting against a headstone, this crazed look of horror on my face, rather than going out to feed. But no one said anything. They went off on their own.

"Well, soon after that night—I'm not sure how long—I became aware of the magnitude of the cravings for blood I had as the shock began to ebb away. I tried to resist them, because, obviously, I didn't want to hurt anyone. But as I headed to the playground—I have always loved to swing—I found a little boy, out after dark. The thirst took over, and I lost control. I grabbed him, covered his mouth, and—" she takes a deep, shaky breath, "—and bit into his neck."

I gasp quite audibly and my hand flies involuntarily to my throat.

"He was…he was…" She gasps too, trying to stop more tears. "He was…delicious. There was no taste of iron, no saltiness. Just sweetness, like milk, like…like life. And I fell into it, and began to get lost. After a few minutes, I managed to stop myself. Emma, you cannot *imagine* how difficult it is to stop drinking someone's blood, especially as a newborn like I was. It's damn near impossible. It's a miracle I didn't drain him dry. God was looking out for him that day. God was looking out for both of us."

She buries her face in her hands once again and cries some more. "I ran. I left him sobbing on the sidewalk, and I ran. I never saw him again. I thought the guilt would kill me. I couldn't believe what I had just done. *I had injured a little boy.* I began to worry if I had hurt him too badly. Someone as small as him could be wounded heavily by such a fierce bite, and I had gotten a lot of his blood—I was surprised at how fast blood can be sucked, how pervasive the wound could be—and I sucked really *hard*. Although I knew it was unlikely, even irrational, I couldn't help but worry…what if he died? He was young, only six or seven. I was terrified and overcome with pain. I still worry about that poor boy. I feel sick when I think of what I did to him." She looks up at me with her huge, grieving, abnormally bright green eyes. "Do you think he's okay?"

I stare at the deck. I'm hovering over her now, leaning against the glass door, my hands clasped behind my back. As I look at her, I realize how full and voluptuous her ruby lips are—and just how deathly white her skin really is. "I don't know."

"It's been twenty-one years. *Twenty-one years!*" She heaves another sob. "I'm not like the others. I hate drinking blood, I feel for victims, I hate being a vampire. Plus my body temperature is mildly higher than theirs."

"What are theirs'?"

"Air temperature. Death temperature. I'm cold, but not *that* cold."

I fall silent.

"Emma, I still feel *human*. I just have a vampire's body. I crave blood, I hate garlic, I have to sleep in a coffin. But…I'm just not like the others. I'm not sure why."

"So, the other night…with that…that thing—"

"That was Jason," she says. "He's one of the worst ones in the graveyard. He's so vicious, so merciless…" Her voice falls. "He rapes and tortures his victims as he drinks their blood. He really does feed on their pain as much as their lives."

"Rape? As in—sex?"

She nods. My head grows light and the world spins as realization of what would have happened to me had Amy not saved me inundates my mind.

"And…his arm bled because your fangs pierced the skin!"

"Right."

"And…when you said I was 'your prey'—"

"It was the only excuse I could come up with. Madam Noctis is very strict about us 'stealing' one another's prey. I knew that Jason wouldn't believe me, because he knows I don't like drinking blood, but it was the best I could do. I think he left because he didn't want to argue; his blood lust was probably killing him, especially after physical contact with you."

Slowly, reluctantly, I sit next to her. She doesn't attack me. Just holds her face in her hands, almost as it I'm not there.

"I have—I haven't been with humans for more than twenty years. The lusting for blood is bad enough when I'm on my own. But meeting you shot it sky-high. Over time I've learned to control it, and I've practiced controlling my feeding on myself and on my friend Elizabeth. She's—she's the only vampire in the graveyard who seems to care about me. I told her I was afraid of what would happen if I ever did lose control, so she let me drink her blood while it was still full of life, life from humans. I can stop when I want to, but…" She inhales deeply. "I've never actually practiced on a human. Just vampires. So…I don't know how much harder it would be to stop."

"Do you…do you think you could?" I ask hesitantly.

"Probably. You don't have to let me near you anymore. My thirst has never been as strong as it was when I met you, and I was afraid I would lose control and—and—I didn't want to hurt you. Even with one bite. That's why I was so unresponsive. And then I realized how susceptible you were, and I told you not to come out anymore."

Shock spreads through me. "Are you serious?"

"Yes."

"Oh my God."

She nods. "I'm sorry. It's just…I've never gotten this out before. I really need someone. I've been all alone for so long. I just…seeing you, speaking to you, the first human I've spoken to since…since *it* happened…and not just a human, a beautiful young girl the same age I was when I was killed…I…I…I just couldn't hold it in anymore. Oh, Emma. I know it sounds so strange. I just…I just…I really need someone to talk to. I really need a friend."

I slowly put my hand on her shoulder, mingled astonishment and sympathy running through my nerves. "You have one."

December

Chapter Eleven

Emma

I bring the permanent marker up and down on the paper lethargically, wishing I could throw it all in the garbage and run away. I've finished about a quarter of the project, and it looks horrible. I groan as Mrs. Larson approaches.

"Emma, Jill, listen. I know you haven't had nearly as much time as the rest of the class on this project, and I'm terribly sorry about that. But the final grades for the second six weeks are due next Wednesday, and I need your projects by Monday afternoon. I will let you take your markers home over the weekend if you don't finish. All right?"

I grumble something incoherent. Now I have to spend the entire weekend working on this piece of nothing. Where is the love?

Jill makes no response, just continues slowly placing dots on her caterpillar. It's only about a fifth done, but it looks incredible.

"That's really good, Jill," I whisper after Mrs. Larson has moved on.

She shakes her head. "It's horrible. I hate it."

It isn't horrible. And Jill knows it.

As I'm brushing my hair at around nine, my eye catches the stippled drawing in the middle of my desk. I sigh angrily and try to place a few dots around the eyes—no. Much too dark. The circles around the eyes in the photograph are lighter than that. My eyes stray to the picture of Mama I have tacked to my bulletin board. She's standing on a paved walkway that runs around various geysers, Old Faithful spewing steam in the distance. Her long red hair and bright brown eyes glisten in the light, her face glowing brighter than the sun behind her. She always loved Yellowstone; this particular picture was taken when she and Robert were on their honeymoon back in 1978. Robert took the picture. I feel the unnervingly familiar tightness clench my chest, and, throwing my pen down, I rocket out of my chair and leap onto the bed, penetrating the silence with my own heartbreaking wails.

Amy

She likes me. She believes in me. She cares.

I feel lost in a mixture of joy and disbelief. I didn't think that anyone would understand me. The actions of the others in the graveyard speak for themselves. And I was almost certain that any human I told would come after me, terrified for her life. But the first risk I took turned out someone who understands, who isn't afraid.

I know some people may think she's just tricking me, luring me in so she can easily kill me. But it's not true. I've been to her house a few times now, and I feel us bonding quickly. She understands that I saved her. She's grateful. And she cares about me.

I wake excitedly right as the sun falls beyond the mountains. It's around nine, I guess, and I know exactly where I'm going.

On my way out the back gate I bump right into Elizabeth.

"Amy!" She starts. "Where did you come from?"

"My grave, of course," I almost laugh. Elizabeth places a hand on my shoulder and leans in to whisper into my ear.

"Are you all right, Amy?"

I nod. "I'm all right, Elizabeth. Don't worry."

She smiles and pulls me in a close hug. She's very cold because she has had no blood yet tonight. But she's so soft. She knows what I've been through, and all the pain of my past seems to just make her care more. "Good luck tonight, Amy. Don't be afraid to protect yourself."

"I won't."

Elizabeth smiles again, lets loose a blood-deprived shudder, and races up the hill toward Sunny Housing. I sigh and turn left for Emma's.

As I ascend her steps, her porch light clicks on, giving the area that eerie, yellow, manufactured glow. I so much prefer the moonlight.

I look through her glass door; she's lying facedown on her bed, her back heaving—she's crying! Concerned, I tap gently on the glass. I try again when she doesn't notice. She freezes, then slowly turns over, wiping her eyes, which widen slightly when she sees me.

"Amy!" She races over, pushes back the door, and steps outside.

"Emma, what's wrong? Why were you crying?"

"Oh, I just miss my mother is all." She tries a weak smile.

"Oh…" I want to put my arm around her shoulders and comfort her, but I don't trust my blood lust. We sit together on the bench and I try to lean away from her. "Oh, I'm so sorry. Emma, that's not nothing. That's nothing to belittle with words like 'is all'."

"I know...I just…I don't know."

After that she doesn't speak to me, doesn't even move, for the longest time. She simply pulls at her cuticles, biting at her skin once in a while. My eyes stray to her neck a few times, and then dart to the wood of the bench. I can't think about it, I have to try to ignore the overwhelming lust filling me from being so damn close to her warm, soft body. I finally pull away a little more, and she doesn't seem to notice.

Emma eventually lets out a sigh as the light turns off automatically. She turns to me, still without speaking, and gazes into my eyes, as if looking for something. Truth, love, emotion, I'm not sure. I can usually figure out what people are thinking by their facial expressions, but not this girl. I can't see anything but two bright blue orbs fixed directly upon my eyes. She's trying to find something in me. But what's there to find in the eyes of the devil?

"So I guess that explains all those rules and ugly crucifixes. I guess Robert and Jaquelina know."

I jerk back to the present. The spell is broken. "Huh. Smart ones."

"I'm just saying. Be careful, 'kay?"

"All right." Silence begins to settle over us, but I quickly break it like blowing dust away.

"If you don't mind me asking about…you mother…"

"Yeah?"

"What…what happened to her?"

"Oh." Emma sighs, and is silent for so long I'm afraid I touched a spot too tender for her. But just as I'm opening my big stupid mouth to apologize, she takes a deep breath and her cute voice fills my ears with a story that reminds me sickeningly of my own.

"When I was thirteen, she went in for a mammogram, right? She came back, and…and she told us they'd found something. I wasn't that worried, I mean, I thought she would get better, you know?"

I nod her on.

"They did everything, but over the next four years she just…she just…she fought hard, but in the last year, she just wasted away." Emma released a shaky breath. "She just died. Slowly. They called it in July, but she was dead long before then. I was sixteen."

"Oh, Emma…" I stare at her sadly, remembering too well the night I realized I'd never see my mother again. "I'm so, so sorry."

"So then my sisters and I…we all moved out here. To live with our father. He left us when I was two. I hate it out here, Amy. I hate him. I hate her. I hate them both and I just…I just…I just want to go home."

I reach over and stroke her hand sympathetically, but instantly wrench it away as her warmth seeps into my skin, through my nerves and into my brain, tempting me, teasing me. "Emma…"

She's silent for a few moments, and I turn away and stare into the stars.

"How long does it usually take?" she blurts out.

"For…for what?" I stutter, taken aback by the sudden change in her.

"For a vampire's victim to die."

"Oh. It depends on how much the vampire sucks on them, where on the body they bite and how much blood is drained, and whether or not doctors get involved. It can take only one night if the vampire hits a vital blood vessel or they stay from dusk to dawn. Bt they don't kill much, because that would pose a threat to us. Killing every once in a while, like once a month, that's not risky because no one really believes vampires exist. Physicians will declare the victim a mystery before suspecting those so-called myths. It's too bad, because so many innocent people could be saved if people would just open their damn eyes. Still, Madam Noctis is intelligent. She's forbidden everyone to kill more than one person every few months. It's just too dangerous if a bunch of people die mysteriously every week like that. A few mystery cases every few months slide, but if a bunch of people seem to die like that, people will start to suspect something, you know?"

"Yeah."

"So we sort of have this system. We aren't supposed to attack anyone more than once or twice, and when we do, we have to be careful about which veins to hit, because that's a big factor in how quickly the victim will lose strength. Some of us, like Jason, love feeling blood gush into their mouths and so they hit the jugular vein and drink for a short time before running to find another victim. Since they attack so many people, they usually bite somewhere obscure, like behind the ear, so that family members won't notice very easily. Others, like Madam Noctis, well, she likes to sort of tease her thirst by taking in small amounts of blood over a very few hours. They usually miss the vital blood vessels or only puncture one. This way, it can take weeks to kill the victim, especially if doctors notice and start blood transfusions. Kind of like Lucy in *Dracula*. I had to read that book for ninth grade English. Anyway, that's what happened to me; because she was planning to kill me, she didn't worry about where she placed the bite. It's horizontal, on the left side of my neck, just above my collarbone. I think she hit my jugular vein with one fang and just pierced whatever smaller veins she could with the other. It took her a week to kill me, because she didn't drink too much before the final night." I groan as regret fills my heart. "I was weak, but we didn't think it was anything more than a bad cold."

"What about the bite?"

"That was a mystery. Obviously we thought it was a bite of some kind, but, of course, I didn't remember getting it. Mom took me to the doctor, but he said I was fine and probably just anemic from my periods. There were no toxins in my bloodstream or anything, so he told me to go home and get a lot of sleep and drink a lot of water." I sigh. "It's amazing, really. How everyone loves seeing the supernatural in stories, but throw any indication of its existence into real life and they refuse to see it. They refuse to even think about it, because it's 'impossible.' That's why we can kill at all."

"Oh, Amy, you poor thing. I'm so sorry."

"It's all right, Emma."

"So—" She stops.

"Yes?"

"So why aren't you like the others?"

I let out a long sigh. "I told you, I really don't know for sure. I can tell you this: it isn't supposed to be this way. Elizabeth told me that."

Emma's silent. Then she asks me yet another question. "You were crying last night. Are all those fluids from practicing with Elizabeth?"

"No. I drink water. I know that one of the vampire myths is that a vampire can't pass running water, but that one isn't true. Not for me, anyway. It may just be part of how I don't like drinking blood."

She reaches over and squeezes my hand. Hers is warm and swollen with blood; I can vividly picture it in my mind, pink with life. My throat begins to swell with lust again, and I try to bite it back.

No. Please. Leave me alone. I need a friend. Don't do this to me.

But it threatens to grow in strength, so I pull my hand away and pretend to sneeze as an excuse.

The night birds chirp as we sit, not speaking, just staring into the night sky.

Early that morning, I find Elizabeth just before sunup.

"Amy!" She hugs me. "How's it going?"

"Not good." My sigh is heavy and my body slouches in her arms.

"Not good?" She pushes me back to an arm's length, stares into my eyes like Emma did last night.

"Well, see, I have this new friend, Emma."

"A new friend? Oh, Amy, that's wonderful!"

"But she's a human, Liz, and it's good because I'm not as lonely anymore. But…but I always have this craving to drink her blood, and I'm scared I won't be able to stop myself if I bite her."

Elizabeth's eyes cloud with sympathy, and she takes me into her arms and rubs my scalp. "Oh, sweetheart. Do you want to practice a little?" she whispers. "It's still a little while before the sun comes over the horizon, and I'm still very full of life. It'll almost be like biting a human."

Sounds good to me. I nod, and she takes my hand and leads me to her grave in the northeast corner of the cemetery, where we'll have a little privacy. Like the kind I wish Sarah and Jade would seek. Behind it, she lies in the grass and exposes the most luscious part of her neck. I feel the monster of unrestrained thirst grab and pull at me—it wants me to lunge at her like a cougar. Instead I take a deep breath to steady myself and lie next to her, where, slowly and carefully, I slip my teeth into her soft, cool flesh. Her blood, still warm from her recent feedings, rushes into my mouth. I swallow once, twice, as she rubs my back rhythmically.

"Okay, Amy," she breathes in my ear, "try to stop now."

I take one final swallow and pull away reluctantly, wishing to stay like this forever.

"Good, Amy," she whispers. "Good. Now do it again, and stop without me telling you."

I do, and she strokes my hair and hugs me close to her. "Perfect, Amy. Absolutely perfect."

Then it's her turn; I feel my whole body relax as she gently opens my skin where she always does—behind my ear, where the scars she leaves aren't that visible—and replaces the blood I sipped from her neck. Tingles caress my body and she finally backs away, leaving me sleepy.

"Good night, Amy. Sleep well." She disappears and I crawl to my feet to go to my grave.

I can only hope these practices will be enough to protect Emma.

Chapter Twelve

Emma

  It's the first day of December and my afternoon is nuts. At first I try to work on my art project, but have no more luck than before. Two years ago I would have loved it. But since Mama's death, school art projects have lost me. Or I have lost them—I only want to draw what I feel the way I feel it. I finally let out a frustrated sigh and stick *Corpse Bride* in my computer's DVD drive instead.

  I hardly pay attention to the screen. I can't get my mind off Amy. The thoughts of what happened to her and what she managed to save me from are all haunting my mind, confusing me and leaving me numb. I end up staring dully at the screen, barely listening to the dialogue. I have seen the movie so many times that it's all playing along in my subconscious, like a sickeningly familiar pop song, as I sit brain-dead in my desk chair.

  At around four, Jaquelina barges into my room.

  "Hey baby. Do you need anything?"

  Baby? What am I, four? "No thank you," I snarl through clenched teeth.

  "Do you want some pecan pie or something?"

  Oh, sure. Try to kill me, why don't you. "I'm *allergic* to pecans, Jaquelina." Stupid.

  "Oh. Well, then, do you want some milk?"

"I'm not thirsty." God, woman. Take the hint and leave.

"Oh. Okay. Are you doing all right?"

I refuse to answer. After a moment, she sighs and the door clicks shut. Then it opens again.

"You know, they may be awful, but that doesn't mean you should treat them like pig shit."

I swivel in my chair to face Annie. "And I suppose you're being a perfect little angel and giving in to their every command?"

"Eat your words, Emma." She thrusts her middle finger in the air. "You know that's not what I do."

"Oh come *on*. Get a life. You're eighteen. Adults don't know everything, you know. You're supposed to make decisions for yourself. You can't just go around acting like a four-year-old and doing everything everybody tells you. You're a legal adult. Get your own values."

"Well, excuse me for liking to stay out of trouble."

"Excuse me for hating someone who abandoned me when I was two years old."

"Creep."

"Jerk."

"Bitch." Annie slams the door. I grumble and turn back to my computer screen.

"So, how's school going for you girls?" Jaquelina asks a little too cheerfully at dinner. "Do you like it?"

I grumble a few words.

"Yes? No? Maybe?"

Shut up and leave me alone.

"Is it fun?"

From the corner of my eye I notice Jill drag her head up and down. She doesn't make a sound, just twirls her fork melancholically in her spaghetti. I know she thinks of school as anything but fun. Same for me. I used to love school, but now I'm getting no enjoyment out of it whatsoever. Even my three art classes seem dull. It all seems so pointless to me now—no pun intended. I want to draw what I feel, and in no conceivable way do my feelings match a butterfly of dots.

"How's the workload?"

None of us answers. Jaquelina seems to give up for the moment as she turns to Kristina to ask her about her life.

"So how're the college applications coming?"

"Fine," Kristina mumbles as Annie reaches for a second serving of spaghetti.

No one speaks for about ten minutes, during which time Annie helps herself to a third bowlful. "Finished," she finally declares as she stands.

"Wow," Jaquelina comments, eyeing the empty serving bowl. No one else has finished her first helping. "You were hungry."

Annie takes her empty plate to the counter and cuts through the family room. I hear the bathroom door close.

Jill, on the other hand, barely touches her food. I manage to eat about half of it, but only because I love pasta. Then Jill and I retreat to our lairs, leaving Kristina to battle with Jaquelina over whatever.

Amy appears in my yard at around ten thirty. I'm so happy to see her; it's starting to seem like she's the only person who understands me (aside from Jill, who barely talks anyway).

We sit on the balcony again. It seems safer than inviting her inside; I don't want to take any risks with Robert and Jaquelina around. If they know about vampires, Amy could be in trouble if they find out about her.

I stare into my lap, trying to think of something to say. "I fought with my sister today," I mention, remembering the brief volley of bad names with Annie.

"You did?"

"Yeah. Annie. She told me I should stop treating Jaquelina so badly. I got defensive. Annie's really the only one I fight with, you know. It's because she and I have the exact same stubbornness and…forwardness, I guess it would be." I laugh. "Mama used to tell me you can't find someone absolutely perfect for you unless you marry yourself, and I said to her, 'Mom, if I married myself we wouldn't last a day.' Kristina's a little less…I don't know. Headstrong. She's more the submissive type, the kind who gets along with hotheads like Annie and me. I suppose she's a little too nice for her own good. Never really stood up for herself much. And Jill…Jill is like Kristina and was always my best friend. I think Annie and I get it from our Mama because she was really, um, confrontational, if you know what I mean."

"I'm sorry you fight with Annie."

"Yeah. Me too."

"Is her real name Anne?"

"Anne Marie. She's eighteen, but she still does everything everyone tells her to do and never questions authority. It's a little strange."

"Huh," Amy begins. "I know people like that. Well, I knew people like that. Now the only people I know are you and…them. If you can even count them as people. Nathan and I fought a lot too, but we loved each other anyway. I missed him terribly after I died. He was only nine when it happened."

I bite my lips, rub my arms against the cool air. Glance at Amy, who is swinging her legs, oblivious to the frigid air.

"Aren't you *cold?*"

She shakes her head. "Can't feel anything colder than my body temperature. I mean, I can feel it on my skin, but that's it."

"Well…do you wear that in the summer too?"

"It's the only outfit I have," she says. "I know it's, uh, gothic. *She* makes us wear them, almost like a uniform or something. It really sucked at first, but I got used to it."

"Do you get hot either? Like, in the summer and stuff?"

"Well yeah, heat still penetrates me. Obviously, because heat is part of what we seek when we drink blood. But I take off my corset and sometimes my boots and leggings…when it's safe, anyway."

"And where did you get that water bottle you always bring with you?" I jerk my head to the Aquafina bottle near the bench. She brings it every night.

"I took it from the gas station."

"You *lifted* it?"

"What choice do I have, Emma?"

"Doesn't that feel bad?"

"Risking my ass every time I get thirsty is worse."

I sigh. She's right—why on earth would she have money? "You know, Robert and Jaquelina love these cold nights. It gives them an excuse to go out to the hot tub on the deck by the sunroom. I don't really want to know what they do out there."

She giggles like a young schoolgirl. "Do you like to swim?"

"I took diving classes a few years ago. I had to give them up when Mama started to get really sick. I miss them. I was one of the best in my class. I'd finally found a sport I loved."

"Well can't you start taking them again?"

I shake my head. "I can't. I won't do as well. They'll bring back too many memories. It'll be too sad."

"I know what that's like," Amy replies. "I never go past my old house. It's too hard. My family is gone, anyway. I guess it was too difficult for them to live there anymore. The house where they found their daughter dead."

My chest grows tight as I let out a shudder. To get my mind off the subject, I pose a question. "Amy. All those vampire myths and stuff—are they all true?"

She doesn't speak at first. "Like what?"

"Um, garlic and crucifixes and stuff."

"Oh. Well, yeah, that stuff's true. Garlic, crucifixes, and sunlight burn our skin on contact. Otherwise, Robert and What's-Her-Face would easily prove how stupid they are!"

I smile. "That's true."

"Anything else?"

"Well, I guess. Are they all?"

"Some. The mirror one is a bunch of bull. I mean, we're living corpses, not ghosts! Our bodies are as solid as they've always been. How could light possibly bounce off us and reach your eyes but not the glass of the mirror?"

"How about the thing about vampires' inability to cross running water?"

"That's not true either. I've seen them cross those tiny rivers that run down the street when it rains."

"What about…"

"What?"

"Is it true that…if a vampire attacks you, you lose your soul?"

She draws out a long breath. "Yes. That—that one's true."

"Oh God. Really?"

"Yeah. It's sort of, like…it's slightly complicated. Do you want me to tell you?"

I nod. "Sure."

"Okay. Well, it's like this. When people hear it, you know, 'you give up your soul for immortality and eternal youth'…a lot of times they just think it's hypothetical, you know, people surrender all their values and morals and whatnot to be a vampire. Kinda like selling your soul to the devil. But it's so much more literal than that. Vampires literally suck out your soul when they're taking your blood. Vampires don't have souls. It's part of what sustains you— not really your body, but it's what brings you to life. A body can't live without its soul; you need it to be really alive, complete. You need it to be unique, you know, who you are. It provides your emotions, happiness and sadness and stuff. It usually leaves the body after death and moves to the next stage of life, that is, what a lot of people think is heaven, but if it's lost before the body is, then that body becomes a vampire so it can search—hopelessly, I might add—for a soul to bring it back. Vampires don't have souls; their bodies are incomplete; their flesh lives, but they are dead as humans, and this is why many refer to them as being 'undead.' Vampires live without life, without emotion. Sure, they can bleed, and they feel emotional pain, but it can't be for anyone but themselves. They don't care about anyone. *Anyone.* Not even their lovers, if they are buried with them. Even the pain that they feel for themselves doesn't come from life. It comes from instinct.

"So, when a vampire sucks your blood, what it's really trying to do is get life, to find a soul to carry. And your spiritual life lives throughout your body. The body of a vampire needs that life because it's so crucial to physical life, Emma, that without it, you die. And that's the thing—since a vampire's own life is lost, it needs others'. It dies if it goes too long without feeding on them. It's almost like we're always trying to complete ourselves, trying to fill that void where our souls should be and bring ourselves back to human form because our bodies miss it so much. When you bleed, you don't lose it because it isn't physical. But when a vampire bites you, your blood becomes a sort of outlet for that life, probably because so much of it is carried in your blood. So when a vampire drinks your blood, what it's really doing is feeding on your soul. Sucking it right out of your body. Leaving you with nothing. Nothing but this distant, impossible hope that someday you may be able to get it back. Hence, vampirism."

My heart is racing as my hand flies to my neck instinctively. "Oh, my God."

"Makes it even worse, doesn't it?" she says half-sympathetically.

"You have that power?"

"I try not to use it. You know that."

"Yeah, but…"

"It's a terrible power. It's sickening. Once, I thought about it too much and I threw up."

"But if a vampire can suck on someone for a week, when does their soul go? At the end?"

Does she shake her head? It's so black out here, I can't tell. "No. Actually, your soul is like a fluid. A little leaves you with every drop of blood. But it does come back to you—very slowly—*if* some of it is still with you. It's like a magnet. If you still have a teensy bit of your soul, the rest will gradually flow back. Once it's all gone, though…it's too late. You become a vampire. Your soul is lost."

"Forever?" I rub at my arms against the chill again; the air is suddenly colder.

"Yes. No. I mean, not necessarily. It depends on when your attacker is killed."

"So when a vampire dies—?"

"They can't move on until they have their spirit back. Only when the vampire that took it is killed does their spirit finally return to where it belongs. Until then, the spirit stays inside the vampire, but we're so soulless already it only provides life for a few hours. One soul provides life for a day, I think, and it's ebbing away the whole time. Once it's given all the life it can, it shrinks away into the dark void and never feeds its captive again. That's why we need a constant supply of blood."

I shift and the porch light blinks on. After about thirty seconds of silence, my hand inches across the smooth wood of the bench and touches her cool one. It's soft, like silk, and I want to never take my fingers away. "Does that mean you don't have a soul, Amy?"

She cringes; I've obviously hit a very delicate spot. "Um, well…God, it doesn't make sense since I don't need blood, but how could I, uh…I try not to think about it, actually, because even the idea of my losing my soul hurts too much." Silence.

I look away slowly, my mouth agape. A charge of fear shoots through me. It's a lot to take in at once, just like a week ago when I first saw Amy's fangs.

"God, that's horrifying," I whisper.

"I know. I'm sorry, Emma. It's really scary. It—it's horrible. I-I'm expected to do it like everyone else. They tease me because I don't suck on some innocent person's life and spirit. I hate it."

I force myself to close my gaping mouth.

"Listen, Emma, I'd better go."

"Yeah, all right."

She approaches the steps, then turns back to me. "I'm sorry, Emma. Just try not to get attacked. It's hard, but you do have slight power. Keep out your crucifix. Lock your door—vampires can harness special energy to unlock doors, but this is only after they've been invited into that house. And close your curtains so you can't look into their eyes."

"What?"

"The spell starts in the eyes, Emma. If you don't look a vampire in the eyes, it can't put you under its spell. So keep your curtains closed."

"O-okay."

She smiles at me. "Good night."

"Good night." I sit for a second, motionless, then leap up to the railing. "Amy?"

She stops, halfway down the steps. "Yes?"

"I-I really like you. A lot."

She lets out a chuckle. "I really like you, too." She continues down.

"Amy?"

"Yes?"

"I think that even if you don't have your soul, you're amazingly beautiful. Personality-wise, I mean. I mean, you're beautiful physically too, but—" I cut myself off.

She grins. "Aw, thanks, Emma." She descends a few steps as she speaks.

"Amy?"

She stops, a sarcastic smile on her face. "Yes, Emma?"

"Thank you."

I can't get to sleep. I'm still trying to take in everything Amy said. The shock and disbelief that there are actually creatures out there that can and will devour your soul—I thought that was just *Harry Potter/Blue Bloods* stuff. Fantasy. I never thought it was actually *real*. The utter terror penetrates right through my bones, keeping my eyes wide open, taking in my dark bedroom. Eventually, out of fear, I pick myself up and go get in bed with Jill.

"Emma?" she asks, turning over sleepily. "What is it?"

I shake my head. "I'm too scared to sleep alone tonight, Jill."

"Why are you scared?"

"Just trust me, Jill. I'm terrified. Let me stay with you."

"...sure." She turns over and goes back to sleep, while the wheels in my head continue to turn.

Something feels wrong...something doesn't seem to fit with everything Amy has said. I think as hard as I can. Amy said that there is no true life without spirit...if she's a vampire and doesn't have a soul, then how can she be so alive, so real? She has emotions. She cares. It...it isn't right. Can't be. She has to still have something...right? Right? How could her body live without blood if she doesn't have her soul? I toss and turn, turning it over and over in my mind. The fact she still seems to have something and the fact she hates feeding on others...is there a connection? It all seems so surreal. It leaves me numb. It's as though the real world I've lived in for seventeen years is gone in a split second and a fantasy world has taken over.

It's three AM before I finally drift off.

Amy

God. Wasn't exactly easy about it, was I? I tried to pad it as much as I could, but I pretty much just gave it to her straight. I just handed her the truly hellish, otherworldly extent of damage that my kind can do. Soul-stealers. Soul-drinkers. That's what we are. We take the spiritual life and let it waste away in darkness to give ourselves just a few hours of sustenance. It's disgusting. And telling Emma like that...was I too rough? She just lost her mother. She's in such a weak state. Can she handle it? Can she handle the danger that lurks just outside her door?

It really is a terrifying truth. To lose the one thing that's keeping you eternally...I know that feeling. I've felt it every night for a week.

Does that mean you don't have a soul, Amy?

I've thought about it so many times over the past twenty years. How could it be that I'm a soulless vampire but I don't need to feed on the blood of the living to survive? I don't want to believe

I don't have a soul. That I'm just a heartless, lifeless being like all the others...no. I'm not. I'm not like them. Not like *her*. It can't be. It isn't true.

"I have a soul!" I almost shout. "I have it! It's right in here!" I slam my fist over my heart and slide down the trunk of the giant pine tree I'm leaning against. Tears fill my eyes. "Right here! I'm not like them! I'm still me, I'm still Amy Wyle...still Amy..." I start to sob. "Still...Amy..."

I don't want to believe it. I can't. I don't. I know who I am. I'm Amy. The girl I've always been. Right?

But the overwhelming truth overpowers me once again. I can try to believe what I want. But I am a vampire. I have fangs and scars on my neck. I have the power to feed on other people's spirits. I have the power to suck on other people, trying to draw in their life because I don't have my own. I even feel lust when I sit next to Emma. The slightest touch and the vampire side of me wants to grab her body and sink my fangs into her neck. She'd be delicious; she has a strong spirit.

And she's the only light in my tunnel of death. How can I tell her about the dryness deep in my throat, the pulsating dryness that her blood would satisfy? She'd surely hate me if I told her. After twenty years, I've finally found someone. But the same thing that left me in darkness for so long is now trying to block the only light that has finally come to save me.

It's too much to bear.

I finish crying, but the moon is still high in the sky and I know the sun won't be up for hours, so I go to the park. The chains on the swings are cool, as always, and feel good on my hands. I sit and push off, soaring higher and higher. The wind it creates brushes under my skirt and awakens the nerves in my inner thighs. My hair blows forward, backward, forward, backward. The ground falls below me, then returns. I let out a sigh. Swinging never loses its magic.

Thoughts of what Emma said seep back into my mind. I groan and try to push them away. I don't want to think about it any more. It's too painful.

But I can't really control them. I have too many awful memories. I push one bad one out of my mind and another one takes over.

Madam Noctis. Darkness. Cold. Pain. Pain. Pain.

My hand reaches to my neck and I finger where she bit me. I'll always have the scars to remind me of those awful nights. And she's still out there, bringing those nightmares to everyone she finds appetizing. She's still out there. Sucking blood. Bringing pain.

I spit into the air. I hate her. I hate her more than anyone else. She used me. She hurt me. She killed me. She took away my family, my friends, my future, my dreams. Left me with nothing but a wretched desire to hurt others. To do the same to them as she did to me.

And she's still using me. Hurting me, killing me. She patronizes me. She threatens me. She touches me—rapes me. I bring some kind of pleasure to her. Am I really that appeasing? Can she not leave me alone? How long will it be until she gives into her undying desire to taste my blood? One more time. Will that ever be enough for her? Or will she just keep after me forever, always just beyond my control, never slowing, never pausing? It sends shivers down my spine.

A bitter taste fills my mouth. Emma. Can she help me? Will she still trust me if I tell her about my urges to feed on her? Is she my only hope?

Chapter Thirteen

Emma

"Meat loaf," Kristina comments as we sit down to another one of Jaquelina's gourmet banquets.

Jaquelina lets out an exasperated sigh. "It was easy to make, Kristina. I have a bit of a headache, so I wasn't up to anything better."

I'm sure fifteenth-century servants got headaches, too. Didn't stop their elegant meals.

"So how are things going with you girls?" Jaquelina asks, five minutes into the meal, in the fakest voice I can possibly imagine.

"Wouldn't you like to know," I mutter.

"Did you say something, Emma dear?"

"No."

"Oh. Well, what about you, Annie?"

"I'm finished," Annie responds curtly, and her chair whooshes across the carpet.

"You are one fast little eater," Jaquelina comments as Annie carries out her practically licked-clean dishes.

"Yeah, sure," Annie says as she hurries out of the room.

"Well, how's school going, girls? Make any new friends?"

"No," I snap. Then a bell rings in my head. *One.* But it's none of her business, especially if she knows about the vampire clan.

"Not really," Kristina mumbles.

"Hmm. Well, what about you, Jill?"

Jill moves her head back and forth slowly as she gets up and carries out her half-empty plate. I follow her closely, mine still full.

I'm never hungry anymore.

Amy and I sit silently on the edge of the deck that night, our legs hanging over between the rails. As she shifts I see her beautiful black hair catch the moonlight, the emerging highlights a lovely faint yet glowing blue. Coupled with her big green eyes and full, bright red lips, she's a goddess of the moonlight. Her graceful hand pushes a lock behind her delicate ear and a tiny white gold stud adds sparkle to her earlobe.

"You're really pretty. Did you know that?" I whisper. She looks up.

"So are you. I always wanted red hair. And I think short and layered is cool, because it looks nice no matter how messy it is."

I smile. "Oh, come on. It looks like a mop. But it does stay out of my way like this."

"Do you not like your hair hanging in your face?"

"I don't like it hanging in my *eyes.* It's Jill who hates her hair in her face. She says that if she cuts it short, she can't pull it out of her face, but if she cuts it too short for that, she looks too tomboyish. So she hasn't had any more than a trim since she was eight. She usually keeps it tied back." I kick my dangling legs through the air. "How does your hair stay so brushed out and shiny like that?"

She lets out a small breath. "I hate tangled hair. I lifted a brush a long time ago."

Quiet pierces the night again until she starts singing an eighties song. I stare at her, dumbfounded.

"What?" she asks almost defensively.

"Wow."

"My singing."

"Yeah, Amy, your voice is incredible!"

"My teacher always said I had the best voice in choir."

"You were in choir?"

"Yeah. I did lots of things. I sang, I played guitar, piano...I loved music. I had this passion for it that most of my friends didn't.

I wanted to be a rock star when I finished school. I know that doesn't sound like a very credible dream because everyone does, but mine wasn't based on a desire for fame and fortune. I didn't care how much I made, as long as I could sing."

"That's how I feel about writing and art. Or, at least, I used to. I really can't do that stuff anymore. It's too hard now." I kick my legs a little more. "So, how are you? Is everything going all right? Are they leaving you alone?"

She exhales heavily. "I guess so. As far as I know, no one knows I don't need blood; they just know that I don't like feeding, and that's good enough for them. They've called me everything from a freak show and a misfit to a blood traitor and a human-fucker."

"But you said that ninety percent of their existence is based on screwing humans."

"It is, but for selfish pleasure, not for love. When they say it to me, they mean I do it without taking for myself."

"Ouch."

"Yeah. It really hurts. They—they even call me a lesbo. They think I'm gay."

"*Damn*, girl, why don't you stand up for yourself?"

"I've never been brave enough, Emma. Ever. I only stand up for my friends…like you." She smiles shyly.

"You should still have the courage to do both."

"I know. I'm passive. I don't like confrontation."

"You didn't seem to be afraid to confront Jason."

"He was going to kill you, Emma."

I tilt my head to that. She sighs and changes the subject. "I had this really awful dream last night."

"Really? So did I."

"You did? What happened?"

"You spoke first."

"Well, I tend to have these nightmares where I'm running through the woods and it's really cold and lonely and scary. Everyone hates me and I feel like a monster. Then a child appears and I'm really thirsty so I attack her. The worst part is…people say dreams are based in truth."

"Amy, that just means you feel that way about your life. It doesn't mean you hurt children."

"I know, but it's always so real, and the blood tastes real when I bite the child."

"But it's just a dream."

"But it's halfway real."

"Amy, I—"

"What was your dream about?" she blurts out.

"Oh, well, uh…" I consider pressing her subject more, but nix that idea as those pleading green eyes look into mine. *Please, Emma. I really don't want to talk about it.* "Well, my mama was there. She was lying in a hospital bed at the end of this long, dark corridor. I had to reach her to save her life, but the more I ran, the farther away she got, and then the floor flew out from under me and I fell into darkness and then…I woke up."

"You jerked awake?"

"Yeah."

"I hate those."

"I do too." I sniffle and run my hand under my nose. "See, it's one of those dreams that's caused by the thoughts and feelings you go to sleep with, not the other way around. One of those dreams that are so vivid and real you sleep restlessly and you're very…*aware* of things."

"That's how mine are, too."

"It's because the things they're about are so touchy and emotional to us. I mean, I really miss my mom. I miss her so bad sometimes I think I'm going to die."

I feel her hand run across my back gently. "I'm really sorry, Emma."

"It's not your fault," I whisper as my heart sinks into my stomach. "I just…I just…" Tears well in my eyes.

She continues to rub my back, trying her hardest to comfort me. "I know, Emma, I know." Her hand slowly moves from my back to my shoulders, then down my arm until finally it gives my hand a reassuring, perhaps even loving, squeeze, and lets go. An exotic sensation speeds through my body. I see her shiver as she takes it her hand away; I drop my eyes in disappointment. I really want her to keep touching me.

I sniff again and wipe the tears from my eyes.

"It hurts, I know."

My lip trembles as I attempt to force a smile. Not that it matters; she can't see it in the dark.

"I remember when my grandmother died," she whispers. "I loved her so much. She was always there when I needed her, and she never let me down. Ever. Then one day she had a heart attack and…and…" She stops. "Before this, it was one of the worst times of my life."

"Oh, Amy."

She sighs sadly. "There's always so much to be sorry about. Never enough to be happy about."

I was planning on going right to bed after Amy left, but the quarter-done stippling that's due in only two days once again catches my eye. The butterfly gazes up at me, seeming suddenly to reach out and pull me in. It's like it's pleading with me, as though its incompleteness is painful and it's begging for me to bring it to full life so it can stop hurting. I brush it gently with my index finger and its effects on me change; now it seems to whisper secrets, Amy's secrets, my secrets. Secrets that we dared to share even though we barely knew each other. Why did we do that? What possessed me to reveal my deepest feelings about Mama? What compelled her to disclose what she became when she didn't know if I'd react with fear or compassion? It slowly dawns on me as I stare at that little black two-dimensional butterfly that there could be a certain spiritual charisma between us. A cosmic connection that just speaks from inside, telling us that it's okay to talk to one another, that if we do, something wonderful might happen. I don't even believe in all that crap, but all of a sudden, it seems so real to me. As real and natural as the pumpkin-colored locks on my head. Is it what made us feel trustworthy of each other in the beginning, and what's keeping that trust alive now? Is fate getting itself involved in our miserable lives, trying to heal our broken hearts?

Or am I just being imaginative again? I shake my head. It doesn't seem to make any difference, as I realize that I suddenly feel a newfound spark of hope, microscopic but existent all the same. I sit in my desk chair and pick up the permanent marker.

Mama came in through the garage door and set her purse on the kitchen counter, sighing deeply.

"Hi, Mom!" I forgot about the Spongebob episode on Nickelodeon and leapt off the couch.

Kristina, at sixteen, was the oldest of my sisters. She looked up from her computer and stood. "How'd it go?"

Mama sighed again. "Well, Kristina darling, we need to talk." She took Kristina and me by the shoulders and sat on the couch with us. Annie and Jill hadn't stood from the matching daybed.

"You girls know I went for a mammogram," she began.

"Yes," Annie urged her on.

"Well, I haven't had one in ten years. I went in for one today, and they found something."

My blood pressure rose. "What, Mom? What did they find?"

"This is hard to tell you girls," Mama continued, "because I love you all so much and I don't want you to worry about me. But…but, unfortunately, it seems I might have a tumor and—and they want me to come back on Tuesday for further examination."

Annie gasped.

"Now don't lose sleep over this, girls. We don't know much about it yet, and it might not be a huge deal. Besides, doctors can do everything these days."

"Not everything," Kristina argued.

"I have full faith in them," Mama countered, "because they saved Maggie last year. After her car accident."

"That was a miracle, okay, Mom?" Annie spat.

"Well, maybe God will be nice enough to grant us another one."

Kristina drew her breath in sharply, and Annie looked like she wanted to kill someone, but I grinned. The doctors could help Mama. Everything would be just fine. Right?

Chapter Fourteen

Emma

I detour to the art room after school to turn in my project, which, after what happened Friday night, wasn't all that difficult to finish. Mrs. Larson is tacking canvases to wooden frames as I come in.

"Beautiful, Emma!" she praises as I hand it to her. "You seem to have a knack for this!"

I shrug. She places it in a bin with a bunch of other student projects.

"H-has Jill turned hers in?" I ask timidly.

"Yes, she did this morning." Mrs. Larson's face falls.

"What?"

"Nothing."

"Was it incomplete?"

She sighs.

"Look, Mrs. Larson, Jill is an amazing artist. She's just lost some of her school spirit and doesn't feel compelled to do artwork for others anymore. I-I'm feeling a little that way too."

"Why?"

"S-something happened and our family is sort of on rapids, that's all."

"Oh, no, nothing too bad, I hope."

I sigh. "You have no idea."

"Oh, Emma." She rubs my arm compassionately. "I'm really sorry. Do you want to talk about it?"

I shake my head, hugging my binder to my chest. I'm not ready to tell anyone else yet.

"Okay, well, I'm here if you need me."

"Thanks, Mrs. Larson." I haven't known any of them for very long, but Mrs. Larson is my favorite teacher.

I sit on the end of the couch later that day, leaning on my elbow and scowling at Robert and Jaquelina, who are putting ornaments on the Christmas tree. Kristina is tacking garland over the archway to the dining room. Jill is sitting stoically on the other end of the couch and Annie is nowhere to be found.

"Are you girls sure you don't want to help out here?" Jaquelina asks like she's the Good Witch of the North.

"Christmas is not my holiday," I reply grouchily.

"Oh, you don't celebrate Christmas, dear?"

"No," I retort. "I'm Jewish. We all are. Didn't *he* tell you?"

Jaquelina frowns and cocks her head. "No, as a matter of fact, I don't think he did."

"*What?*" I rocket to my feet, outraged. "You left us twelve years ago and you haven't even told your wife you're Jewish? What, have you just been celebrating Christmas with her without giving Hanukkah a second thought?"

Robert stands erect and stumbles over his words. "Well, um, see, um, actually, Emma—"

"Nope." I close my eyes and signal him to stop. "I don't wanna hear it. Just tell me where you keep the decorations."

"I-I'm afraid I don't have any decorations, Emma."

"I knew it! You converted, didn't you? You left your religion with us, didn't you? I don't care if you were already Christian when you met Mama. You left Judaism like you left the rest of us. You are *pathetic*." As angry tears dance on my eyelids, I rampage upstairs and slam my door. He is so sick. He just wants to erase every trace of us from his life. He doesn't even want to celebrate the best holiday of the year anymore. No doubt Christmas became the big thing again when that…that…*other woman* came into his life. I kick my bed in anger before falling on it and drowning in spinning darkness.

Amy

I knock on Emma's door and she comes out silently, projecting a strong, negative air.

"What's wrong, hon?"

"Nothing. I just won't be celebrating Hanukkah this year. That's all." Her voice is bitter with latent sarcasm.

"Why not?"

"Because Robert gave up Judaism when he left us. He just *had* to leave everything behind, didn't he? He couldn't even keep his religion. He couldn't even hold on to the spiritual belief that he shared with his wife and daughters. He had to cut off the last connection there was—the spiritual one." She falls onto the bench and buries her face.

"Oh, Emma." I sit next to her, frantically racking my brain for something to say that will make her feel better. "But…were both your parents Jewish, or did one convert when they got married?" Apparently the best I can come up with.

"Mom was always Jewish. She told me once that Robert converted for her."

"Well, Emma, once your parents got divorced, he probably felt most comfortable returning to his old religion. It probably felt wrong to him to celebrate a holiday he wasn't native to if he wasn't with the people he celebrated it for."

"Whose fault was that?"

"I know, Emma, I know. But you know, you don't have to let this keep you from celebrating. Can't you and your sisters celebrate?"

She cracks her knuckles. "Yeah, I guess so, but we don't have a menorah or anything."

"So buy a cheap one. Or improvise. Nothing should keep you from celebrating your religion, especially at a time like this."

"But there's really no point, Amy. I like Hanukkah, but in my family, the holiday was as much about religion as having fun. After what happened to Mama, I lost faith. I won't celebrate a holiday for a god that isn't there."

"Oh, no, Emma, don't. Don't isolate your spirit like that. You need God, Emma. You need to believe that God's there, because then you can believe your mom is, too."

"How can I believe in God? He killed my mama."

"I believe in God."

"But how can you? He let that—that monster—"

"But that's just why I believe in her." I consider all the things "that monster" had done to me that Emma isn't even aware of.

"Her?"

"I think God is a woman."

"I didn't think God had a gender. Why should you assign such a human characteristic to an entity? Why favor one over the other?"

"I don't know." Really, it's because I've never really seen a lot of beauty in males, aside from my father and Nathan, so when I think of the beauty that's supposed to be God, I think of a female. "Anyway, now that I'm dead, she's the only hope I have." I gaze into the stars. The little blue-green dots create an artwork of their own, the unique composition creating hypnosis without movement. I wonder how far away they are from the sun, from each other. What about the stars behind them? And the stars behind those? Is the universe eternal, like the life I'm now doomed to face? If it curves in on itself like some scientists say it does, will I eventually curve in on myself too? Because honestly, I think I already am.

"I miss my mom," Emma whispers out of the blue. "It hurts so much sometimes. Like this really tight feeling in my tummy that won't go away."

I rub her back lightly, quickly, before my thirst gets too strong. "I know how much it hurts. I missed my mom so badly after it happened. I missed everybody. And I still do."

"I'm sorry," she says. "I suppose it must seem so trivial compared to your problems."

"It's not," I hear my voice blurt out. "Not one bit. You're going through a lot, Emma. Don't minimize your problems by comparing them to others'."

"You're really sweet, Amy."

"Tsh. Thanks." Sweet. Never thought I'd hear a vampire be called sweet.

She starts to cry a little. I begin to feel concern waxing inside my abdomen. I want to embrace her comfortingly, hold her in my arms and feel her close to my heart, but I can't. I know her life will be too much for me. I can always feel the lust deep in my throat strengthen when she is near. What if I lose control?

But, before I know it, she's in my arms and I'm sitting perfectly still, letting her cry it out right onto my sleeve. Her body is so warm with her life. It radiates from her skin, seeping into mine and making my spine tingle. It awakens lust, desire, a need to become one with her blood, one with her life.

Yet another feeling awakens with it, a more innocent feeling, one that almost seems to burst out of, and bring with it, a human side I know I don't have. Weak, and immediately overshadowed by the promise of blood, but present all the same.

And that need for blood explodes in my cheeks. Strong, fierce. I bite my tongue as hard as I possibly can and drown in the succulent taste that fills my mouth. Yes. It's sending it away.

But it returns as quickly as it leaves. Strong, powerful. It's taking over. I don't let her go. I can't.

I clench my teeth hard, squeeze my eyes shut, and try to fight it. Instinct tells me to do it. *Now. Her neck is right there, just inches from your mouth. She's warm, full of life. Do it. Do it. DO IT!*

No! I fight back. *No! I can't! I can't do it! I can't!*

Emma is gone. I can't feel her in my arms anymore. I can't see her, hear her, smell her. It's just instinct and me. Fighting. Fighting. Fighting.

Do it!

No!

NOW!

Go away! GO AWAY!

Fighting. Fighting. Fighting. I'm losing. I'm being consumed by the need for human life. *No. Not Emma. Please. Not her.*

"Amy?" a far-off voice calls. "Amy, are you all right? Answer me. AMY!"

I open my eyes. Emma is grasping my right arm and staring at me appallingly.

"Huh?" I pull away. The thirst lessens just a bit. "Oh, I'm all right."

"Amy, you were talking to yourself. And you were crying a little, too. What's wrong?"

"N-nothing. I-I just…"

"What?"

"Tell me."

"It was nothing—"

"Now."

"I-I just was having this disturbing recurrent memory, is all."

She keeps staring at me. "You don't lie much, do you?"

"I'm not lying."

"*Amy…*"

I groan. She has me. "No," I confess. "I hate lying." Especially for the significance it has in the success of devils like me.

"Okay. So what really happened?"

A wave of guilt passes over me. What am I doing? Why am I hiding this from her? I'm coming to see her every night and I'm not even telling her how close to the surface my dangerous side can be. How can I call her my friend if I'm subjecting her to such danger? I draw out a long breath. "I was fighting my instincts."

"Instincts? What instincts?"

"Instincts for blood."

"What—"

"As soon as I touched you, they came back to me. Stronger than they have in a long time."

"Oh, God. Me? My blood?" Her hand flies to her neck.

"Yeah. Every time I see you it grows stronger, and I need to fight it off. You don't need to hang around me anymore. It-it could've happened. I've never had to control such a strong urge before."

"Oh, Amy, why didn't you tell me?"

"I-I was afraid you wouldn't want me around anymore. That I'd lose the only friend I've had in twenty years."

"Oh, Amy…" She falls silent.

I sigh. "I think we should stop this, Emma. I don't want you to feel unsafe, and I don't want to bite and hurt you." When she doesn't respond, I sigh again and stand to go. It's for the best, and we both know it.

"Wait!"

I turn to face her.

"Don't go, Amy. That—that's the nicest, most unselfish thing anyone's ever done for me."

"What?"

"Amy, you've been alone for twenty years, and you've finally found someone who believes in you. Someone you can talk to because she trusts you and you trust her. But you're afraid you will bring her harm, so you decide to leave to protect her. Amy, don't you realize how unselfish that is?"

"Are you serious?" Now I am the stunned one.

"Dead serious, Amy. Please, stay with me. Didn't you say you'd learned to control your feeding?"

"Yeah, but I haven't actually tried on humans, so—"

"But you let that little boy go. And that was with no practice at all. So now, after all these years…I trust you, Amy."

I trust you, Amy. It's sweet, but at the same time, it punctures my heart like a flaming iron dagger would. What if I can't control myself? I express this concern the moment it enters my mind.

"Please, Amy, you're my only friend, too," is how she responds. "I don't want you to leave. I need you as much as you need me."

I feel my lower lip quiver, and in gratitude, I throw my arms around her neck. She gasps in surprise, then pats my back gently.

"Thank you, Emma! Thank you, thank you a million times over!" The thirst tugs strongly at my throat. *Shut up*, I snap. *Don't spoil this for me.*

And I don't bite her. We sit together for what must be two hours, and the overwhelming urge to feed on her life lies inside me the entire time, stronger than it has ever tugged. But I manage to keep it at bay.

Maybe, just maybe, I can do this.

Chapter Fifteen

Emma

Amy arrives at nine thirty. I grin ear-to-ear and open the door to let her in, where she instantly wraps me in a warm hug. We sit together in my closet now because it's grown far too cold outside.

"How are you, Amy?"

"I'm doing all right." She sits down in a corner and pulls my Powerpuff Girls blanket over her knees. "How are you?"

I roll my eyes. "They're as annoying as ever. And"—my heart grows heavy—"my mommy...."

She strokes my cheek in sympathy. "I know, Emma, I know."

"It's just that, every day, it's like waking up and remembering how bad everything is, and you feel sick to your stomach and don't want to get out of bed because sleep can be so much easier than facing the day."

"No kidding. I know exactly what you mean."

"I'm sure you do."

Her eyes light upon something on my chest. Mine follow her hand as it moves from my face to the tiny gold cross that hangs around my neck. She fingers it gently, a faraway look in her eyes.

"That doesn't harm you?" I ask.

"Huh?" she starts, as if waking from a trance.

"Doesn't touching that cross hurt you?"

"Oh. No. As a matter of fact, I'm kind of drawn to it," she replies, frowning and turning the tiny charm over between her thumb and middle finger.

"That's strange. I thought vampires hated crucifixes."

"They do. Madam Noctis cautioned me of them early on, and I've overheard a lot complaining about them. I've also seen scars in the shape of crosses on some of the others. They burn the skin."

"Then how come they don't hurt you?"

"I don't know. I have no idea why I'm so different from the rest of them, Emma. Garlic burns me. Sunlight burns me. But I don't need blood to survive. It's like I'm only half-vampire or something." She folds her arms tightly over her breasts. "Why are you wearing that, anyway? I thought you were Jewish."

"I am. But back when I was in middle school, the only real best friend I ever had moved away. She wore it around her neck all the time, and gave it to me as a keepsake."

"What was her name?"

"Rachel."

"Aw, that's really sweet—"

"Emma!" Jaquelina bursts through the door. I poke my head out of the closet as Amy lies down and pulls a blanket over her head.

"What are you doing in there?"

"Oh, I'm just looking for something."

"Well, I can see that your crucifix is out."

"Of course it is."

"Good night, darling."

"Whatever."

Jaquelina sighs and shuts the door behind her.

Amy peeks out from under the blanket.

"It's all right; she's gone. Amy?"

"Yes?" She throws the blanket off.

"What was your life like?"

She sighs.

"Well, it was wonderful. I had a great house, a wonderful school, a loving family. Nathan was seven years younger than I was, but we were best friends nonetheless. Since neither one of our parents came home until at least five PM, I always waited at the bus stop while the bus finished the middle school route and picked up the elementary kids. Then we walked home together. He was a bundle of joy, Nathan—very playful, great sense of humor. He was also an energy bomb." She laughs a little. "Sometimes I'd get annoyed because our rooms were separated by one wall and he'd always kick it when he couldn't sleep."

"Sounds like you really loved him."

"Oh, we had our moments—we fought over how you hold a pencil. But we were best friends all the same. Actually, I—" Her voice catches in her throat; she takes a deep breath and continues. "I saw him again a few years ago."

My eyes widen in curiosity. "Really?"

She nods. "I was going downtown, and as I was leaving the neighborhood, I saw him opening a car door, and he saw me. He's really grown up now, and I almost didn't recognize him, but he was under a streetlight, and as he stared at me I-I knew it was him."

"Damn." My eyes drop to the carpet. "That must have been freaky."

She smiles. "Kinda. But I was glad to see him again, even just like that."

I grin back at her. "So what else?"

"Well, I had a group of close friends at school—Mike, Regan, Bryan, Matt, Kelly. Kelly was actually my girlfriend; she was one of the last people I saw before I died."

"You're a lesbian?"

Her eyes drop to the floor, shamed by her confession. "I'm sorry I didn't tell you a few nights ago, when I said the other vampires think I'm gay. I was—"

"You weren't sure how I'd react, I know."

"You understand?"

"Yeah…I…I know what it's like because I'm kind of questioning."

"Really?"

"I don't know. It's a long story. But I want to hear yours first."

"Well…we got teased a lot. Homosexuality isn't as big of a deal now as it was in the eighties."

"How do you keep up with the times?"

"I overhear things from the others. I see the newsstands, and Elizabeth keeps me up to date. She knows I'm gay. She hears things from her victims and sometimes parties at nightclubs. Nightclubs are like vampire paradise, you know. Lots of heat and alcohol and sex. And no one misses you."

"Yeah, that makes sense."

"Well believe me, they have no trouble 'keeping up with the times.'" She tugs at the loops of the carpet. "When I came out, some of my friends ditched me. I found Regan and everyone as I looked for people who would accept me for who I was. My parents didn't take it as any big deal; they just loved me as they would any other child they had. Nathan didn't care at all; he was a bit too young to understand the significance of my situation. All he knew was 'Hey, my sister kisses girls instead of boys. That's just who she is.'"

I smile. "Have you ever kissed anyone?"'

"Kelly and I kissed all the friggin' time. It was like we were addicted to each other. We even made out on her bed once—don't worry, we kept our clothes on!" she exclaimed as I raise my eyebrows. "She was really pretty. Soft light skin, blue eyes, and curly dirty blonde hair. She was really nice, too. But…she's just a memory now. Oh, I would kill to see them all again. Just once more. Just to know they're happy."

"I'm sorry, Amy."

Amy grins slightly. "I know that homosexuality is still a major issue in society, and that the world is still full of homophobes and other people who don't accept it and want to change you just so you can be like them. But believe me, things have gotten a lot better since the eighties. Not many of us came out back then—too much fear. But my family was always accepting, and I really did believe there was nothing wrong with me and I had nothing to be ashamed of, so I went forward and joined the only gay support group in the city. It was small and quiet, but it was good for me." She blushes. "It's where I met Kelly."

I stare into the corner, where a spider is trying to spin a web Jaquelina will sweep up in twenty-four hours. Or fewer.

Amy reaches into her pocket and pulls out a wallet-sized photo. "This is her." I

reach out and take what turns out to be a school picture and gaze into the face of a beautiful young girl with pink lips, straight white teeth, and soft blonde hair that curls gracefully just past her shoulders. Pangs of recognition shoot through me at the sight of her, but I can't place my finger on who I know who looks like her. "Wow," I whisper, tracing the outline of her face. "She's beautiful, Amy."

"She really is."

"How did you get this photo?"

"They buried me with it."

"I think I have a crush on your girlfriend," I laugh, handing the photo back to Amy.

A sly smile crosses her face. "Oh really?"

"*Psht*. Shut up. Anyway, my story. I think I'm lesbian. Really! I'm pretty sure, anyway. Thing is, I haven't had anything to prove it yet. I just...I get these huge crushes on girls, and the only crush I've ever had on a boy turned out to be fake, just this tiny wish I had in the back of my mind. I never looked at him and felt like floating. Last year I fell desperately in love with my art teacher—and I wasn't exactly obscure about it. I got labeled a 'stalker' after a while because I just could never stop following her around and talking to her." I giggle. "She always liked me as a student, but I think she got a little tired of my constant visits."

"So what would you do if a girl friend of yours kissed you?"

I consider this scenario for a moment. "I'd probably let her kiss me. I may even kiss her back."

"But you wouldn't be mad?"

"No, not at all." I look at her slyly. "You're plotting."

"No! No, Emma, not at all."

"Oh, come on," I tease, rubbing and squeezing my breasts and smooching into the air. "You know you want me."

This leaves us both laughing joyfully on the floor.

I wake to a full bladder at three AM and groan. I'm exhausted and the last thing I want is to get out of bed. I reluctantly step into my slippers and walk cautiously through the dark hallway to the bathroom.

But someone else is in there. The door is shut, and light is coming through the crack by the floor. I can't hold it for much longer, so I race to use the bathroom downstairs.

The upstairs bathroom is still occupied when I return. I notice that the door is slightly ajar, and I can hear gagging from inside. What's wrong? Is one of my sisters sick? I place my hand on the doorknob and slowly peek in.

Annie is in there. She's kneeling on the floor in front of the toilet. And her fingers are down her throat.

A charge shoots down my spine. Annie is puking. On purpose. In shock and fear, I turn on my heel and race back to my bedroom.

I sit cross-legged on my bed, my eyes wide, my mouth slightly agape. *Oh my God* keeps racing through my mind. *Oh my God.* It takes me a few minutes to start thinking clearly. The first thought that crosses my mind then scares me to tears. *My sister has bulimia.*

Is it bulimia? Or is it something else? Was it a one-time thing? Or does she do it all the time? The more I think back on how much she eats (and then runs to the restroom), the less I can deny the awful truth. Bulimia.

The rest of the night and the next day are a nightmare. I don't know what to do or how to handle it. It's an awful dilemma. I have to tell. I know I do. But I'm far too scared. I studied bulimia in health in the sixth grade. Annie would hate me forever. And what would those two idiots who call themselves our parents do for her? How would they handle it? Plus, bulimia is a subject I've always had trouble talking about, for some reason or another. What can I do?

Amy comes in at around ten PM that night. I'm sitting cross-legged on my bed, fumbling anxiously with my Star of David earrings, which, together with the Santa Clauses I have in the first holes and the red-and-green bell headband, give me a very festive look that ironically contrasts drastically with my mood. Although I look like a Christmas tree, as a girl in my school put it, I feel like the goth elf of death. I don't know if I can possibly feel more depressed, angry, terrified, and just plain mixed up. Amy reads the fear on my face almost instantly. "What's wrong?"

I burst into tears of stress at her words.

"Emma!" She races over and pulls me into a warm hug. "Oh, Emma. What happened, Emma?"

Once I calm a bit, I'm silent for a moment. Should I tell her? But I know our trust is sealed. I can't break it. "Annie has bulimia."

Amy looks rather surprised. "Really?"

I nod. "I saw her forcing herself to vomit last night."

"Oh, my God. Have you told anyone?"

"No."

"You know you should tell an adult."

"Yeah, but she'll hate me forever if I do. And what will those two nut jobs who call themselves our parents do about it?"

"Emma, you have to tell. They'll get her therapy of some kind. And she won't hate you forever. In time, when she recovers, she'll be grateful to you for helping her."

I wipe a few remaining tears from my cheeks. "How do you know?"

"My best friend, Regan, had bulimia."

I stare at her.

"Yep," she continues. "In the sixth grade. When she got help, she had a lot of trouble, but eventually began to recover. She was still in therapy when..." Her voice trails off sadly. "I don't know what happened to her," she whispers eventually. "I hope she recovered and didn't starve to death. But I wouldn't know, because death snatched me away first."

I know I have to tell a grown-up about Annie, but I don't who to tell. I don't trust Robert and Jaquelina, but if I tell a teacher I know the first thing she'll do is report to them, as they are our guardians. Why waste time? I finally decide to tell Jaquelina, for while she is an airhead, she isn't a traitor, unlike Robert.

I approach her at around three PM, as she's folding laundry in front of the TV in the living room. A story about a surgical procedure plays through on *Discovery Health*.

"Shouldn't you be watching *Sex and the City?*" I grunt. She frowns.

"I hate that show, Emma. It has no substance whatsoever."

I raise my eyebrows. I didn't think she was any deeper than such a show. I move on to the important; I want to get this over with and hightail it of there. "Um, Jaquelina?"

"Yes, darling?"

I wrinkle my nose but shake it off. "I need to talk to you. About Annie."

"What about Annie, sweetheart?"

"Well, she...she's not doing so well."

"What's wrong?"

"Well, the other night I got up to go to the bathroom and I found her in there, making herself puke."

"Whoa. Intentionally?"

I grit my teeth in frustration. "Yes."

"Oh my. Are you sure that's what she was doing?"

"*Yes!* I think she's sick, Jaquelina. You see how she always wolfs down her meals and then heads for the restroom."

Jaquelina nods. "I'll talk to her. Thank you, Emma. You did the right thing, coming to me."

"Okay." I turn and start back to the stairs, then turn back. "Don't tell her it was me."

"I won't, Emma."

"Good."

It was short but sweet, and I'm going to make sure Annie gets help, even if I have to call a therapist myself if Jaquelina doesn't keep true to her word.

As I wander downstairs to grab a Popsicle that evening, I overhear Annie, Robert, and Jaquelina arguing in the living room.

"Annie, we know this isn't your fault. It's a common illness. My sister is struggling with it. But it's dangerous to puke so much, and we want to get you help before something bad happens." Jaquelina's voice is sickeningly sweet; it's the kind of voice you use on an ill four-year-old, not an ill eighteen-year-old.

"I already told you, I don't have a problem!" Annie insists, furious. "What on earth caused this to come up so suddenly? *You!*" she shouts suddenly as I turn through the archway to go back upstairs. "What did you tell them?"

"No-nothing!" I blurt out. "I don't even know what's going on!"

"Don't lie, Emma. I saw you, and you know it. You told them I have bulimia and I *don't!*" Her cheeks are flushed and her face shines with tears.

"Annie—"

"You are such a liar, Emma! I hate you!"

"Annie! Annie, calm down!" Jaquelina grasps her shoulders. "You're really overreacting!"

"You're a fink, Emma! You're a dirty, rotten fink! I hate you! And *you*—" she yanks free from Jaquelina—"you're both stupid and naïve for thinking you can do *anything* to help me!" She tears though the living room and shoves me aside as she bolts up the stairs. Her bedroom door slams.

I look to Robert and Jaquelina, feeling tears coming on myself. Jaquelina moves toward me. "Emma—"

I turn away. "Forget it. It won't do any good."

"Emma, I—"

"Stop trying to be our mother, Jaquelina. Just stop, okay? You aren't our mother, you'll never be our mother, and if you're trying to be our mother, you're doing a shit-poor job. Just stop acting like a preschool teacher and stop trying to speak to us like we're four years old. Just leave us alone. Please."

Tears fill Jaquelina's eyes; Robert looks from me to her and then back to me. "Emma, that was cruel. Please apologize to her."

"No. You're no better at parenting than she is, and you can't tell me what to do."

At this, Jaquelina buries her face in her hands and runs, sobbing, up the stairs. Robert follows quickly, stopping once to turn around. "Go to your room, Emma."

"With pleasure." I start upstairs.

"You're grounded for the next week," he continues, in a weak voice that makes it obvious he doesn't want to ground me but thinks that, as my "father," it's his duty.

Oh, horrible. Grounded from *what?* TV? I can watch DVDs on my computer. I have no friends to go out with, and if he tries to confiscate my computer, I'll steal it back and hide it.

Anger is coursing through my veins. Doesn't that idiot realize that our mother is dead? That we're depressed, and we're going to have breakdowns? That by grounding us, he's just making it worse?

Amy is peeping through the door when I return. I smile sadly and hug her when I let her in.

"Did you tell?" she asks me.

I sigh and motion her into my closet. "It's a long story. Come on, I'll tell you what's happened."

Breast cancer. I felt fear jolt through my body at those two harsh words. Breast cancer. Cancer. It had meant nothing to me before, but in one month, it had become the scariest word in the world.

It was big. The tumor was big. And the cells had spread. Blood tests and CAT scans showed tumors in all different parts of her body. They said it had probably been there for at least seven years. Since I was six. How come no one noticed before? They said she'd need surgery, radiation, and chemo, and still her chances of recovery would be slim. They said that depending on how the first rounds of treatment went, she'd only have a few years.

I was eleven years old. I couldn't lose my mother to breast cancer. I needed her. I loved her and I needed her love. As I laid in bed, I realized what I needed to do. I closed my eyes tightly and prayed to God.

Please, Lord, please. Help my mother get through this. Don't let this happen. We need our mother as much as she needs us. Please help her to recover. Please, God, I'm begging. I know I haven't exactly been loyal to you, but I don't think you'd ever hate someone for their beliefs. Please, God. Help me.

I then went to sleep, crossing my heart and hoping that it would work.

Chapter Sixteen

Amy

As December moves through, the temperature drops brutally. Even the five minutes it takes to get to Emma's house turns me into an ice sculpture. When I got to her house, she began to shiver when she touched my hand, and eventually she began having a hot water bottle and a blanket waiting for me when I got there.

One day midway through the month, I know I have slept late into the night the second I emerge from my coffin. Based on the feel of the air and the look of the sky, it has to at least be midnight. Regret and anger surge through me as I move slowly through the woods, trying to decide what the best move is to make. Should I just leave Emma for the night, in case she's sleeping? Or is she worried about me, and should I go to assure her that I'm all right?

I move very slowly, trying to put all my energy into thinking. I'm thinking that maybe I should just rap lightly on the glass if her room is dark, when I feel a cold, ruthless hand clasp my shoulder. I stop dead in my tracks and turn rigid. Not tonight. Please, not tonight!

"Amy."

I don't reply, closing my eyes in pain and fear. I'll never be able to fight her.

Her hand moves slowly over my back and her lips graze my cheek. I grit my teeth in agony. Why must she always do this?

"How's it been?" She whirls me around and pulls me into her right side, moving her fingers over my breasts, pinching my nipples through my shirt. I cringe in pain and gulp back tears, wanting so badly to force her off but finding myself immobilized. I close my eyes again, pretending to watch a sunrise I haven't seen in over twenty years.

"I never see you anymore. You're like a little ghost." As she utters "ghost" with a ghastly sweetness that makes my stomach turn over, she sweeps her hand over my hip and then my crotch. "Tell me, how do you receive your victims, Amy? Are you sweet and seductive, or do you take the demonic approach?"

The demonic approach? Which approach isn't demonic?

"You are so sexy, Amy, that with the right charisma, you could probably easily get the guys. But of course…" She kisses my cheek, her cold lips sending a violent shiver through my body and a terror that would rip through my soul had I still possessed it, "…being the way you are, you wouldn't want to."

She knows. Oh God, she knows.

With a sharp sweep of her long, pointed, silver fingernail down the side of my neck, she lets me go. I must have gone limp in her arms, because the moment my body is free, I fall to the earth. She lets out a blood-curdling laugh and fades into the darkness. A second later I'm on all fours, supporting myself as best I can as my stomach lurches violently.

My esophagus clenches angrily, bringing waves of water from my stomach. The sick splashes to the leaves and gathers in a puddle. I heave a second, then a third, until there's nothing left. Then any water left in my body comes out as tears as I fall to my side and weep, desperately clutching my burning stomach. My abdominal muscles twist from the vomiting and it's only added hurt to what I already feel.

I sense a presence above me. I cringe, believing it to be another vampire, but the creature lays a warm, gentle hand on my shoulder and speaks in a soothing yet worried voice. "Amy?"

Surges of relief pour through my veins. Emma.

Emma

When Amy doesn't show up by half past midnight, I begin to worry. She's never been so late before. As the seconds tick into minutes, I stay up and bite my nails apprehensively. It's one thirty when I decide to go look for her.

It isn't a safe idea, and I know that. But I'm so worried about Amy it doesn't matter to me. I pull on my down coat and head out.

I look all through the forest, and for the longest time have no luck. The darkness closes in as my cheap flashlight dims to nothing. I can hardly see, but I stumble on, completely losing my sense of direction. I try my flashlight again every once in a while, but its light just keeps fading out until it refuses to light up at all. The cold night air nips at my cheeks and my nose grows numb. I don't know where I am. But I need to find Amy.

After a while, I see a little clearing in the distance that's punctuated by the moonlight. I look around the trunk of a tree and can just make out shadows. There are two of them—one is holding the other and appears to be touching her sexually. I squint a little, trying to tell who they are and what the first is really doing to the second. She seems to be bringing her hands over her hostage's chest, and at the same time ever so slightly leaning into her neck. I stand stock-still in the darkness, not daring to breathe. The second figure isn't moving; she just stands there, enduring it all. When the first finally releases her, she falls to the ground like a dropped stuffed animal. The first gives a horrific laugh and seems to simply vanish into the night. Then the second pushes herself up. Her back heaves, and it takes me a moment to realize she's vomiting. I approach her cautiously as she continues to puke into the leaves, until there is nothing left to come out. At this point she falls sideways and moans, clutching her stomach. The moonlight catches her long black hair. I let out a tiny gasp and kneel, laying my hand on her arm.

"Amy?"

She turns her head slightly. "E-Emma?" She lets out a gag-cough.

"Yes, Amy, it's me. Come on, let's get you out of here." I pull her to her feet and lay her arm across my shoulder for support. She coughs a few more times as she stumbles into position.

"Come on, Amy, come on."

"Emma—can't—be—out here—too dangerous—vampires around—"

"Shhh," I say. "I don't care. You obviously need help."

She coughs again and begins to cry and gasp. I pull her along, her weight causing me to stumble a bit as I follow the general decline of the hill, knowing I'll end up, at worst, somewhere along Penny Lane. She's almost too weak from utter terror and the pain of vomiting to walk. I pull her through the forest and, at long last, we reach Robert's yard. With great effort, she climbs the wooden steps to my deck and I sit her in my closet and drape over her shoulders the comforter I received from Mama for my eleventh birthday. I sit next to her and she proceeds to reveal one of the most horrifying secrets I've heard from her.

Amy

Once we're inside her house, Emma sits me on the white carpet and drapes a down comforter over my shoulders.

"My mama gave me this for my eleventh birthday," she says, hugging me. I sniff it; it radiates her scent, a lovely combination of lavender and vanilla. The desire to drown in her heavenly aroma pulls at my heart.

"Are you feeling any better?" she asks. "Do you need anything?"

I shake my head.

"I saw what happened, Amy. I saw you with that other…creature…and I saw you puking, too."

I nod. "But most vampires puke up blood." I hear myself stumble on the word. The very idea of vomiting blood makes me want to puke again.

"Who was with you? It looked like she was…how do I say this?…sort of feeling you up."

I let out an involuntary shiver. She clutches my shoulders supportively. "That," I whisper, "was Madam Noctis."

"Madam Noctis?" she gasps. "That was *her*? What was she doing to you?"

I shake my head. "She was touching me. She does that a lot, Emma."

"Jesus Christ. She *molests* you?"

"Yes. She touches me, she feels me up."

"How much?" I can tell Emma's anxiety level is shooting sky-high.

"Not very often. I try to avoid all of them. But when she can, she comes up to me and—acts like I'm her sex toy. "

"How?" I hear the fear and anger building in her voice.

"She strokes my neck, rubs my hips, touches my breasts…" Emma's cheeks flush bright red at this, which almost makes me smile. "She also uses verbal abuse. She speaks in this extremely suggestive manner about things like my feeding rituals. Then she usually threatens to bite me…again."

"Oh, no—"

"Tonight she ran her hands down my arms and squeezed my breasts. It—it really hurt. But it's been worse."

"*Worse?*"

I take a deep breath, expel it, and close my eyes. "When I had just turned seventeen, she…she raped me, Emma."

Emma's gasp is loud enough to wake the whole house. Her hand flies to her lips and she whispers shakily, "What did she do to you?"

"She just penetrated me. You know, with her finger. Nothing worse. But…but goddamn, I cannot tell you how much it hurt. It felt like she was tearing me open and taking everything that was left of me. She was invading something that was private and special to me. A place I loved and felt only I deserved to touch, until a lover came along." A tear falls from my eye as the ghost of the pain returns to my vagina. The first time was by far the worst. "She was touching a place she had no right to even see."

I realize as Emma speaks that I am in her warm arms. "And…since then…"

"Dozens of times, Emma. Once every few months, really. She'd do it more, but I hardly enjoy it, and she'd rather spend her time with someone who will receive her. But she says I'm just too gorgeous to ignore. And she says I'm her favorite of her victims, and that I have the richest, most delicious blood she's ever tasted, and she wishes she could 'have me' one more time."

"*Have you?*"

"Suck my blood."

"Oh, Amy…" She pulls me closer, her body's warmth seeping through every pore. The cravings are pulsing, but they're overcome by a different feeling, a new one, of surging desire and passion. I close my eyes, enjoying the feeling of her body against mine. Her breast against my arm. Her hair tickling my cheek. "Oh, Amy, I'm so sorry." She falls silent, as though lost for words. Her fingers run soothingly down a lock of my hair.

"I'm so afraid she'll give into her cravings. Emma, the pain of having your blood sucked can't be compared to anything. It's hell. To feel those terrible, sharp fangs penetrate your skin, the stab of rapidly losing your blood, your life, to each terrible suck...you start to feel lightheaded, weak, and depressed. And it seems like it will never stop. It happened to me every night for an entire week. I don't want to feel it again."

At my words, she lays her head on top of mine and begins to sob. "Amy, oh, my dear, sweet Amy..."

"It's always been like this, Em. From the very beginning. And it doesn't look like it'll ever change. But I'm tired of running from her in fear."

"What's she like, exactly?"

I sigh, trying to find words to describe that soulless witch. "She's creepy. She's slender, curvy—a man's picture of the perfect female. She has long, silvery-white hair and glowing blue eyes. She has really long, sharp fangs. She keeps her nails filed to a point and painted to look like crystal in the moonlight. We all have this haunting beauty that attracts our victims, but she's...she's...God. So many young, innocent victims, Emma. She rapes her victims and she takes guys and she takes girls. I don't know if she's bisexual or *what*...I don't think she cares. She just wants life, regardless of gender. She wants their blood, their bodies, and their souls."

"She sounds awful."

"You never want to see her. She leaves a scar in your soul and you'll never forget her. I'm not talking big. It's just the truth." I shudder. "She's a living nightmare. If it weren't for her, I could—I could—have a family by now."

Emma rubs my back sympathetically. "Did you want children Amy?"

"I wanted a little girl."

She lets out a gasp as she pulls my hair behind my ear. She's spotted them. "Oh, God, is that where she—"

"Yes."

She inhales in awe, places her index and middle fingers over them gently. It makes the skin on my neck tingle, not with blood lust, but with natural desire. "Those look horrible. How much did it hurt?"

I shake my head. "I've told you how much it hurt me. It was unbearable. I really did think I would die of the pain. But…it was always too much, and I usually passed out before she finished for the night." A nervous laugh escapes. "Thank God for that."

"But, is it like that for everyone?"

"It depends on how it's done. When Elizabeth feeds on me to replace the blood she lost to practice, it's amazing, sexual, almost. The kind of thing where you just want to get lost in it and never want it to end. She's taught me to do it that way, too. You just have to be really careful, really gentle, and caress and soothe your victim a lot."

"Mm." She nods. "Well, I'm not going to let you hang out in the night with her doing this to you. You stay in here instead. It's safer for you, and I'm not sure I'll be able to sleep knowing you're alone out there with that creep. You can stay in my room with me. I have a lot of books and stuff. I have movies, too—*Harry Potter, The Nightmare Before Christmas, Underworld*…I'm not sure how much *Underworld* will appeal to you; it's about a brutal war between vampires and werewolves, but whatever interests you. Just stay with me, Amy. Stay here, where you'll be safe."

"Oh, I don't know, Emma…"

"Please, Amy. You have to. I don't want my best friend lost in the night with someone like Madam Noctis around."

"But what about your family?"

"I'll take those chances. My sisters will be shocked, but they'll probably accept you. And Robert and Jaquelina—fuck them. If you stay in my closet and leave before sunup, chances are they won't find you. Oh! Hang on." She stands and retrieves her crucifix. "Tap this and see if the fact that a dead Jesus is on it makes any difference."

I laugh and follow suit, first tapping it, then placing my thumb and index finger on it for a few seconds. "Nope."

"Here," she says, placing it in my hand. I'm as much drawn to it as the little golden cross on her necklace, despite the fact that it's a hundred times uglier. "Use this if you need to."

"But what about you?"

"I'm sure Robert and Jaquelina have others."

"Well," I begin, handing it back to her, "I'll take this tomorrow, when I'm sure you have another one."

"All right. Now you just stay here until you absolutely must go. Okay?"

I smile gratefully. "Thanks, Emma." I reach up and stroke her cheek. "You are so amazingly beautiful."

She grins sheepishly, takes my hand in hers. Amazing, blissful feelings—feelings I haven't felt in over twenty years but recognize nonetheless—are causing my heart to swell as I stare at her beautiful, freckled face surrounding those amazing crystal blue eyes. I'm slowly starting to realize something. I'm in love with this girl.

Chapter Seventeen

Emma

Now that Amy's staying with me and she has a crucifix, she seems much more relaxed. Getting a new crucifix turned out to be insultingly easy; all I had to do was go straight to Jaquelina with the excuse that my crucifix must have been knocked off my bedside table because I can't seem to find it. A quick trip to the basement on her part and a stern caution on being careful not to lose it, and Amy was armed against those creeps. Amy, being the protective, loving friend that she is, made sure I had a new one when she arrived the evening I was to give her mine.

We love all the extra time together. We watch movies and talk and laugh, and I can already see she's not as depressed as she used to be. I sometimes stay up with her until I can't keep my eyes open any longer, even if I have school in the morning. I don't care if I fall asleep in physics. She's worth it.

"You know, Emma, I think maybe you should apologize," Amy says to me the night of the sixteenth.

"To whom?"

"Jaquelina. For that incident a week and a half ago."

"Why?"

"I dunno. But if she was crying, it obviously hurt her feelings, and that's a good enough reason. She's probably doing the best she can, Emma. She's never had a child before, let alone four teenage girls. It must be really hard for her. I'm not saying you have to like her. Just tolerate her. And respect her as a human being.

She's obviously trying, even though she's failing miserably. I think you should at least try to make amends so that you don't build a giant wall."

"But it was ten days ago! I'm not even grounded anymore!" Not that there had really been any grounding. I was banned from the television, but I already had the best episodes of my favorite shows on iTunes, and when Robert caught me watching *Deal or No Deal* on NBC one night, he didn't try to stop me.

"I know, Emma, but it's never too late to apologize." She smiles and squeezes my hand. Intense tingles run through me, and, instinctively, I take her in my arms. I recognize suddenly that the feelings I have for Amy are the same ones I felt for previous individuals I had a crush on, like various rock stars, teachers, and friends, only stronger and more intense. Do I have a crush on Amy? I must, and it's pretty strong—stronger than any that I've felt before.

Christmas break is approaching at breakneck speed, and the teachers are piling the work on like we're all going to be shoved into the real world come the new year. Mrs. Larson said our textural animals are due on Monday—no exceptions. Jill and I worked somewhat on them; I'm not much interested or good at it and Jill still has no initiative to draw under someone else's instruction. Mine sucks. The lines are all so dark and I just can't get the hang of it. I have to force so much out of my pencil; despite my wonderful burst of inspiration on my butterfly, which is now on display in the rotunda by the entrance, I am still desperately lost to art. I don't feel like I can do any of it correctly anymore. Jill's animal is beautiful, but she's taking a really long time.

I'm sitting on my bed on Friday night, trying desperately to finish my sucky drawing, when I hear a knock on the door. I look up and feel my heart leap; Amy is smiling from the other side. I jump off the bed and pull her inside in a giant hug.

"Amy! You just saved my life!"

"How?"

I point to the drawing on my bed.

"I thought you liked drawing."

"This project isn't 'clicking,' if you know what I mean."

"Ah, yes. Like a piece of music I just couldn't play well."

"I guess so."

"So, how are things with you?" she asks as she leads me to the closet.

"Jaquelina served chicken for dinner for like the fiftieth time this year."

"Ooh."

"Yeah. I'm sick of it."

"What about Annie?"

I heave a heavy sigh. "They found a therapist. She's grumpy and keeps saying she's not going to go. And she's not speaking to me anymore. I tried asking her a few things, but she just frowned at me and walked away. It makes me really sad."

Amy gives me a sympathetic look. "She'll come around eventually. Regan did."

"I know. But it's like I've lost her too. And Jill never talks anymore. It's like I'm losing my whole family."

"Oh, Emma," she sighs.

I shake my head sadly. We need to stop talking about this. "So, do you want to watch a movie or something?"

"Um, okay. What have you got?"

"A lot of stuff you probably won't have heard of. I don't have many movies, but I'll bring you what I have." I leave the closet and yank seven DVD cases off the bottom shelf of my bookcase. *Titanic, Little Miss Sunshine, The Nightmare Before Christmas, Corpse Bride, Over the Hedge, Mean Girls, Legally Blonde.* I throw them in to her and go to retrieve my MacBook.

She's scanning the backs of all of them when I return; I sit and wait for her to pick one.

"Don't you have more?" she finally asks me.

"Well, yeah, three more, but they're all vampire flicks."

She shrugs. "I don't mind."

"Really?"

"No."

"Okay then," I say doubtfully, collecting the DVDs and leaving to trade them for

the vampire movies. *Underworld, Underworld Evolution,* the *Dracula* with Gary Oldman. Amy looks them over too, finally settling on one and tossing the others aside, handing it to me.

"*Underworld?*" I ask. "Are you sure? It has a lot of brutality in it. Brutality you're probably too familiar with."

"It's fine," she replies curtly.

"All right." I pull the DVD out of the case, stick it in the side of my computer, and run to turn out my bedroom lights.

"Wow, watching movies has changed since I was a little girl," Amy jokes as the opening warnings and logos shoot through. "Does anyone ever use cassettes anymore?"

"For movies? Well yeah, but they'll probably be gone in ten years. I don't think they're sold anymore."

I feel her hand slide across my lower back and gently caress my outer thigh as the darkness setting of the movie flows onto the screen.

"Are you *flirting* with me?" I ask incredulously. She grins mischievously. "Maybe."

I give her arm a playful punch, and we both shut up as the narrative begins.

Not ten minutes into the picture, Amy pulls me into her arms and I don't resist. Lying with her, the contours of our bodies fitting so perfectly, makes me feel safer and happier that I've felt since I lived in Maine. Intense rushes of feelings pour through my chest, but I have trouble telling exactly what they are. As the first battle scene ends and Selene storms angrily through the mansion of partying Death Dealers, Amy rubs my scalp a little and a warm feeling of content settles over me and I smile a little. I really can't remember the last time I felt this good.

"All right, class, your sketchbooks and textural animals are due today," Mrs. Larson announces at the end of the period on Monday. "Please make sure that if you haven't turned them in already you get them into the box by four this afternoon. Otherwise it will show on your report card."

I sigh and bring both up to the front of the room. They're crap. I have less than half the minimum sketchbook dates because of my utter lack of motivation to draw, and the things I managed to come up with look like something I would have done had I been given two minutes to draw a picture. I sigh, not really caring. I'm sure I'm dumping in all my other classes, too, but I prefer not to think about it.

Jill comes up behind me. Her animal is incomplete.

"Don't you want to finish that over lunch, Jill?" I asked her genially. She merely shakes her head.

"Why not?"

"I hate it," she whispers. "It's awful. It'll get a bad grade regardless."

"Jill, come on, it's good and you know it."

"No it's not. I don't know why I don't just dump art class altogether."

"But you used to love art class."

She glares at me. "So did you." Then she turns and stalks out off the classroom, leaving me staring after her sadly.

The first surgery went well, and as her radiation began and they got her settled into a routine, things seemed to look up for us suddenly. I lay in bed one night, reflecting on the last three months while waiting for sleep.

Things were difficult at first, but the success of the first surgery seemed to lift a black blanket of doom from the family and life looked to the sun. I was optimistic about Mom, and my sisters were the happiest they'd been in a long time. Jill had even told some great jokes at the dinner table that evening, and we'd all laughed ourselves into stitches. It was at that meal that I thought, This is right. This is how a family is supposed to be. Surrounded by my sisters and mother, eating a good dinner in a warm house and laughing.

I said a silent prayer of thanks to the Lord as I fell into a deep, contented sleep.

Chapter Eighteen

Emma

We go to Robert's parents' house in the mountains about forty miles outside the city for a Christmas Eve celebration. About two hundred others who are apparently my relatives on my father's side are also there, including a screaming, drooling baby, a businessman with a cell phone glued to his ear, an overly-chatty dumb-sounding redheaded college girl who is even more weighed down with fashion than Jaquelina is, and a geeky thirteen-year-old girl with frizzy hair, large braces and even larger glasses. Her name is Jenna and she spends the whole day playing on her Gameboy Advance XP.

Jill and I find the crowd of strangers—er, relatives we haven't seen since we were toddlers—very disturbing, so we stay in a corner and pretend to not exist.

Most of the food is devoured during the meal, so any leftovers were left with the grandparents. It's after eleven when we finally get home, and after giving Amy, for whom I'd left a note and the door unlocked, a quick hug in greeting, I collapse and sleep like a log until ten AM. I swear I feel her pat my back sometime during the night, but I might have only dreamt it.

Christmas is everything, and Hanukkah isn't given a second thought. Robert and Jaquelina call us down on Christmas night for a gift exchange. I look around under the tree; not counting the packages relatives sent from Maine, I have six presents. I wonder if the two that aren't from my sisters will be any better than the awful too-tight fashion clothing I got from Robert's parents the night before.

"So, who wants to go first?" Jaquelina chirrups as we all sit cross-legged around the commercialistic tree. When no one answers, she hands a present to Jill. "Here you are, Jill dear. I hope you like these."

Jill rips off the paper lethargically, revealing three canvases, a set of acrylic paints, and a set of assorted brushes. I catch a glimmer of delight flash across her face and don't think anyone else sees it.

"Do you like them, sweetheart?" Jaquelina is beaming like the Cheshire Cat.

Jill nods quickly before falling back into her own world.

Kristina takes a package, then Annie. Once we've gone around a few times and hidden our eyes from an unpleasant scene of affection between Robert and Jaquelina after they exchange a necklace and a tie, the last present is thrown into my lap. It's from Robert and Jaquelina.

"I think you'll really like this, Emma," Jaquelina says as I yank off the paper rather impatiently.

I suppress a gasp. *The Silver Kiss.* One of my favorite books. Library-bound, with a better cover than the cruddy paperback copy on my bookshelf. Something I've been searching for forever and was never able to find. I can hardly believe my eyes. How on earth could they possibly know how much I wanted this?

Jaquelina must have read the shock on my face. "Robert and I have had some trouble figuring out what you like, Emma. It took us forever to come up with this. I hope you're happy, darling."

I stare at the box, open-mouthed. I can't believe it. They actually came up with something I'd like, nothing like the itchy sweater that I threw behind me from the other package from them. "Th-thank you," I stutter.

"We would have gotten you something more suitable than a sweater for that other package, Emma," Jaquelina continues, "but we just couldn't figure out what else you wanted."

A rush of different emotions pounds through my chest as I gather my other gifts to return to my room. I expected some sort of halfhearted stumble to present me with a worthwhile gift, but never did I expect them to actually *succeed*. I dump my presents on my bed and pull on my coat to go sit on my balcony and wait for Amy.

The moon shines above my head as I try to sort through the tidal wave of thoughts washing through my mind. They did it. They gave me what I wanted, and they worked hard to get it for me. But...how did it happen? People who do what he did tend not to do that sort of thing for you. They just *don't*. So does this mean they love me? If Robert truly loves me, then why did he leave me behind all those years ago?

Someone places a cool hand over mine on the bench. I look up, surprised. "Amy!"

"Sorry, did I startle you? I can't imagine you didn't notice my approach. My boots make a lot of noise."

"I was sort of...out of it."

"Oh." She sits next to me; I hear her skirt rustle and her hand tickles mine, generating a pulsing between my legs. "Aren't you cold?"

"Nah. This coat is down."

"Oh. Well...what's on your mind?"

"What? Oh, just...well, Robert and Jaquelina gave me a special copy of *The Silver Kiss* for Christmas."

"'Sat a book?"

"Uh-huh."

"And?"

"I've wanted that copy for forever, but no one except Jill knew because I don't express excitement the way I used to. I know Jill would never say anything to them, seeing as she hardly even talks to me. Jaquelina said they worked really hard to get me something I would appreciate, something I wanted."

She leans on her shoulder. "It sounds like they really love you, Emma."

"Really now? If Robert loves me, then he wouldn't have left. He would have been there for me throughout my childhood. When I cried at night, wondering where my daddy was. When I needed a daddy most. All the times he wasn't there."

"Maybe there's more to the story, Em. Maybe you just need to dig a little deeper. He may have had a good reason for leaving, you know."

"Maybe so. But never coming back?"

"Which is why you have to ask him."

She and I look into the dark sky. I suddenly remember a very special time when I was around four or five. The memory had been pushed to the back of my mind, but now it returns, vivid and overwhelming.

"Girls! Girls! Come outside!"

"What is it, Mommy?" Annie put aside her reading flash cards and ran out to the deck, where Mama was standing. Kristina followed. Mama said something to them and pointed to the sky. I heard a distinct "woah" escape Annie's mouth.

"Emma, Jill, come on out!" Mama insisted. "You girls have got to see this!"

Jill and I looked at each other, then hopped off the sofa and ran out.

"Look up in the sky, girls," Mama said, placing her hand on my back and pointing up at a bright streak in the sky.

"What?" I asked.

"It's a comet, Emma!" Annie squealed, hopping around. "A comet!"

"A comet?"

"That's right, Emma," Mama said. "A comet. I'm not sure which comet it is, but here we see it."

"There are 'pecific comets, Mommy?" Annie asked, now peering through the deck telescope.

"Sure there are, dear," Mama answered. "They have names and move around the sun, just like the planets do."

"Are they as big?" Jill asked.

Mama laughed. "No, silly. Not quite." I sit still, letting the memory pour back. The more I think, the more I remember. I didn't think that comet such a big deal, but Annie was so ecstatic. The comet was all she talked about for a week. I'm not sure which comet that was, although if I ask Annie, she might be able to help me find out. That is, if she ever speaks to me again.

"Christmas night always reminds me of Kelly."

"What?" I snap to attention.

"Kelly. The Christmas before I died, she and I went to the park at around nine in the evening. We were sitting on the bench and...and...I had my first kiss there."

"On Christmas?"

"Yes. She kissed me. From then on, we were inseparable." Amy sighs sadly. "I loved her so much."

"Oh, dear, Amy—"

"I do miss her. I miss everybody."

"I'm really sorry."

"I know."

She puts her arms around me and emotions explode inside. "Emma."

"Yes?"

"Don't you worry about...my kind. I'll never let them hurt you. Ever. I promise."

"Thank you, Amy." The corners of my mouth twitch as I snuggle into her arms like a little girl. "Amy?" I ask, slightly nervous, when we stop snuggling and I sit back up and she throws her hair back.

"Yes?" She winds her right arm around my back and pulls me into her body as much as she can. Our faces are so close our cheeks are almost touching.

"What does it feel like? Being...kissed?"

Amy looks at me, then smiles. "It feels...it feels just like this." And she places her left hand over my cheek to turn my face to hers and tenderly puts her lips to mine.

Her lips. On mine. It's surprising, it takes me a moment to realize it's happening...but it is, and it's...it's...dynamite. My whole body begins to flower, like a bud bursting into bloom, and my hand moves over hers and I let myself fall into the beauty of the moment. Her lips don't move, just hold mine, for three, five, ten, twelve seconds. The whole time I'm thinking,

Don't pull away, Amy. Oh, please, God Almighty. Don't you ever pull away.

And yet she does, and it's over. My first kiss. My fingers explore the new wetness of my lips wonderingly, the place where hers were not a moment ago. Her full ruby lips light her face with a smile and her glowing green eyes gaze into mine with a tender affection that sets my heart on fire. "Happy Hanukkah, Emma."

And the tingles are coursing into me, washing through me like a tsunami, and suddenly the only thing I want in the whole world is her. A foreign emotion pours through me, and I fling my arms around her and pull her body back into me, too eager to once again feel that wonderful soft mouth on mine. I kiss and she kisses back and I kiss some more, and after a few moments she opens my mouth and our tongues gently graze. Then and only then do I realize that that foreign emotion is one long lost, one I haven't known since my mother's days of life. It is joy. Joy, excitement, bliss.

My whole body trembles as her breasts press into mine and her fingers spread over the small of my back. "Do you know how long I've been wanting this with you?" she asks between kisses.

"Nope," I reply and she giggles and kisses me again. I feel like I'm releasing all the energy that has been building inside since the day I met her, and only now does it occur to me what all that energy really is. It's more than just a really strong crush. Oh, so much more.

It is love.

Chapter Nineteen

Amy

    I lie all night in Emma's closet in a daze. I didn't remember how good kissing feels. Is my memory fooling me? Or did kissing really not feel this good with Kelly?

    Kelly. My girlfriend from 1985. Am I betraying her? We were in love when I died. Does she still consider us in love?

    Oh, this is silly. Kelly would be thirty-eight by now. Surely she has another partner, perhaps even children. And she wouldn't want me to be alone just to please her memory. She'd want me to love Emma beyond my fullest extent if it made me happy, especially when my life is so unimaginably miserable.

    I don't know what possessed me to make that move. I had wanted to for a long time, but I was so afraid—afraid that I'd put her off me, afraid that I'd lost control and bite her. But when she asked me how kissing feels, it was too perfect, and it was happening on its own.

    The first one, the delicate touch of love I laid upon her tender, virgin lips, was sudden but wonderful, and I found myself never wanting to pull away. Her lips were soft, damp, and the moment I touched mine to hers her warmth was flowing into my body, passing through my skin and awakening every nerve. And she didn't push me away. She pulled me into her and kissed me back—passionately. Something must have erupted inside her—she was probably as anxious to release this intensity as I was. We touched, rubbed, kissed—and finally we stopped and I pulled her into my side and neither of us really knew what to say.

"Only if you want to," I'd finally whispered, fearful still of rejection. "Only if you want your first relationship to be with...something like me."

"You're not a something," had been her reply. "You're a someone. Someone very special. And...I can't think of anyone I'd rather be with right now."

"You really want to take that risk?"

"Amy...I really do. I want you. When you kissed me...I realized...I want you so bad."

It was the most beautiful thing I'd ever heard.

Most romance stories involve a man and a woman, and those are the ones our society tells us are the classics, the picturesque definition of love. But the loving bond that Emma and I share, girl to girl, is amazing, wonderful, and can't fit my definition any more perfectly. Two women kissing, two women making love...how anyone can think that is disgusting is beyond my realm of comprehension. If you ask me, it's truly heaven on earth. It's the most beautiful thing in existence.

I smile a little as I lie in Emma's closet, turning it all over in my head. I'm a lesbian. And I love it like the burning desire it leaves within me.

Emma

The next day is heaven for me. All I can do is lie in a daze, daydreaming about Amy. The feeling of her soft kisses lingers on my lips all day, making me tingly and excited. Sometimes I squeal and hug myself tightly. I never realized how powerful love could be.

"Emma?" Kristina asks me at dinner.

"Yes?"

"Are you all right?"

"I'm all right."

"You seem slightly dazed."

"No, it's fine."

"What, no witty comments, no insults to throw?"

"Not really."

"You are very smiley, dear," Jaquelina agrees. "Has something exciting happened to you?"

"No," I lie in a high-pitched voice. Kristina looks at me suspiciously, then a cunning smile crosses her face. She says nothing, just looks me in the eyes and spears her broccoli. She knows I'm in love. She's had so many boyfriends that the symptoms of lovesickness are second nature to her.

Annie pushes back and carries out her plate. "Don't go to the bathroom, Annie," Jaquelina calls out. Annie simply frowns at her and turns to cross the family room.

"Annie! Annie, come back here! Don't puke, Annie, don't. No!!"

"You can't make her stop, Jaquelina," Kristina says.

Jaquelina lets out a groan. "I wish your father didn't have to go back to work the day after Christmas."

Gagging sounds come from the bathroom. Now that word is out, Annie isn't trying to hide it anymore. On the contrary, she seems to enjoy flaunting it just to spite Robert and Jaquelina. And me.

The lock turns in the door and Robert bursts through, clutching his briefcase in one hand and a stack of papers in the other. "Hello, dear," he says to Jaquelina, kissing her quickly before setting his stuff on the counter. "Sorry I'm so late tonight." He grabs a plate from the overhead cabinet and serves himself from the various pots and pans on the stove.

"I'm finished," I announce to Jaquelina. She smiles.

"Carry your plate out, dear."

"All right, Emma, spill," Kristina orders, cutting in front of me as I head back upstairs.

"About what?"

"Come on," she says, crossing her arms and leaning against the railing. "I haven't seen you smile so genuinely in two years. Who's the lucky guy?"

I laugh a little. "I don't know what you're talking about."

"Oh, I think you do." Kristina grins slyly. "There's someone. Come on, who is it?"

"Someone special." I smile broadly and race to my room.

Annie starts therapy the next day. I'm watching Discovery Health reruns in the living room when Jaquelina leaves with her.

"I'm taking Annie to an appointment," Jaquelina calls to me as she pulls her purse over her shoulder.

"Fine," I say as I put a huge spoonful of ice cream in my mouth.

"We'll be gone about two hours."

"Uh-huh."

As they walk out the door, Jaquelina gives me a warm smile; Annie throws me a death glare. I stare out the window as they walk across the gravel to the garage. So they have Annie signed up for therapy, and without a flick of half-heartedness. My mind flits back to *The Silver Kiss*. Maybe they do care about us, if only just a little. But how can they expect us to ever care for them?

The next night Amy arrives early, at around eight thirty.

"Amy!" I leap forward and hold her in my arms, both of us let out small sighs of contentment, and then we kiss like we did last night. Never in my life have I been in love. The closest person to me who is my age was always Jill. I'd never had any idea that anyone else could be so important to me, so much a part of my life.

As I rock her, I let her lips touch my neck without a trace of fear. This is no vampire holding me. This is a beautiful young woman, a free spirit trapped in a world of darkness. A girl wanting nothing more than any human longs for: touches, kisses, love. Her hands are reaching up my shirt and gently rubbing my back and they're so cool and soothing on my skin when—

Creeeeak!

I whip around to see Jill and Kristina standing in the doorway. I glance around the room awkwardly, pulling away from Amy.

"What is it, guys?"

"Uh, well, I needed to use some tape and Jill was just opening the door when I came up but..." Kristina frowns. "Who's your...friend?"

"C-close the door! You know the rules about letting people in after dark!"

"Uh, sure. And don't worry, I won't tell." She closes the door and turns back to me. "*This* is your special someone!"

"Y-yeah."

"Wow, Emma."

"What?"

"Just...wow. I had no idea."

"Well now you do. You know there's nothing wrong with it, Kristina, Aunt Maggie is—"

"Emma, Emma, no, of course not! It's just...surprising, is all. You know. I never really saw you as a lesbian." She approaches me and cocks her head at Amy. "Wow, she's a cutie. What's your name?" She extends her right hand.

Amy glances around wildly, looking everywhere but at Kristina and keeping her hands clasped tightly behind her back. "Um, it's uh..."

"She's really shy, Krissie," I interject. " It's Amy. Just, uh, you know."

Kristina takes the hint and slides back. "That's a pretty name."

A faint pink flashes into Amy's cheeks, barely visible, giving her face a hint of childlike cuteness. I touch her cheek and take her hand in mine. "She's a really special girl, guys. Please don't tell Robert and Jaquelina about her. They...they might not like it. You know. That I'm with a...another girl." It seemed easier than explaining the real reason they wouldn't like this.

"Don't worry, sweets, my lips are sealed." Kristina gives my hair a ruffle, winking at me. I remember the time I kept her boyfriend a secret for her, back when she was thirteen.

I look at Jill, who isn't nearly as surprised to learn my first love is female because she knew about my questioning sexuality.

"You won't tell, right Jill?"

Jill's head snaps up, as though I've pulled her from a trance. She shakes it and looks away.

"Well...thanks for the tape." Kristina motions to me with the tape she's pulled from my desk and heads out with Jill on her heels. Jill gives a final glance over her shoulder before she closes my door behind her. As their footsteps fade and silence settles over the room, I'm overcome by a rapid of emotions as I stare into Amy's perfect face, and gently reach out and pull her into my arms.

I remember when Mommy lost her hair. It was about a year after her illness was discovered, soon after she started chemotherapy. She kept it for as long as possible, but when it was just too thin to look convincing, she disappeared into the bathroom and came out thirty minutes later, a towel wrapped around her head and tears in her eyes. When she finally unwrapped her towel and threw it aside, I burst into uncontrollable tears and threw my arms around her, heaving sobs.

"Darling." Mama patted my back and rocked me. I couldn't believe my mother's beautiful, luscious red curls, the ones that had fallen to her waist and caused so many men to ask for her number when she went out, were gone. *All gone*. Mama held me for a long time, trying desperately to calm her Emma, her youngest child, telling me she kept her hair and was going to send it to be made into a wig. I still couldn't catch myself in my piteous tears. *My mommy lost her hair. My mommy really was sick.*

My mommy really was dying.

Chapter Twenty

Emma

2007 is coming to a close. I haven't been told what we're doing to celebrate New Year's, but I seriously hope it doesn't involve a car. Actually, I prefer it not involve "quality family time" at all. I want to spend it with Amy. With my *real* family.

Coming out of the bathroom New Year's morning, I notice Robert and Jaquelina's door is shut. I would think that's a sign that something that I do not need nor want to know about is going on in there, but there is no laughter, no suggestive sounds or moans. I move a little closer to the door, only to hear whispering coming from inside.

"Robert, listen. We've had them here for two months. Do you know how many innocent lives are taken in that time period? We need to take action soon or we'll be lucky to get through Valentine's Day without an attack on our family."

"I know, baby. I know. But we have no idea how many there are. We can't possibly kill them all. We don't even know which cemetery they're coming from. They could even be coming from different ones. Vampires exist all over the world. What if they work in cults, and if we kill one the rest come after us? They're like any other murderer. You can punish the individuals, but we can't possibly rid the world of all of them. We've supplied the girls with crucifixes and we have plenty of garlic in the basement. It's about the best we can do for now."

"And if a vampire attacks?"

"If a vampire so much as approaches us, it'll be history in a matter of seconds."

Shit. *Shit!* I pull away from the door. SHIT! If they catch Amy, if they find out she's a vampire...and that fact is rather obvious to anyone with their knowledge... I'm appalled this didn't hit me before. Of *course* they know about vampires—the rules and the crucifixes! And of *course* they'd kill a vampire if she were near their family. Why wouldn't they? I guess I was too caught up in the fact that I'd finally found joy, I didn't let myself believe that. Goddamn it, I can't risk her life like that. I have to keep her away. Tell her that if she continues to come back, her life will be in jeopardy. It kills me to think about doing that, now that I've finally found love. But if I want to save her life, I have to.

Amy

When I knock, Emma opens the door abruptly, a wild look in her eyes, and doesn't even invite me inside.

"Amy, you can't come here anymore. You have to leave. Now!"

"What? Why?"

Emma's voice is as hard and intense as I've ever heard it. "I overheard Robert and Jaquelina talking! They know about vampires, duh, those crucifixes, and they say that if one ever so much as comes near this house, they're gonna—they're gonna—kill her."

"So?"

"Amy, if they catch sight of your fangs, they'll think you're attacking us and they'll come after you. They'll try to kill you!"

"Oh." I step back, thinking. Do I mind if they try to kill me? I've tried to commit suicide several times, staying up through sunrise and always running at the last minute. I even put a long, sharp strip of wood to my chest once, but dropped it in dismay. So now I have a choice. Do I want to steer clear of Robert and Jaquelina and go back to my old lonely existence living for God knows how long, or do I want to risk my life for happiness? For the chance to hug, kiss, laugh, and talk with my sweet, sweet redheaded angel, and then, if I die, finally escape myself?

The answer is obvious.

"Emma, please," I whisper. "It isn't worth it. If I stay away from you in order to stay safe, then I'll go back to being lonely and afraid with nothing good in my life. You're the first thing in this damned life worth living for. Do you really think I'd go back to living as I did, without any joy, so that I'd know I could keep living it forever?"

Emma casts her eyes to the deck. She doesn't have anything to say to that.

"If I die, it's all over. All the pain and suffering is over. I've tried to kill myself, but I'm too scared. If they kill me, I can't chicken out of that, and it's over. I don't care if they kill me, Emma. Not if you're the tradeoff. Okay?"

"But what will happed to you if they do?"

"My soul will be free."

"But isn't Madam Noctis still alive?"

"Yes."

"You said she has your soul."

"I guess."

"Then you couldn't truly be free until she's killed! You said so yourself."

"I know."

"What will happen to you until then?"

I shake my head. "I guess just a gap in my consciousness. Sort of like a long, deep sleep. When my spirit is freed, I guess I'll wake up."

Emma's voice holds a waver as she utters her next words. "I'll kill her for you."

"*What?*"

"I'll kill her for you. If you die, I'll kill Madam Noctis as soon as I possibly can."

"But-but Emma, you can't! Killing a vampire is *extremely* dangerous, and you don't even know which one she is!"

"Then you tell me."

"I can't let you do that. I won't let her turn you into a vampire, too."

"Please, Amy. This is for you."

"I won't let you risk your soul for mine."

She pushes out an unsteady breath. "Please, Amy. Please."

"No. I can't. I just can't. End of story. Promise me that you will never chase after that woman. Because if you don't, you leave me no choice. I'll leave you. To protect you."

Tears well in her eyes, and I take her hand supportively as she lets out a shaky sigh. "Okay. I promise."

"Good." I lean over and hug her comfortingly as a few sobs escape her. "Now come on. Let's go inside." I take her in my arms—she's shivering from the cold by now—and push her back through the door and towards our little hideout.

"S-something doesn't make sense to me," she says. "I was thinking about what you said, and it seems weird…didn't you say someone's emotions and ability to care for others are part of their soul?"

I nod. "Yeah, so?"

"Well then…that's weird. You're really kind, and you obviously still have emotions. Not just emotions, but *strong* ones. You care about both of us, and you cry for me when I cry. You were so scared about hurting me that you were ready to give up your only friend in twenty years for her own safety. The way you hug me, the way you kiss me…it's so strong, so devoted. How can you do that if you don't have a soul?"

I shake my head. "I'd like to believe that I still have it…that I'm not like Madam Noctis, a heartless, evil vampire, but…but…"

"But you're not. You're real, Amy." Her hand comes to rest gently on the side of my neck. "You're not like the others. You're not."

I shake my head. "It's so confusing. I died. I became a vampire. How could it still be there? She…she took it. She killed me."

"That can't be right. That can't be true. It just doesn't work. I feel your soul every time we talk, every time we hug and kiss, every time I think of you. I feel it, strong and alive inside you. You're the most alive person I've ever met. I feel it all. Right here." She places her palm over my heart, and I become painfully aware of her hand right between my breasts.

"It makes no sense."

"Does it have to?" She blesses me with that warm embrace that has already become so second nature for us. "You have your soul, and it doesn't matter how," she continues as our lips part.

"Some things just can't be explained. Try not to dig too deeply into this."

I smile, warmth seeping through my chest. We sit in silence for a while before I speak again, a new subject on my mind.

"Now I can't even tell her to lay off a little bit."

"Has she touched you from the beginning?"

"No, it was a few months after my death before she made any advances on me. But when she started, she didn't stop and"—I wipe a tear away—"I never did anything about it. So really it's kind of my fault in the first place—"

"Oh, Amy, shut up!"

I stare at her, surprised at the sudden angry outburst. Her eyes immediately take on a look of shame and she pulls me into her arms.

"Oh, I'm sorry, darling," she whispers. "I'm really sorry. I just got annoyed. You know it's not your fault, and I get tired of hearing you say it is."

"But, well, I know, but really, I should have done something about it long ago—"

"Listen, Amy. If someone is raped, is it her fault?"

I shake my head reluctantly.

"No. It's the rapist's fault, even if she doesn't fight back very well. She didn't want it, so it's still rape and it isn't her fault. What makes you any different?"

I don't answer. She sighs.

"I think the problem is that you know in your head that it's not your fault, but you don't know it in your heart and soul. In *here*." She pounds her chest with her fist. "You know it, but you don't believe it. You've got to believe it."

"Even if I did believe it, what difference does it make? I can't make her stop. I'm not strong enough."

"But you can be. You have to believe you are strong enough to stop her. It's the only way you'll ever be strong enough to protect yourself. You have to believe in yourself. It's clichéd, I know, but that's because it's true."

"Well…I don't know—"

"So answer my question. What makes you any different from any innocent girl who's been raped?"

I shrug.

"The only thing that makes you different is that you're drowning in self-doubt. And the more you blame yourself, the weaker your spirit gets, and the easier it's been for her to harm you. Twenty years of lying in self-blame and hopelessness…Amy, that's enough to weaken anyone's spirit. You just need to remind yourself that you aren't at fault for what you've been through. And you need to stand up for yourself to prevent any more." She kisses me. "Do you think you can do that?"

I shake my head.

"Of course you can. You just need to try."

"Emma?"

"Yes?"

I take a deep breath. "I lost my virginity on my first night as a vampire, and it wasn't to her."

She freezes. "What?"

"It was to Jason. That guy who caught you about a month ago? He just sort of caught me while I was trying to return to my coffin, and, well…that was my first time."

"What happened?"

Just as I'm approaching my grave, trying to figure out how to return to my coffin beneath the surface, something seizes my neck and forces me against my stone. I let out a yelp of surprise and pain. "So you're the new girl," a young blond man observes, lying on top of me and breathing in my ear. "Damn, you're sexy. I wish I'd found you before Madam Noctis did."

I shudder and tell him to please get off me.

"Come on, baby, there's some time left before the sun rises. How about a little one-on-one time before, you know, we have to spend thirteen hours alone in our caskets?" He runs a hand through my hair and another over my chest.

"No, please, don't—stop!" He isn't listening, and before I know it, his lips are all over my face and neck and I'm screaming and crying. His hand pulls my shirt from my skirt and slides over my abdomen, freezing on my bare skin.

"Mmm, you're warm," he whispers in my ear as his hand slides north, toward my breasts. He kisses my face again, licking my salty tears from my cheeks. He reaches under my bra, and I can feel his disgusting, clammy hand clutch at my breast. That's when I stop struggling, stop trying, and let myself fall away. I can feel a hard pain, a piercing pain, that seems to pulse to the beat of his thrusting, but I try not to pay attention. Instead I close my eyes and see my mama. See Nathan. See Kelly. She's kissing me, and it doesn't feel dreadful like this. It feels so good…

Then a searing, on my eyelids, all over my face. The sun. We both scream in agony, Jason leaps off me, and I disappear from the surface, the painful burning sensation on my cheeks, neck, and legs pulsing to nothing rapidly, along with the angry pain in my vagina. I cry and cry and cry, only half-realizing what just happened to me.

"Good God," Emma moans when I finish my story. "That's so awful."

"Yeah." I massage a lock of my hair.

"This was before Madam Noctis raped you?"

"Yeah. But for some reason, when she did it, it was so much worse. Maybe because she was my killer and I was much more scared of her. Or maybe it was because she used her hands."

"Has Jason ever attacked you again?"

"Well, not really. He threatens me sometimes, but I don't think he really wants me that much. He likes the bodies of the living better. They can give him human life at the same time." I think back to that night when he tried to take Emma from her driveway and shudder.

"Have you heard of voluntary virginity? Where a girl is a virgin until she says she wants to give it up, whether she gets raped or not?"

"Hm? Oh, yeah, but I never really believed in it. I mean, you're a virgin once, and if someone's been inside you, you're not. End of story."

She shakes her head. "You have to believe in it, honey. After all that's happened to you…it's probably one of the only things that can remind you your body is still yours. And you still have ultimate control over it. Loss of virginity shouldn't mean having sex for the first time. It should mean making love for the first time."

She smiles. I shrug. As I gaze at her, I begin to wonder if just maybe I will get to make love in this lifetime.

As the night drags on and the clock checks off the hours, first twelve, then one, then two, I grow tired of reading and watching movies. I venture out of the closet and sit on the carpet between the curtain and the door, leaning my head against the cool glass and staring out at the night. The full moon shines over the wood and casts that usual silvery blue glow across the lawn. I think about what Emma said. Her insistence that my soul is still inside me, even though there is no way it's possible. Her belief that I have weakened myself through blame, and that I need to regain my strength and stand up for myself. I let out a sigh, stand, and approach her bed. She's lying on her back, breathing slowly and deeply. Her face is soft with sleep, her eyelids meeting gracefully, the lashes intricately woven. I reach up and stroke a lock of hair from her face gently; she twitches and the corners of her mouth pull into a smile. Waves of passion inundate me as I gaze at her. Her warm, gentle smile, her soft, caring touch, and her tender, compassionate kisses. Rushes of feeling pour through my body. I have never been so deeply in love.

Love. I'm in love. I look at Emma, and I feel pure, unselfish tenderness deep inside my heart. I can't do that. Not without a soul…it's not possible…is it? I just don't know how I could possibly still have my soul. That's part of the definition of vampires. Soulless, undead creatures that wake at night to drink the blood of the living.

I start back to the window, but Emma moves abruptly and I turn. She sits up and sees me there.

"What is it, Amy?"

"I just…got tired of reading. I've been thinking."

"Are you tired?"

"A little."

She gets up and locks her door. "I can't believe it took me this long to notice this," she tells me. "I didn't have a lock on my door at Mama's house." She gets back into bed, pulls back the covers on the other side, and pats the empty space beside her.

I don't think about it; I go right over and lie under the covers and place my body in her arms.

"Emma."

"Yes?"

"I won't let any of them hurt you. I won't let any of those demons near you. I'll protect you. I know I've said it before, but I'm saying it one more time. I'll keep you safe. I promise."

"Aw…" She squeezes me gently. "Happy new year, Amy." She beams contentedly and kisses me softly. "I love you." Then she closes her eyes, a smile warming her face.

My heart swells. I haven't heard those words in over twenty years. *I love you*…so soft, so sweet. And now a beautiful young girl has said them to me, and I'm lying in her arms right now. I smile a little and kiss her. "I love you too." It's been so long since I last uttered those words. She rubs my back in acknowledgement.

I lie awake for quite some time, watching her sleep. Her back rises and falls with her deep breathing, creating a hypnotic motion that tempts my consciousness. When the sandman finally comes along to close my eyes, I'm already dreaming about her.

It's the most peaceful sleep that I've ever fallen into.

January

Chapter Twenty-One

Amy

Out of instinct, I wake just before sunrise. I try to free myself from Emma's arms, which are cool from being against me all night, without waking her, but to no avail. Her eyelids flutter open, revealing those crystal blue irises that are partly responsible for my feelings for her. They stare into mine with that intense, empathetic curiosity that always seems to be gracing her soul. I smile compassionately and bend down to bid farewell.

"Good-bye, my love," I whisper as the kiss ends. She reaches up and caresses my cheek, then closes her eyes again.

"Good-bye, sweetie," she whispers, closing her eyes again.

I return to the cemetery and fall into my coffin, joy pulsing throughout my body. Sleeping with Emma was like heaven.

I hug myself tightly, still feeling her lips against mine and her fingers on my cheeks. I feel that familiar desire between my legs, but for the first time in as long as I can remember, it's unaccompanied by an overcoming lust for human blood. I reach between my legs and bring my fingers in circles over myself until orgasm sends tingles and emotion throughout my body, then I relax and reposition.

And for once, no pain comes with the aftereffects of self-sex. No fear, no cold, no loneliness. All I feel is content. Content and happy. Madam Noctis does not defile my mind or the experience (Jason's crime against me doesn't have any effect because the experience was so physically different); masturbation is once again pure and liberating, as it was when I was alive, when thoughts of Kelly highlighted it. I lie there happily for a long time, thinking about nothing and no one but the girl who is bringing life back into my veins.

I slowly drift into a heavy sleep, Emma's image lulling my mind.

The park has grown tiring, but it's still very early and I do not yet want to return to my grave for sleep lest I wake before the sun is down and feel the desperate need to stretch. I sit against the fence surrounding the graveyard, the cold iron bars pressing into my back. Sensations of fear rush throughout me. Even though it has been five years, the idea of my life as an undead still terrifies and pains me. I miss home. I miss Mommy, Daddy, Nathan, and Kelly. I miss all my friends at my school and all my distant relatives. I know they miss me, too. Oh, why did I have to be taken away from all that I held so dear? Why, why, why?

Voices echo behind me. I gasp and try to remain positively frozen, clasping one hand over my mouth. Soon, the voices become coherent, and I strain to hear what is being spoken.

"I'm telling you, Madam, I think that Amy girl is incomplete."

"And whatever makes you say that, Jason?"

"She's just not like the rest of us. She's never visibly stricken with thirst for blood, she never speaks of her feeds, she's terrified of everything. I've also seen her swinging at the park and when we speak to her of drinking blood, she cringes and pushes us aside. It's like she hates being undead. I think she's still part human."

"No vampire, complete or otherwise, can still be 'part human', Jason. Now you know I am the one who took Amy and that I never let any of my victims become incomplete unless they are anemic. You know my rules. And believe me, I am quite familiar with anemic blood. There is no possible way Amy is anemic; her blood is some of the richest I've ever tasted."

"But what about her constant fright?"

"It's just the way she is. Lay off, all right? Amy's fine. End of story."

I wake with a start, drenched in a cold sweat. I had completely forgotten that night! Its memory must have been lodged deep in my brain in such a place only a hypnotic sleep could reach to retrieve it. *An incomplete vampire is one that still possesses his soul even though he has been turned.* My eyes widen in realization. Could it be? I throw myself into the night immediately. I have to tell Emma.

I take the steps two at a time and rap on the glass of her door. She opens it quickly and we share a brief kiss before I step in and hurry her into the closet.

"Listen, Emma, I just remembered something."

"What?"

"I was sleeping and dreamed about a memory in the back of my mind."

"What is it?"

"Okay. About seventeen years ago, when I was around twenty and still grieving a lot, I overheard Madam Noctis and Jason talking. Jason was insisting that I was what he called 'incomplete', and Madam Noctis was insisting to him that there was no possible way I could be."

"What do they mean by 'incomplete'?"

"I don't know. But I think he was using it as a reason for my…strange behavior. Do you think—"

"Maybe." Emma stands and fetches her computer. "I think I'll do a Google search on it."

"A what?"

"I'll search for it over the Internet."

"What good will that do?" Emma taught me what I didn't already know about how to use a modern computer so I wouldn't be bored at night, but she never showed me that she had Internet.

"Listen, Amy, it might have been a tiny little thing back in the eighties, but these days it's the biggest info source on the planet. You can find an answer to almost everything with it—the problem is knowing which info is correct, because anyone can put websites up. Now since vampires are considered fictional, our findings won't be proven or anything. We'll have to believe what makes the most sense to us." While I gawk at how advanced it all is, she goes to some…page, types in "incomplete vampires" and hits her "return" key.

"You sure the word they used was 'incomplete'?" she asks as the screen goes blank.

"Positive."

All kinds of blue titles rain down the page. She clicks on one and it takes her to an entirely different site.

"Damn," I breathe as she clicks a tiny arrow and the page of titles reappears.

"Man, so many links are useless," she groans. As she scrolls down the titles goes to the next page of results. "Oh, this looks suspicious." She clicks on something. "It's an article." She pauses a minute, then continues. "It says that the 'first recorded incomplete vampire kept a journal. He said he described himself as anything but what he knew he was—a vampire. He had all the physical characteristics of "normal vampires," but he didn't feel like one. He lived off water and his body, though not as warm as a living human's, was much warmer than the temperature of utter death, the temperature of most vampires. He cared about humans; was not afraid of crosses, but, on the contrary, drawn to them; he loved blood but hated hurting people to get it, so he hardly ever did."

I swallow. *Hard.*

"'There have been many others since then. It is believed that this condition of being "incomplete" is caused by the vampire having not lost all of his or her soul, dying from the attack before their predator has taken it all. In turn, the rest flows back to what is left in the body after death. There are two known reasons for this "death-before-death" phenomenon.

"'One. When the attacking vampire isn't around, another comes to feed on the victim. It can't, however, draw life, because the other has already laid claim on the victim's soul and it cannot be fed on by someone else until it all returns. So, if the newcomer feeds long enough, said victim will die of blood loss before all spiritual life is gone. The rest of the spiritual life comes back after death.

"'Two. The victim is anemic, and so dies of blood loss before all spiritual life is gone. The rest of the spiritual life comes back after death.'"

She looks to me. "You're not anemic?"

"No."

She looks back to the article. "So that means…"

"No one else fed on me, Emma! I remember everything, and no one else came!'

She raises an eyebrow. "Are you sure you remember everything, Amy?"

"Well, some nights are still blurry, but—"

"Blurry, eh?" She eyes me skeptically. I groan.

"Look, we don't even know if that article is accurate."

"Assuming it is? Like I said, vampires aren't scientifically proven to exist. We can't go by fact. We have to rely on legends. Especially if one is as explanatory as this."

"But…" I turn away. "It all seems so…unreal. It's hard to believe. If this is true, if I'm incomplete, then what happened? Who else attacked me? Was it another clan member? Did they do it unknowingly? Or was it…a stranger?"

She shrugs, returning to the search results page. "Just to be sure, though…" As she passes through a bunch of pages on her computer, she comes up with a few more documents, all bearing striking resemblance to the one we first looked at. "Yeah, Amy, I'm pretty sure this is what's going on here. Someone else must have attacked you. Because as far as I see, it's the only way unless you have anemia." She closes the program.

I put my hand over my heart. If it's true, if I'm incomplete, then…Emma was right. I do still have my soul. I'm not like them. I'm still Amy. I'm still human. Emotion inundates my chest and my eyesight blurs.

"What's wrong?" Emma closes her computer and sets it aside. "What is it, darling?"

"M-my soul." I feel myself start to shake. "I still have my soul." I barely get out the last word before bursting into tears.

"Amy! Oh, Amy!" Emma hurries to cradle me in her arms.

"It's just…it's just…so amazing. So incredible, so hard to believe. It's just…I've spent the last twenty years believing I lost my soul and thinking that I'd never get it back, and now I find out I never lost it in the first place…it's-it's-it's wonderful. I mean, I'm—I'm—I really am different. I'm not a monster. I'm a human, Emma! A human!"

Emma lets me cry into her shoulder, then she lifts my face and kisses me, causing me to relax and my cries to cease momentarily. I see that tears have begun to fall over her cheeks, too.

We cry together for a long time.

Chapter Twenty-Two

Emma

"Hey girlfriend," I beam at Amy when she comes over Saturday night. "I have stuff for you."

"Stuff?"

"Here." I hand her a foot-tall plush doll with plastic blue eyes and short red yarn hair. I show her mine, with green eyes and long black hair.

"Oh my God, Emma," she says, taking both the dolls. "They're adorable! Where did you get them?"

"Some locally-owned toy store in the mall."

"They look just like us."

I grin at her like we've been granted the ability to live forever. "That was the plan."

Amy

I sleep like a log and wake to a sliver of a moon. The January air chills my skin like the touch of a ghost as I get up from my grave and start toward Emma's. As I near the gate, Madam Noctis appears from nowhere, grabs my wrist, and jerks me towards her.

"Oh, Amy, I haven't seen you in a while..."

Oh, just fuck off, will you! The scent of blood and stolen life invades my nose and my stomach does another one of its classic backflips.

"I hope everything is going all right..." she says in a tauntingly sweet voice.

"It'd be a lot better if you'd leave me alone," I snap, immediately shocking myself with my sudden burst of courage. She laughs and begins to stroke my neck threateningly.

"Oh, come on, darling, be nice. You know, you are still one of the best I've ever gotten..."

"Yes, I know," I seethe.

"I do wish I could have you, just once more..."

"You have 'had me' far too many times," I snap.

"Oh, baby, I don't know why you get so uptight about our relationship. I've never done anything to hurt you. Think about it. I've given you eternal life. And you know I only touch you because I *love you.*"

Emma loves me. You are a monster. I grit my teeth and feel the tears well up inside as her hand moves toward my inner thigh. *Use the crucifix,* I command myself. *This is why Emma gave it to you. Use it.* But I can't. It's right there, in my pocket and within easy reach, but I can't use it. As usual, I'm paralyzed with fear. I want to kick myself for being so helpless.

"Is it really that bad, Amy? Is this—" her hand moves between my legs—"really so terrible?"

She pulls the elastic of my skirt away from my body and reaches down. And something inside me snaps. *Not again. Never, ever again.*

A piercing pain charges through my hand and up the middle of my arm and she stumbles backward, clutching her cheek with both hands. For a dreadful instant, the universe seems to stop as we stare at each other, shock shooting through the air. Her stunned expression curls her features into something more inhumanely beautiful than I've ever seen.

And I'm running.

The words just keep racing through my mind, over and over and over. *Never, never, never again.*

"She *what?*"

"Oh, Emma, I just…I just…I don't know what to do!" I sob. "She was going to do it, but I just couldn't let her anymore, because you're right, my body is mine and I should have ultimate control over it, but I'm afraid of what she'll do to me when she sees me next…God, what am I going to do?"

I'm lying in Emma's arms, my head resting on her shoulder. She strokes my hair, rubs my back, kisses my head, and rocks me until my crying slows. Even as I sob, I'm hyperaware of her breast nestled in the curve of my neck.

"What am I going to do?"

Emma props me up higher against her chest. I rest my chin on her shoulder.

"Would she hurt you for what you did?"

"I-I don't think so. She doesn't beat us or anything, but I'm afraid she might be a little more aggressive now."

"And you're sure you can't hide out in my basement?"

I release a single, forlorn giggle from deep in my chest. "No. I'm sorry."

"Then I'll come out with you. I'll walk you down there and make sure nothing happens to you."

I knew she knew what my answer would be. I'm surprised she even asked. *"No."*

"What about the crucifix I gave you? Maybe you should carry it in your hand instead of your pocket. Or wear it around your neck."

"Maybe."

"But she won't harm you? I mean, more than she already has? Your life isn't in danger or anything?"

I shake my head. Madam Noctis would never kill us.

"Thank God for that." Emma lays a kiss on my ear. "I am so proud of you, Amy," she whispers.

"Huh?"

"You defended yourself. You didn't let her do that awful, awful thing to you." She kisses my cheek. "Can't you see it? You're getting stronger."

"It was instinct."

"But still you did it. You're so special to me."

I look into her eyes, smile. "You're special to me, too."

"You still have your crucifix, right?"

I pull it out of my pocket.

"Maybe you should carry it in your hand instead of your pocket when you're out there."

"Yeah. Maybe. So ironic that such an ugly little thing shields us from the devil." I sigh heavily. "God, I'm so damn sick of this life."

Later that night, having finished *The Silver Kiss,* I pick up a flashlight and search Emma's bookcase for new material. I'm looking on the bottom shelf when I come across a stack of paper; with a little examination I recognize it's a manuscript. I pick it up. Pulled in by the first paragraph, I return to Emma's closet and begin to read the rest.

It's about a girl, young, just a freshman in high school, whose parents are abusive and whose sexuality is in question. She has a boyfriend, but she's never turned on by his affections. Then she gets kissed by a girl in the bathroom, and her whole world is turned upside down as she realizes what she is and doesn't know how she's ever going to tell her conservative, divorcing parents. Captivated, I read through the entire thing that night, but it ends just as the girl is about to come out to her mother and I'm left hanging from the edge of a young woman's tale cut short.

"Did you write this?" I ask Emma the next night when I arrive.

She takes it from me and scans it, then frowns. "Where did you get this?"

"I found it on your bookshelf yesterday."

"I…was writing it," Emma sighs, setting it on her desk, "But I quit about a year ago, when things got too tough for us."

"But it's extraordinary!"

"Not really. It's a real mess. I wrote all the time up until last year, but…"

"But what?"

"I don't want to anymore."

"Why not?" I insist, picking it up again.

"Because…I've just lost the spirit I need to write, to do art, read, and pretty much anything else I used to enjoy. It's just all meaningless for me now. I just don't like it anymore."

"How much did you used to enjoy it?"

"I used to feel that writing was my number one talent. It was all I ever did. I came home from school, tossed my backpack aside, and wrote. Then, at school, I drew pictures to go with the story. Sometimes I snuck a flash drive into English and wrote during class. Then at dinner, I imagined my characters eating the food. And at night, I daydreamed myself to sleep. But that's all history now."

"When was the last time you wrote?"

"I honestly don't remember."

"You don't remember? Then why don't you give it another chance? You're such a talented writer, Emma! And you really loved it!"

"'Loved' is the keyword there. I don't know, Amy. I just don't feel motivated."

I throw the manuscript back on her desk. "You know, I used to get bored with my guitar."

"Really?" She doesn't seem surprised at all.

"Yes. And a lot of the time, I had to force myself to practice. It wasn't easy and it wasn't always fun. But you know what? Because I made myself do it, I went to the top of my class in music. It really was one of my number one talents. And it seems like writing is one of yours. Just force yourself to sit down and write. I'm sure your brain feels dry right now, but a little pushing might force it free again."

"I doubt it."

"Just try it. You might be surprised."

She shakes her head. "I don't know."

"Come on, Emma. What do you have to lose?"

She sinks to her bed, buries her face in her hands. "I can't write if I don't feel motivated to."

"Just do it."

She sighs. "I guess I could try…"

"Please do." I sit next to her and kiss her on the cheek. "You are really good."

"Thanks." She twiddles her thumbs, changes the subject. "Did you finish *The Silver Kiss*?"

"Yeah, it was amazing."

"Have you read the *Blue Bloods* books? Or what about *Tantalize*?"

"What are those about?"

"Vampires."

I snort. "You're really into vampire lore, aren't you."

She digs her toe into the carpet. "Yes. And it's not because of you. I've been into vampire stories since the eighth grade. That doesn't bother you, does it?"

"No, no, of course not!" I laugh.

"Well…okay…" She glances over to her door, her beautiful red locks dancing around her head. It's too sweet, and I tackle her, pushing her back onto the bed, and smother her with kisses.

I was eleven when the truth first occurred to me. I was sitting in the bathtub, staring at the dripping showerhead above me and thinking about the new girl at school. Hallie, the tall one with deep chocolate skin and long black braids. Bright outfits, even brighter eyes. She wasn't afraid; by the second day, people were voluntarily eating out of her hand. Three days after she'd arrived, she'd sat by me while I waited for Mama to pick me up after Girl Scouts. She'd spoken first, and ten minutes later, when Mama's car pulled up, she'd learned all the basics about me and I'd known more about her than I'd ever expect to out of the new girl at school.

The attraction I felt as I thought about her, basking in the warm blue bubbles and toying with my developing breasts, caused me to launch upright so fast water splattered everywhere.

"Mom!" I called out, alarmed, my eyes nearly popping out of my skull. The familiar thump-thump of her moving downstairs reached my ears and soon she was in the bathroom, staring at her naked daughter with the waist-long red hair plastered to her skin sitting in the middle of the sea of blue bubbles.

"What is it, Emma?"

"Mommy?"

"Yes, darling?"

"Mommy, I-I-I think I might be gay."

Mama looked surprised. "Really? What makes you say that, darling?"

"Just a feeling."

"Well, sweetheart, you're only twelve. It can take people half a lifetime to figure something like that out. Almost everyone faces that question at some point. However." She knelt by the tub and took my slippery hand between hers. "Homosexuality is a beautiful, beautiful thing, sweetie. Aunt Maggie is gay, you know."

"I know."

"If you're gay, I will love your girlfriend like my own daughter, no matter who she is. And never let anyone with their stupid, naïve comments against gays get to you. They're wrong."

"Naïve?"

"It means ignorant."

"Oh."

"You may be gay, but there is nothing wrong with you, baby. You're just special. If you are a lesbian, then God gave you a wonderful gift that not everyone is blessed with. You shouldn't be ashamed, you should be proud. Proud to be a lesbian. Proud to be Emma Kathleen Levesque."

I smiled and she kissed my forehead. *"I love you, sweet baby."*

"Love you too, Mama."

She smiled and opened the door, flipping the light switch and leaving us in complete darkness.

"Oops!" Light flooded the room once again and Mom laughed. *"I wonder how many times I'm going to do that to you girls."*

I giggled as Mom closed the door behind her.

Chapter Twenty-Three

Emma

With Amy's words in mind and nothing better to do on a slow Saturday afternoon, I pick up my computer and open my old story. It's rusty in my mind; I've forgotten where I am and what changes need to be made, and I don't want to bother trying to sort it out. So I turn on iTunes and open a new document, and after only a few words, inspiration strikes. I put my fingers to the keys and begin a new story, one about a lonely teenaged lesbian with a dead mother and a traitor father, who meets and falls deeply in love with a beautiful yet miserable vampire. Before I know it, Jaquelina is calling us down for dinner and I have four chapters written.

Jaquelina continues with her usual stupidity at dinner, but for some reason, I don't really mind. Although Annie gulps down her food, looking as miserable as ever, I feel a smile force its way through my wall of death. It isn't showing on the outside, but I can feel it in there, and my mood responds accordingly. After I finish my meal, I head into the living room to watch *Extreme Surgery*. Jaquelina comes in about halfway through the show and opens a blue photo album in her lap. I think nothing of it as I keep my eyes glued to the screen. But as the show ends, something Amy said to me quite a while back echoes suddenly through my mind. *She's obviously trying, Emma, even though she's failing miserably. I think you should at least try to make amends so that you don't build a giant wall.*

I sigh. Amy is right. I should apologize to Jaquelina. But it's been such a long time. Would she even remember? I want to wait to ask Amy, but I already know what her answer will be. *It's never too late to heal wounds, Emma.* I turn to shoot Jaquelina a quick "I'm sorry" when I notice the pictures at which she is looking. I recognize those photos. A brunette child reading first-grade level books, a little girl with a ponytail learning to ride a bike, a toddler with red pigtails scribbling with Crayolas, another redhead smearing strawberry ice cream over her mouth…it's my sisters and me!

"Oh my God," I exhale, staring.

Jaquelina grins a mile a minute. "You girls were so adorable," she says. I gape at her.

"He has these?"

"Sure he does," Jaquelina says. "When we got together about seven years ago, this was one of the first things he showed me. He said that these were his daughters, that he missed them so much but he didn't want to go back. He didn't want to risk hurting you girls. But he looked at these a lot, and I became quite attached to them too. I wanted children desperately, but he told me that we couldn't, that he couldn't risk the same things happening."

What things?

"It hurt me badly, but I tried to look on the positive side. Still, I looked at this a lot, wishing every day for my own. I thought you girls were so adorable. You can't imagine my ecstasy when I found out you were coming."

I frown at her. Her eyes widen.

"Oh, no, Emma, don't take it that way! I know what you've been through! I just was so happy to know there would be teenagers in the house." She sighs. "I know you think I'm annoying and that I'm trying futilely to mother you, but I'm really inexperienced with teenagers. Having four suddenly appear at my doorstep is kind of hard. I'm trying the best I can. I just want you to know that."

"Yeah, you're still kinda young for teenagers, don't you think?"

"What? Many women have teenagers by my age."

"Yeah, those that became pregnant at fifteen."

She almost laughs. "Whoa, are my Clinique bonus bags really doing that good a job? My God, do you have things twisted. I'm thirty-eight! Did you think I was younger?"

My jaw drops to the floor. "Thirty-eight? I thought you were, like, twenty-seven!"

"Wow, really? That's flattering."

"You don't look any older."

"Well, thank you. I've been working hard to keep myself well. I try to eat well and exercise a lot. I wish I had exercised more in high school and college, but I was too devoted to my studies."

"Huh?"

"My studies. I majored in sociology and, because of my hard work, graduated close to the top of my class. Then I went for three years of law school." She laughs. "But it didn't benefit my thighs, that's for sure."

I couldn't be more shocked. "*Law school?*"

Jaquelina grins wickedly. "Betcha thought I majored in fashion merchandising and became one of those stick-thin models, huh?"

"Well, um—"

"Or maybe you just thought I avoided college altogether." She's practically having hysterics now.

"What makes you think that?" I ask, embarrassed.

"I know more than you think, Emma. After law school and a few years of work, I scored a partnership in a law firm in Denver. I was still working there when I met Robert. We lived there for two years in this small house, and we were really very happy, but we had to leave a few years ago because of an emergency. We moved here and then I worked in a firm here until last September, when I took leave to help care for you girls. Believe it or not, we've only lived in this house since August."

"August?"

"Yeah. Our jobs were paying off, but we were happy in our condo. It wasn't nearly big enough for six, though, so we bought this monster." She laughs. "Anyway, when the courts gave us the news, Robert was still a little worried about history repeating itself, but I assured him that he had turned his life around and it was time he gave you girls—and himself—a second chance."

"What are you talking about?"

"What do you mean?"

"What history?"

Her eyes widen. "You don't know?"

"Know what?"

"Why your father left, sweetie."

"He left because he didn't want us anymore." It's out before I can stop it. Jaquelina simply shakes her head.

"On the contrary, Emma, he wanted you more than almost anything. But the one thing he wanted more than you was for you to lead happy, healthy lives. That's why he left."

"What on earth made him think his leaving us would make our lives better?"

"I think you'd better go ask him, darling," Jaquelina says. "It's not my place to tell you about a past I wasn't involved in. It's his and only his. He's in the den."

"All right." I stand and head for the other arch in the living room, the one that leads to the family room, then I turn back.

"Listen, Jaquelina, I'm sorry about what happened a month ago. Things are rather difficult for us right now, you know?"

Jaquelina grins ear-to-ear. "I know, sweetheart. Don't be too hard on yourself. What you said hurt, but it did open my eyes. I've been trying to be less annoying since you told me that. In fact, I wish you'd done it earlier. I can't know if I'm hurting someone unless she tells me."

I shake my head and pass into the den. Robert is in there, reading glasses on and book open. He's leaning on his elbow and prominent bags hang heavily under his eyes.

"Um…Robert?"

He turns. "Hey kiddo."

"Hey, listen, do you have a minute?"

"Sure." Looking only too happy to, he shuts his book with a *puff* and turns off the desk lamp, taking off his glasses. "Whatcha need?"

I sigh. "Tell me the truth. Why *did* you leave so many years ago?"

His face falls.

"Come on, Robert. Tell me or the grudge I have will only worsen."

"It's a long story, sweetheart."

"I have time."

"Mom never told you?"

I shake my head."

"Come sit on the couch with me." He gets up and sits on the plaid futon. "Listen, Emma, I didn't want to leave. I really didn't. I loved you girls and I loved Celina. But that's precisely why I had to go. I really had no choice."

"What are you talking about?"

"Well, I had a serious problem with alcohol. By the time Celina was pregnant with you and Jill, I was already downing three bottles a night. Things were getting out of control. When I passed out on the night of your first birthday, Celina took me to a specialist. Unfortunately, two years of therapy were not helping at all, and I was getting worse and worse." He sighs, puts his hand in his head like this is the most difficult thing he's ever done. "I would go out to parties, drink countless shots or bottles of whatever. I liked whisky and vodka and lager, although it was the gin I really loved. I'd then come home at around midnight dead drunk."

"*Dang.*"

"Yeah. Your mother would confront me the next morning, but by then I was so hung over that I could hardly remember anything. My addiction was also draining us of the money that should have been going to the care of you girls. One night after you had gone to sleep, your mother caught me in front of the TV, three bottles of gin at my feet. She lost it and began scolding me about irresponsibility, lack of self-control, and being a bad influence, and I got violent. I stood up and shouted back at her, and we began…screaming…and then I lost control and…and I hit her."

"You *hit* her?"

"It's not something I'm proud of, love. She stared at me for a second, shocked, and then we heard a tiny, frightened voice. 'You hit my mommy,' it said. It was Kristina, standing on the steps, looking mortified." Robert wipes his eyes and I feel mine widen. Is he *crying?* "That-that poor child, barely five years old and witnessing violence between her parents. Celina managed to get Kristina settled down and back to bed, then she told me that she couldn't stand to see her babies witness such things. She told me to leave, to cut off all ties and not to come back until I gained control of my life again. I blew up and stormed from the house.

"But despite the lager I took at a night club later, I remembered everything the next morning, and I knew your mother was right. I couldn't expose my daughters to such horrors as

177

violence and alcoholism. So many children suffer through that, and your mama and I had made a vow early on that you would never grow up in a family like that. Yes, I had been trying to get it under control—I really had—but it just wasn't working and I didn't feel like I could stop it. I moved out here to try to get a fresh start, to try to get my life back on track. But when I finally managed to quit, go to grad school, and get a respectable job, I was too afraid to go back. Too afraid to face the awful past, too afraid I would lose control again. So your mother and I got divorced." His eyes shift to the floor. "We kept it clean, quick, secret—we didn't want you all caught up in it. I knew you were older and I didn't want to take any chances, so I thought it best to just burn off the severed ties and let you girls live your lives without me. I really thought it would be best for you."

I have trouble finding words; I had no idea Robert had a real reason for leaving, let alone such an important one. "But—but it wasn't. It really hurt us. Jill and I didn't really remember you, but we used to look at your photographs, hoping that someday you'd come back. I thought you'd left because you didn't care about us. That's why I don't address you as my dad and I don't really trust you."

"I was scared when I found out you were coming, Emma. I really was. I missed you all terribly, but I just didn't want to risk things flying out of control again. I didn't want to hurt you. Now that you've come and I've seen what wonderful young women you all have become…my God, I was terrible to let you go. I'm really sorry I missed your childhood. I'm sorry I couldn't be there for you. I just really messed up big time. And I'm sorry I didn't celebrate Hanukkah with you girls this year. I know that you probably haven't celebrated Christmas much in your lifetime and you probably felt like you'd missed the best holiday of the year. I'll get a nice menorah and we'll celebrate it next year, okay?"

I nod and glance at the clock on the wall. It's approaching eight. Amy has a tendency to show anytime between eight and ten. I have to get back to my bedroom. I stand and approach the door.

"You know, there are some instances where 'I'm sorry' just isn't enough, Robert."

"I know, Emma. I've been trying so hard to take good care of you. You have no reason to forgive me, no matter what I do for you. I just hope that someday, you girls will find it in you to forgive me and accept Jaquelina as your stepmother."

I nod. "We'll see."

Our report cards arrive in the mail mid-January. I open mine, expecting the worst, but almost drop the paper upon seeing it.

COLDWATER CENTRAL HIGH SCHOOL
1856 N REGAL DR
SALT LAKE CITY, UT 83732

PARENT OR GUARDIAN OF:
EMMA K. LEVESQUE
1823 E PENNY LANE
BOISE, ID
83731

MID QUARTER GRADES FOR
EMMA K. LEVESQUE
GR: 09
TERM 03
YR: 2005-06

GP1	GP2	GP3	S1	GP4	GP5	GP6	S2

DRAWING 1-2   B   C+
CHRZASTOWS

PRE-CALCUL   C   C
BURKE

PAINTING 1-2   B-   C+
CHRZASTOWS

PHYICS I   C+   C
LEWIS

PHYSICAL ED   A-   A-
WEVER

ENGLS 9 HON   C   C
BUTERA

| LATIN III ROE | B+ | B |
| ST GLASS I SMITH | A | A |

TERM 3 GPA: 3.056
SEM 1 GPA: 2.069

I'm stunned. I was sure my card would be all Ds and Fs. I was an A student up until the end of tenth grade, but after Mama died, I was striving just to keep my GPA above a D. So having 3 Bs is like a miracle for me.

Later that night, I show Amy my report card, along with my previous one from my old school, and she giggles. "I should reward you for this," she says, a mischievous grin on her face.

"Oh really?" I beam, sitting on my bed and crossing my legs sexily.

"Oh yes." She dives for me, landing on top and pushing me back onto the bed. Our kiss grows passionate and as she strokes my inner thigh, my feelings turn serious and intense as her hands start to feel really good on my body.

"Amy?" I whisper as her finger strokes my cheek.

"Yes love?"

"I—" This is a hard thing to request, considering her wretched past, but—"I want to have sex with you."

She sighs heavily, her eyes dropping. This is a whole new step in our relationship. "Oh, Emma. You know I want it too. But sex is a big thing, you know? I don't want to get into it too fast. It might hurt you."

"What about you?"

"Emma, I'm thirty-six."

"But would it be scary for you? Would it remind you of...of her?"

She gazes at me. "You kiss me. You touch me in the same places. She never crosses my mind. I only think about you."

"Yes, but—"

"Let's not rush. Let's let things happen, okay?"

I nod, smile crookedly and glance at the scars Madam Noctis's bite left Amy with. I move over to her, put my fingers to them lightly, then my lips.

"Whatcha doin'?"

"Erasing it," I respond, kissing the bite again.

"Oh." She smiles weakly and runs a hand through my hair softly. "Sometimes it feels like just being with you has already erased all of it."

Chapter Twenty-Four

Emma

My eyes widen in horror as I pull my fishnets out of my pile of laundry at around four in the afternoon. They're ripped at many crossing points, leaving giant holes all over. I freeze for a second, mortified, then cry out in anguish "Jaquelina!" as I speed from the room.

She's in the living room, watching a soap opera as she sorts laundry. I storm up.

"*Which* cycle did you wash these on?" I demand.

"What are they, dear?" she asks me.

"They're my fishnets! Did I not tell you to put them on delicate?"

Her face falls. "Oh, I'm sorry, sweetie, I'm afraid that must have slipped my mind. I threw them in with your others."

"On *regular?*"

"I'm afraid so."

I turn away and examine them, rage and sadness filling my heart.

"Emma? Are you okay, sweetie?"

"I was finally starting to forgive you guys," I say, my voice shaky. "But my mama gave me these on the sixth night of Hanukkah a year ago, right before she died. She gave them to me, because even though she was slightly alarmed at my growing interest in Goth culture, she knew I'd like them. How can you expect me to forgive you if you tell me the truth one night and do this not even a week later?"

"I'm really sorry, Emma. I—I didn't know—"

"How can you have graduated at the top of your class?" I howl, whirling around with hot tears burning in my eyes. "How could you have when you don't even know that fishnets are delicates and should never be washed on fucking regular?"

"Emma—"

"Just shut up, okay? Shut up and get out of my life!" I storm back upstairs and slam my door as hard as I possibly can.

Amy

"I HATE them!" Emma storms. "I hate their guts!"

Not having really slept well in the last fifteen hours, I let out a deep yawn and rub my eyes, remaining silent while Emma rants.

"They can just go and destroy every last piece of what I loved without giving a shit about it! What the hell is their problem?"

I twiddle my thumbs.

"How can they expect me to forgive them when they do something like this?"

"Emma."

"I just can't!"

"Emma."

"My mother gave me those—"

"Emma!"

"What?"

"I'm sure Jaquelina didn't mean to harm your fishnets."

"Oh yeah, she just happened to throw them in on regular, thinking they were as tough as denim!"

"Maybe they were hidden in a shirt or something."

"She said she threw them in with my other clothing! She saw them! I'm sorry, but people who graduate with honors do not throw fishnets in on regular! They just don't!"

"I'm really sorry, Emma. But things were getting on so well. Everybody has brain lapses. I know this is hard because your mother gave you those. I know that, baby. But just try to forgive her, okay love?"

"Why are you always telling me to do that? Why can't you just listen for once?"

"I don't always tell you to do that! Out of all the times you've complained to me, I've only told you twice! And I have been listening! You know I listen!"

"So why are you always taking their side?"

"I'm on your side!"

"Then act like it!"

"Emma, come on. You know that all this grudge is doing is hurting you. You saw how happy you were when you were on the brink of forgiveness. I ask you to forgive them because that's key to your content while living in this house! That's what I want for you! I want you to be happy!"

"Yeah, whatever! If you're so logical with helping me, why can't you help yourself a little, huh? Why can't you just tell Madam Noctis to fuck off for once?"

Mingled surprise and hurt well in my chest. I can't believe I'm fighting with Emma. I can't believe she just said that about me. And worst of all, I know she's right. How much can I help her if I can't even help myself?

"Unless you want to get raped *again*, you're going to have to find that strength! What has just lying there, hoping she'll forget about you, ever done for you? It's only made things worse!"

"For the love of God—"

"Just go away."

"What?"

"Just *go,* okay? Get out of here! I don't care where you go! I just don't want to be with you right now!"

I don't want to be with you right now. Tears well in my eyes and I back towards the door. "Stop being a bitch."

"Oh, fuck you!"

"Well…fuck you too!" The tears fall from my eyes, and I run. I run from her room and out into the cold, harsh January air. I cry all the way down to my grave, and once inside, I let the wails out.

What happened? Those harsh words we threw at each other—were those real? Could those words have come from the mouth of my dear, sweet Emma? And could I have actually had the cold hear to hurl them right back? As I remember her soft lips against me, I can't believe I said what I said. I think I did the right thing in telling her to try not to let it hurt her so much, but I could have been gentler about it. I could have been more sympathetic, less blatant and icy. I feel my heart grow with love for that girl, then waves of sorrow pour through my veins and my tears grow stronger. I turn over and leave my grave. I have to get back to Emma and apologize. I have to kiss her and comfort her. I have to let her know I still love her, that I will always love her, no matter what, and that everything will be all right. I look around for any of the others, then take off through the cemetery and into the woods.

I'm coming, my love.

Chapter Twenty-Five

Emma

Devastation rises in my chest as Amy runs from the yard without looking back. What have I done? She's my only friend. She's more than my only friend. She's my love, my spirit. She was only trying to help me. And I shunned her for it.

And what I *said!* Telling her to fuck off? Telling her I didn't want her around? I can't believe it escaped my lips, the same lips that assured her that everything would be all right, and that kissed her adoringly to soothe her tears. It was my moment of stupidity, weakness, when anger got the better of me and a monster spoke with intent to hurt. Hurt my darling Amy. How could I be so heartless? Dear, dear Amy. How could I be so stupid? I want to break down, I feel so horrible.

Instead, I lock my door, stuff pillows under my sheets, grab my flashlight, turn out the light, and hurry outside. I have to find her. I have to run to her, apologize, and kiss her and love her and tell her that everything's all right, that I'm here for her and I'm not mad at her at all.

I look everywhere for Amy: through the woods, around the playground, even along the streets. But she isn't there. I decide to try the graveyard, no matter how risky it is. I head through the back woods, since it's safer there and I might find Amy. I've passed the hill and am almost to the cemetery when it happens.

"Hello, little girl."

I freeze in my tracks and chills run up my spine. What was that…that haunting echo? I look around at the dark silhouettes of the trees and the starry black sky, the silence ringing across them and pounding in my ears. Am I hearing things? A small terror of the dark shakes me and I shut my eyes for a moment, pretending to be safe. In bed. In Amy's arms. Our lips touching, our fingers laced.

"Come here, little girl." My eyes shoot open and a tiny gasp escapes my throat. I heard it again. It isn't just my imagination. The voice is haunting, terrifying, yet beautiful and mesmerizing. "Come, come to me. I will not harm you." The terror in my heart begins to ebb, replaced by a longing to seek the voice, to find and become a part of it. I turn slowly around.

At first, I see nothing but the dark outlines of trees. But then, by one of the dark trunks, a woman materializes seemingly out of nowhere. Her sheer beauty immediately shocks me into complete submission. I can see her staggeringly well in the darkness—as though she casts her own glow. Her straight, silver hair falls to her waist and the ends curve in slightly. Her blue eyes glow, and her long, silver nails on her white hands are sharpened to a point. Her lips are bright red, and she's tall and slender. She must be wearing a black dress and black shoes, because her skin is set around darkness in the shape of a sleeveless dress and thin-strap heels.

I can't look away. And, without my even realizing it, my feet are moving in her direction. It's as though they aren't connected to my brain—my mind is lost in the splendor of this goddess.

As I float toward her, she stares into my eyes, right at my soul; she shifts a bit, causing the moon to reflect silver glitter on her dress. "Come to me, come…" She speaks soft, calming words, and I long to be in her arms. Just a little farther…I reach out; she takes my hand and pulls me in close, so that I'm laying my head on her shoulder and our chests are pressing into each other.

She holds me firmly yet gently as she slowly reaches up and gently pushes my hair off my neck. She runs her ghostly fingers up and down my throat…it sends a chill down my spine and makes my insides tingle, but in an excited, sensual way. She leans in; I can feel her cool breath raise the fine hairs on my skin. She puts her lips, soft and cold like water, to the base of my neck, and…

The pain that follows is the shearing bite of the devil himself. It's as though these two sharp daggers penetrate straight into my soul, and then something beautiful, but horrible, is sucking something wonderful, something vital, from my body. The stabbing pain branches from my neck to my shoulders and deep into my chest with each excruciating suck. I'm blinded from the very start by the unnatural, unearthly pain.

I also feel something else: a strange, sickening sensation; a feeling that all the wonder and love is being sucked from every cell of my body. All the joy I know seems to be plummeting to depression like a thermometer suddenly placed in icy water; the pain is so ghastly I'm barely aware of the cries I'm letting out and the tears that are drowning my face.

My head must fall back, for the next thing I know, I gain enough eyesight to see another girl, upside down, staring at me through the darkness. She's one hundred times as beautiful as the one holding me, but, although this is true physically, the beauty I see comes from her soulful eyes and the emotion they reflect: intense fury and terror.

She pulls something from her skirt and advances; the pain in my neck grinds to a halt, replaced by the much duller pain of someone screeching like a banshee in my ear. The world spins as I hit the ground, too weak to move. Someone's yanking me to my feet...

Looking up, I see, in the gentle moonlight, that beautiful, soft face I've kissed so many times. She's pissed. She's screaming. She's...pulling us away.

"Oh...Amy..." I moan with all the strength I can muster.

"Shhh. It'll be all right, baby. It will be all right." She manages to pull me off the ground, and, carrying me like a child, she struggles to walk away from the horrible scene. I feel my head begin to spin again; my eyes roll back and close as I slip into unconsciousness.

Amy

I try to go as fast as I can, but I don't get very far before ear-piercing shrieks stab at my eardrums. I assume they're coming from a house up in Sunny Housing, but as I get nearer to Emma's, they grow louder until they're consuming the air around me. I round a tree and see Madam Noctis feeding on a girl imprisoned in her arms. I have to silently move closer before I can see who it is. When I can, the truth pierces my spirit and makes my blood turn to ice.

Emma.

In one split second, I forget everything that came between us that night. I forget all the bad words that we hurled, all the mean things we said, and all the apologies we owe each other. All that matters now is us. The love between us, and the love that is in danger if this demon should succeed. All that matters is that in the arms of this red-eyed beast is my Emma. My lover, my soul, everything that means anything to me. All resting in my hands now.

I shove my hand into my pocket and withdraw the crucifix Emma gave me. Our only hope rests within this tiny carving of Jesus on a pine wood cross. So small, so simple, yet the only thing that can save Emma's soul.

I lunge at Madam Noctis, the crucifix clutched tightly in my outstretched hand. Emma's head tilts back and her big, beautiful blue eyes, so full of pain and fear, lock onto mine for a fleeting moment before I hit Madam Noctis head-on with the cross. She shrieks in agony, and we all three fall to the ground with the force of my blow.

"*Leave her alone*," I demand, pulling Emma off her and up with me. "Don't you ever come near her again. If you do, you will be sorry."

"Little bitch," she sneers. "How shall I be sorry?"

"If you ever touch her again, if you *ever* so much as come close to her, I will kill you. Literally. *Kill you*."

She laughs. "Kill me? *Kill me*? I am the leader of this clan! I made you into what you *are*! What makes you, a small, defenseless girl, think that you can control *me*?"

Emma's wonderful, thick blood, the blood that should be bringing life to only her, drips lusciously from Madam Noctis's fangs. As I gaze at them, horrified, I feel the sharp pain at the base of my own neck—the pain Madam Noctis made me suffer twenty years ago and the pain poor Emma endured only moments ago. It's too much. I want to lunge at her, bite her, rip at her flesh, cause her as much pain as possible. But I don't. The words fly from my mouth before I even know what they are. "I can hold a crucifix." With that, I draw the crucifix again and she cringes. I shove it in her face and she screams, covers her eyes, stumbles, and falls once again. I move slowly back, dragging Emma with me. *"Leave her alone,"* I repeat. *"Or you'll be sorry."*

I put my crucifix back in my pocket. "Oh…Amy…" Emma groans weakly as her

head falls against my left breast.

"Shhh. It'll be all right, baby. It will be all right." She's so heavy…can I manage to carry her home? I can. I have to.

Madam Noctis does not follow. Emma lies in my arms, her eyes echoing an excruciating emptiness, for a few minutes. Then slowly, sadly, they close and her face falls to echo a pained sleep. Fear speeds through my body as I start to lose too much energy to carry her. Normally, I have superhuman strength. But in my fatigue of so much sleep loss over the past few days, I find I am no stronger than any average girl. And Emma grows heavier with every step.

Oh, God. The others are rabid right now. They won't care if I'm with her—they'll take me down to get to her. I can't fail. I can't.

Finally I collapse about ten yards into the forest around the northwest corner of the cemetery, holding her tightly and gasping for air. "No…" I whisper. "No." This can't be happening. I can't lie here, leaving us cold and vulnerable. I have to go…

But it's hopeless. I try to stand again but my legs wobble and I fall. Finally I just hold her protectively and cry into her shoulder as I wait for my strength to return.

As I rest my ear on her chest, her heart begins caressing my ears. That beautiful, strong heartbeat. That force that's keeping her with me.

Dreadful images force their way through my mind, images of Emma's blood dripping from Noctis's fangs; images of her sad, spiritless face twisted in agony; images of the night that woman took me, how terrible the pain was; images of Emma dead, lying pale and lost in a casket somewhere, doomed to a fate worse than death.

God, I can't let that happen. I push myself up, my mind racing for a way out of this hell. Then I hear a little tone playing and realize just before it stops that it came from Emma's coat pocket. Reaching in, I feel my hand close around a cool plastic object with a few buttons on the side. I wrench it out. A little display has lit up on the front, giving the date and time, and recognition shoots through me as I stare at it.

I held this thing once before, back in Emma's room. She even told me a little about it. It's a cell phone!

I flip open the display desperately and the screen and all the little numbers and symbols light up. The little tone plays again, with a small "Battery Low" sign covering the screen. Then it disappears and the date and time, displayed in white against a beautiful red floral background, take its place. Who can I call? Who will help me out here? I don't know anyone around here. No one…do I have no choice but to call the authorities? I don't even want to think about the horrible consequences of that.

After fumbling for a few moments, I finally manage to pull up the address book Emma told me about, and I flit my eyes over the short list of names. Annie, Jill, Kristina—of course! Jill and Kristina! They can help me, can't they?

But asking them to come out here in the middle of the night, with all those vampires about…dare I risk it? I have to. Dear Emma depends on it. After pressing what I've figured out is the select key one more time, I see a "CALL" option and hit it.

One ring. Two rings. Three rings. Fo—

"Hello?" an exhausted voice drones.

"Hi, uh, Kristina?"

"Yeah?"

"It's Amy. You know, Emma's girlfriend? I really need your help!"

"Wh-what? Amy? What are you talking about?"

"Listen, Kristina. Emma and I are on the north side of the graveyard at the bottom of your hill, right outside the fence. You've got to help us, Kristina! She's unconscious and I can't carry her home by myself!"

"Wait—*what?* Emma's *unconscious?*"

"Yeah, and it's dangerous out here. You have to help me get her home!"

"What happened?"

"We were…taking a walk and she…passed out." Oh dear, I have to choose my words carefully. Don't want them calling 911 on me. "She saw…a dead deer, and it was really gross, and she let out this little shriek and just sort of fainted. I checked everything, and she's fine, she's breathing normally and all that, but I can't carry her home. It's really dangerous out here at night, Kristina, please be careful! Bring Jill so you're not alone! And we'll need all the hands we can get."

"Do I need to call an ambulance?"

"No, no, I told you she's okay, I just need help getting her home. And whatever you do, don't bring Robert and Jaquelina."

"Why not?"

"If they find out about me, we may not be able to see each other anymore!"

"Okay! Okay, we'll be there as fast as we can!"

"Kristina!"

"What?"

"Bring those crucifixes Robert gave you."

"The cruci—what? Why?"

"Just bring them, okay? Pull them out if someone attacks you."

"Amy—"

"Just do it! Now hurry!"

The time between my hanging up and Kristina and Jill coming into view seems like a trillion years. When I finally see their silhouettes coming around the gate of the cemetery, I call out and flash the light of the phone their direction.

"Amy!" Kristina shouts and they both break into a run and arrive in seconds. Jill lets out a cry as her flashlight shines on Emma's limp body. Not wanting to panic them, I hid Emma's neck by pulling the hood of her jacket over her head.

"Oh my *God*," Kristina exclaims. "Are you sure she's okay?"

"She's fine, Kristina, how many times do I have to tell you?"

Kristina checks her vitals anyway, and she and Jill hoist Emma between the two of them and as we start off, guilt and fear encompass me completely.

We manage to get her up the hill, across her yard, up her steps, and into her bedroom. They laid her gently on the bed and I turn on a light and realize too late one of them has unzipped her jacket already, exposing the streaks of blood. And the sight of them awakens a thirst in the back of my throat that I thought was gone for good. Oh God.

A sharp intake of breath, and the blow falls. "You told me she just passed out!" Kristina screeches.

"Shhh! Kristina, quiet!"

I grab a Kleenex from a box on Emma's nightstand, dip it in a glass of water sitting on a coaster next to the box, and place it on her neck. The tissue soaks up the blood instantly, and I wipe her neck off as best I can, trying my hardest not to shudder with blood lust.

And there they are. The most horrible things I have ever known. The two punctures at the base of her neck from which Madam Noctis sucked her blood, life, and soul. I close my eyes in dismay. I can hardly bear to look at them.

"Oh my God. Something bit her."

"Well, no shit, Kristina," I snap.

"Why didn't you *tell* me that?"

"Because you might have gone ballistic and called 911."

"So? I think we *should* have!"

"No, Kristina, shut up! Listen, both of you!" I let out a sigh. "Hang on just one more second, okay? Could one of you get some soapy water so I can wash this?"

I turn back to Emma. The bleeding has stopped. I gently take off her shoes and pull back her covers. She's stuffed some pillows under her comforter; I remove them and place them behind her head. Then slowly, lovingly, I cover her with the blankets and kiss her cheek.

Something pokes at my arm, and I realize Jill is behind me with a Tupperware bowl full of soapy water, a washcloth, and a towel.

"Oh, thanks, hon," I say, taking them from her.

"What bit her?" Kristina presses "And *there?* What kind of animal were you guys messing with? God, that's so close to her jugular, one more inch and she could have bled to death!"

"If that had been the case, I would have called the hospital myself." I put the Band-Aid Jill had wrapped in the towel over the bite, not because the bite needed it, but to keep the Polysporin from rubbing off.

"Okay." I turn around and sit on the bed. "I want you guys to listen. And don't interrupt me until I'm finished."

Kristina sits next to me with another nervous glance at Emma, whose hair is being stroked affectionately by an anxious Jill. "Are you sure she'll be all—"

"*Yes*, Kristina, she hardly lost any blood at all. A full inch from her jugular, remember? Now do you want to know what's happening here or not?"

"Fine. Talk."

"Okay. Look." I pull down my shirt collar to show them my scars. "I have those bite marks too. I got them over twenty years ago. Emma and I were both attacked by the same person."

"Wait. *Person?*"

"Yes. Person." I proceed to explain to them that their guardians gave them those crucifixes for a reason, that there are vampires around, and that Emma was attacked by one when she was outside looking for me after our fight. I try the whole time not to open my mouth enough to show my fangs. Through the whole story Kristina and Jill's faces became more and more panicked and disbelieving.

Finally, when I finish, Jill whispers, "Does that mean she's a vampire now? Does that mean—oh my God—are *you* a vampire?"

"No, Jill, she's not a vampire. That's just a fairy tale. She wouldn't be a vampire unless that woman had drained her dry."

"*Dry?*" Kristina asks incredulously.

"Well, enough for Emma to die of blood loss, anyway." I let out a sigh.

"But…are *you* a vampire?" Jill whispers again.

I let out a tenacious sigh, looking into their faces. "Yes, I am." I no longer bother to hide my fangs as I say this, and they both jump back in horror.

"Holy shit!" Kristina's voice has become a shaky whimper and she scoots away from me as all the color drains from her face in the shock of the truth.

"I'm so sorry, Jill. Kristina. I never wanted to get you caught up in this. But I couldn't carry her up the hill myself and—"

"Amy, how do we know for sure that you didn't attack her?" Jill asks savagely.

I sigh. "Emma and I have known each other for two and a half months. Don't you think if I'd wanted her blood I'd have taken it by now?"

Jill shrugs, dropping her eyes.

"Or, if you think I was just playing my cards, waiting for the right moment, don't you think I would have just drained her if I'd gotten my chance tonight? Rather than calling you guys and begging for help? I didn't bite her, and I never, ever will. I love her, Jill. She's the most wonderful person who's ever been in my life. I would give my soul for her in a heartbeat."

Kristina nods. "I overheard you one night, when I brought one of her laundry baskets up. Telling her how much you love her."

"Emma's going to be fine. But I'm gonna watch her closely all night. Okay?"

Finally, Kristina nods, and motions for Jill to follow her out. But I swear I hear at least one of them set up camp right outside Emma's door, as though testing me. Making absolutely positive I'm not going to hurt their sister.

Have to be grateful for it, I guess. It shows how much they love her.

I look miserably at her face, so sad and pained. Her cheeks are streaked with tears. I feel cries of my own well in my chest. I want to hug her, comfort her, tell her that everything is all right. That I'm sorry about everything I said and I love her so much and never want to lose her.

I pull off my boots and fishnets, turn out the light, and get under the covers. I slip my arms around her shoulders and tenderly touch my lips to hers. "I love you so much, Emma, and I'm so sorry," I whisper as tears fill my eyes. "I promised you I wouldn't let this happen to you, and—and—I didn't keep my promise. I'm so sorry, Emma. I'm so, so sorry."

Chapter Twenty-Six

Emma

  The first thing I see when I wake is pitch blackness. Someone is sleeping next to me, her arms folded around my shoulders. I feel stiff and weak. A dull pain throbs at the base of my neck and I put my hand to my throat instinctively. The sudden movement wakes the person holding me. We both sit up in the darkness.

  "Emma! Oh, thank God!" Amy leaps over and hugs me so tightly I think for a moment I'll choke. Then she kisses me and rubs my sides.

  "Wha-what happened?" I ask, feeling my neck. There are two tiny punctures there.

  Amy sits back and sighs. The joy is gone as soon as it came. "I'm really not sure how to put this…"

  She doesn't have to "put it." I press on the hurting area and an unbearable pain shoots through me like a lightning bolt. It starts where I press and branches in rays, first in my neck, then through my shoulders and into my chest. And it brings back memories. Dreadful memories. Memories of the fiery depths of hell.

  "Oh, my God…" I put my hand to my mouth. "A-Amy, I-I was attacked."

  She touches my hand empathetically. "Oh, sweetie."

  "Who…who was that?"

  She sighs. "Madam Noctis."

"That was Madam Noctis?"

"Yeah."

I look away, shocked. The memory is emerging in my mind with more and more detail. "I couldn't stop myself. It was like someone had taken over me."

Amy nods. "That's how the spell works."

I put my hand back to my neck. "She sucked my blood," I whisper, astounded.

Amy massages the top of my hand gently. "It's all right, Emma darling. You're safe now."

A horrifying thought strikes. "My soul—"

"Don't worry, Emma, you haven't lost much. You'll feel stronger as what she did get comes back. You'll be happier."

My eyes widen as I remember more. The girl...the eyes, the soothing, loving voice. "You saved me!' I gasp.

"You remember?" she asks.

"Yes! You attacked her and we all fell to the ground."

"I used the crucifix you gave me."

"What were you saying to her after we fell?"

"I was just...I just told her that if she dared to do that to you again, she'd—she'd—be in for it."

"What do you mean?"

"Well, I told her I was going to kill her. She was skeptical, but...oh, my God."

"What?"

"She knows, Emma. She saw that I can hold a crucifix. She saw what I did for you. I exposed myself tonight! She knows now that I'm incomplete!"

Fear penetrates my heart. "What will she do to you?"

"I don't know. I don't know if she can take my soul now. If she can, she...she might."

"How?"

"By feeding on me again."

"Can she do that?"

"I don't know. She might be able to. Oh, *God!*" I feel her curl up and fall over next to me.

"Oh, Amy!" I pull her into my arms and squeeze my eyes shut, forcing the tears to fall. We cradle and rock each other for the better of ten minutes, trying to calm down but without avail. All kinds of thoughts pour through my mind. I can't lose her. Tears explode from deep inside and burst out in heartfelt sobs. If Amy loses her soul, then she'll—then she'll—I imagine my beautiful, dear Amy doing to some innocent person what Madam Noctis did to me.

"No," I whisper once we've finally managed to regain control of our emotions. "Not possible. No, Amy, she can't!"

"Yes she can!"

"But you…walking around, feeding on others! I saw Madam Noctis' eyes! They were cold, full of deceit and hunger. That's just not you! Not the Amy I know and love!"

She strokes my hair gently, sending a wonderful tingling sensation throughout my scalp. "It wouldn't be me, sweetheart." She's calmed a bit, but I can still feel the utter terror radiating from her body. "It would be my body, taken over by a demon. I wouldn't be in control; I'd be waiting asleep for my soul to be freed from my captor."

"How do you know that's what has to happen for a lost soul to be free?"

"I don't know. It's just common vampire belief that our spirits are gone once we've become true vampires, and that they can escape once their captor is killed and move on when their only link to earth—their body—is killed. It's like our religion or something. I've just been relying on it particularly hard, because for all those years I really had thought I'd been drained of my soul. I really couldn't understand why I was still so full, but the belief that I would eventually get it back and go to someplace better—where God is—is the one thing that kept the pain from crushing me."

I cry harder, squeezing her tightly. Her soft hair is cool against my hot, wet cheeks. "Oh, baby girl…oh, I wish I could make you human again…and we could grow up together and have children and live happily…and you would be safe…"

"It's not possible," Amy says, choking up. "My body is dead. My heart has stopped beating."

"Oh, Amy…please don't let it happen…I need you so much. I want to be with you for the rest of eternity."

She pulls back and kisses me profoundly. Like nothing could ever mean more to her than this kiss, this moment. "No matter what happens, Emma, you will be."

"How?"

"My spirit will always be with you. Even if Madam Noctis captures it. Now that I know you, I could never leave your side."

"That's clichéd."

"Because it's true. I love you so much, my darling girl. I—I can't believe this

happened to you. I can't believe that you have to be in such danger for us to be together. I can't believe I'm part of this horrible existence. Sometimes…sometimes I just wish this disgusting body and these disgusting fangs would just go away!" She's weeping again. I hug her tightly and let her cry for a few minutes before trying to soothe the pain.

"That's not true, Amy. No matter what happens, your body is still yours. No one else's. Not even the demon of a vampire's."

"But I am a vampire. And I hate it!"

"But I love you the way you are. I don't mind your vampirism one bit. Really. Every part of you is you, and every part of you is beautiful."

"These fangs? These fangs and lips—this mouth—are you saying it's *beautiful?* Why do you think my lips are so unusually red? More blood flows to them to make bloodsucking easier. And the teeth—without the teeth, you can't feed!"

"Amy, girl, listen to me! If I didn't think your mouth, your fangs, were beautiful, would I French kiss you so passionately every night?"

Amy shrugs, remaining as silent as a little mouse. "All your lips have done for the last nineteen years are wonderful things, Amy. They've provided air for you, even when you don't need it. They've kept a steady supply of water in your blood. They've spoken soothing words to calm me and harsh ones to save me. And they've kissed me like an angel's. Listen to me. You may be a vampire, but that makes your body no less wonderful than before, because it still has your spirit guiding it. I've touched and tasted your fangs. They're amazing. I don't care what they were meant to do; the point is that they don't do it. They saved me from Jason, remember? They saved my life. And I love them as much as I love the rest of you. Your fangs are beautiful. Your lips are beautiful. You are beautiful."

She lets out a sniffle.

"Don't doubt your worth, Amy. Don't doubt it for one second. It's just a stupid waste of your time."

She inhales abruptly, exhales deeply, and kisses my cheek in gratitude. "Thank you," she whispers. I feel a small giggle rise in my chest.

As she pulls back, she accidentally hits the bite, and I gasp in sudden agony that burns out as quickly as it flared.

"Oh, Emma, I'm sorry! Did I hurt you?"

"Oh, no, you just hit my neck a little too hard."

"I'm sorry," she squeaks. "This is my fault. I promised you I wouldn't let anyone hurt you, and-and-I let it happen to you."

I stroke her hair gently. Soft black hair. Silky, gorgeous. "Oh, come on, Amy. What could you do? You didn't 'let' it happen at all. The second you found out what was happening to me, you rushed to my rescue. I was asking for it, wandering out there alone."

She touches the bite gently, her cool fingers soothing on my inflamed skin. Then she kisses it tenderly and rests her head right above my bosom.

"You were out looking for me, weren't you? If I hadn't started that argument...if I'd just listened rather than criticizing you..."

"Don't even go there! You're right, I need your support, but what good does support do if I'm never going to change? You were sympathetic while I was most vulnerable, and now you're trying to help me fix my problems. I shouldn't have been so defensive. I—I can't believe what I said to you. I'm so sorry, my love, I can't believe I hurt you like that." I rub her back strongly as if to emphasize my apology.

"I'm weak. You're the strong one, not me."

How can she say that? After everything she just did for me? "Amy, no! You just fought that woman off to save me! You are *not* weak, okay? You stood up to Madam Noctis. You revealed the secret that was protecting your soul to save me. That isn't weak, that's *strong*. That's the strength that comes with love."

She lets out a sob.

"You are the strongest person I know, Amy. You are beautiful and loving and brilliant. You saved my life." I cradle her as she continues to cry. It's pitch black in my bedroom, but I don't care. I can see all I need to see with my body. "I will never stop loving you, baby. Never, ever, ever. I promise with all my heart and soul."

I slowly pull her back to the lying position and we tangle our legs and kiss once more. I can just picture her lovely face, sad and stained with the horror and grief of her past. It makes my heart clench. Why did this have to happen to her? She's such a wonderful person. She deserves to live. I would give myself fully to Noctis if it would give Amy her life back. She has such a miserable existence. And it's the last thing in the universe she deserves.

Amy

The moon is unusually bright tonight; it's shining in my eyes and covering everything—the cold ground, the barren trees, even me—with a hard coat of silver. Tears leap from my eyes as I run, the harsh laughter pounding in my ears. The trees reach out for me, the moon smiles menacingly.

"Stop it! Leave me alone!" I cry in despair. The laughing only becomes harder. Louder. Colder.

"Why can't you leave my alone? Do you think I *want* to be this way?"

The cackles are overwhelming; I give up and continue to let out the cries of a little girl as I turn and race through the evil trees. Where am I to go? What am I to do? How can I escape this sphere of torment?

There she is. The little girl near one of the trees. My throat throbs and I race toward her, desperate for anything to distract me, anything to kill the thirst. She's curled into a ball, staring at me over her knees with bright blue eyes. I can't wait to taste her blood, feel it trickle down my throat. My legs can't seem to pump fast enough.

Her body is soft and warm in my arms. I pull her in close without even bothering to put her under my spell and put my lips to her neck, her soft, warm neck, tempting me maddeningly with its life. My fangs linger on her skin for only a moment before they take the plunge, and she's screaming and crying and kicking, but I'm drinking. Oh, life. Sweet blood. Sweet life.

Amy.

I stop drinking and lie still. Nothing seems to have changed; the laughter is still pounding in my ears, and I can feel the moon and trees above me.

Amy.

I look up. The tree is still there, the same as before, but the little girl is gone from my arms, and standing above me is a beautiful redheaded angel in a lovely silver gown. Her eyes are the same as the little girl's, a deep bright blue, but they're smiling at me warmly; her hand is reaching out for me and her light is shining through my eyes and into my heart. She's inviting me in rather than shoving me down with the cold glare the girl gave me. I'm frozen on the icy earth; a wind kicks up and blows my hair over my face. Her beautiful dress and hair blowing to her right, she reaches down with a perfectly shaped hand, and slowly I take it and begin to push myself up.

She's warm. She pulls me the rest of the way to my feet and laces her fingers with mine, and I smile at her and she smiles at me. We begin to walk together through the trees, to a destination I know of not.

"I'm not like them," I whisper to her. "I'm still me."

"That's my girl," she whispers back. She pats my hand and waves her arm through the air as if to create a rainbow over our heads. A world of light opens in front of us, at the end the dark hallway of trees. At last, I have found the escape I thought I'd never see.

"Come on, honey." Angel pulls my hand and we approach the light together. Right before we step in, I look back.

The moon and trees are no longer laughing. They're unemotional and unmoving, just the way they should be. I turn back around, smile at her, and we step into the light. Together.

I wake with a smile on my face. I'm lying in Emma's arms in her bed, just as I was when we fell asleep after we talked about what happened. The sky is getting lighter; I slowly slip out of bed and pull Emma's covers over her shoulders for her.

"Thank you, angel," I whisper in her ear. She smiles and nods, as if to say, "No problem," even though she's asleep and likely in an entirely different world. I kiss her cheek and silently slip out the door.

Something tells me that nightmare will never again haunt my mind. I squeal and jump in ecstasy as I race down Emma's steps and into the woods.

Chapter Twenty-Seven

Emma

I'm still slightly weak in the morning, and I don't want to get out of bed. Jill and Kristina come in at around nine. "Hey sweetie," Kristina says, sitting next to me. "Robert and Jaquelina are gone for the day. They won't be home till suppertime. How are you feeling?"

"Do you think I'm sick?" My voice comes out shaky and hesitant. I don't want to lie to them any more than I have to.

"Oh, Emma." Kristina rubs my knee. "We know."

"What?"

"We know about Amy."

"You mean—"

"We had to come out to help her carry you home," Jill explains. "We know she's a vampire. And we know you were attacked. Amy…Amy was desperate to get you to safety, honey. It's amazing how much you two love each other."

I feel tears sting my eyes. "I…I…"

"Emma." Jill takes me in her arms and rocks me back and forth. "If you need to cry, cry."

And I do. Knowing that they know, and that they don't blame Amy, and that they understand what horrors their little baby sister has faced…all the grief of the night before finally hits me, and I lose control, falling apart right there in Jill's arms.

I stare at my sheets in shame. Jill reads it immediately.

"Don't feel guilty, Emma. You put yourself at risk to help a friend, and that's brave." She smiles. "Braver than most could even dream of." She puts her arms around me and I close my eyes and let out a relaxed sigh.

Amy

I lie in my coffin, nursing my burns and crying rivers. I don't know whether it's the physical trauma of the garlic burning into my skin or the emotional trauma of what happened at Emma's house that's making me sob more heavily.

When the garlic touched my skin, the pain was so blinding that for a moment the rest of the world was swallowed in darkness and all I knew was the searing pain on my hands and face. None of the garlic remained on my skin long enough to cause third-degree burns and bleeding. But there are quite a few second-degrees and the skin is blistering quickly. The wounds sear with every touch, and moving my hands is torturous.

My ears still ring with the horrible things Emma's parents shouted at me.

GET AWAY FROM HER, YOU SAVAGE BEAST!

GET, YOU BLOODTHIRSTY MONSTER! GO! NOW!

THAT'S RIGHT, KEEP RUNNING, YOU SICK LEECH! NEVER SET YOUR FILTHY FEET IN OUR HOUSE AGAIN!

The tears slide over my face and drop onto the purple velvet. As if I want to be a vampire! As if I want to be obligated to suck out someone's blood, their life, their soul—to suck it all away until there's nothing left! As if I want to do that terrible thing to *Emma!* Reduce her to worse even than what I've become! I love Emma. I love her with all my heart and soul. I just saved her from that awful fate. Why is everything so screwed up?

Emma was still in bed when I came over. She was on her laptop, and when I tapped on her door, she pushed her computer to the side and came to let me in.

"How do you feel?" I asked her as she and I sat on the bed.

"Better," she replied. "And Robert and Jaquelina were gone all day, so they have no idea." She points to the bite. "I hid it with makeup in case they come in before I go to sleep."

I smiled, glad to see she was strong and happy. Her smile sparkled in the lamplight, her face glowed golden, and she radiated a warmth that I had never sensed so strong in her before. This sudden rebirth sent waves of relief through me. I was worried I would find her still lying in bed, too sick to get up.

I leaned in and our lips met in a tender, devoted display of adoration; hers were unusually soft. She kissed me gently, her affectionate, warm hand cradling my cheek.

"Thanks for saving me," she whispered.

"I love you. I would never let such a horrible thing happen to you. At least, not without a fight." My face fell. I had already let it happen to her.

She read my thoughts. "Oh, drop it already, Ames," she groaned. "I can't see how you can blame yourself for everything that horrible woman does. Why do you do that?"

I opened my mouth to answer, but at that moment, Jaquelina came into the room without knocking first.

She halted in her tracks when she saw me. A look of shock crossed her face as a ringing silence fell over the bedroom. Then bomb dropped.

"*Robert! Garlic!*" she screamed as she lunged for my wrist and wrenched me off the bed. I stumbled on the carpet and fell backward, bumping me head against Emma's nightstand. "Yow!" I cried.

"*Amy!*" Emma shrieked, rocketing to her feet and reaching for me. Jaquelina held her back as Robert burst into the room, a string of garlic flowers clutched in his left hand. My eyes widened when I saw them and I began to back away.

"Get away from her, you savage beast!" he shouted, yanking a flower off and hurling it toward me while Jaquelina shielded Emma as though I were holding her at gunpoint. Behind him, I saw Emma's face transform in terror. "*Run, Amy!*"

"Get away, Emma, Now!" Robert shouted as I lurched to avoid the flower. Jaquelina continued to stand in front of Emma like a pawn to a queen. Emma didn't move.

"Go, Amy! *Go!*" she shouted at me.

"*Get away, Emma!*" Robert insisted.

"Robert, Jaquelina, stop it!" Emma pleaded, trying to hold Robert back as he ripped another flower from the necklace and lunged for me . "She's my friend, and she'd never hurt me!"

Robert shook her off like she was water and threw garlic at me like the flowers were snowballs. I dodged again, and they missed my face, hitting my arms instead and bouncing onto my exposed hands. It ate through my skin like acid, and I screamed in agony, cringing and holding my arms to my face for protection.

"Amy!" Emma screamed.

"Get, you bloodthirsty monster! Go! Now!" I couldn't see anymore, could only feel screaming penetrating deep into my brain. Practically tripping over myself, I turned and blindly found my way out and onto the balcony, feeling the back of my legs burn as more garlic slapped my skin. I followed the railing down the steps, and once I felt the firm grass and soil beneath my boots, I sped toward the forest.

"That's right, keep running, you vicious leech! Never set your filthy feet on our hill again!" Their voices chased me, even after I disappeared into the woods.

I flew down the hill, weaving in and out of the trees and tripping here and there. The run seemed to take forever. I fell out of the trees at the base of the hill, the back gate yards before me. I hurried through the gate and across the grass and hurtled myself towards my grave. I hugged it and found myself moments later in the satin lining of my casket. There I lay, gasping for air out of habit. Even though the air inside the coffin had long since been nothing but carbon dioxide.

My hands burned like fire. I turned over and buried my face in my pillow, weeping like a baby.

My hands are the only parts of me that the garlic hit. For the first time in my life, I'm thankful for my outfit. But my hands hurt so badly, I can't even wiggle my fingers. They feel raw, dry, and swollen with blisters. I kiss them to try to make the pain go away, but it only makes it worse.

As I touch my mouth to my wounds, I notice a familiar texture on my lips. One of the burns is bleeding after all. The distant pang of the yearning for blood throbs at the back of my throat. I can't believe that even my own blood triggers it. What's the point in resisting? It's my body.

I gently lick up the thick, crimson fluid gathering around the sore, and my thirst turns ravenous. I lick more, and more, and when that isn't enough, I give in and sink my fangs deep into my wrist.

Blood spurts into my mouth like a fountain, oh, heavenly blood, and I shove my free hand between my legs and bring myself to a fast, hard orgasm. Finally the lust subsides and I roll onto my side.

That was monstrous. That is what every one of the others does every night. Feed, and when that isn't enough, rape too.

I'm tired of this. I don't want this anymore. I want this devil in my heart gone forever.

Another tear slides down my cheek. It isn't fair. They hurt me because they thought I was going to hurt them when I wasn't. They thought I was a heartless, soulless monster voraciously hunting the life in their daughter. It isn't true. It isn't right. I love Emma. I want to give her life, not take it from her.

The whole incident makes me sick with anger. They discriminated against me. No, they were merely protecting their family. But it still stings in my chest like discrimination. And now I'm terrified to return to the one place I felt safe, comfortable, human once more.

But I have to. I can't just let this one incident keep us apart. She's all I've ever wanted, the light in my dark sea of despair. I love her. She loves me. We need each other, now more than ever. And I'm terrified of what might happen if I don't go back. Emma might come looking for me, and if I'm not there for her if something happens...

Visions of her beautiful, shattered face at the hands of Madam Noctis, of her blood dripping off Madam Noctis' fangs, and of the deep red liquid flowing off her limp neck overcome my mind, bringing waves of unsolicited nausea through my stomach and head. I moan and turn over, clutching my ribcage. I gag, and, realizing what's about to happen, surface quickly and lean on all fours in the grass.

The muscles seize. I gag, cough, choke. Water streams over my tongue and into the soil.

After a bit, a hand rests on my back as I finish my heaving, then it moves to my arm and yanks me up menacingly. Its owner pulls me tightly into her arms. "I know you can hold a crucifix, Amy," Madam Noctis whispers in my ear. "And I also know all about being incomplete. If you are incomplete, I can fix it. Given only one night, I can make you normal easily. All I need is your neck. Your beautiful, soft neck." She pushes my hair away from my throat. I struggle, but she's too strong, especially with my paralyzed hands. Memories come flooding back to me. Memories of the nights she attacked me. In my own bed. Fear shoots through me as she wraps her arms tightly around me and rubs my sides.

"Some vampires are special, Amy. For them, holding a crucifix is no problem. But they aren't incomplete. Just...blessed, shall we say. Blood is a powerful thing, " she says. "Do not waste it." With a laugh that shoots chills through my core, she releases me. I fall to the ground.

"I long for you, Amy," she says. "If you're incomplete, your blood should be just as delicious as it always was. You know I don't like to feed on members of the clan, but I am perfectly willing to make an exception. Don't make me. After all, considering how rich and delicious you are, given a good reason to do it, I may not be able to resist. You are the most delicious creature I've ever had."

I breathe heavily even though I don't need to.

"You don't want me to finish you? Then prove to me that you are blessed, not incomplete. *That* should be interesting to see." With a soul-chilling cackle, she turns and walks away.

I lie in the grass, staring after her. My breath comes out quickly out of habit. I seriously thought she was going to do it. I lie there for the better part of ten minutes, too terrified to move. When finally I manage to pull myself to my elbows, I cough and my head spins. I stand as best I can and start off toward Emma's house. I don't care what they'll do to me. I need her.

Chapter Twenty-Eight

Emma

Amy races from the room, screeching in agony. I'm still wrestling Robert, who just threw the entire string of garlic at Amy's calves, back. He had lunged at her with the string and I had stopped him just in time, constricting him with much more force than I did the first time.

"Let go of me, Emma!" he snarls. "Let go right now!"

Jaquelina is already out my bedroom door, no doubt to try to catch Amy out the back door downstairs. Robert manages to pull free of my grasp and bursts out the door, and I follow like wind chasing fire.

"Goddamn it, Robert, stop it!" I scream at him. "She wasn't trying to hurt me!"

He whirls on his heel and catches me by the wrist. "Get back in the house, Emma! Get back right now!"

"I'm not going in unless you both come with me and promise not to chase her!"

"I beg to differ." Jaquelina materializes beside me and takes me from Robert, her grip angrier than a rabid bear. "Don't let her get away!"

Robert turns and chases away into the woods. Jaquelina yanks me towards my steps. "My God, do you know how much danger you're in?"

"Yes," I snap. "None at all."

"None at all," Jaquelina scoffs. As soon as we cross the threshold into my bedroom, she jerks me around and shakes me. "Do you know that was a vampire? And don't give me any crap because I know all about them!"

"Yes, I've known for a long time!" I holler right back. "And she's my friend and she'd never do anything to hurt me! Leave us both alone!" She holds me firm by my shoulders and yanks the collar of my turtleneck down.

"Damn beast got away," Robert growls, coming in through my door.

"Oh my God," she whispers. "Robert." She motions him over. "These marks are fresh."

I twist out of her grip. "Yeah, because I was bitten last night," I retort. "But that's *not* Amy's bite! Amy's not like the others because she still has her soul and doesn't need blood to survive! This is Madam Noctis' bite!"

Jaquelina's eyes bore through me. "Madam Noctis?"

"She's the leader of Amy's clan! I was out in the forest, looking for Amy, when she bit me!"

"*What?* You were out in the night *alone?*"

"Yes. Amy and I had an argument and I was trying to find her and bring her back."

"We have strict rules against that, Emma!"

"Yes. Rules that are much less important to me than the safety of my friend. I had to get her out of the night! It's just as dangerous out there for her as it is for me!"

"You're grounded!" Robert hollers. "No TV for a month!"

"Fine! See if I care!"

"Did you know she was a vampire?" Jaquelina insists.

"Maybe."

"And you say she didn't bite you?"

"She *saved* me from Madam Noctis, you morons!" I cry. "Now get out of my room!"

Jaquelina looks to Robert. "That thing could be behind everything she's saying. We can't trust any of it. We can't hold her responsible for anything. Though why that thing would let her remember and be able to tell us that it's a vampire is beyond me."

"I'm not under anyone's influence!" I screech, that hopeless feeling of never being able to prove myself washing over me. "Amy is my best friend!"

"Their motivations are never clear, Jaquelina," Robert continues, completely ignoring me. "Anyway, we don't need to discipline her if we can't trust what she says. We'll just protect her. And everyone else in this family."

"Vampires don't attack unless everyone in the house is asleep," Robert says to me. "Otherwise, they can't cast the spell and we'd hear you screaming."

"Therefore, we'll leave you alone until we can decide what to do to keep you—and the rest of our family—safe." Jaquelina says. "But in case what you say is true and you *did* disobey us and leave this house, we want you in the living room."

"But—"

"*Downstairs!*" Robert bellows.

"Fine!" I grab my computer and storm past them.

Jaquelina comes into the living room about fifteen minutes later. "Come on, Emma," she says. "You're staying in Jill's room."

"Why?" I retort, knowing the answer all too well.

"Because we can't risk that cretin biting you."

"You are so fucked up."

"What did you just say to me?"

"You heard me."

"Excuse me, young lady, but I fear you've forgotten that we still have authority over you. You live in our house under our rules. This is for your own protection."

"How many times do I have to tell you? Amy is my friend. She won't hurt me!"

"Do you really think that—that *thing* is your friend?"

"That *woman* is the best friend I've ever had. She loves me, Jaquelina. She'd never, ever hurt me. She protects me from the other vampires! Not that it's any of your business."

"The protection of your soul is my business," Jaquelina snaps. "Now get in there with Jill before I ground you for a week."

I sigh angrily, grabbing my computer. "You wouldn't hold to it, but I'm not going to fight back tonight." I stomp up the stairs.

"That creature has really messed with your brain, hasn't she?" Jaquelina says to my back.

Only halfway up the stairs, I turn. "She hasn't messed with my brain at all. I think I know who bit my neck, Jaquelina. Why won't you believe me?"

"Because that monster could have told you to say all of this. All we know is that you're the victim."

I thrust my middle finger in the air and sprint to Jill's room, not listening to whatever Jaquelina is screaming at my back.

Strings of garlic and crucifixes are hung around every door and window upstairs. The stench isn't awful, but it's there, and I bite back a retort. When I leave for the bathroom, I see Jaquelina is stringing garlic along the staircase, too. God, this has gone too far.

I worried about Amy from the moment she ran, but as soon as I get settled onto the bed with Jill, it begins to overpower me.

"So leave her a note outside your door," Jill suggests when I express to her my concern. "Tell her to throw a rock at this window when she gets it or something. To let you know she's okay."

"All right. Do you have a scrap piece of paper?"

Jill reaches over to her day calendar, rips a day off, and hands it to me. I scrawl a note to Amy, grab a piece of tape and stick it to the note, and head out the door.

Guess who's sitting on the floor right outside Jill's room?

"Where are you going?" Jaquelina asks as I close Jill's door behind me.

"I need something from my room."

"I'll come with you."

"Hey. Just because I've been hanging out with a vampire doesn't mean I need a bodyguard. I'm just getting a book. It'll only take me a few seconds." I hurry into my room, shut and lock my door, and race to unlock the sliding glass one.

I feel weird being in a room into which I'm not allowed, especially since that room is my own room. My own bed. My own stuff. Jaquelina begins knocking loudly.

"Emma Kathleen Levesque, you open this door!"

I stick the note securely on the outside glass of my sliding door, then I close it along with the curtains. I realize that I left my baby blanket, which always helps me sleep, on my bed—how foolish—and retrieve it as well as a book as cover-up for my lie before reopening my door and pushing past Jaquelina.

"Emma—"

I turn and look her in the eyes. "Can't you just leave me alone, Jaquelina? Please? Haven't you done enough tonight already?"

She frowns at me for a second, then sighs. "Fine. Back to Jill's room. And I don't want to see any more of this behavior, young lady. I want you to get back in there and go to sleep. If you need anything, *I* will get it for you. And don't even think about trying anything, because we're staying up tonight."

"Fine."

Jill's light is already off when I return to her room. I get into bed silently and close my eyes.

"I love you, Emma," she whispers from the other side of the bed.

"I love you, Jill." I kiss her hand and turn over, clutching my blankie. Soon her slow, rhythmic breathing lulls the night, but I can't go to sleep so easily. I'm too worried about my Amy. Is she okay? Did the garlic hurt her badly? Is she trying to come back? Is Madam Noctis hurting her? Raping her? Sucking her blood? I close my eyes, only making the awful images clearer. My eyes shoot open. It occurs to me that when I was in my bedroom, I could have run away after Amy, but then I realize no doubt Jaquelina and Robert would go after me if I did. And what if they took garlic with them and found Amy first? I squeeze my eyelids shut again, and this time, tears leak out.

Oh, Mother, dear Mother, please help me. Please keep Amy safe for me, okay? Guide her safely back to me. I need her. She needs me. Please, Mommy. Can you hear me? I miss you so much. Please help me, Mommy. Please. I want my Amy back.

Eventually I hear Jaquelina close her bedroom door. And I know I'm clear if Amy gets the note.

Amy

I run across the yard and try to silence my footsteps as much as possible as I ascend to Emma's door. The room is dark and a note is taped to the glass.

Amy, my dearest love—

Robert and Jaquelina are on super-alert and have put me in Jill's bedroom. It's too dangerous here for you now. I don't want you here. They'll hurt you, Amy. I think the safest move would be for you to return to your coffin.

I hope you are all right! If Madam Noctis approaches you, PLEASE use your crucifix. Protect yourself. Please. I love you, my darling.

I'm really worried. When you get this, throw a few stones at Jill's window so I know you're okay. It's the window farthest west (to your right, if you face the house) in back of the house.

Hugs and kisses, Emma

I pull the note off the door and kiss it. I can almost feel her touch lingering on it.

I grab a few stones from their gravel driveway and run around back to Jill's room, where I hurl them at the first window on the far right. Pain sears through my blistered hands as the stone flies away.

Click.

A few tense seconds pass, and I throw another.

Click.

I'm about to hurl the third when the window opens and a silhouette pokes out. "Amy?" it whispers.

"Emma?"

"Oh, Amy! Are you all right?"

"Yeah, don't worry. I'm fine."

"Hang on. I'm coming out."

"Emma—"

She's already gone from the window. I walk back over to wait for her at the bottom of her steps.

"All right," she says, coming down with a flashlight. "Let me see your injuries."

I hold out my hands and she takes one in hers and shines the flashlight on it.

"Oh, my God," she breathes, gently touching the wounds with a soothingly cool finger. "Oh, baby. I'm so sorry."

"They'll heal soon. It'll only be a couple days." She kisses the burns softly and lets my hand drop from hers.

"I don't know how long it's gonna be like this. They're all hyper-alert and have garlic up everywhere. It might be a while before it's safe for you again. Will you be okay, out there without me?"

Tears threaten my eyes as the implications sink in. "I'll miss you."

"But will you be all right?"

Fighting to keep the tears in, I smile, nod weakly. "Yeah, don't worry about me. I've been fine the last two decades."

She gazes into me. "You were tortured repeatedly the last two decades."

"Emma, don't worry, I'll be okay."

"I don't want you coming back here, Amy. Not for a week, at least. Check again then, okay?"

I nod again, letting a tear free. It slides over my cheek reluctantly and finally comes to rest along my jaw line.

"You promise?"

"I promise."

"Okay. I love you."

We don't move after that, just stare into each other's eyes, for a good ten seconds, then she pulls me into her and presses her lips to mine.

"I love you too," I reply as she pulls away.

"Now go. I'll see you in a week."

I can't move. I don't want to. I don't want to leave her, even if it only is for seven days.

"Amy, now. The longer you're here, the more likely we'll get caught. They could really hurt you."

"I've told you before. I don't really care."

"But *I* do. Please. Do this. For me."

I stare at her for a few moments, then slowly, hesitantly, back away and turn into the woods with a final, soft, "Bye."

Each step that brings us farther apart punctures another hole in my heart. I can feel it bleeding inside of me as I ponder. How much more time do Emma and I have together? How long until they move, or I die? How on earth can Robert and Jaquelina be so cruel?

I know that they don't realize I love her. But I can't help but hate them for it.

Emma

In drawing on Monday, having finished all my projects, I find myself sweeping the floor for Mrs. Larson. It really needs it around the abandoned cabinets in the back. I sweep the broom furiously around the corners and through the crevices, imagining each dust bunny is Robert and Jaquelina. *Swipe. Swipe. Swipe.*

The floor is clean long before the end of class, but I keep sweeping anyway. There are no dust bunnies left, but I don't care. I imagine them there. Robert and Jaquelina. *Swipe. Swipe. Swipe.*

"You're going to put a hole in the floor if you keep that up."

I jump and let out a tiny shriek. I'm not startled that often, but when I am, my reactions aren't tame.

Mrs. Larson smirks. "Scare you?" She takes the broom from my hands. "Thanks, Emma. I needed that done."

"No problem." I head back to my seat and put my head down. I'm unbelievably tired.

I must fall into a coma, because the next thing I know, Jill is shaking me violently.

"God, Emma," she says when I finally lift my head. "I thought you'd died. Come on. Class is over."

I groan and lethargically gather my sketchbook and pencils.

"See you girls," Mrs. Larson says as we sweep past her on our way out. I flip my hand up in a fast, silent good-bye.

Our second-to-longest visit with Aunt Maggie, succeeded only by the stay leading to Mama's death, was in the fall Jill and I turned fourteen. Mama underwent a terrible operation followed almost instantly by weeks of intense, constant radiation. We were with Aunt Maggie for three months and Mama was still immensely weak by the time she came home. She agreed to stay with Aunt Maggie so that the hospital would release her a few weeks earlier than if she'd had no one to nurse her. The medical bills were soaring beyond our budget and family members were starting to give us cash by the hundreds.

Seeing Mommy so weak and pale, lying alone in Aunt Maggie's king-sized bed that made her look so tiny and insignificant, tore my heart to shreds. I could almost see the blood from its many ruptures pouring through my chest cavity and suffocating me with pain. I came in ten times a day to kiss her and hug her and to generally give her love. At first she slept all the time, then her eyelids began to flutter more and color slowly began returning to her face. Still, two weeks passed before she could walk without support, and another two before she was well enough to gather herself and take her four loving daughters home.

Sleeping once again in my own room was strange—I had become so accustomed to my room at Aunt Maggie's—but soon it grew warm with my presence and began to feel like home again.

The closest label you could slap on my religious beliefs by now was pagan. I no longer believed the God-is-the-Man theory. Still, I thought there was God out there, some universal spirit being there for you, but I believed he must be a woman.

Oh, God, please tell me the worst is over now. You'll make her better now, right? Surely you've punished me enough for whatever it is I've done! Let us get better now, please!

February

Chapter Twenty-Nine

Emma

"Please, Jaquelina, let me stay in my own room tonight," I plead. It's February third, and I haven't seen Amy in a week. The physical and spiritual strain of not getting to be close to her is becoming as intensely painful as if I were burning at the stake.

"No, Emma. I'm not letting you stay in there until I'm sure it's safe for you."

"But I want to sleep in my own bed!" I have tried again and again to convince her that Amy loves me very much and that she has no intention of hurting me, and that Amy is incomplete and therefore doesn't need blood, but she won't listen.

"Forget it."

"How long are you going to keep this up?" I ask her. "You and Robert took shifts staying up until Thursday, and no one came. You've been sleeping outside the door since then, and *still* no one has come. Why can't you just let me back into my room?"

"Because you really seem to have a thing for this Amy," Jaquelina says, "and if I let you back into your room, she'll probably just come in and try to suck your blood. Besides, how can we be sure she hasn't been coming back every night, only to find that you're not there? The second you go back she might attack you."

"Oh good God!" I groan. "Please!"

"I saw those marks on your neck. I know you've been bitten and you are not going back into that bedroom until we know it's safe for you."

"And how long will that be, hm? A month? A year? *Never?*"

"Stop it, Emma."

"I've already told you, that's not Amy's bite!" I shout. "It's Madam Noctis'!"

"Right, right, it's Madam Noctis'." She's given up fighting about Madam Noctis. She doesn't believe me and she knows I know it. "Tell you what. Since no one has attacked and you seem antsy to get back to your room, Robert and I will stay in our own room tonight. If all goes well, then in a few days, you may return to your room, and I'll stay outside your door, but you must leave those garlic and crucifixes around your deck door. And you shall not remove that garlic, for should it not be strung exactly the way we left it, you will be in such big trouble your head will spin."

"Joy."

"Don't be sarcastic with me or I'll reconsider."

Robert and Jaquelina have slowly weaned the garlic away from the bathroom and staircase, but they still insist on leaving it up around all the bedroom windows and doors. I pray that this won't have too much of an effect on Amy as I wait for everyone to go to sleep. This is the night we'd promised she'd check back.

As soon as everyone has retired to their bedrooms and all is quiet, I leap out of Jill's bed and sneak back to my room. I unlock my door and slide it back slowly.

She's sitting on the bench. Our eyes light upon each other and she shoots to her feet.

There are no words. No greetings, no exclamations. Moments after our eyes lock we're in each other's arms, hugging, kissing, loving.

"Oh, Amy," I breathe as we rock back and forth. "Oh, Amy. I've missed you so desperately."

"Oh, dear God, I've missed you, too, Emma. It's been so horrible."

"I'm so sorry," I whisper. She pulls me down to the bench and we sit there, hugging gently, until finally she rests her arms

around my neck and begins to weep bitterly into my left shoulder. I stroke her hair gently, waiting for her to regain control.

"Why are you crying?"

"It's just...it's just...it's too much. My feelings for you, and us not being able to be together peacefully, and me being a vampire, and...and...M-M-Madam Noctis threatened me. She told me that she knew I was incomplete, and she made it clear that she was going to 'fix it'. She told me that if I didn't want that, I needed to prove myself as one of the 'blessed ones'."

"'Blessed ones'?"

"There have been legends, and they're about as credible as any, of a few complete vampires can hold crucifixes." She wipes her eyes. "But no one really believes that. She's just torturing me. She lives off my pain, and she's going to get me. Oh, Emma, what am I going to do?"

I find myself half-paralyzed at what she's told me. "No..." I whisper. "No, oh, please no..." I put my face in her hair and begin to weep myself.

"What are we going to do?" Amy begs.

"I don't know," I sob. "I don't know. I can't lose you, Amy. I need you so desperately."

"I don't want to lose you, either. The first person I'd attack would be the one I recognize the most, and that would be—that would be—oh, dear Emma, I would rather give up my body and soul forever than see myself attack you!"

I take some shaky breaths. "So you haven't seen her since then?"

"No."

"Okay, that's good."

"But I can't dodge her forever!"

"I know. Oh, baby, I know. Listen, Jaquelina says that if I'm not attacked by next week, she'll let me back in here. There's garlic everywhere, but it doesn't hurt you unless it touches you, right?"

She snivels. "Yeah."

"Okay. We'll just have to be really careful. I think you should stay in your coffin as much as possible until then."

"I can't confine myself like that. But I can go downtown where they won't find me as easily."

She nods. "All I can do is continue what I'm doing."

She kisses me then, and it's the most arousing one she's ever given me. I open my mouth to ask about sex, then close it again. No point, we can't have it now. But I really want to, and the way things are going, it's becoming obvious that we can't put it off forever.

We could be torn apart at any second.

Everything in the hospital was so light. The walls were white, the floors were white and light green, every nurse and doctor was dressed in white, light blue, or light green.

"It's like a sea of manufactured light," I grumbled, digging my toe into the floor.

"It's so they can see blood more easily, darling," Aunt Maggie said, kissing my head.

"Yeah, I know." Aunt Maggie smiled at me and squeezed Natasha's hand. Natasha was really beautiful. She had these big, bright green eyes, and her hair was bright red, like mine—only it was curly.

Aunt Maggie looked toward the corridor and sighed. Natasha saw the pain in her eyes and turned her head and quietly kissed her lips. A tear fell from Aunt Maggie's eye as she returned Natasha's love tenderly. I felt surges of desire and pain at the sight. It was so beautiful. I wanted love too.

I never felt this way when I saw a guy and a girl making out at school, though. Just when I saw two women doing it. I was seriously beginning to think I was gay.

Kristina was leaning against the wall, arms and ankles crossed, frowning at everything. Annie was trying to read A Farewell to Arms *for school, and Jill was asleep, resting her head in my numb right arm.*

"Aunt Maggie…"

"Yes, Emma dear?"

"I'm so scared."

"Oh, darling." Aunt Maggie ruffled my hair. "She'll be fine, don't you worry."

"Miss Hayes?"

"Yes?" Aunt Maggie replied, looking up at the tall young nurse looking down at us.

He sighed. "I have some news. You might want to…"

Taking the hint, I shook Jill gently and she stirred.

"Wha—?"

I indicated the nurse and she sat up and smoothed her hair.

"Miss Hayes—" His gaze took us all in, even though he was addressing Aunt Maggie. "I'm afraid your sister—Celina Levesque—well, I'm afraid she's very sick."

"No shit," Kristina muttered. The nurse glanced at her sadly and continued.

"There's not a lot more we can do. It's just spread too far. She's slipping in and out of comas, and I'm afraid she isn't expected to live much longer."

Jill started crying into my shirt. I rubbed her back, feeling no tears myself.

"We're expecting she'll live for about five more weeks, just as a rough estimate, but she could go any moment. She's awake, though barely. If you want to talk to her, it's now or never."

"She's only fi-fifty!" Jill sobbed.

Kristina groaned and uncrossed her arms. "Well, let's go, then."

When we entered her room, It seemed like Mama was hooked up to about two million machines, about one million more than I'd ever seen on her.

"Mama..." I approached her and stroked her head. Her eyelids fluttered and she looked around the room at her family, her sister, her girls. I could swear I saw a smile in her pale, lifeless face. "Mama..."

"Baby..." She could hardly speak, and I took her hand and squeezed it gently.

"Oh, Mother!" Jill was still sobbing uncontrollably, and the others were gazing at Mama in sad silence.

That was one of the most soul-searing ten minutes of my life. When my sisters were done, they slowly filed out. Aunt Maggie and Natasha lingered in the door.

"Coming, Emma?"

"Can you give me a moment?"

Aunt Maggie smiled and nodded. She and Natasha closed the door.

"Emma." Mother's voice was small and crackly, barely audible.

"Oh, Mother!" I squeezed her hand and kissed it.

"Baby...I love you, darling."

"Oh, Mama, please don't do this! Get better and come home, okay?"

I could see the glint of laughter in her eyes. "Oh, sweet."

"I love you, Mama. I want you to stay with us."

"I'll-I'll never leave you, baby. Never."

"Then come home."

"Oh, Emma." She tried to squeeze my hand, but was too weak. Aunt Maggie opened the door a crack.

"Emma darling, we need to leave."

I nodded at Aunt Maggie.

"I'll see you tomorrow, Mommy?"

Mama smiled as best she could. "Yes. Tomorrow."

"Love you, Mama."

"I love you, Em."

I smiled and let her hand go, standing and approaching the door. I took one glance back at my frail, dying mother, blew her a kiss, and stepped through the doorway.

It was the last time I saw her awake.

Chapter Thirty

Emma

I wake at around three AM but can't figure out why. I groan and sit up, rubbing my eyes, and it's then I notice that moonlight is flooding the room. I look up, realizing too late that the curtains are open. My eyes flit past them and settle on a pair of bright blue eyes that gaze in from my balcony.

There she is, standing just beyond the glass like a goddess. That beautiful, silver-haired, blue-eyed woman. A pang of recognition passes through my chest; I know I've seen her before, somewhere...

She calls out to me. Her voice is like water, a distant echo from long past.

"Good evening, little girl," she calls. "Could I come in?"

I sit up and continue to stare at her.

"Come, let me into your house, into your world. Let me in."

I can't stop it. I'm mesmerized, trapped. Slowly, I step out of bed, move hypnotically to the door, unlock the handle, pull open the door, take her hand, and lead her over the threshold.

She takes it from there. She leads me to my bed and lets me lie back down, then she's on top of me, her mouth to my neck. It feels so amazing. She kisses me there a few times, even licks me. It sends tingles down my spine. She's gentle, careful. I feel something coming as she caresses my back with her long fingers. I can sense it's something otherworldly, something that would leave me awestruck. The wonder and anticipation build inside me until I can no longer take it. *Just get on with it,* I think fiercely.

Then, from far off, a wail reaches my ears. A male's voice reaches my ears, and this woman on top of me says something to him. They exchange a few words, and then a girl starts to scream and beg. I can't make sense of any of it.

And then an unbearably sharp, gruesomely agonizing fire pierces my neck and into my body. I scream in anguish, but no one comes to help me. As the pain grows in intensity, my sense of existence begins to disappear…it's just the pain, encircling, taking over until it's a part of me, then all of me. And I can't stand it. I can't.

It stops for a minute, and I open my eyes and gain recollection of my surroundings. Something warm and wet is running over the base of my neck. I see Amy, held tightly in the arms of another and struggling and begging for mercy. Her wailing voice echoes a broken heart, and my soul weeps for her.

"Do something with Amy until I'm finished with this girl," the woman holding me commands. I feel a tingle in my scalp, realize her long fingers are woven through my hair. "And if you go back to Annie, don't finish her. Two deaths in this house will look far too suspicious."

"A-Amy," I struggle. "Amy, help me…"

Amy's eyes, those beautiful, glowing green eyes, flash to a heart-wringing look of mingled horror and insufferable pain. I can tell her heart is dying, her spirit is being ripped in two. *"No, please, stop it! Please! Take me instead! Take me!"*

The woman holding me only laughs. "Why would I do that? Her blood is so thick, so rich…" Her finger slide down my neck, sending a shiver down my spine. "…next to yours, it's the best blood I've *ever* tasted." Nausea inundates my stomach as I stare at Amy, who still tries desperately to force free of her captor's grasp, tears breaking her beautiful white face. Poor, sweet Amy. I can't bear to see her like this.

And the unbearable, death-bringing pain returns. I scream and cry, struggling futilely to get loose. But every stab of pain brings me further into darkness. Amy's shrieks become more and more distant, and, after what seems like an eternity, the pain disappears again.

Amy

The screaming hits me like a truck. It's sudden, shrill, and blood chilling. I bolt upright immediately and cross the room at a half-run. Emma doesn't seem to be stirring, even though the cries are ear piercing. My stomach gives a nauseating lurch. That can only mean one thing.

I fly into the hall and follow the wails to the other end, where I see an open bedroom door. What lies beyond confirms my fears and I squeeze my eyes tightly shut. No.

It's happening to one of her sisters, but I don't know who's doing it. I don't really care either; I lunge my hand into my pocket, and to my dismay, discover that my crucifix is missing. Did it fall out of my pocket in my coffin or in Emma's room? Or somewhere between the two? There's no time to consider, because instinct pushes me into the room, and before I know it, I'm pulling at the vampire's sides and trying hard to yank him off her.

"Leave her alone! Get off, you sorry, filthy, worthless creep! *Get off!*"

Whoever it is won't let go, but instead tries to shake me off. I throw myself on the bed, and try with all my might to push him away. He won't stop. It's as though he doesn't notice me.

"Get off of her! Get off! *Get off!*" I'm screaming now, and as pushing and pulling aren't working, I resort to my last instinct and begin pounding my fists on his back as hard as I possibly can. I reach out my fingers and rip at his throat.

He catches me by surprise. Just as I reach around to tear at his skin once more, his arm flies up and clutches my wrist.

"Hello, Amy."

I feel a rush of anger at his calm, collected tone. He lets go of the girl and slowly sits up as I try feebly to wrench out of his grasp. It's hard to see in the dark, but I just barely catch a fresh stream of blood running from his mouth. The straight, ear-length hair and awful, chilling voice immediately give him away. "Jason!" I shriek, pulling with all my might. "Let go of me, you bastard!"

He merely chuckles. "I knew it. Protecting sweet, innocent humans, are we? I knew it all along. You're incomplete. You are a pure, miserable, incomplete child. Foolish girl."

Emma's sister moans behind me. "Wha—? Who are you?" She tries to lift her head to get a better look at me, but the fresh pain in her neck forces it down.

"Shut up, Annie," Jason snaps.

Annie. The one with bulimia.

"We all tried to tell Madam Noctis," Jason continues. "But she just wouldn't listen. 'Oh, no, I would never leave anyone incomplete. I'm too perfect for that.' Well now I have you, Amy, and it won't be long until you"—he grabs my other arm—"are"— he pulls me off the bed—"complete." He yanks me against him and, though behaving menacingly, makes no attempt to hide the magnitude of his delight at feeling my back pressing into his chest. "Madam Noctis is in the house," he continues. "She's been looking for that girl you saved ever since that night she first got her. She told me the story—of how her blood was as tasty as yours, that her soul was as pure as they come. She told me you'd saved her with that crucifix of yours, and that she's been trying to find her ever since. She told me what she looked like, to keep my eyes out for her. I found Annie yesterday morning, and I went to see who else lived in the house after my feed. Imagine my shock when I saw that this was the house where that girl lived. I told Madam Noctis, and we came here together tonight. I asked if that girl was the one, she said yes, and after Annie unlocked her window for me, I came in here, pushed back the curtains for Madam Noctis so that Emma could see her when she woke her."

By now, fear is shooting through my veins, and I'm cursing at myself for having had on headphones tonight and the majority of the night before. I also curse Robert and Jaquelina for taking down the last of the garlic and crosses two days ago. What if Emma's in there right now, being seduced once again into Madam Noctis' hold? Just imagining my dear sweet girl in the arms of that…that *thing*…I suddenly feel like someone has taken a wrench to my gut.

At this point, Jason drags me into the hallway, back toward Emma's room. "In my opinion," he continues, "all those who are incomplete either need to be finished, or, if that's not possible, killed. Because the incomplete are abominations—dirt in the bloodlines—and we can't have that." We reach her door and he shoves me against the wall and leans into me, pressing into my chest. "Good God, are you lucky, girl." His lips graze my ear and his breath is repulsive on my skin. 'You can be completed. There's hope for you. Madam Noctis told me a few nights ago that someone else must have fed on you because she knows anemic blood and yours sure as hell wasn't anemic. I'd do it myself, but Madam Noctis should enjoy having her favorite victim"—a hint of bitterness befalls his voice—"one more time. Besides, I have that girl. I've barely started on tonight's feed."

His lips touch my ear and the dreadful wetness makes me shiver. "Remember that night all those years ago, Amy? It was fun. We should do it again after she's finished you."

"That wasn't something *we* did, Jason. It was something *you* did to *me*."

"When I make you my bride, we'll see who's wanting what."

"I'm a *lesbian*, Jason. You know that. Even if you did make me forget everything you've ever done to me, I'd *never* do it willingly."

"Well, we'll just have to work on that, won't we?"

He drags me right into Emma's room, and when I get in there, an involuntary wail escapes when the sight, illuminated by Emma's porch light, meets my eyes.

Madam Noctis is lying in Emma's bed, that special world that's our home together. Emma's folded tightly in her arms and is silent, transfixed, her fluff of soft hair falling around Madam Noctis' hand. Madam Noctis brings her mouth from her neck when she feels our presence. She hasn't bitten yet; I would have heard Emma's screams. Madam Noctis grins, her long, horrible fangs glistening in the light.

"Good evening, Madam," Jason greets, bowing slightly.

"Good evening, Jason," she replies. "Having a successful night?"

"Well, I was, until Amy here intervened." He yanks at my right arm.

Her smile only widens. "Ah, yes. How are you, Amy?"

"Go to hell," I snarl.

"Are you going to finish both of them?" Jason asks her.

"Yes, as we both agreed Amy is incomplete, if I have time, I shall finish her off tonight too. Pity," she says, looking to me, "I guess you'll just have to watch helplessly as I feed on your poor little friend here. Oh, but don't worry, sweetie, you'll be next."

"No!" I shriek. "No! Please! Don't!"

"But before I do," she continues, as though unable to hear my desperate wails, "Please tell me, what is so special about this human girl? What is it about her that possessed you to expose yourself to me? To stand up to me like that and save her? What on earth could possibly make you want to do that?"

Silent tears drip from my eyes. A look of wicked realization spreads over Madam Noctis's face. "Oh, no," she mocks. "Don't tell me…you love this girl, don't you Amy? She your girlfriend? Your lover?"

I shut my eyes tightly. No. Please, please, no.

"Well, you poor, poor dear. Let's see how love can withstand this sort of blow." Madam Noctis gives a wicked grin, showing clearly her glistening, sharp fangs, and slowly puts her lips to Emma's neck.

"No, please! Stop! I'll do anything! You can have me right now! Just don't hurt Emma, please!" I kick and flail my arms frantically, but I can't hit Jason hard enough to make him let go.

Madam Noctis nibbles Emma's neck tauntingly, bringing her fangs to and from the skin rapidly, not enough to break the surface, but enough to cause me to die inside. "Don't worry, Amy," Madam Noctis continues. "I'll make sure she's buried in our graveyard with you."

"*No! Please! Stop it!*" I kick and scream and flail my arms and legs fanatically. But it's too late. Emma's deafening, excruciating scream shoots through my ears and shoves a dagger through my heart.

" *Emma! No! Stop! Please! Let her go!*"

My cries weave with Emma's screams as we both struggle, each trying to free ourselves of the vampire holding us. It seems like hours before Madam Noctis finally looks up again.

"Do something with Amy until I'm finished with this girl," she orders. "And if you go back to Annie, don't finish her. Two deaths in this house will look far too suspicious." She strokes Emma's hair and I feel my stomach heave. Blood trails freely down Emma's neck and onto the carpet. Her eyes open, reflecting pain, fear, and rapid loss of life as she utters a few feeble, desperate words.

"A-Amy…Amy, help me…"

Her words are like a million long steel claws, forcing their way deep inside me and tearing in all directions. *"No, please, stop it! Please! Take me instead! Take me!"*

Madam Noctis grins yet again, this time her fangs bright red with—oh God—Emma's innocent blood. "Why would I do that, Amy? Her blood is so thick, so rich…" She runs her index finger down Emma's neck. "…next to yours, it's the best blood I've *ever* tasted." And she begins feeding again, and, despite everything, I'm glad when Emma's wails cease, signaling the end of her consciousness. At least she can't feel the pain.

Jason yanks me out the door and onto the balcony.

"Emma! No! Let me go!" I snap, trying to wrench free of Jason's grasp. "Let me go, you filthy goddamned fucking—"

"You shut up," he snarls. "You can just wait here while I work on that other girl." And, before I can do any more, he jerks me, I feel a sharp pain in the back of my head, the world spins, and everything goes black.

Chapter Thirty-One

Amy

I wake to a dull pain in my side. I moan as a sharp voice above me snaps, "Get up. It's sunrise. Hurry back to your grave."

I lie there, unaware of where I am or what's going on. When I finally open my eyes, the world spins and the back of my head throbs. I'm sitting on a balcony—Emma's balcony—and the sky is turning dark blue. As the night returns to me, horror crushes my sense of reality and I leap to my feet and dash inside.

Emma's lying in her bed like a dead maiden from an old English novel, a dark shadow staining her pillow around her throat.

"No." I'm already sobbing as I rush over and begin to check her vital signs. Pulse—her wrists are as cold as ice— heartbeat, breath…breath? She seems perfectly still. I practically have to touch her lips to make out the very faint breathing. Oh, my God. I have to do something. She's dancing on the border between life and…and…my heart bleeds as I lunge for the phone and dial.

"Nine-one-one emergency."

"Please help me! My girlfriend is dying! She's hardly even breathing and I'm scared she's going to stop and help me ple-e-e-ase!" Tears begin to stream down my face and I don't even try to hold back the sobs.

"Miss, are you at 1823 East Penny Lane?"

They must have a caller ID service or something. I don't know the address, and I don't have time to check. "Um, I think so. W-w-we're on Penny Lane, at the top of a big hill with a gravel driveway just off S-Smith." I'm beginning to choke on my saliva.

"Okay. We'll send help immediately. Just stay calm, miss."

I slam down the phone and fall down next to Emma, sobbing hysterically. Every few seconds, I check her breathing and heartbeat again. I'm almost too terrified to even do that. What if they stop? What if Emma's soul is already lost? In some rare cases, the body of the victim has a delayed "death." Oh, God. Oh, God, oh God, oh God.

Minutes seem like hours. My head begins to spin. Where are they? Emma's growing weaker by the second. What if—

"*Annie! Annie!*" It comes from another room. Oh God. Jason really did go back to her, and he must have lost control.

I cover my ears and shut my eyes tightly. I can't listen. This isn't happening. This isn't happening. I'm dreaming. It's all a dream.

The darkness encircles me, but I can still hear everything. More screaming. Yelling. Pounding. In the house. In my head.

And the next thing I know, someone is dragging me to my feet by my hair. "Get off of her, you monster." I screech in pain as I'm hurled across the room. "Oh, no, Emma, no…"

I hear voices, many voices, coming from downstairs.

"She's just up the staircase, come on…"

I open my eyes. Jaquelina is bending over Emma, checking her just as I did. She sits up and calls out, "Wait! Another girl is unconscious in here! Same condition!"

I crouch behind the bed as paramedics burst through the door.

"Out of the way, ma'am," one says as he and his partner hoist Emma onto a stretcher. Jaquelina chases after them as they run out the door, Emma in between them.

I don't wait. Jumping up, I fly out onto the balcony, down the steps, and around the house into the front yard. The sight is terrible.

The red and blue lights illuminate everything, and I can see both Emma and Annie being carried out the front door. I bite my nails as my tears stain my cheeks and watch as the paramedics put them both in the back of the ambulance. Radios buzz and people shout. Robert follows closely behind and the ambulance doors slam shut.

I wring my hands and fidget nervously, praying to a God I'm beginning to think doesn't exist after all. *Oh please Lord please not Emma please keep her alive don't let die don't let her become a vampire oh pleasepleaseplease…*

All I can do is watch as the vehicle zooms over the hill and out of sight, rushing my whole world to the ER.

I stand there for a long time afterward, watching as the crest of the hill grows lighter with the sun. It's as the brilliant colors fill the sky that I finally realize what I'm doing. I turn and sprint back towards the woods, going as fast as I can to get back to my coffin.

But the sun isn't my main concern. Even as I race to the graveyard, thoughts of both Annie and Emma fly through my mind and I'd continue crying had I still any tears remaining.

I don't sleep at all. I've already decided that if Emma becomes a vampire, I will have to find the courage to kill her as quickly and painlessly as possible, then I'll have to kill Madam Noctis, and then myself. That's the only way I can see our reunion if she's turned.

"Not Emma," I whisper, a few final tears flowing over the bridge of my nose. "Please, Lord, not Emma. She doesn't deserve this. She doesn't deserve to be a vampire. Not my Emma, Lord, please. I'll give anything. Take anything from me. *Anything.* Just not her."

I return to the house as soon as I possibly can. The sun is barely down as I bang heavily on Emma's door, praying that someone will hear. I think it too risky to use the front door.

After a few minutes, a harassed-looking Kristina comes to the door.

"Amy!"

"Kristina! Oh my G—Emma!"

Kristina reaches out and pulls me inside. "She-she's doing all right, I guess. I left the hospital at around noon. Jill and Robert and Jaquelina are still there. Jill—Jill had to give Emma her blood."

"What?"

"Yeah. She and Emma are the only ones in the family with O negative."

I stand back, for I was leaning in to talk to Kristina. "Take me to her."

Some might say it's a bad idea. Some may refuse for their own safety. But not Kristina. All she does is straighten up and whisper, "Come on. I have my own car."

We're silent most of the way. Were the situation not so terrifying, I may be mesmerized. It's been twenty years since I've ridden in a car. But all I can think is Emma. Emma, Emma, Emma. Dear Emma. Dear heart.

My stomach is wringing itself out. What will I find when we get there?

The thick rubber soles of my boots create a dull *thud* that echoes eerily throughout the dark stairway. We race up two flights and stop at the landing of the second floor.

"She's here," Kristina whispers. "Right in here."

If my heart could still beat, it would break a heart monitor. I can imagine it thudding against my chest like a drum in a parade.

Kristina and I walk down the hallway, and she stops at room B136. The door is open slightly; Kristina looks in to be sure the coast is clear, and we enter hesitantly.

My heart would stop.

A pale redheaded girl lies in the bed breathing through a tube, a heart monitor at her side, an IV taped into her arm, tubes strung up her nose. Oh, Lord in heaven. I barely recognize her.

Jill is sitting in a chair by her bedside. She looks up upon our arrival.

"Oh, hi," she says in a weak voice.

"Robert and Jaq with Annie?" Kristina asks.

Jill motions to the door with her left hand. cradling her head in her right. "Yes," she says wearily, "except Robert went out to get some dinner for us and gifts for them, I think." She looks exhausted.

"How's Emma?" I ask, hurrying to Emma's bedside.

"She's stable," Jill replies. "They say she'll be all right."

"What happened?" I stare at Emma's face. It's haunted with death. With loss of life. Loss of spirit.

Jill looks up. "They rushed her to the ER, and…and…it was a nightmare."

I stare intently at Jill.

"She was suffering extreme loss of blood," she continues. "She needed a blood transfusion right away. I had to give it to her, because, due to some extreme operation, their blood bank was low on her type and I'm the only other one in the family with O negative blood."

I stare at Emma's face; the sprinkling of freckles along her nose and cheeks contrast greatly with the ghostly pallor of her skin. Emma. The girl I love. I feel tears fill my eyes. How could I let this happen?

"She almost died," Jill whispers.

Almost died. A tear spills from my left eye.

"I watched it happen," I blurt out. "I was there, but the vampire that attacked Annie held me and I couldn't get free."

"Were you the one who called 911?" Kristina asks. "I called on Robert's orders, and they said they'd already received a call."

I nod. "It was all I could think to do."

Jill look up, smiles, and reaches across the bed to pat my hand. "Oh, thank you, Amy. You saved her. If it weren't for you, she might have died before the ambulance arrived. But she didn't, because you made that call. You saved her."

I shake my head. "I can't believe you guys still trust me after all this. How do you know I'm not the one who attacked her? Both of them?"

"M-mm," Kristina shakes her head. "We know you made that call, Amy. I didn't and Jill didn't and Jaquelina says neither of them did."

"Mother gave all of us her fault of trusting everyone a little too much," Jill adds, with an unhappy giggle.

"Yeah," Kristina begins. "I once told a girl I barely knew a deep dark secret, and the next thing, the whole school knew." She laughs a little. "I sure learned my lesson."

Jill's head falls to the edge of Emma's bed, her shoulders slumping.

My hand moves to Emma's. Her skin is as pale as mine.

And I'm a vampire. Theoretically, I'm dead.

I lift her hand between my palms and hold it against my cheek. Silent tears fall like giant raindrops onto her covers. Dear Emma. Dear, sweet Emma. My lover. My friend.

Kristina must sense the emotion between Emma and me, because she announces, "I'm going to go check on Jaq and Annie," and leaves the room. Jill seems to be dozing off in that hard chair by Emma's bedside.

Poor girl, I think. *She's so weak from giving Emma her blood.*

Emma's eyelids flutter. I draw in a sharp breath. They open slowly, and her eyes are clouded for a moment before they fill with recognition, then sorrow and love. "Amy…" She can barely manage a whisper.

Suddenly, the tears fall one after another onto the blankets. I begin to hiccup. "Oh, Emma."

Her strength allows a very weak smile.

"Emma…Emma…" I'm lost for words. The fact that she was stabilizing told me before that her soul wasn't lost, but I don't truly believe it, I don't truly feel an ecstatic sense of relief, until she opens her eyes and her face fills with adoration as she recognizes me.

"A-Amy?" Her voice comes out a crackly breath, but it's a warm one. Full of affection and gratitude.

"I love you, Emma," I choke. "I love you so much." I cradle her hand in mine, wanting to never let go. It feels as though our connection is keeping her alive, that my hands are holding onto her spirit so that it can't leave.

She manages to reach up and put her right hand to my cheek. "I-I love you, Amy."

Her sweet voice, her sweet touch…she melts my heart. She's so beautiful. So caring. I lean down and gently put my arms around her, and, with a little sigh, she lifts her arms and places them lightly around my neck. For how long can I protect her? What if Madam Noctis finally gets the better of us?

"I'm sorry, Emma." I nearly have to force the words from my throat, which is almost choked shut. "I tried. I tried so hard." I'm on the verge of a breakdown, and I want badly to cry out loud and let my feelings go, but I can't make it happen. I'm screaming on the inside. Emma begged for my help, and I couldn't do anything. Now she's on life support because I couldn't get Satan to let go of me.

"No," she whispers. "I saw how they held you down. Don't be sorry." she strokes my cheek gently. "None of this is your fault. None of it."

I drop my head. She strokes my hair weakly. "Come closer, Amy." I lean in a little. "Closer. Closer." Our lips touch, only for a moment, then she lets out a weak sniffle. "My darling. I love you." Her eyes close and sleep resumes, her chest rising and falling with her strong, steady breathing. She looks so peaceful. So wonderful. I want to send her my life, to make her better. I want to carry her away. Away to a safe, happy place. For eternity.

It's outside the hospital that I finally lose control of my body. I fall to my knees on the sidewalk in a fit of hiccups and cries, not giving a shit who turns to stare.

"Amy! Amy...Amy!" Kristina falls next to me and rests her hands on my back and abdomen, trying to support me. "Come now, it's all right."

Her futile attempt to calm me only makes my wails louder, my spasms more violent.

"Oh, Amy, it's all right, you've got to believe me..." She finally manages to pull me to my feet, but as hard as I try, I cannot control the sadistic wave of emotions pouring from my soul. I tried to hold them in for way too long, and now the consequences are raining down on Kristina and me as she tries her hardest to comfort me on that yellow-lit sidewalk in front of the hospital in the middle of the night.

"I-I-I-I'm s-s-s-sor-ry, I-I-I j-just c-c-can't he-he-help i-it! I-I-I c-ca-can't—"

"Shhh...shhh...I understand. It's all right, Amy, it's okay." She pulls me into her arms in a placating effort. "Just get it out...just get it all, all out."

She waits for my howling to calm before she speaks to soothe the tears. "She'll be all right, Amy. They were able to save her life. She'll be fine; she'll come home and go back to school and laugh and cry and...and l-live." Now Kristina's the one choking up. "They both will. Th-they both w-will."

"I-I love her, Kristina. I-I can't lose her. I love her."

"I know you do. I know."

I catch my breath as much as I can. "Th-th-they think it was me. R-Robert and J-J-Jaquelina. They think I d-did it to her."

"If there's one thing I've learned about Robert and Jaquelina, it's that they are strong in their opinions and will not sway for any reason. They are also pitifully wrong."

"I-I didn't, K-Kristina. I-I would never do anything like that to Emma."

She looks deeply into my eyes. "I know you wouldn't. You love her. I know. She loves you too. You have no idea. She is happier than she's been in two years. Her face glows, she smiles so much, and when she's just around Jill or me, all we hear is 'Amy Amy Amy.' You have made a big difference in her life. She was very depressed after our mother died—we all were. But she and Mother were so close, and her death was just devastating for poor Emma. But you've helped her get through it. You've given her her life back. She's discovered love, and love can overcome anything, no matter how miserable. It's the most powerful thing in the universe, and you've given it to her. You've given meaning back to her life, and that just means the world to me." Kristina hugs me tightly. Her kind words and her heartfelt embrace are enough to start the tears again. I sob and sob until I'm sure I'll drown in my own river of tears, like Alice almost did.

My crying eventually gives way to panting, than a yawn and sigh finish it and leave me sleepy.

"Are you ready to go now?"

I nod and she walks me back to the car, her arm around my shoulder to provide support. We both climb in, thanking God for saving the girl we'll both love eternally.

Chapter Thirty-Two

Emma

Annie and I both have to stay in the hospital for a week. We share a room, and given a lot of time to just lie around, we soon begin discussing what happened that fateful night.

"That was the second night he attacked me," Annie explains.

"Why didn't you tell us?"

"Because he told me not to." She takes a deep breath. "At the end of that feeding, he told me to not utter a word of it and try my hardest to hide the bite, which was easy, because I wear so many turtlenecks."

"So how come you're telling me now?"

"When he came back to my room after wrestling that girl—I think her name was Amy—out, he began feeding on me immediately. He didn't stop, and I went unconscious before he could tell me not to do anything."

"Why didn't you use the garlic and crucifix when he came back?" I know that the first time, she was been under his spell.

"I couldn't move, Emma."

I look down at my blankets. "Madam Noctis attacked me at the same time. That male vampire that was attacking you held Amy and made her watch. That's all I really remember."

"Jill told me Amy called 911 at around six. Why'd she wait that long? I can tell you that Jason came back to my room hours before that."

"He must have done something to her, because I heard Madam Noctis telling him to 'take care of her' until she could finish with me." I sigh. "Listen, Annie, Amy and I have been really close since November, and she's been visiting me. She's…do you think you can handle this?"

"Sure."

"She's my girlfriend."

Annie's eyes widen. "You're—you're gay? Oh, Emma, why didn't you tell me?"

"Because I was keeping Amy a secret, for obvious reasons, and I don't…I don't know, Annie. It's hard, coming out. Robert and Jaquelina discovered her a few weeks ago, and that's when all that craziness began."

"And you're dating a *vampire?*"

"She's not a vampire, Annie. Not in the way you're thinking, anyway. She doesn't drink blood."

"How is that possible?"

"It's a long story. And Robert and Jaquelina don't believe me, which is why they do what they do. I'm scared, Annie. It's going to be really difficult for me to see Amy after this, and it's really dangerous for her at night."

"How?"

"The other vampires in her clan—the ones that do drink blood, like the one that attacked you—they hurt her. Badly. A lot."

And I guess Jill and Kristina know?"

"It's not my place to say."

"Oh." Annie gazes into her lap for a moment.

"For how long have Jill and Kristina known?"

"About Amy? A long time. They walked in on us and that's how they found out…about me. About us. As to her vampirism…about a month, I guess. They helped Amy get me home the first time I was attacked. Back when Robert and Jaquelina freaked out and garlicked up the whole house. That's what that was about. I got attacked in the woods, but they thought Amy did it."

"You've been attacked before?"

"Once, yes."

"Oh, Emma…how come you never told me? About any of this?"

"Listen, Annie, I wouldn't have told Jill or Kristina either. They kind of found out on their own. If you found out, you'd probably have gotten mad at me for breaking the rules."

"Well, yes, but…" Annie falls silent and stares at her covers. "I would have told. And then God knows what may have happened." Annie sighs sadly.

"Listen, I know you follow the rules because you want to be a good person. Don't beat yourself up for it. I haven't been really understanding of your feelings recently."

"I know, but…you're right, adults don't always know best, and what if Robert and Jaquelina had tried to hurt Amy if I'd told? She might not have been there to save us."

"All you can do is your best. I think you should abide by what you believe in. You're eighteen, and I think that once you get into college and have a little more freedom, life will be a bit easier for you. You won't feel so bound by rules and regulations and…maybe you'll relax a bit."

Annie shakes her head. "I know you only told them about my illness because you cared, Emma. It's just that when Mom died, school became so difficult. I had trouble concentrating, but I knew I had to maintain my good grades, and then I began to notice how fat I was getting, and it was just too much."

"You weren't getting fat! People envy your body."

"Yeah right. Anyway, food was a comfort. Then, when I realized I'd eaten too much, I threw up so that I wouldn't be sickeningly bloated." She buries her head in her hands. "And therapy is so difficult. It's taken so long for me just to begin to accept the fact that I have bulimia, not to mention to try to turn things around. I'm sorry I've been so mean to you, Emma."

I grip the white sheets. Poor Annie. Things are so difficult for her. Is there any real hope left for any of us?

We come home Wednesday morning, the 22nd. I hurry up to my room and leap onto my bed. It's so good to be back, out of the sterile hospital room and free of tubes and needles.

I think a lot about Amy. Is she all right? Does she know when to come back? When will she? I'm afraid. I need her to come back as soon as possible, if only for five minutes. I just need to thank her and tell her I love her.

My prayers are answered at eight that night. I'm playing online when I hear a cautious rap-rap on the door. I shoot off my bed and lunge for the handle.

"Amy!" I throw my arms around her the moment I wrench the door open. "Oh, Amy!"

"Emma!" She squeezes me like a teddy bear. "Oh, Emma, I've been so worried!"

"Me too." I feel tears fill the corners of my eyes as I kiss her tenderly. "I missed you so much!"

After a few minutes of hugging, kissing, and crying together, I lead her inside, as it's freezing out. Amy cringes a little at all the garlic that's strung up around; since Annie's in one of the most secure rooms in the house and she was attacked, Robert and Jaquelina decided that there's really no safe place to put us, so they set a bunch of vampire traps instead and vowed to leave them up until the end of eternity.

Once she and I are nestled in each other's arms inside the safety of my closet, I warn her that she can't stay long because as soon as the family goes to bed Robert and Jaquelina are going to start monitoring the rooms.

I stroke her hair soothingly as she recounts, with some difficulty, what happened.

"Oh, baby. I can't believe you were forced to watch her hurt me," I whisper once she's finished.

Amy shakes a little. "I screamed and cried and begged her to let you go, but she didn't. She knew it hurt me. She knew I loved you."

"Amy," I whimper. I can't bear to imagine her in so much pain. "I'm so sorry."

"There-there's something else. Jason told me something about 'the incomplete', like me, being 'dirt in the bloodline' or something and he said that we must either be completed or killed. He said I was lucky because I could be completed. I think—I think it means that there are some that can't be finished, and that the only way to 'purify the bloodline' or whatever is to kill them."

"The anemic ones?"

"Probably, since that's the only other way to be incomplete."

I reach around and pull a small leather-bound book out from under a stack of blankets on my shelf. "It's a book of vampire legends," I explain as Amy looks on with curious eyes. "It was recommended on the site where we found that article. Kristina helped me order it." I flip through the index, find "incomplete" and turn to page 367. "Look at this," I say, waving Amy over. She peers over my shoulder and I follow the words with my index finger. "It says 'if a vampire is incomplete due to anemia, his incompleteness is irreversible. He must either live forever as an incomplete or he must die. It is impossible to complete him by drinking his blood, for lack of blood is what killed him in the first place, rather than the loss of life from the vampire's bite. If another tried to complete him, he would die of blood loss long before his soul was lost, especially since blood loss is much deadlier to a vampire than to a human.'"

Amy sits back gravely. "So that's what Jason meant by 'lucky'. I'm not anemic, so I can be completed." She puts her palms to her eyes. "Oh, Emma, I wish I were! I would die painfully an infinite number of times before letting some terrible creature like one of them steal my soul."

I close my book and put my arm around her shoulders sympathetically. "There, there, baby, it will be all right. It will be all right."

"How do you know?"

"Because we may be two against all of them, but we have one great advantage that they can never have."

"What's that?" she inquires, wiping some new tears from her pretty green eyes.

"It's this," I whisper, and kiss her, touching her cheek lightly with the tips of my fingers and wrapping my arm around her lower back. "Love conquers all. It's the strongest force in the universe—you said so yourself. As long as we hold our strong bond, we can save each other." I weave my fingers with hers. "We can win." And for the first time in over a year, I truly believe what I'm saying. I truly believe in love.

Chapter Thirty-Three

Amy

Emma tells me on the second night of her return that, since Robert and Jaquelina are staying awake at night to make sure no vampires return and she doesn't know when they'll quit, it's probably better if I don't come to her house until things are looser around there, and so, with a heavy heart, I leave her house and go to the playground as it's an unusually warm night and no one's much of a threat to me there. I go back every night anyway, just to check, and if the coast is clear, Emma comes to the door, shakes her head, and sometimes, if it's not too late, opens the door enough to touch me or give me a kiss. And then it's over.

As I'm heading back to my grave at sunrise a week later, I get lost in my head, going over all that's happened for about the hundredth time. Madam Noctis knows. She said she'll do it. Is she really planning to? Is she just standing around, lurking in the shadows, waiting patiently for the perfect chance to jump out and nab me? And will Emma and I, two lonely girls, really be able to win this ongoing battle? For Emma and me to finally douse the flame victoriously, Madam Noctis will have to die. She won't give up on me; it just isn't in her nature. In twenty years, she hasn't stopped raping me. Why should she stop chasing me for completion of what she started so far back? The only way to win would be for us to kill her.

What is there even to win? Even if we did defeat Madam Noctis, I'll never be welcome in Emma's household, and I'll never be able to live a lifetime with her. She'll grow into old age and I'll still be so young. Not that it'll matter, at least, I hope it won't, but it just won't be the same anymore. And then she'll die, and I'll be left alone here…

I walk wearily through the woods, the constant feeling that Madam Noctis is going to grab me burning through any sense of security. Glancing into the shadows and trying to put myself on high alert hardly calms the gnawing fear.

And Emma. Dear, sweet Emma. I can't let her help me kill Madam Noctis; I can't put her in that much danger. But I can't kill Madam Noctis by myself, either, because it will take more than a crucifix to keep her weak long enough to run a stake through her heart. It will take garlic, a substance that I, as a vampire, cannot come into contact with.

I hang my head sadly and turn into the cemetery.

"Amy." Pain rips through my back as I'm forced against the iron fence and she pins me.

"Amy. I've been looking for you, but you really are like a little ghost, slipping in and out without a trace. It's so hard to find you sometimes, but I've finally caught you. I know you're incomplete. You're incomplete in the same way I was. And I know how horrible it is to live that way. But I was saved from it, and you can be, too." She leans into me and her lips graze my throat. "All you have to do," she whispers menacingly, "is hold still."

The tips of her two sharp fangs press threateningly on the exact same spot they pierced twenty years ago, causing a small sting to tingle in my skin. I can just picture the menacing deep blue of her eyes. She's hurt me over and over, attacking me, raping me, feeding on my blood and my pain. The whole time I've just laid there and watched it happen, praying for what I know won't. Now she's trying to do the same thing to the one beautiful thing I have left, the sweet redheaded body of courage and hope on top of that hill. A surge of strength and rage shoots through me like electricity and forces a reaction to burst from my tortured mind and body.

"Get *off* of me, you sick freak!" I bring my knee into her crotch and, with a burst of strength, heave her off.

"*Why* did you do it? *Why* did you hurt her? Why her? What does she have that everyone else you've ever attacked doesn't?" I can't believe what I'm saying. This isn't me. This is someone else, someone I've never known, even in my days of life.

Madam Noctis almost laughs. "Why does she mean so much to you? She's a *human*. You, as a vampire, are supposed to feed on her blood. But instead you go to her house and hug her and kiss her and God knows what else, and then you save her from your own kind. And why do you do this?" She lets the suspense build in silence, her eyes and smile mocking every part of me, before going on: "Because you *love* her. You love a human girl. Only an incomplete vampire can love a human. And you, who must have had some idea of what I would do if I found out, tried your hardest to hide it from me for twenty years. But then, when I attack your girlfriend, you relinquish all concern for yourself and undo the facade you've worked so hard to build up. Just so you can save her."

I give her a continuous death glare as she circles me and places her hands on my shoulders. "Piteous, what love does to the mind."

I slap her away. "Our love is beautiful, the most wonderful thing I've ever known! And you made me watch as you drank from her soul! Why do you get so much pleasure out of other people's pain?"

"Shut up!" She brings her hand through the air, but I swerve to avoid her slap.

"Are you really that pathetic? So sad and soulless that you love feeding on others' misery? Most vampires enjoy humans' misery, but not even a 'normal' vampire loves it the way you do!"

The others are wandering over. I don't care what they see, and I don't care what Madam Noctis does to me for this. She's crossed a line and isn't making it back across unscathed.

"Fool!" she screeches. "You don't even know pain! You think you've got it so bad. 'Oh, poor little me. I've been hurt and violated and now I'm going to sit here and cry and cry and cry and not try to do a thing about it.' You go suffer through what I know and then come talk to me about misery!" She lunges for me, but I dodge and she misses my face and swipes my ear instead. Pain shoots through it and, instinctively, my hand flies up to make sure my earring hasn't been ripped out.

"I used to live in paradise. Nights of luxurious feeding and then hours with my husband. But then he was slaughtered and soon I avenged his murder by starting this clan with the two people who killed him." She throws an accusing finger at Rose and Sam. "*Them.*"

A few people suck in sharp breaths upon hearing this truth, ripped open like a wound. Rose and Sam stand, paralyzed, as her eyes shoot venom at them. She's lost control. Demons, not the vampire, but the other ones, the ones that must have been nesting in her mind for decades, fly to the surface and she knocks them both to the ground in one swipe of her hand. Sam's hand whips to grasp Rose's.

"Don't you think I feel like he's been avenged yet. You don't deserve to live as vampires. You don't deserve to live at all." Rose cowers, shivering violently; Sam stands protectively over her, face to face with Madam Noctis. She raises her hand to slap him again, but I jump forward.

"No! Leave them alone!" I push her so hard that she loses her balance and topples into the grass. I storm over and placed my right toe between her breasts, applying the slightest pressure. She cringes, then glares at me menacingly, grabbing me by the ankle.

"Watch it, little girl. Or it could mean the end for that little redheaded human girl you love so much." She pulls me down, but I immediately sit up and yank out my crucifix, which I found lying in my coffin.

"Don't lie. You'd kill her anyway. Don't you ever go near her again. And do not pity us. Emma is the best thing that has ever happened to me. And you—you're the worst." I shove the crucifix over her heart; she recoils. "Don't you *ever* touch her again"—I place it on her bare skin; she screams in agony, and I let her suffer for a moment before pulling it away—"or I will kill you. Do you understand?"

She stares at me, the strain of physical pain reflected in her eyes.

"Do you?" I hover the crucifix over the burn, ready to strike again.

She nods in desperation. I stand and kick her in the side and back away, my crucifix still out. She lies, gasping even though vampires don't need to breathe, trying to recover.

"I will kill you," I repeat as I back toward my grave. "I swear on my soul."

Elizabeth is the first to start. She slowly brings her hands together to make a single clap, then repeats this action with increasing speed and strength. Slowly, the others follow suit, until Jason and Mary are the only two not clapping and cheering for me. I do nothing but continue to edge toward my grave, my crucifix still held in front of me threateningly.

Once there, I place my hand on my headstone and disappear from their view. The clapping and cheering continue, muffled greatly by the six feet of soil above me.

No longer am I afraid of her.

Elizabeth is different. Elizabeth is a ghost. Elizabeth leaves too early and returns too late. Which is why I'm surprised when she steps out from behind a tree and yanks me aside.

"Ouch!" I whisper severely as my arm snaps back into its socket.

"Sorry."

"What is it, Elizabeth?"

"Well, see, it's just that…it's sorta that…I'm really proud of you, Amy. You stood up to her like no one else could. You stood up for yourself and the woman you love when no one else could find the strength to do so."

"What the—wait…how on earth did you know?"

"Well, just the way you spoke about her, the anger that filled your eyes as you said it…I assumed you loved her. Plus, and I know that this isn't a very reliable source, but…Madam Noctis said to us, 'That bitch is in love with a *human* girl.'"

I laugh a little. "For once, she spoke the truth. But…how come everyone was clapping for me back there? Why do they care?"

"Oh, Amy. Most of the others don't hate Madam Noctis, but no one really likes her either. They just get so tired of her pushiness. They want a little power, too, and they just all get so sick of her running everything like a queen. The main reason they have sex with her is because she's so seductive, so beautiful, and they can't resist. No one likes her, even in a selfish manner."

My face falls. "What was that thing with Rose and Sam all about? He was shielding her, like he was ready to give his life for her."

"It's instinct, honey. Left over from their human relationship." She smiles sadly. "I understand they were more important to each other than anyone or anything." She sits on a log and pats the spot next to her. "We need to talk. There are some things you should know."

I sit slowly.

"Her full name is Victoria Regina Noctis. It's funny…when you put her middle and last name together, they mean *queen of the night*. And Victoria means victory. It's Latin."

"Yeah, I suppose that is rather funny."

Elizabeth's mouth twitches in a half-hearted smirk. "Madam Noctis grew up in the late 1800's in a rich family of about eight. She had her two parents, two brothers, and three sisters, I think. Apparently she was a very nice person; you know what it says about her on her grave, right?"

"Yeah, something about a charitable selfless youth." I snort.

"Right. Anyway, when she was approaching her twenty-fifth birthday, something

happened. In the middle of the night, when everyone was asleep, a man by the name of Count Mortimer came to the house. He found her and took her as his own.

"Apparently Mortimer had a small clan himself, because someone else came for her that night. He fed grossly on her for a long time, but he couldn't get her soul because Mortimer had already laid claim on her. When he left, Mortimer came back, so two different vampires attacked her in one night. By morning she was deathly ill and unable to remember anything. Her family called the doctor, who said she'd somehow lost a lot of blood and needed a transfusion from her mother. Of course, that didn't replace her lost soul."

"And then?"

"Count Mortimer, ignorant of the traitor's appearance, came back. Only this time, he had his eyes set on more than just blood. Regina's father was out with her little siblings, so she, her mother, and her twenty-some sister were alone in the house. She was lying on the sofa in the drawing room when he came in. Far too sick to even walk, all she could really do as he raped and killed her mother and sister was close her eyes and try to pretend it wasn't happening. Then he raped her; she passed out and died later that night, and was left incomplete."

"So she *was* incomplete."

"For a while, yes. During that time, she was terrified, unhappy, and desperately alone. About a year after her death, she learned where her mother and sister were buried; they were in different cemeteries because she wished to be laid to rest with her fiancé, who had died of cholera two years before. She looked for them, praying she'd find them as she remembered them. But when she did, they were feeding on young, innocent victims, namely children and teenagers. She was unable to bear seeing them like that, and of course she didn't want any innocent people—especially children—to be condemned to such an awful fate, so she sharpened a wooden stake, returned the next night, and killed both of them."

Elizabeth pauses; I become aware that I'm gaping slightly. "That-that-that's *horrible!*" I gasp, shocked.

"I know. It killed her to do it; she had been very close to both of them. She told me, and I quote, that she 'felt her spirit die that night,' and she lost herself. After he learned what had happened, Mortimer came back to her. He told her that pain was natural, that he understood what it was like to lose people you love, to have to take their lives to save them from a fate worse than death. He hypnotized her, took advantage of her broken state. He told her that he could make it all go away. That they could marry and live happily together, and that she would never have to feel like this again. All she had to do was let him drink from her neck just one last time."

"And she did?"

"She did. The temptation was too great. She said yes and he bit her fiercely—I think he punctured her jugular vein with both fangs—and drank rabidly. She said it hurt like hell, but he didn't stop, and by morning she was complete, they had shared wedding vows, and all traces of Victoria were lost.

"Then, around 1915, Victoria's cousin Rose figured out what was going on and she and her husband Sam set out to kill them and save Victoria's soul. They managed to accomplish their first task, but Madam Noctis escaped and, enraged and drowning in the death of her husband, she avenged him by killing them both and forcing them to start this clan with her."

"Oh, God. That's so awful."

"I know. It's been over a hundred years, and her broken soul, the beautiful light that was Victoria, still waits for the day her body is killed and she can finally be free."

"That must be what she was talking about so long ago…"

"What?"

"Once, a while back, I lost control and cried to her that she was hurting me. She screamed at me that she had once felt pain too, when she first became a vampire. Do you think that was the year she was incomplete?"

"Probably."

"Wow. So was her marriage based solely on sex?"

"Yes."

"And she told you all this?"

"Yeah. She sees me as one of the 'trustworthy' members of the clan, so she told me her back story."

"Oh."

Elizabeth's teeth begin to chatter.

"Elizabeth? What's wrong?"

"I-I'm just a little deprived of blood, is all. Th-that brings me to the next thing. You know you're incomplete, Amy."

"Yeah. I'm incomplete. My girlfriend and I figured it out a while back."

Elizabeth smiles. "Very good. You're incomplete in the same way Regina was. You're incomplete by another vampire. I'm incomplete because I have anemia."

Shock and understanding shoot through me. Elizabeth is incomplete. Why didn't I see it before? I knew since I first met her that she was chronically ill with a blood disease. When she died, the doctors said it was anemia, although they didn't understand why she suddenly lost so much blood. By that time, I was ten, and old enough to understand what she was sick with. Why didn't I realize it when Emma and I found out about me? "So that's why you're always gone!" I exclaim.

"I need a steady amount of blood for the better part of the night, Amy. Otherwise I get really sick and eventually die."

"Doesn't it hurt you to attack others?"

"You have no idea." She slips a stray curl behind her ear. "I try to make it pleasant for them the way I've made it pleasant for you. But I don't suppose you know who else attacked you?" she continues, surprising me with the sudden change in subject matter.

I shake my head. "I have no idea."

She's silent for a few moments. "Amy, i-it was me."

"*What?*"

She nods, a little shamefully. "I sucked your blood. I made you incomplete."

"You-you-you mean, I—"

"Do you remember how close we became when I babysat you?"

"Ye-yes."

"I just…I love you, Amy. You were always such a sweet, loving little girl. And…and…the night before you died, I ran into Madam Noctis and she told me she was about to kill a girl at your address. She said her name was Amy and she had long black hair and green eyes. I knew it was you. I didn't want you to die, to lose your soul, and I knew you weren't going to survive. You know her…once she starts, nothing, *nothing,* ever keeps her from finishing her victims, especially on the last night. She takes after her husband in that way, and I think all these rules she's made were originally his. I knew it was too late, and the only way I thought I could save you was by feeding on you." Her voice starts to waver. "I wouldn't get your soul, but you would lose more blood. So I went straight to your house and fed on you for about thirty minutes—I tried to make it as painless for you as possible—then I slipped out. I'm so sorry, Amy."

Tears fill my eyes. "Elizabeth…"

"Back then, I wasn't as skilled at biting people painlessly as I am now…I don't think it was too bad for you…for one, you weren't losing your soul, so that cut away half the agony, and I tried not to penetrate your neck too deeply. Because I wanted it to be peaceful for you, I didn't suck very hard, though the urge to do so was horribly strong."

"I don't remember it," I whisper, a tear falling from my eye. She tried to make it peaceful for me. She knew the pain Madam Noctis was putting me through, because she'd suffered it herself, six years before.

She lets out a sob. "You…you didn't scream or cry. In fact, you remained perfectly silent, even as I sucked the blood from your veins. I hoped that meant you weren't in much pain, or something…you were clutching me to you like I was some kind of lifeline."

I close my eyes, trying to remember.

She bursts into tears. "I-I'm sorry, Amy! I'm so, so sorry." She wipes tears from her face. "Oh, had there been any other way—any other way to save your life—believe me, I would have—I would have jumped through flaming hoops for it—"

I stare at the ground, then look into her eyes. "Thank you," I whisper.

"What?"

I slip my arms around her. "Thank you, Lizzie. Thank you so much." I can't remember the last time I called her Lizzie.

She's shaking like a leaf. I'm not sure if it's from her crying or need for blood, or a mixture of both. "You-you—don't you hate being like this?" she asks me.

"I do, but I'd rather be like this than a complete vampire."

"Well, at least you…at least you…don't need to drink blood constantly to survive. It kills me to hurt innocent people. I never attack anyone more than once."

"Oh, Lizzie…" I look into the sky and feel a stab in my heart. A full moon. "That's the most wonderful thing anyone's ever done for me. You saved my soul."

She rubs my hair gently. "I love you, Amy. I could never let such a terrible thing happen to you."

I smile and close my eyes, and for a moment, I'm four again, lying in her arms while she runs her fingers through my short black curls and sings me to sleep gently. Our hearts beat together, and our heat makes us one.

But a quick recognition destroys that momentary bliss. Elizabeth is anemic—she's incomplete in the other way. The way no amount of feeding can fix. She can never be a complete vampire the way I can—the only way for her to escape is death. And Jason made it clear he hates creatures like us, and I have a nauseating feeling in my gut that if he finds out Elizabeth is incomplete, he'll try to kill her for sure. Oh, no. I have to make sure that doesn't happen.

"Elizabeth."

"Yes?"

"It's Jason. You can't let him know you're incomplete. You—"

She nods. "I already know."

"You do?"

"Yes. Like I said, Madam Noctis tells me everything. Jason has sworn to either complete or kill anyone like us. I've been working so hard to hide myself, and I think I'm doing a pretty good job, but there are no guarantees in life. We have to take what is thrown our way."

I look to the ground, sobs shaking my shoulders. She reaches under my chin and pulls my face upward. "I'm not afraid of death, Amy. I hate living like this, and after what Madam Noctis did to me, I am not afraid of the pain of being killed, either." She hugs me. "The only thing I worry about is you. Watch out, all right? I love you and I don't want them to hurt you any more than they already have. Although"—she laughs—"you seem to be doing a pretty damn good job when it comes to looking out for yourself. But constant vigilance with Madam Noctis. I can guarantee she will not be happy after tonight."

I nod, tears blurring my vision. Elizabeth smiles warmly. "Now go be with the girl you love."

"Emma."

"Yes. You need each other."

I nod again and walk away hesitantly, looking back quite a bit. Elizabeth stands there, watching me go. I know she can't possibly know very much about my relationship with Emma. How does she know she needs me as much as I need her? I almost laugh. Elizabeth can always see through me. It's as though she's psychic. I realize slowly as I head up toward Emma's that perhaps she's been guarding me the entire time, that she's been there from the day she learned of my fate. I hug myself. It feels so wonderful to have an angel protecting you like that.

Chapter Thirty-Four

Amy

I arrive at Emma's door and peek in. No one is in there with her, so I knock timidly and she looks up with a look of excitement and relief that breaks my heart. Why does it have to be this way?

"Oh, Amy," she whispers, heaving open the huge glass door and throwing her arms around me. "I can't take this anymore."

"I could never take it, Em."

"They're starting to get a little looser, but not much. You have to go. I'm so sorry." As she pulls away I catch a tiny tear lingering on her cheek and reach out to catch it on my finger.

"Don't worry," I find myself saying. "Everything will be all right."

My mind is whispering too.

Yeah, right.

In the end, it's a painful nine nights before Robert and Jaquelina finally stop taking "anti-vampire" shifts and return to their room for a regular sleep schedule. But the night they finally do I see the happiness in Emma's face and, after two more unbearable "safety nights," we're finally together again.

The garlic is still prominent in the bedroom. "You get used to it," she explains when I wrinkle my nose and ask her how she can stand it.

"It might not be that way for me," I reply. She agrees and leaves the door open with the curtains drawn and the screen locked so that the room can air out, at least to a small degree. She also locks her bedroom door.

"So they can't come barging in," she explains.

"But won't they wonder why your door is locked?"

"Well, I can say I'm changing."

"And if they try again later?"

"I can say I'm...masturbating. I'll take my clothes off to make it more convincing."

I hadn't laughed in nearly two weeks, and it was almost foreign as it escaped from deep inside my chest.

"Or I could escalate it a bit. 'Go away Jaquelina. I'm having sex with a vampire.'"

My laugh grows even harder.

"But they could still come barging in at any time of the night. They've done that a few times. To make sure you aren't here."

"Should I not stay the night?"

Emma falls silent.

"I guess the danger is kind of equal all around. I'll stay in here."

"Come on." She takes my hand and sits with me on her bed. I tell her what happened that morning I stood up to Madam Noctis.

"Elizabeth sounds amazing," Emma says when I finish telling Elizabeth's story.

"I do love her."

Silence settles and for about ten seconds the room is dead still. I detect modern jazz wafting from the living room like the stench of a dead animal. I always hated jazz.

"You know, Emma, your mother isn't really gone. She's still with you spiritually."

"Yeah. Why don't you spit out every other cliché in the book?"

"Oh, Emma. Listen to me. Her body is dead, but her soul will live forever, and I don't think she's left any of you, not even for a second. Don't you ever look into a corner and feel her presence there? You know, you see the objects in the corner but you know you aren't looking through empty space to them because something is there—some palpable force that you just know is there because you can feel its energy in the air?"

"No."

"Well, after my grandma died, I always could. I could feel her spirit, strong and steady, right next to me, in my room, on the porch swing, even at school. I think the spirit is always there with you, but you don't really notice it until you think about it. You should try it sometime. You might be surprised."

She sighs. "I don't know."

"Come on, Emma, just give it a chance. If you feel it, you might feel less alone, perhaps even like your mother is with you again." I fall into her and she ruffles my hair.

"We'll see," she whispers.

"What do you think will happen to us?" I ask after another long silence.

"What do you mean?"

"I mean, look at this. You're a healthy high school girl with a great future ahead of you. And I—I'm a vampire who risks her very soul every time she leaves her grave. We don't know how long I have, because Madam Noctis won't stop until I'm finished. And even if we do kill her you'll grow up and I'll still be only sixteen."

"I don't care if I'm eighty and you're sixteen."

"I don't either. But then you'll die, and—and—I'll be alone again. For eternity."

Emma strokes my face sympathetically. "If that is what the future looks like for you, then you should turn me."

I nearly jump out of my skin. "What!"

"If we defeat Madam Noctis, and it looks like you'll live forever, eventually without me, I want you to kill me. I want you to suck my blood until I'm a vampire like you. Elizabeth could feed on me too so I'm incomplete like you are. I want to be with you forever, no matter what it takes."

"Oh, Emma, are you nuts? I could never do that to you! Don't you realize what I'd be doing to you? I'd be taking your soul, and I could never do something that atrocious, to anyone. I would never condemn my sweet lover to such a terrible fate." I kiss her cheek. "I guess if you die before me, I'll have to work up the courage to try to kill myself."

"Oh, dear, Amy, don't say that!"

"Now that I have you, life without you just doesn't seem worth it anymore. It didn't before, but that's just the thing—you brought meaning back to my life. I just want to be with you forever and ever."

"Then bite me. Do it now, even! I'm not scared."

"No!" I sigh. "Thinking about just how much danger we're in makes everything seem surreal. Like it's all so scary I have to remind myself that the world is still turning."

"I know. I've felt like that a lot over the past few years. Believe me, I know."

"I love you."

"I love you, sweetheart."

Emma

It's later in the afternoon the next day that my world turns completely upside-down. I'm on my way to the bathroom when I notice that Robert and Jaquelina's door is shut. I put my ear to the door to listen.

"I knew we should have taken stronger precautions with that room. I knew we should have torn down the deck or taken it for ourselves or something."

"I know, Jaquelina, but vampires can get in through second-story windows easily. I'm not sure that would have made much of a difference."

"Listen, Robert, we've discussed this at least a hundred times in the past few days. I'm sure it was her. I bet that little bitch was just toying with Emma's affections. Waiting a while before she hurt her. We have a very educated guess. We know she's been inside this house with Emma. She was targeting her. And unless another vampire has been let into this house…"

"What about Annie, Jaquelina? Who attacked her?"

"It is possible that she attacked them both. Regardless, we need to get rid of her and as many of the others around here as we can. They are all evil, all bloodthirsty, and either we kill them or eventually they will kill us, along with dozens of other innocent victims."

Robert sighs. "The minute I found out about Celina I knew it would come to this," he says. "I knew it."

"So why didn't we do it sooner? Why didn't we try to find the source of those horrid creatures before?"

"I don't know, Jackie. We were stupid. We were foolish. But there's no time for

that now. We need to act. We need to go out at night and wait in the graveyards for them to appear. When they do, we will mark the graves and then when we go back with our armaments we'll surprise them as they rise. What are the most likely cemeteries?"

Oh God. They're planning to kill her.

"Well, the one at the bottom of this hill, of course, and then there's the one about a mile away on Tenth Street—"

"And the one on Crystal Springs Avenue—"

"And the one near the swimming pool. Those are the most likely ones."

"They probably all came from the one right down there. But even so, we can't leave the girls alone in this house while we do that. Maybe we should just wait for one to come up and attack her then."

"Jaquelina, vampires put the house under their spell before entering. They'd know and run away before we would even notice their presence."

"Can't we wait outside?"

"Vampires have acute night vision, Jackie. They'd see us and run off."

"Maybe we could hide?"

"They'd sense us."

She sighs. "You're right."

"As far as we know, that Amy is the only one who has attacked this house. Perhaps we should try to get her out of the way first?"

"Great idea, Robert. There are only two hundred Amys in those cemeteries. We don't even know if Amy is her real name—"

"It wasn't Amy!" I shriek, storming through the door.

"Emma—" Jaquelina sounds startled. "Have you been listening to us?"

"It wasn't her!" I insist. "Amy would never do that to me!"

"Do you know who it was, then?"

"Madam Noctis!"

"Her again?" Robert groans.

"How do you know it wasn't that girl?" Jaquelina demands. "Do you remember?"

"Yes! There were two other vampires in the house. One—the one that attacked Annie—made Amy watch while Madam Noctis sucked my blood."

Jaquelina shakes her head.

"Didn't Kristina tell you that when she called 911 they told her she'd already gotten a call?"

"Yeah, she said that right after she called. We assumed it was Jill."

"Jill? *Jill?* It was *Amy*, dumbass! Just ask Jill! Just *ask* her!"

"She doesn't speak to us, Emma. You know that."

"Even if she told you, would you believe her?"

"Emma, I don't care what kind of delusions you or any of your sisters have about that vampire," Robert scolds. "Vampires are killers. That's all they are. They will do *anything* to earn your trust—trick you, lie to you, pretend to be your friend, even brainwash your family. But all they're interested in is your blood. And they'll continue to trick you after they've fed on you, so that they can keep you. They make you a slave, Emma. They make you theirs, and they hurt and rape you, and eventually they kill you!"

"Not Amy! Amy's not like that!"

"No vampire in history has ever been like what you say Amy is," Robert counters. "But plenty of victims have described their attackers just like that. You're under her spell, Emma!"

"How do you know?"

"We've done extensive research, dear," Jaquelina explains timidly.

"Not as much as I have, if you think all vampires are soulless monsters!"

"We don't care how *confounded* you are, Emma!" Robert shouts. "It's our job to protect you, and we're gonna do everything in our power to do just that!"

"No! You don't understand! I'm in *love* with her!"

They both gawk at me.

"You...you're in love with her? You love that vampire girl?" Robert sounds stunned.

"With all my heart and soul."

They gape at me, astounded.

"What? Do you have a problem with that? The fact that your daughter's a lesbian?"

"No, no, that's not it at all, Emma—" Jaquelina begins.

"Then what? *What?*"

"She fell in love with this vampire," Jaquelina mutters to Robert. He nods.

"Oh *God!*" I cry. "Please!" I beg, looking back to them. "Please, don't hurt her! She's my whole world now, and I want to be with her! I want to see her and love her and…and she's the one who has made me so much happier around here! Why on earth would you ever want to take that way from me? Your *youngest daughter?*"

"Emma, listen," Jaquelina begins.

"No! I won't until you both promise me you'll believe me and you'll leave her alone!"

"Emma—"

"Promise me!"

Jaquelina sighs.

"Please." Tears are turning Robert and Jaquelina into a vast blur of colors. "I'm begging you."

"All right, Emma," Robert says. "We promise."

I gaze back at them, the tears spilling over the rims of my eyes. "What will it take to make you guys believe me?"

I race back to my room, terrified rivers falling down my cheeks. They're going to try to kill every vampire they can, right? That could possibly include Madam Noctis and Jason. That thought is good.

But not Amy. They can't kill Amy. She's my heart and soul. She's everything I live for. The love I have for her is so real, so true. All those nights lying in her arms, whispering to her and comforting her and her comforting me have done nothing but return me to the girl I used to be. I can't lose her.

I take baby steps over to my full-length mirror, where I pull back the collar of my shirt.

There they are. I gently place my fingers over the two tiny scars on the base of my neck, wider now because they were reopened.

Amy.

She has them too.

It isn't fair. Amy doesn't deserve any of this. She's so caring and kind; she has such a wonderful, loving soul. She deserves to *live*. Live a long, happy life. Like I probably will if Madam Noctis doesn't attack me again.

I feel a lump in my throat. *Why?* I want to scream. *Why Amy? Why?*

I fall on the bed, weeping.

Jill hears me and comes in. "Emma? What's wrong?"

She sits on the side of the bed and begins to rub my back. "What's wrong, honey?"

"They—they think it was Amy," I sob. "They think Amy almost killed me. And now—and now they want to kill her. I tried to tell them she's different, but they won't believe me."

Jill says nothing. She just keeps rubbing my back.

"How can they do this? What if they kill Amy but not Madam Noctis? They'll only kill the one thing that was truly protecting me, that saved me both times I was attacked! They think they saved me—what a joke! I bet that if Amy hadn't been there to call when she did, I would have died in the ambulance! And no matter how many times I try to tell them, they *still* don't believe me! I hate those self-righteous bastards!"

"Oh, Emma…"

"You have to tell them, Jill! You have to tell them you didn't make that call!"

"Emma…I already did."

I turn over and gaze into her eyes, astonished. "What?"

"I heard your argument—I think the whole neighborhood did—and after you ran out I went in there and told them that I didn't make the call."

"And?"

"They didn't believe me."

"Oh…" I moan as nausea clenches my stomach and bury my head in my pillow. I listen to the thump-thump-thump of my sisters walking around in the hall. How are they doing? Surely they don't feel half of what I do, even if they know about my situation.

I lose track of my consciousness after a little while. Sometime in my delirium, Jill leaves my room. My worries carry me into darkness, and I'm awakened by a loud knock on my sliding door. Amy is there.

Amy

As I make my way back to my grave at early sunrise, a scary thought nagging in the back of my mind becomes uncontrollable worry and takes over. Now that Emma is back from the hospital, what if Madam Noctis comes back, and I am unable to defend her? What if she gets to Emma's house before I do? What if?

I remind myself of why I haven't been able to see her all week. Of why the putrid garlic smell bothers me all night. I remind myself that Emma now wears that little golden cross around her neck constantly.

It doesn't help me. I toss and turn in my coffin, trying hard to sleep. I can't remember the last time I slept well, but it's especially hard now. I'm not just worried. I'm terrified.

I sprint straight to Emma's as soon as darkness falls. Even if she does have garlic and crucifixes to protect her, I feel like I need to be there for her too, or something awful will happen.

But, despite my panic, she's the first to speak when she lets me in.

"Amy! Amy, we have to do something! They think it was you! Robert and Jaquelina think you were the one who attacked me. I tried to tell them, but they don't believe me. They-they—" She stops abruptly.

"What, Emma?"

Her voice drops to a whisper. "They-they…they want to…kill you."

My eyes widen. "*What?*"

"They want to kill every vampire in your graveyard."

"I'm partial to that," I remark flatly without thinking.

Emma grabs my hand, tears dancing on her eyelashes. "I can't lose you!" she cries. "I can't!"

My face softens. I fold my hand around hers and gently draw her in to me. "I love you," I whisper in her ear as I shut the door with my free hand and pull her onto the bench with me. She begins to bawl.

"I've never loved anyone as much as I love you!" she weeps. "I never knew love before you came into my life. I've always been so introverted that I never built any real relationships! I couldn't even imagine real love, the love I feel for you now. I can't lose it!"

I smile sadly and lift her face to mine. "Oh, Emma. You have so much to learn." I let her chin go and hug her again, resting my head on her shoulder. "No matter what happens, you'll never lose me or my love. I swear that no matter what happens to me, I'll always be with you and I'll always love you. Always."

"But what if—she—completes you?" Emma says "she" as though she's an over-devout Christian uttering the word *fuck*.

Her arms clutch my midsection desperately and her back rises and falls rapidly with her gasps. I weave my fingers through her hair and can't help but notice how perfectly my hand fits over the crown of her head. "I will still love you, Emma. My body will give in to evil, but my spirit never will. Your soul is who you truly are, and no vampire can ever change that."

"Oh, Amy!" She can't stop crying. "Sometimes I think your love is all that keeps me going!"

"Same here. You've changed me. Over the two decades I've been a vampire, I forgot how to live, to love, to be happy. You taught me how. You brought me to life."

I lift her face to mine and rub my thumb over the beautiful line of freckles that spill over her nose and under her eyes. Her tears catch on my skin and I pull her back into me.

"My darling," I whisper. She rubs my back and buries her face in my shoulder.

Emma

About half a week later after dinner, I'm sitting on my bed, trying to catch up with my homework, when a spell of exhaustion slowly comes over me. I set my books aside gently and lie down for a catnap. *It'll only take a second,* I think. *Only a second…*

And there's Mama. Cold, alone, at the end of that awful hallway in a sterile hospital bed.

"Emma!" she cries out desperately. "Emma! Come over here, baby!"

My heart clenches and I run, but it's as though the hall is moving with me, and Mama isn't getting any closer. Then slowly, mockingly, the walls and floor separate and fall away and I'm pulled into the blackness…

...which becomes the cold, hard earth and the velvet blanket of night surrounding it. I look up, at first seeing nothing. Then an ear-piercing shriek throws me from my own skin and I scramble to my feet.

And there's Amy, closed tightly in the arms of that horrible woman, that Madam Noctis. Madam Noctis grins evilly and slides her hand between Amy's legs; Amy cringes, then shrieks as Madam Noctis moves her fingers over an area no one but Amy should be allowed to touch; I practically gag, unable to watch such a horrible thing happening to her. Madam Noctis places her other hand on Amy's breast; soon, prominent tears begin to fall and stain Amy's precious, innocent face. Then Madam Noctis rests her fangs on Amy's neck; I cry out, but it's too late; her fangs pierce Amy's beautiful skin, and Amy's screams shoot through me like death. Blood seeps from the wound and runs over Amy's shoulders and soaks into her shirt; Madam Noctis slurps as she drinks without any sign of remorse. Amy falls suddenly silent, her lovely green eyes dull with numb apathy. Madam Noctis's hand slides from between Amy's legs and into her skirt, and when Amy lets out another blood-chilling shriek, it doesn't take a rocket scientist to figure out what Madam Noctis has done. Amy's tears are creating visible rivers in the soil; I try to run to save her as I'd tried to save Mama, but it's no good; this time, instead of them moving away from me, the ground becomes frictionless and I slide around. Blood pours from Amy's neck, over her body, onto the ground, and into the air. Everything becomes thicker and redder; soon I feel myself swallowing, choking on, drowning in the blood of the girl I hold so dearly in my heart...

I start. I'm lying on my stomach, drenched in a cold sweat. My face is wet with tears and my stomach heaves angrily. The gag brings nothing up. My clock reads eight fifteen, and my assignments still lie on the unused side of my bed, although one loose piece of paper has slipped off and floated to the floor across the room.

I sit up, clutching my chest and panting. My God. I have to sneak out. I have to be there for my love when she rises from her sleep.

Perhaps it's foolish, but I don't care. All I care about is the horrific danger she's in, and I don't care how much danger I'm putting myself in to help her. I leap into my sneakers and coat and fly out the door.

Chapter Thirty-Five

Amy

On Wednesday night, I wake from a long, heavy slumber and press hard on the lid of my coffin. A second later, I sit up on the grass overhead.

I start and look to my right, where a dark blue silhouette falls to its knees next to me. My eyes bulge. "*Emma?*"

"Amy!" She throws her arms around me like I just came back form the dead.

I push her away and leap to my feet. "What on earth are you doing out here?" I instinctively pull her close and whirl my eyes over the area. "It's so dangerous!"

"I was worried about you."

"That never brought you out here before!"

"Well, I had this dream and—"

"Amy."

My feet leap out of their boots, arms crush Emma against my chest, and my head spins to look right into Jason's lust-laden face.

"Jason!" A petrified ghost of a voice.

"Hasn't Madam Noctis taken care of you *yet?* It's been two weeks. *Two fucking weeks!* If Madam Noctis hasn't gotten you by now, she's not going to. And I will."

Thoughts of that first night barge into my mind. I say nothing, just cling to Emma

"And is that your *girlfriend?*"

"You can't have her," I snap immediately. "You leave her alone. She's done nothing to you."

He gives a blood-curdling laugh. "What makes you think I want her? She's Madam Noctis's victim."

"She's not *anybody's* victim! And you *can't* have her!"

"No," he replies, "but I can have you." He reaches out to grab me, but a woman's desperate scream halts the action.

"*No!*" Elizabeth leaps from the darkness and rams him. They both topple to the ground and spring back up, regaining composure as soon as they lost it.

"You leave both of them," she spits. "You leave them both alone."

Jason cackles again, advancing on her. "Oh, Elizabeth. The greatest threat of all."

"*What?*"

"Man, and to think that all these years we've been trying to hide from humans." He releases a hellish cackle that makes Emma cry out and buckle and is by far the most frightening thing that's ever penetrated my ears. "At least they won't produce incomplete freaks like you do. And we can't have creatures like you driving the true vampires from existence."

"What are you talking about?"

"I have something for you." He grins, showing off his awful, glistening fangs, wet with blood from a recent victim.

"Oh my *God!*" Emma whimpers, stumbling back like a tiny child.

With one sweeping motion, Jason produces a yard-long splinter of wood and points it directly at Elizabeth's heart. With a tiny shriek, I lunge forward to help her, but he, this time prepared for attack, shoves me back so hard that I stumble into Emma and we both sprawl to the ground.

"You're incurable," he whispers to her angrily, advancing as she steps back, "and you're also responsible for Amy's condition. And that is an unforgivable sin."

"*No!*" I shriek, but it's too late; Elizabeth's shrill screech of agony pierces the cool night air before I've even gotten to my feet. She falls to her knees and slumps to her side and then her back, the stake shoved directly through her heart.

"Good-bye, Elizabeth," Jason says in a slick, emotionless voice and evaporates into the night.

"*Elizabeth!*" I scream, falling to my knees by her side. I feel a sudden, overwhelming urge to vomit, the sight of her blood pouring from the wound, running over her leather-covered chest, and soaking into the earth causing my stomach to flip over in horror. Her eyes bulge with pain and a futile effort to live, her mouth wide, trying to catch air although she doesn't need it, probably as a reawakened reflex.

Tears of desperation stinging my eyes, I grip the wretched, splintered stake and yank it furiously from Elizabeth's chest. She groans, tears creating lakes in her eyes.

"Oh, Elizabeth…" I exhale shakily, touching the blood gently. Her eyes dart to mine, and, though still mangled with pain, open to a look of love and she smiles.

"Amy…"

"Don't worry, Lizzie, it'll be all right, everything will be okay…I'll get help…"

She nearly laughs. "No, don't b-bother, Amy. I-I'm not going to make it, sweetie…" Each forced word comes with a desperate gasp for the nurturing comfort of oxygen.

"Oh, God, …no…please…"

"Don't worry," she whispers. "It's all right, sweetheart"—she gasps—"it's all right. I'll be fine, honey. Just let me go, and try to stay safe. Please."

"Oh, Elizabeth, no, don't go, please…" The tears in my eyes spill over the rims and fall off my cheeks to mix with the rivers of thick red fluid on her shredded leather outfit. If I lose her, I will be alone in the cemetery. Utterly, desperately alone.

"Oh, Amy," she breathes. "You sweet girl. Please promise me you'll be happy."

"But—"

"Please, Amy."

I hesitate a moment. How can I make a pledge of happiness when Elizabeth is dying? But my eyes dart to the blood, now flowing freely over her neck and into her beautiful blonde hair. "I promise."

"Is this her?" Elizabeth makes a slight motion with her hand; I didn't even notice Emma, kneeling next to me with her head on my shoulder. I give a sad nod.

"Hi, Emma."

"H-h-hi."

"Oh, Amy," Elizabeth breathes, reaching a shaking hand to stroke Emma's cheek. "She's so beautiful."

I nod again, taking Lizzie's hand and holding it against my cheek.

"Take care of her, and never forget, I love you and believe in you."

"Oh, Elizabeth..." I'm so choked up I can hardly breathe to speak. "Please, don't leave me here, don't leave me here all alone..."

She smiles and, with what seems like all the life left in her, motions to Emma, who's holding my shoulders and seems to be crying a little herself. "You're—not—alone, sweetie. You're never—alone. I—I love—you, sweetie."

"I love you too, Elizabeth." I press her hand to my wet cheek. The smile still gracing her face, she closes her eyes and lets her arm falls limp in my hands.

"Elizabeth?" I gasp. "Elizabeth!" I shriek when she doesn't even twitch, shaking her hand in despair. "*Elizabeth!* Oh God...oh God, no...no no no no no..." I moan, letting my head fall to her bloody torso. "No! *No!*" I clutch her hand as though I can hold her spirit in her body. Emma lays her head on my back and rocks me as I weep.

"Oh, baby," she whispers. "Oh, dear Amy..."

Her gentle, shaky words only make me sob more violently.

A triumphant smirk reaches my ears. We both look up; Jason has returned, looming above, smiling evilly.

"Too bad about your little friend," he says, leaning down and pushing Emma aside, "but I'm afraid I did what I had to do." His menacing smile indicates no remorse whatsoever; his treacherous fangs gleam in the moonlight and blinding rage seizes me.

"*Don't you ever touch Emma again!*" I feel my mind fall, lost, into a dark void, a demon I can't control taking over. Using my body, it seizes the stake, still fresh with Elizabeth's blood, from the ground at my side. My vision blurs and I merely watch as it shoots to its borrowed feet. I become conscious of what it's about to do, but I can't stop it; I don't *want* to stop it. The demon tightens the muscles in my arms and pushes the stake onward forcefully; the wood slashes through air, hits a wall of flesh, and grinds to a halt with the new friction.

The demon dies. And for a moment, the world freezes. No one moves, no one speaks, no one breathes. I open my eyes slowly, reluctantly, and my soul screams out at the horror before me.

Jason's eyes have taken on a look of mingled shock that quickly turn to rage as they glare into my terrified ones.

"You—fool—ish girl—" he struggles out. "Now you— you'll be lucky if M-Madam Noctis lets you l-live—even as a complete vampire." That's all he can manage; the next moment, his head droops; he falls backward and collapses on the ground, and the man who forced himself inside me so long ago is as dead as dust. His blood covers my hands, cold and clammy on my skin. And we continue to exist, Emma on her knees behind me, Jason and Elizabeth's bodies collapsed in the grass, and me—my knees bent slightly, my back arched, my arms still holding the stake outward, now wet with Jason's blood as well as Elizabeth's. My eyes stare into the empty space that Jason's head occupied only moments ago; incredulous, I slowly drop them to the dripping stake. After a few moments, the stake falls from my paralyzed hands, and a few more, and time starts again. My muscles collapse, causing me to sink to my knees and lose any control I had left over my mind, body, and spirit, and convulsive weeping takes its place.

The next moment passes and Emma's arms are around my shoulders and she's pulling me to my feet, her soft chest pressing against my heaving back. "Oh, baby girl," she groans. "Come on, honey. Come on." She jerks around suddenly. "*Back off!*" I look up at her sudden outburst; a few of the others are coming closer to us, and she's facing them, a crucifix clutched tightly in her outstretched hand. Her left arm holds me tightly. Feeling the consequences of the presence of the crucifix, they move back slowly. "Come on," Emma whispers into my hair, setting me on my feet but keeping her left arm under my breasts for support. "Let's get you home." We start moving away, Emma still grasping the crucifix for protection. I'm so distraught, I barely realize that she referred to her house as my home.

Chapter Thirty-Six

Emma

I pull a messy, sobbing Amy into my bedroom and sit her in my closet. Her body is hunched over and rigid and she's bawling uncontrollably, like a child crying for her mother.

"Shh…shhh…it's all right, dearie, it's all right." I kiss her head comfortingly. "Come on, sweetie, relax." I get up and turn the radio on loudly so that no one can hear Amy's sobs.

I then return and put my arms around her shoulders; in her despair, she grips me so tightly I can barely breathe.

"Elizabeth—" she chokes. "Elizabeth—she's—she's—she's dead…my God…Elizabeth…d-d-dead…"

"When my mother died, her mother told me to stop crying, that my Mama was in a better place. That really hurt me because it made me feel like Mama was happier without me and that my tears were selfish. But it's not true, Amy, it's not. You go ahead and cry. That's right, get it all out…" I kiss her head again and stroke and rock her until she finally calms down.

"I killed Jason," she whispers. "I killed him. Oh, my God. I'm a murderer."

"No, Amy, you're not a murderer, okay? You ended his life as a vampire—you didn't *kill* him. You gave him the first step to heaven."

"But—but—but I killed him. And now the others—the others—"

"Shhh…" The fear of that is already pulling at my stomach, but I try to push it away. One thing at a time…

I sit back and look her over. Her hands, face, and clothes are covered with mingled tears, dirt, and blood. Her hair hangs in oily, muddy snarls around her shoulders, her hands caked with dried blood. "Oh, darling…" I touch her messy face. "Let's get you cleaned up first. Wait right here." I hurry out of my bedroom and look over the railing. Robert and Jaquelina are watching TV in the living room, so I dart into Kristina's room.

"Kristina!"

"What?" She turns from her desk, where she's going over college applications.

"I need you to get Robert and Jaquelina out of the living room long enough for me to get Amy into the bathroom. Can you do that?"

"Sure." She doesn't question. She stands and goes right downstairs. I race back to my bedroom and bring Amy to my door.

"And I need some help finding it," Kristina is saying. "So could you two come down and help me look? It'll only take a little while if you help me."

"Sure, honey," Jaquelina says. She turns off the TV and all three head downstairs.

"All right," I whisper to Amy. We hurry down the hall and I shut and lock the bathroom door at the other end.

She falls over the toilet and begins violently heaving. I hurry over and pull her hair away from her face as the few contents of her stomach empty into the bowl. When she finishes, she leans her head against the seat and weeps. I fill a paper cup with water for her to rinse with, and when she's done that, I flush.

"Do you think you're going to puke again?"

She shakes her head, the misery of grief and stomach cramps mangling her face.

"Okay." I turn her leg over and untie her first boot.

"What are you doing?" she moans.

"We need to get you into this shower, sweetheart," I reply, pulling the boot off. "You're filthy."

She nods and begins unzipping her corset. I pull off her boots, fishnets, and skirt; she pulls off her corset, shirt and bra.

Then I turn on the fan, help her to her feet, and let her take off her underpants while I get the water running.

Since I need a shower, too, I strip quickly as she climbs in, taking off everything but the cross necklace I now wear at all times. I get in after her.

We've never been naked together before. It's a bit of a shock at first, to see her breasts for the very first time, round and hugging her chest gently, and the dark, curly hair between her legs.

"You—you're so beautiful," I say.

She nods, wiping tears from her eyes. "So are you." She lets out an isolated sob.

Then I stretch out my arms and hug her; she slowly puts hers around my back and we stand, our bodies against each other, for about a minute. The warm water pouring over us, her soft skin touching mine tenderly, our naked breasts pressing with the force of the embrace, my right hand holding her head through her wet hair.

Slowly, hesitantly, I let my fingers touch her breast. The skin is smooth, inviting, growing softer than anything I've every touched around her nipple, which is a soft baby pink. As I touch it gently, I swear I hear a tiny laugh rise from her chest and I feel her fingers spread lovingly over my lower back.

At last we manage to pull away from each other back and I grab my shampoo, turn her around, and begin to tenderly wash her hair. I run my hands through it and massage her scalp with the tips of my fingers; it gradually grows softer as I work the dirt and blood out. Then I put some conditioner in her hair and wash her skin gently with my Bath and Body Works gel, massaging it the same way I did her scalp, my fingertips gently pushing and pulling the surface. It's soft and beautiful, like an angel's.

Once I've washed, I turn off the water and dry with my own towel. As she waits in the tub, I pull our biggest, fluffiest one out of the linen closet for her to use.

"Thank you," she says in a watery whisper as I drape it over her shoulders lovingly and kiss her cheek. As she dries off, I check outside for signs of Robert or Jaquelina. Luckily, I hear them chatting in the den, so, taking with me the hairdryer, I smuggle Amy back into my bedroom.

"Do you mind wearing my underpants?" I ask her as I open my undies drawer.

"No."

"'Kay." I throw a pair over to her, grab some for myself, and turn around. We put them on and I let her borrow my cloud-patterned pajamas while I wear my purple nightdress.

"Did you like that?" I ask her as I blow-dry her hair a few minutes later.

She nods. "I haven't had one of those in so many years. And you're a good masseur...uh, masseuse, I think."

I smile as I blow her hair into my free hand. She lets out a hiccup.

"Amy, you have to understand that you haven't done anything wrong. Absolutely nothing." I turn the dryer back on and blow her hair a little more.

"I killed Jason."

"You set him free."

"It still feels like murder."

My face twitches into a sad half-smile as I turn off the dryer and reach for a brush and tie so that I can braid her hair. "I'll wash your clothing," I tell her as my hands separate and plait the long black tendrils.

"Thanks."

"You did the right thing, Amy. Jason has killed so many people—he almost killed Annie. I'm glad you did what you did. And now no one else will be hurt."

"What do you think they'll do to me?" she whimpers.

"I don't know, honey." I feel tears spring into my eyes. "I really don't. Maybe I should walk you to your grave and bring garlic to fight them off?"

"*No.*"

"But I'm so scared for you."

"But you can't come down there with me. Not even with garlic."

"We could stay out until the sun comes up and—"

"Emma, I have my crucifix. I'm not completely helpless."

"I never said you were!"

She groans, her face flushed with mingled anger and sadness.

"Listen, I'm gonna go get your clothing into the washer. Will you be all right by yourself?"

She nods. I stand, gather her clothing from the corner, and carry it downstairs.

After asking Jill, who's doing homework in the family room, to watch the machines in the bathroom closely for me, I put the shirt and fishnets in the washing machine (on delicate!) and the skirt in the dryer for a dry-clean cycle.

"Make sure Robert and Jaquelina don't open those machines, okay?" I whisper to her as I exit the bathroom. "They're Amy's clothes. Call me down when they finish their cycles."

She nods and I go back to my room with a wet cloth to clean Amy's corset and boots.

It's pretty late by the time everything is finished, and I'm really tired. It's right as I'm getting in bed that Amy starts sobbing again.

Turning over, I begin shushing her gently and wrap myself around her, praying that my affectionate actions will soothe her. Luckily, she isn't wailing anymore; she's gasping, but not bawling. After a little while, even the tiny sobs she's letting out cease, and only silent tears remain.

"You're wonderful, Amy," I whisper into her ear. "Don't you ever let anyone or anything tell you you're not."

She doesn't speak, so I continue.

"Everything you did tonight…protecting me and holding Elizabeth and freeing Jason—Amy, I didn't think it was possible for me to love you more, but now I do."

I kiss her soft, wet cheek. Fatigued by the dreadful experience, she lays her head on my shoulder and cries herself to sleep as I stroke her hair. I lie with my arms around her for a while longer, my eyes wide and staring into the darkness. Maybe I should try her trick? I stare at the ceiling and imagine my mother's spirit is there. *She's right there, smiling at you.* But I feel nothing. There's just me, the ceiling, and the empty space between us. Sighing, I turn to look someplace else. Still, nothing. Maybe you really do have to believe a spirit is there for it to work. And I don't really believe my mother is there. I mean, I do think she can see me, and I believe she's watching us and guiding us from wherever she is, but I do not feel like she's really *with* me. I don't feel like there's any superior being protecting me from the evils of the world, not my mother's spirit, certainly not God. I sigh, kiss my partner's cheek gently, and slowly fall asleep, feeling so lucky to still have someone I can call the most important person in my life.

The next day, in the late evening, we went back to see her, but the nurse said she had slipped into a coma during the night. She lay in her bed, the tubes hooked up everywhere, the heart monitor beeping loudly. I rushed over and shook her hand. *"Mother! Mother!"*

She didn't respond.

"Mommy! It's me, Emma! Mama!"

Her hands were like ice, and her face was stoic with death. I had never seen her like this before.

"Mother!"

Still no response. Annie reached out and stroked Mama's once-existent hairline. *"Mom. Mom."* Tears played on Annie's eyelids. *"Mom, oh, Mother…"*

The doctor said this was probably it. She'd never wake. I took one last look past her pale, translucent eyelids as we all shuffled into the hall.

When we got home, Aunt Maggie forced a smile, telling us we should probably get to sleep if we wanted any hope of getting through school in the morning. It was already eleven thirty, and we were all so tired there were no protests to this. I was the last one out of the bathroom, and when I emerged, the house was dark. Annie and Kristina's door was closed, and I passed it and the study before reaching Aunt Maggie and Natasha's door. It was slightly ajar, and, hearing crying, I looked through.

Natasha and Aunt Maggie were both in their nightclothes, standing in the middle of the room. Natasha was holding Aunt Maggie, rocking her back and forth gently. Aunt Maggie was sobbing uncontrollably in her arms.

"I'm losing my sister! She's never going to wake, Natasha! She's g-gone!"

Shock spread through me as I saw the two of them grieving together in the middle of their bedroom. I had never seen Aunt Maggie cry. Jill and I were in the next room, and I slipped through our door and leaned against it.

The room was dark; Jill was lying in our bed already. I heard her turn over. *"Emma."*

And it happened. For the first time, I knew it, and I believed it. My mother was going to die. They weren't going to save her. And there was nothing we could do about it.

I slid to the floor and lost any remaining composure. My rigorous cries echoed out our window and pierced the silky black of the night.

March

Chapter Thirty-Seven

Emma

Time is the strangest thing. It moves fast if you're having fun, slowly if you're bored or scared. And sometimes, it seems like it can never move slowly enough.

Sometimes I sit in her arms, wondering at how, after all that's happened, we're here, we're still together.

No matter what happens, I don't want to risk putting it off any longer, so when we're lying on my bed together very late into a cold Friday night, just talking about life, love, feelings, et cetera, I take a deep breath and get ready to ask.

"Amy," I whisper to her, holding her hand in mine.

"Yeah?"

"Amy…will you…will you marry me?"

She lets out a short bark of a laugh, like someone who's just seen something pathetically stupid on television. "Emma, what on earth are you talking about?"

"I want you to marry me."

"But when? How? You're still so young! And I'm a vampire, when would we do it? Not to mention we're both girls…"

"I never said it had to be all government-endorsed, Amy. Just marrying you right here is good enough for me."

"But…but how would that be official? I mean, everyone performs weddings in their own home, just for fun. Kelly and I did it once, as a joke."

"But that's just it. This wouldn't be a joke. Our love is real, and this is real, and marriage is just a bunch of bullshit if it isn't real unless the government endorses it. I mean, marriage is about love, isn't it?"

She nods slightly. "I see what you're saying. I didn't know that's what you meant by 'marriage.'"

"That's all I'm ever gonna mean. That's all marriage is to me. A bond of love. Which is why it can be between you and me. Screw laws. Screw dictionaries."

She smiles, squeezes my hand gently.

"I got you something." I reach into the drawer of my nightstand and pull out two little boxes. "I got these at Macy's. They aren't anything special, but I thought they'd do."

Amy opens it. Her eyes widen as they light upon the tiny gold ring inside.

"It's not like I have money to buy big fancy rings," I continue jabbering. "I mean, I could if I really wanted to because I have life savings but it just seemed kinda weird, you know, because we're both so young and—"

"Shh." Amy puts her finger over my lips. "Let me see your ring."

"It's just like yours," I provide as I hand her the box. She opens it, takes the ring out, and slips it on my finger.

"Lovely," she exhales, and brings my hand to her lips. "Here. My turn."

Her ring slips onto her finger like it was made just for her. The gold band sparkles against her white skin, and before I can say anything she's pushed me back on the bed and is kissing me all over my face. "My wife," she whispers. "My beautiful wife." Her lips are soft and warm against my skin and I let myself relax, let her take over. She reaches into my nightshirt and her hands cup my breasts gently, and suddenly I realize what has to happen. Here. Now.

"Amy," I whisper. She stops, pushes herself up so she's on all fours above me and her long hair is hanging down over her face, the ends just barely tickling my cheeks.

"Yes?"

"It's time."

Understanding fills her eyes, warm green in the lamplight, yet she still asks me, "It's time?"

"For us. You know. To go all the way."

She's speechless for a moment, lets her mouth open while she thinks. "A-are you sure, love? You can't just have sex on a whim. It's too risky."

"This isn't a whim. I've thought about it for, like, six weeks, ever since that night…that night, when I realized that we might not have time to wait…that…" I choke up a little. "That…fate may tear us apart before we can find out. Before we can know what it's like for the two of us."

"Emma…" She reaches up and wipes a solitary tear from my eye.

"We don't have to do anything viciously intimate," I continue. "We can just…we can just take off our clothing and touch each other, if you want. I just want to know."

She nods. "I want to know too, Emma." She kisses me. "I just want you to be sure you're ready first. I don't want our first time to hurt you. I want it to heal your pain, to make you happy."

"It won't hurt me, Amy. It will make me happy. I'm positive."

"All right, darling."

Amy reaches out a graceful hand and runs her index finger down my right cheek gently, letting it smooth my jawline, trace the contour of my neck, and finally come to rest on my shoulder. "You're beautiful," she whispers.

My lips pull tight with a semi-excited, semi-nervous smile. "Thanks," I whisper. She smiles back and strokes a lock of hair out of my eyes, then leans over and kisses me slowly, tenderly. And I realize right then just how gentle and tender this is going to be. Not like in the movies, where they're always forcing everything and panting like they're on Everest. No, this is going to be tender and gentle. Almost like a sleep.

She pulls back and unfastens the buttons on my nightshirt, slowly loosening every one until she reaches the bottom and it's open to my chest and tummy. She pushes the fabric away from my front and touches my breasts gently, treating my body like it's sacred.

We're undressed before I even realize it's happened. As her lips grace my neck, I reach around and unhook her bra, freeing her breasts from their restrictive hold. She plays with my hair as I leave a line of slow kisses down her neck and over her chest, finally sucking on her nipple like a baby.

"Emma…" she says, her hand coming to rest on my back. "How far do you want this to go?"

"Let's play it naturally," I suggest. "You know, do what feels right and stop when that feels right."

"Okay." She pulls me back up and kisses my lips again as she slides her hand under the delicate lace lining the top of my underwear. Her hand moves over my thigh gently, slipping the cloth out of place, and out of reflex I'm doing the same for her. It's just as my hand is sliding over her inner thigh that she freezes and turns away.

"Oh God."

"Amy? What is it, darling?"

"Oh God. Emma, love, I'm sorry. I just can't do this. I can't."

"Amy." I take her hand and hold it to my lips. "It's me. Not her. Me."

"I know, I know, it's just…I'm so scared. Really, really scared."

"You don't deserve to die thinking of sex as the most dreadful thing that's ever happened to you."

"I know, it's just…I'm sorry, Emma. I'm really, really sorry."

"It's okay, love," I say to her, and kiss her in comfort. "It's okay."

I'm just about to turn out my lamp when she reaches up and pulls me back on top of her.

"Amy? Wha--?"

"No, Emma, you're right. I have to face my fears. I can't let that woman ruin our sexuality." To emphasize her point, she slides her hand between my legs, parts the skin, and touches me gently. My eyes widen in surprise, my breath stops in my throat, and I feel my body fall limp over hers. God. Already, so amazing.

"Come on," she urges. "You too." She takes my hand from her cheek and guides it down between our bodies, leaving it rest on her lower tummy. *You take it from here.*

So I do. Slowly, carefully, I slide my right hand over the soft, curly hair and between the beautiful, slippery, blanket-like folds of skin between her inner thighs. She gasps too, out of the same shock that I felt, the shock of feeling someone you love touch some place a lover has never touched before.

I move my fingers slowly along the lovely hidden world, sweet as sugar, exploring the final part of her that I had not been able to reach. It's just as amazing as the rest of her; the area is wet and slippery, soft, tender, and warm. I can't believe that this is a human body; surely our simple, seemingly average forms don't really hold this many secrets. Is every human like this? Do all women and men, be them ugly or pretty as they may, as grouchy or friendly, have this same aura of wonder about them?

She finds it first. Deep down, where only a lover should be able to reach. I let out a quick breath, ready for the big move, yet she hesitates, as if waiting for me to turn back, to sit up and say, *"What the hell? Amy, what are we doing? This isn't right, we're only seventeen, for God's sake! Let's just put our clothes back on and go to bed, okay?"* But I won't. I'm enjoying this. I'm enjoying her. And thanks to her hesitation, I find the same place and teeter, waiting for the one move that will change my life forever.

"Honey," she whispers. "Are you sure?"

As I take my free hand from her back to stroke her cheek, I realize I'm shaking and tears are filling my eyes. What's happening? I don't feel like Emma anymore. I feel like a new person, as though my soul has been reborn and is just waiting for me to start its life. I only pause for a few seconds; the intensity is waning, and I tighten and relax my muscles and squeeze my eyes shut, causing the tears to spill. Her fingers stroke me deep between my legs, eager yet hesitant.

"Please, Amy. Please."

Yet she waits, so I carefully make the first move. I do what only monsters have done before. I enter the place that should have always been hers, that should never have been taken by Madam Noctis or Jason. And then I wait. Wait for her to cry, wait for her to pull away. Wait for a sign, anything, to tell me that what I have just done is wrong.

But instead I get a subtle relaxing of her muscles, and then the same thing. She's followed suit. And it feels so amazing—we're truly together now. We're one. I am touching her soul, and she is touching mine. And that's the way it should be.

The strength of the feelings growing deep inside my body is foreign; I didn't know such power in touch could even exist. The feeling of her inside of me doubles my tears; they create steady rivers on my cheeks and I find I'm actually sobbing a little.

She places her free hand supportively behind my head and kisses my cheek lovingly, licking the tears away. "Emma…" she whispers, "are you all right?"

"Don't stop," I whisper hoarsely, and she continues, her movements quickly becoming stronger and more passionate. I try to imitate what she's doing, but it's hard when such amazing sensations are running between my legs. Nevertheless, she lets out a little cry as we move, and I try to breathe steadily, letting the climax arrive as it wishes…

Stronger, heavier, stronger, heavier, stronger, stronger, stronger…

It comes. I relax and let my body drown in what feels like a tidal wave spreading throughout every inch of me; tingles followed by a nice, soft warmth radiate through my limbs and I want to scream my lungs out in ecstasy. I manage to remain silent save a few tiny moans as Amy licks my lips tenderly and massages my scalp with her free hand. The blood pulses around my lower abdomen, around and through the area graced by Amy's soft, delicate skin. My heart pounds wildly in my ears.

As Amy moves inside me and the climax nears its end, a small cry escapes my mouth. So soft. So close. So sweet. So tender. So perfect.

Then it's over and I feel small pangs of regret, not wanting it to end. It slows, fades, and ceases to exist save the general pulsing that sex leaves you with. I let my breath out and fall limp. She takes the hint and slowly slides back, rubbing a sensitive spot and sending a final wave of love throughout my body. I sigh and relax; it was the most amazing feeling I'd had in my life. Now I can focus solely on bringing her to the peak to which she so tenderly brought me. Without having to think about my own intensity, I am able to give her what she needs much more effectively; I close my eyes and give all my attention to the soft, wet, amazing part of Amy that surrounds my fingers. As I rub her and her body moves beneath mine, I can't imagine anyone thinking something as beautiful and spiritual as this is morally wrong. Amy's body is full, soft, and strong. She takes a few deep breaths and, crossing her legs around my lower back, hugs my midsection with her lower body. After a few minutes, I begin to realize she's not really coming this way, so I reposition my hand so that I'm also stroking that tiny place outside the vagina where women feel the most pleasure.

"Emma," she breathes. "Emma…"

It takes a little while for her to hit the zenith; for a minute, I'm afraid it won't occur. Then it surprises me; she pants and moans as quietly as she can, her coming body surrounding me like a blanket. Her legs are crossed tightly over my back, her arms, my neck; her lips are folded with mine and I remain inside her for the duration of her orgasm. I can feel her climactic rush of sexual love all over my body.

Finally, she relaxes and I slip away, give her body back to her. "Oh, oh, Amy," I sob, wrapping my arms around her neck and falling to pieces on her shoulder. She holds me close and kisses my head again and again, her hands caressing my back. "I love you, I love you, I love you."

"Emma," she speaks. "Listen, baby. Nothing, I repeat, nothing, will ever take me away from you. My baby. Never."

"Never?" I squeak.

"Never, never, never."

As she wipes a few final tears from my cheeks, I realize just how good I feel, how warm and relaxed and carefree and…happy.

I lie with her and slowly cry myself to sleep in her arms, laying my head between her breasts and feeling her soft hand woven through my hair and following the gentle curve of my head. Her distant voice, a tired whisper, calls from far off.

"I love you, Emma. Dear God, I love you."

Chapter Thirty-Eight

Amy

I open my eyes slowly, letting out a deep yawn. I'm lying in Emma's bed; her covers are like silk against my bare legs. We're still wrapped in each other's arms, her naked body feeling like heaven against mine. Memories of what we did inundate my mind, and I let out a little gasp and then smile widely. Sex. I had sex with Emma.

After lying in her arms for a while longer, enjoying the feeling of our bare bodies encircling each other, I check the clock (five fifty) and yawn, moving to get up.

She sleeps deeply; even when I slip from her arms and stand, causing the bed to creak slightly, she doesn't twitch. My clothes are pretty cold from lying on the floor all night; I flinch slightly as I put them on.

After zipping my corset and lacing my boots, I turn back to Emma. In the moderate warmth my spirit provides my body, she kicked off the blankets; they lie around her ankles, exposing her soft, delicate figure. I feel my heart fill as my eyes scan her in the small amount of light illuminating the bed. She lies on her side now, one hand under her head and her knees bent ever so slightly; her feet, lying gracefully among the blankets, could be those of a water-nymph's. The bright red curls gracing that so intimate area between her legs barely show past her strong thighs. In this position and lighting, she could be a model on the cover of a magazine. Not that that's really fair to say; I'm her girlfriend and I think she always looks like a model.

I lovingly place the blankets around her sleeping form and lean over and turn her head to kiss her tenderly. Memories of the wonderful experience we had fill my mind and tears of happiness threaten my eyes. Not wanting to leave but forced to by the clock that now reads six, I whisper a tiny good-bye, unlock her bedroom door, and slip into the cool, early-morning air.

I always try to leave Emma's as late as possible as I can't lock the door behind me and I don't want any others attempting a last-minute attack on her. The sunlight is slowly grazing the horizon; I sprint down the stairs and into the forest.

When we agreed to have sex and were lying in her bed together, waiting for it to happen, I kissed her tentatively and touched her a little but was scared to go much further. Madam Noctis's dreadful face, that feeling from when she entered me, was stuck in my mind with Superglue. And it wouldn't leave me, not when I was this close to doing it again.

Even though this was voluntary. Even though it was with someone I loved.

But I played forth anyway; I kissed her mouth and cheeks and neck; our soft lips left tender tingles in their wake; my whole body began to shiver with desire as she placed her lips here and there and blew into my ears, her palms massaging my scalp and her fingers running tenderly through my hair.

Soon the hindrance of the physical world slid off our skin and was cast haphazardly aside to await our return to society, when we decided to hide our wonderful world of love and sex again. She was so warm, her skin so soft, and I couldn't keep my hands off her body or my lips off her lips. Her soft, gentle hands made playful movements around my tummy, chest, breasts, shoulders, and back. Our legs entwined in different patters, our hips dancing together as though at a wild party. Slowly, our hands moved south toward the forbidden area, the one we had avoided because culture had ground it into our minds that letting someone else down there before age twenty was wrong. But we had tossed that aside with the cloth symbols that now lay in heaps in another dimension and we didn't worry about morality now. After all, how could something that felt so good be so wrong?

But just as she was about to touch my lips, to cross that point of no return, I felt my muscles clench in terror, and I fell away.

"Amy? What is it, darling?"

I told her how terrified I was, how the last time someone had touched me down there, it was awful, like I had been meeting the devil himself. How I was so scared my experience with her wouldn't be right, because I would remember her.

"It's okay," she whispered to me, even though I could feel the disappointment flow from her body.

And I realized how silly this was, how ridiculous it was to let that woman deny her—deny me—*the right to love each other as we so desperately wanted to. For how much longer was I going to let this woman control me? Take charge of my action, rule my soul? No, that was wrong. So wrong. If I didn't fight it, I would never win. I would never be free.*

So I reached for Emma's hand and pulled her back into me, then placed my hand between her legs, just inside those two gentle folds of skin. She was soft, warm. She was my Emma. And since she hesitated in confusion, I sent her in the right direction.

And we were doing it, we were making love, and it began to hit me just how much we weren't little girls anymore. We'd grown up, we'd changed, and we were young women. Doing what was right for us.

Though I asked her, once I'd found the tender opening to her beautiful virgin body, if she was sure she wanted this and she'd replied yes, I couldn't make my fingers move. There was just too much fear I'd somehow hurt her. In response to my hesitation, she forcefully made the move, and I gasped out loud as the realization of what she was doing hit. She then paused, as though afraid of what I might think, but I no longer felt any pain, any fear; to deliver this message to her, I entered her too.

And she caressed me, both on the inside and the outside, and after a few minutes the familiar tsunami of feeling, only twenty times stronger, overtook me and I hugged her as tightly as I possibly could.

And she was crying. No, not just crying; she was sobbing. I wondered if she hurting, but she told me no, to keep loving her. And I did, and she came, and I felt myself cry a little too. And I came, and any horrible memories of being raped were washed from my mind, as though swept away by true love's tide. This was what sex was to me now. It was Emma.

I soared. It felt like I was weightless, flying through the sky with no one but my Emma. Her warm body touching mine, our eyes gazing forever at only each other.

Then it was over and we both lay there, breathing heavily and bathing in the bliss of being so close. After only a few minutes we both fell into a deep sleep that was only disturbed hours later by the instinct of the coming of the dawn.

295

I twist the little gold ring on my finger. My mind is racing with disbelief and ecstasy. I cannot believe that we finally did it. Even more important, I can't believe how *good* it felt. I mean, it's only ever been pain before, with Madam Noctis and Jason…I hadn't thought it would be that amazing even once. I knew it probably wouldn't be *terrible,* like it was with *them,* but it really is incredible how much your feelings can affect something, isn't it?

I remember asking my mother, when I was about eleven, if sex was fun.

"With the right person," was her response.

I've known Emma's "the one" for a long time, even though we've only known each other for four months. I've just had this feeling deep inside, this feeling that as long I'm with her, everything will be all right. Problems will sift their way to nothing and we'll just be closer because they'll strengthen our relationship. The sex just gives more evidence to prove it. Which makes me wonder: if I'm twenty years older than Emma, why are we soul mates? In our society, couples who are more than ten years apart in age are generally frowned upon. *Greatly.* Like, "She just married for money," or "The older one is just seducing the younger one." Surely that can't be true for all of them—since when has everything society says is true been true in the eyes of God and Mother Nature? Just look at Emma and me now. Both girls, loving each other like a girl and a boy are supposed to. Human standards are far too strict to work peacefully with our instincts.

But then another thought strikes me. *If I hadn't been immortalized as a vampire so far back, would Emma and I have met?* Perhaps, but not likely. *If we had, would we have fallen in love?* Probably not. *Would the support you've provided for her have been nearly as intense?* Probably not. *Would she have been able to help you with your problems, whatever the hell they may be, the way she can because you two are together?* Probably not.

So maybe my birth was for Emma's sake. Maybe the reason God let me become a vampire is that it's the only way that I can really be with Emma, so that she can be with me. I believe that soul mates are always able to find each other, even if it isn't on earth. *Maybe God meant for us to find each other on earth.* But then why were we born so far apart? Why can't she have been born earlier, or me later? *Because it did not happen that way. Accept that. Accept the truth, Amy Leanne Wyle.*

This is the way it happened. You were killed and you've been undead for over two decades. You and Emma found each other when life was at its hardest, when you needed each other more than ever. And that's the way it is.

And I become suddenly aware that being a vampire isn't hurting me as much as it used to.

Emma

Bittersweet. That's the best word to describe how I begin to feel about sex after dinner that evening. I lie in a deck lounger I dragged up from the patio earlier this week, watching the sunset and going over everything in my brain. I felt so good this morning; I was bright and happy and, for the first time in as long as I can remember, didn't wash between my legs in the shower because I didn't want any remaining traces of the night, of Amy, to be rinsed away. But as the afternoon fatigue drifted in, I began to feel depressed about the entire thing, and mixed with the elation I've felt all day, I'm left confused and storming with mingled emotions.

It was so amazing. I'm so happy we did it, so happy that I did such a beautiful, beautiful thing with such a beautiful, beautiful person. The thought of the tender intimacy with which we touched each other lulls in my mind, causing a fuzzy feeling that makes me want to squeal and hug myself. I'm so happy that I let my darling, the girl who has become the center of my universe, grace such a tender, personal area inside and outside my body, the feeling of the woman that I love so much entering that forbidden world as many believe only a man could. It's like a whole new secret I've let her in on. And she let me in on her secret, too. And it's one of the best things that's ever happened to me.

And yet...I miss my virginity. I feel like I've been reborn since last night, and I miss the girl I used to be. I'm sure that if I stated this to people, some might disagree, saying that I'm a virgin until I have penis-in-vagina intercourse (which I know will probably never happen). But I feel differently. Although I really don't know what defines a virgin male, I believe that a virgin girl is anyone who has not let another person, male or female, penetrate her with any part of his or her body as a sexual act. And so, by my own belief, I gave Amy my virginity last night when I let her slip her fingers inside of me. It was astounding, it felt incredible, but it also stole away my virginity, and I miss that.

I feel tears sting at the corners of my eyes. How can something so breathtaking hurt so badly? How can being as physically close to Amy as I possibly can be, something that I've wanted since the day she first kissed me, in fact, since the day she met me, have such a heavy impact on my heart? How can it leave me feeling so full, yet so empty? I let out a yawn and go inside to lie on my bed, trying to clear my brain as I let silent tears lull me to sleep.

I see Mama. She's not in an inaccessible hospital bed. I'm not running to her in vain, running to try to, just once, beat the floor and reach her before it fades into darkness, carrying me with it. No, this time I'm in her arms, and she's rubbing my hair and consoling me.

"Oh, darling," she whispers as I cry into her shirt. "Oh, my Emma. My sweet daughter. My darling baby girl."

"Oh, Mama, I thought you were dead!"

She laughs. "Not quite, love. I'm right here with you. I'm always with you. You just have to see."

I let out a sob.

"Listen to me, Emma," she croons. "You and Amy are so close and your love is so real. This is a real time of peril for you both, and you need each other more than anything. Listen to me, sweetheart. You're right to miss your virginity. You really are. It shows that you value your spiritual being highly and realize the consequences of life-altering decisions. But don't feel bad that you had sex with Amy. You loved it. I know you did and you know you did. You be with Amy in every way that you can. Every moment matters in true love. In no way have you disappointed me. I'm happy that you had such a delightful experience last night. And I think you'll very soon come to realize that that experience did more for you than you know." She kisses my head. "I love you, baby," she whispers. "Now go be with her."

And she's gone, replaced by the smooth white texture of my bedroom walls. My heart sinks into my knees. It was just a dream, nothing more.

I'm writing my story later when I'm pulled from my fantasy land by a familiar rapping on the glass of my door. As I cross the room to open it, all the thoughts and feelings of earlier suddenly flood back to me. Seeing her face as I pull back the curtains only makes it worse; I feel my broken heart bring a flash flood of emotions as I slide the door open with medium effort. I can't control so many all at once; as soon as the cool night air hits my face, I feel myself break.

"Oh, Amy!" I gasp as I fall into her arms and let the first wails out. She pulls me over the threshold and closes the door. We sit on our bench and she strokes my hair and lets me cry into her shoulder.

"Oh, baby," she whispers, kissing my head and trying to soothe me.

I let out a rather violent hiccup.

"Please tell me what's wrong, darling."

I keep on weeping.

"Did something bad happen to you today?"

I shake my head. "No?" She rocks me for a few more minutes, then sighs in understanding. "It's sex, isn't it?"

I nod, coughing and blubbering.

"Oh, sweetie pie." She pulls me closer to her and continues her soothing actions.

"I really wasn't ready, Amy," I sob. "I j-just th-thought I was."

She nods and we were silent save the meaningless sounds from my lamentation. When I finally get myself under control, she holds my hands and looks into my eyes. "What is bothering you specifically, Em?"

I shake my head. "Everything. Just…everything." I hiccup a little more. "I just…I'm just so emotional right now. I don't know if it's that I *wasn't* ready. I mean, I was ready to share myself with you, but…but…I wasn't ready to lose my virginity."

"Mm-hm."

"When I woke up this morning, I was so happy, and I still am. You touching me down there…feeling our hands in such an intimate part of me…such a tender area…it was so wonderful, it felt so good…" I clutch her hands and hold them up to my cheek. They're so cool against my hot, wet skin. "When you entered me, when you…penetrated me…" I run my fingers in circles along her cheek as I speak, "…just…just feeling your delicate fingers inside my body…it felt so beautiful, so magnificent, and…I was sure I couldn't be happier." Amy gives a bit of a melancholy smile at the lovely memory. I put my arms around her neck and gaze intently into her eyes. "But now…now I miss my virginity. Since you did that, I feel like I've been reborn, and I don't feel like the person I used to be. And I miss the person I used to be."

"Emma, darling, how are you different?"

"Well, I just…I just don't feel like myself anymore. I feel like someone completely different. I want to be who I used to be, not who I am now."

"But you *are* who you used to be. What you've said to me just now proves to me that you're exactly as you always have been. You just feel different because you did something big last night, something you've never done before. You passed a milestone in life. It's like going to college or getting married. You've taken a big step. Everyone feels different after a big step. But after a little while they adjust to the changes it's made for them and they begin to feel like themselves again. The only change you have now is that you know how wonderful sex can be, since we're both women and I'm a vampire so there's no chance of disease. And that's a positive thing. You don't really need to adjust to anything. No one can stay the same forever, sweetie. I think that since I met you, you've changed a lot. Much more than you have since yesterday."

"I just don't get it. I love you so much. I love every part of you, everything you do, and everything you've given me. *Everything*, including last night. I know it's all natural, that sex exists to keep the human race going, so…so…why does it h-h-hurt so badly?" I feel myself start to bawl again. "How could it be so wrong? How?"

I feel her lips touch my head. "Honey," she whispers. "Listen to me. The thing isn't so much that it's wrong, I guess, it's just that…it's just that…it's life altering."

"But how? When you get down to basic physics, it's just one thing entering another! It's like we've been doing all along, only in new areas!"

"But this is also about more than just physics. In the natural world, when a woman goes that far, she is telling her mate that they need to stay together because they need to be prepared to have a child. You know, dedicate the next two decades of their lives to working together twenty-four–seven to putting another being into the world correctly. So doing it alters you emotionally by default, because if I were a man, Emma, there is a fair chance that you could get pregnant, and then…you know. So you need to feel like your life has changed because were those the circumstances, it could change. *Forever.* And don't say 'Well we're both girls.' It's all the same in nature's eyes."

I know all of this already. But I overanalyze so much sometimes that I forget to keep my spirit in the equation. "I still miss my virginity."

She kisses me again. "I know, darling, I know. But you know what? You've only lost your virginity in one sense in the word. I once heard a doctor say that you, as a woman, are a virgin until you let a man enter you with his penis. And you've never done that. If you really are a lesbian and not bi—"

"I'm a lesbian, Amy."

"—so you probably never will. So you'll always be a virgin, sweetie, always."

"But that's not how I view virginity."

"But your view may change, or if it doesn't, I assure you that you will adjust to your new body, which isn't really new at all."

"And what if I'm raped?" I clench my teeth against the question that will dig so deeply into Amy she might break down right in front of me. I expect her to cry, or gasp, or *something,* but she's just silent for a long moment before letting out a tiny laugh and speaking again.

"Your virginity is more than just physical. It's mental also. If a man rapes you, he has done something to you that no one deserves. And since your losing your virginity is something you should decide and something that you should be ready to do, he can't take it from you by just raping you. The only way you can lose it is if you give consent to sex. That's the only way. Take it from someone who knows, love. I lost my virginity last night too. To you."

"Oh, Amy!" I throw my arms around her neck, shocked at how far she's come, how much confidence she's gotten back since we met. The pre-me Amy would never have said something like that.

"One more thing about that, Emma. You know how people say that virgins are beautiful and pure, the white flowers and wedding gowns and all? And that once you've had sex, you're desanctified, you're no longer pure? Even if your first time was with someone you truly loved?"

"Yeah?"

"Well that's total crap. Why do they want to make love sound so…evil? So *wretched?* Why does society treat sex like some kind of murder? Emma, what could be more pure than two people loving and caring for each other forever? What could be purer than them becoming one, sharing themselves with each other? What?"

I shrug. She kisses my lips and puts hers to my ear.

"Love is the purest, most beautiful thing there is, baby. Every time you make love with someone you know you love with all your heart and soul, someone you would die for—every time you have sex with that person, Emma, you're becoming more pure, whiter, brighter. You're becoming an angel. When you were coming last night—when I was holding you and kissing you and loving you, and you were at that point—did you feel dirty? Or did you feel beautiful?"

"I felt…I felt like we were both in heaven."

"And there is nothing impure about heaven. If a virgin is a girl who is pure, you're more of a virgin than you have ever been." She sits back. "The sex we had, the sex we felt…that was the most beautiful thing in existence."

"Yeah," I squeak in agreement.

She kisses my head, right above my ear.

"I wouldn't change it though. I'm glad we did it. It's almost as though, with all the pain and anguish that's been eating away at us, our lovemaking sort of…cleansed us. Remember how I started crying?"

"Yeah."

"They were tears of joy, love for you, good feeling, all that stuff. But they were also releasing the pain that has been building up. Remember—remember when I came?"

Even though the porch light has gone out, I know she's smiling. "Yeah. You should have heard yourself weep."

"Because it was as though your entering me opened a window in my soul, and all of the pain flew out. I felt so much better as I fell asleep in your arms, like I had been reborn. So I guess I sort of feel like having sex with you was good for me, and I guess, if given the chance to go back and change it, I wouldn't." *I think you'll very soon come to realize that that experience did more for you than you know.* My eyes widen. It was just a dream. But it makes so much sense. Is it possibly not a mere coincidence?

"I think it may have done the same for me. Whatever it did, it purified my opinions of sex." She kisses my head again. "It doesn't mean torture so much anymore. It means you."

"Amy?" I ask, lifting my head.

"Yes?"

"I wonder…see, I had this dream a bit earlier. I saw my mother. She held me and comforted me and you know what she told me?"

"What?"

"She told me that I would realize what I just did. That our lovemaking did more for me than I thought. I don't really believe that dreams are anything more than just meaningless thoughts that run through your mind. Do you?"

She thinks for a second. "No."

"No?"

"I don't think dreams are just meaningless thoughts. I think they're more of a gateway to other universes, those we cannot touch physically. I mean, all science can show is that they're meaningless data in our heads, but, you know, those tests are earthly and carried out by waking scientists. There's only so much they can prove. Maybe in some dreams, our spirits leave our bodies and visit different places. Sometimes I wonder…sometimes I wonder if dreams are how humans visit heaven."

"Really?"

"Other times, I suppose, they give us the full picture of…what's the word?…turmoil, I guess, that we face. You know, without the outside world to really distract you. Of course, those are only theories I have."

I nod. "That's an interesting point."

"I love you, baby." She begins stroking my hair affectionately and we lie in each other's arms, touching very intimately at times, not speaking but just enjoying each other's bodies, for what was probably well over thirty minutes.

Chapter Thirty-Nine

Emma

Everyone says that being in love can lift you into heaven or burn you in hell. But I wonder if anyone else feels the pain I'm going through worrying about Amy. I know that many, many people worry about the lives of their loved ones, but I wonder how many people find the person they love facing brutal death on one side and a monster stealing their soul on the other. Amy is a sweet, innocent girl, and my father and stepmother want to kill her because they think she tried to kill me. The vampires that surround her want to take her soul so she will be like them. The mere thought of either happening to her sends me reeling.

All I want is to be with her. For her to be safe, for the two of us to be together. Is that really so much to ask?

I've tried everything, time and again, to convince Robert and Jaquelina of Amy's innocence: reason, pleading, even screaming and threatening, but to no avail except almost landing myself grounded. It's been three weeks since that afternoon when I found out they're planning to kill her, but they haven't taken action yet because they aren't sure where she is or how to hunt vampires without leaving us alone in the house.

Unfortunately, the next night, only two nights after Amy and I first had sex, they find that opportunity. Right after dinner,

Kristina takes Jill to a movie that Annie doesn't want to see, and I know better than to leave Robert and Jaquelina here at night. I'd think they'd want us all out of the house before they went vampire hunting, but I stay downstairs, just in case.

As I lie on the couch, trying to read *Anna Karenina* as an English assignment, my eyes begin to droop from the profound exhaustion I've experienced lately. *No,* I think, fighting to stay conscious as I begin to lose my sense of reality and the objects around the room became meaningless dream-like swirls of color and form. *I can't go to sleep. I need to watch to make sure Robert and Jaquelina don't leave.*

But the darkness begins closing in, and it's becoming harder and harder to bring myself back into reality every time I slip. *Must stay awake,* I keep telling myself, but it hardly takes effect as that sentence, too, becomes an element of my dreamland as I forget everything and slide rapidly into unconsciousness.

I wake with a start. I didn't have any dreams; it was just pure blackness. Now I realize I'm in the basement—how on earth did I get down here? Remembering everything within a split second, I bolt upright and check my watch.

Eight thirty. Oh no.

I don't think. I react. I rocket off the sofa; Annie's at the desk by the stairs, textbook open.

"Annie!"

"Eh?" She turns the page, leaning on her elbow wearily.

"Where are Robert and Jaquelina?"

"They went on a walk, and put us down here for safety."

"*What?* When?"

"They left about twenty minutes ago."

"Oh…" I feel my head spin for a moment.

"Emma?"

"Oh..." I shake my head rapidly and launch myself up the steps and to the closet under the stairs where I wrench on my sneakers. Not even bothering with a coat, I blast to my feet and speed like a bullet into the dark, cool night.

Amy

Something awful is going to happen. I can feel it as I try to go to sleep in my coffin. I don't know what, but it's going to happen, soon. I pray that whatever it is, it doesn't involve my Emma.

I'm restless the entire day. I try to sleep, but I can't. I just can't shake the feeling that something is wrong. What's coming? Does it have to do with what happened with Jason and Elizabeth? I grip my crucifix tightly, asking God to protect Emma and me. When it's finally safe to go out, I materialize from my grave as quickly as possible.

I don't even see what happens.

Pain rips through my spine as I'm forced against something hard. A powerful hand is clutching my neck, holding me to my stone. Two other hands take hold of my legs. I struggle, but they have a strong grip. I can barely see, but I can smell the life. Two humans are holding me down. I try desperately to re-enter my coffin, but, as I'm in physical contact with humans, I can't. Another vampire hindrance. If you're touching a human being or another vampire, you can't return to your coffin. I've always hated it because of what...that monster...is able to do to me as a result.

"You almost killed our daughter," a male voice seethes. "You almost killed her."

I shake my head as best I can. "No, I didn't."

"You were lying next to her when we found her, lying unconscious on her bedroom floor. She had lost so much blood, so much spirit, her body was reduced to almost nothing. The doctors were able to save her, but she came so close to death. And *you* did it to her."

Then it strikes me, and I know who these people are. Robert and Jaquelina.

I feel the sudden presence of a cross. Oh, God. It's what Emma warned me of. They're going to kill me. Despite my desperate need to die, tears fill my eyes. They pool quickly and begin to fall down my face.

"She almost died. You almost killed her," Jaquelina says.

I try my hardest to shake my head. "No-no, I didn't—" I choke, trying my best to pry loose the hand around my neck. "It was—someone else—the same one who killed me—" I try to get my crucifix from my pocket and show it to them to prove my innocence, but I can't reach my pocket.

"You dirty little liar," Jaquelina sneers. "You toyed with her, tempted her, chewed her up, and spit her out." Robert presses on my neck harder, choking me off.

"There's only one place for monsters like you," Robert spits. "It's called hell." With that, he reaches for something with his free hand and I feel a poke on my chest, right over my heart. Fear shoots through my body. A stake.

"No…" I gasp. "Please no…oh, God, mercy…"

The hands on my legs release me and, a few seconds later, hold my shoulders firmly against the grave. The hold on my neck eases away and the stake hovers a little as the one holding it moves, undoubtedly for the hammer. Tears stream down my face. Not here. Not now. Emma still needs me.

But it's too late. I sense Robert lift the hammer. I close my eyes against the pain that's about to shock through me. My life is going to end, this time for real. Good-bye, Emma darling. I'll love you forever and ever. My dear.

"*Stop!*" a girl calls from far off. A second later, the point of the stake lifts. "*Get off of her!*"

"Emma!" Robert gasps, astonished. "What're you—"

"Stop!" Emma hollers again.

I open my eyes. Everything's a blur of forms. A cry of pain and, not a minute later, the hold on my shoulders lifts. I scramble to my feet, my eyes focusing.

"Amy!" Emma cries. "*Run!*"

I hesitate. "*Now!*" Emma insists. "Before it's too late!"

"But—"

"Damn it, Amy, *go! Now!*" The exact same thing I said to her when I was holding Jason off so long ago.

I take off, weaving through gravestones, pushing against time to reach the back entrance. It looms ahead, the darkness of the forest threatening beyond. But I'm not going anywhere—as soon as I pass out of the cemetery, I turn back and try to see them. It's dark, but Emma's voice tells the entire story.

"She didn't do it!" she screams. "You can't kill her! I love her!"

"Emma, you—"

"No! She's not like the rest of them! If you kill her, you'll have to kill me too!"

That's all I hear before a pair of strong arms grasps me and begins pulling me away.

"Hello, Amy," Madam Noctis whispers. She holds me just as she has so many times before, my back pressing against her chest. "I've finally found you, and I'm afraid I can't wait any longer. I heard about what happened between you, Jason, and Elizabeth. I must say I'm surprised at you, but I wouldn't have put it past you not to kill him. I know you're incomplete, and I am going to finish you. Your succulent blood will be a warm relief from all the mediocre, average stuff I've been experiencing."

"No!" I cry, struggling. I shut my eyes tightly as she leans over my neck. *No. Emma needs me!* If Madam Noctis succeeds, I can't be with her until my spirit is freed. And that could take an eternity. And what if Emma tries to do it and Madam Noctis turns her?

I feel Madam Noctis push my hair back and lean in all the way. "You will thank me for this, Amy," she whispers, her lips slithering like a snake over my neck with the words.

"Please no…" I beg. "Please…"

"See you on the other side, Amy." It's all I knew before her fangs pierce my throat, bringing back searing memories of pain and horror that time had never erased.

Chapter Forty

Amy

The sharp fire is more overwhelming than I ever knew. My screams tear my vocal cords apart, and I let them, perhaps hoping someone will hear me, perhaps trying to drown the pain in them, perhaps trying to make Madam Noctis let go of me. Or perhaps I'm just willing myself to die.

I feel my body plunge slowly into depression, weakness, darkness. I'm losing my soul. She's sucking it away, and with it, my ability to love Emma. What will become of her when I am complete?

It continues forever, surrounding me, engulfing me, stealing away my soul. It's all pain. Pain, pain, pain.

"Oh my God! Get off her, you monster! *Get off! Now!*"

The smell of garlic penetrates my senses—*revolting*. But at the same time, Madam Noctis lets go and begins screaming as though she's been thrown into a fire. As the pain in my neck dulls, I fall, losing consciousness as I hit the cool, dark earth.

When I open my eyes, all I can see are silhouettes, struggling, screaming, falling. I try to move, but my arms and legs won't budge. Both Madam Noctis and Emma shout and scream as they attack each other; finally, the taller one forces the other against a tree and Emma's shrill screams pierce the night like the echoes of a million banshees as the taller form thrusts its face into its opponent's neck. I shut my eyes for a second and do the last thing in my power to help my sweet love—I pray.

Oh, please, God, Jesus, please. Don't let this happen, don't let this monster win...please, please help us...you can't let this happen, you can't let this demon take both of our souls and leave our bodies for hell...please, please save us, even just one of us, even just her, please...

As a few other forms burst through the trees, a new scream, one shrill enough to waken the dead, slashes through the air. The taller one falls to its knees, writhing. The smaller pushes off the tree and the newcomers close around it. It breaks free and approaches the dying creature lying on the ground.

Emma stares for a moment at Madam Noctis before yanking the stake from her body, hurling it into the darkness, and approaching me and touching my face with her cool, soft hand.

"Amy..."

"Oh, Emma..."

I'm not sure what all happens next; I think Emma tries to carry me, but I seem to keep falling. Then Jaquelina is reaching for me and I feel my body shrink back in terror. She says something about not hurting me, then Emma smiles at me sadly. "They won't hurt you, love."

The world spin again, and soon the dark forms swirl together like Gothic cotton candy and thrust me into darkness.

Emma

The night air tickles my face as I speed through the woods, praying I won't veer off course. The dirt thuds beneath my feet, and the moon shines on my face.

My breath soon grows ragged; I'm not exactly a marathon runner. But no matter how much I gasp, sputter and choke, I keep pushing myself to run faster. There's no time to wait for my lungs. There isn't even time for me to sprint down the hill, praying Amy is all right and that I'm not too late.

I run in through the back entrance and race toward the center. What I see when I approach her grave is two dark shapes, probably Robert and Jaquelina, kneeling on the ground. I don't stop running. If there is still a chance, if I'm not only a minute too late, I can't waste it.

"Stop!" I hear myself cry as I lunge at the dark silhouettes. "Get off of her!" I collide with them, and not half a second later, I'm struggling to hold Robert back while trying to kick Jaquelina to make her let go of Amy.

"Emma!" Robert hollers, appalled. "What're you—"

He doesn't have a chance to finish. Because as I struggle, my knee flies up involuntarily and hits him right between the legs.

Howling, he doubles over, and I exploit the opportunity by racing over and pulling Jaquelina off Amy. Jaquelina tries to shake me off, and the scream escapes my mouth. "Stop! Amy, run!"

Amy's standing now, but she doesn't move. What the hell is she doing? "Now!" I shriek. "Before it's too late!" She still doesn't move—"damn it, Amy, *go! Now!*" She hesitates another second, then splits. I continue to struggle with the two monsters that I'm supposed to call my family.

"Emma—" Recovered, Robert pulls me off Jaquelina. I push him back and lunge for her.

"Emma, what has gotten into you?" Jaquelina asks.

"I'll handle her!" Robert shouts, seizing my wrist. "You go, Jaquelina! Don't let that beast get away!"

"No!" I scream. "You can't hurt her! She didn't do it! You can't kill her! I love her!"

"Emma, you—"

I cut Jaquelina off. "No! She's not like the rest of them! If you kill her, you'll have to kill me too!"

A scream penetrates the night from behind us. "Amy," I gasp, wrenching free of Robert's grasp, yanking at the first weapon I see—a necklace of garlic—and taking off toward the back gate.

"Come back here, Emma!" Robert roars. "Come back here this instant!" I can hear him start to chase me.

Then I hear Jill's voice. It comes out a frantic screech. "No! Stop!" She must grab him, because I hear struggle ensue behind me. But I don't even glance back; Amy's wailing and screaming sends fear and adrenaline coursing through every nerve of my body and I just keep running. Across the cemetery, through the gate, and into the forest.

The scene that greets me nearly knocks me from my body. Madam Noctis is holding her tightly, her face to her throat. Her long silver hair falls over her face, but I can still see the blood trickling down Amy's neck.

Her blood. Her life. Her soul. I feel my head go faint. This can't be happening. It can't.

Madam Noctis is completing her.

Chapter Forty-One

Emma

I don't think. I can't think. I can only react. "Oh my *God! Get off her, you monster!*" I wail. "*Get off! Now!*" I fly to them, the garlic necklace clutched tightly in my hand.

I have to be careful. I can't hit Amy. I dive for Madam Noctis's ankles and wrap it around her right one, and it burns her skin like fire. Screaming, she stumbles backward, dropping Amy at my side. Amy moans in pain and lies still.

I jump to my feet and, moving like lightning, toss the strand around her neck. She falls to the ground, writhing in pain. I turn frantically, trying to decide what to do. There Amy lies, seemingly unconscious; I hurry over and I'm just bending to pick her up when Madam Noctis, having freed herself from the burning misery that is the garlic, grabs me and flings me away. I barely have time to recover before she's on top of me. I push her back as much as I can and knee her between the legs as hard as possible. It doesn't have nearly the effect it would have were she a man, but it hurts enough for her to stumble back, giving me time to stand.

"You miserable little wretch," she spits, her hand barely missing my face. I try to slap her back, but she's too quick.

"Why can't you just leave us alone?" I shriek. "Why do you keep torturing us like this? What have we ever done to you?"

She doesn't reply, just takes another swipe at me. I leap back and desperately throw a kick in her direction.

"*Robert! Jaquelina!*" I scream. "*Help me!*"

The words have barely left my mouth when Madam Noctis forces me against a tree and pulls me to the ground, and in a moment of fleeting terror I remember I took off my cross for swim practice at school—and forgot to put it back on. As I hit the earth, I spot what looks like the stake Amy used to kill Jason lying near the base of the tree—the other vampires must have thrown it back here. I reach for it desperately as she puts her face to my neck and whispers in my ear.

"You strange couple of stupid little girls," she seethes. "Fancy thinking you, a mere human and an incomplete vampire child, could defeat me! Me, the woman who not even two adults could manage to kill! You're both a couple of miserable fools, and by the coming dawn, you will both be sucking the blood of others to survive, just like the rest of us, and soon you will both learn to love it, to bask in the beauty of a life of seduction and sex. Good-bye, Emma." Her dreadful fangs pierce my flesh and I screech in anguish, but, though the pain of her bloodsucking is hellish in its severity, I manage to keep my mind on my attempt to reach the stake. It seems the only hope for Amy and me. I stretch as much as I possibly can as she begins to suck in the awful manner with which I am now so familiar. Its splintery wood dances on the tips of my fingers; I push as hard as I can and twitch my fingers to get it to roll toward me.

The wood is cool in my palms. Relief surges throughout my body. I have it. The pain of everything she's done to us in the past and of what she's doing to me now driving every move—the images of Amy's beautiful body, broken and tormented by the fear of her; the ghastly look on Amy's face as she sucked my blood; the constant sexual assault and rape of Amy—I force the stake under her chest and strike with as much force as possible, channeling all my energy into the blow.

Direct hit. She lets out the scream that seems not only to echo her physical torture but also the forgotten cries of the hundreds of lost spirits she has held captive. She stumbles back as blood pours from the wound; I jump up and hold the stake tightly until her cries lose energy and cease, her struggling stops, and her body lies still. I hold that stake until I'm sure of what Amy and I have dreamed of for so long. Madam Noctis is dead.

And that's it. Her face falls from the hard, terrifying expression of a dying monster to the soft, peaceful one of a young woman, barely over twenty-four.

And, for the very first time, I see something new in Madam Noctis, something I didn't think I'd ever see, something I have been unable to even imagine. Innocence. Innocence and beauty, not haunting beauty, loving beauty, not unlike the one I see in the face of the girl I love so much, the one that still lies motionless a few yards from me. I can't believe I'm still staring at Madam Noctis, the woman who tortured us, raped us, fed on us…and then it hits me. This isn't Madam Noctis. This is Victoria. Victoria Regina Noctis, the caring, loving woman who had to kill her own mother and sister and was then manipulated into someone she wasn't with her own pain. I see it now. I see, to its fullest extent, the horror that vampirism is, just how much it victimizes the human race with its own selfish need to bring hell upon the earth. And a question blows through my mind as I suddenly remember my studies of ancient civilizations' torturous customs, of slavery, of World War II, of the Holocaust, the wars and genocides that rage to this day: do you really need to be a vampire to carry out hell? Perhaps vampirism is merely an exaggerated symbol of what humans are capable of doing, of what they have been doing since they began to evolve.

I feel tears fill my eyes as the look of innocence on the woman's face becomes more and more prominent. Poor Regina. Poor Amy. Poor everyone. Everyone on earth, victimized by the horrific side that we can never get rid of, no matter how hard we may try. In a burst of desperate fury, I yank the stake from Regina's chest and chuck it as far away as I possibly can. The fury quickly dies, leaving me burdened with a feeling of emptiness and futility in my soul. I stand, shaky and cold.

The next thing I know, Jaquelina's arms are tight around me; Jill squeezes her arms around my belly and weeps. Robert wipes some of the blood off my neck with his hand and kisses my head.

"Oh, Emma, oh, darling, darling baby…" Jaquelina sobs, her face buried in my hair. Robert pulls us both close to him and I feel him slowly rocking me back and forth.

"I love you, Emma," he says softly, his strong hand rubbing my shoulder. "I love you so much."

I want to fall apart now too; I want to break down and let all of it out, all the spite, all the anger, all the pain of the past and the horrors of the present. Just cry it out in Jaquelina's shirt, cry and cry and cry until my soul is cleansed and I can start anew.

But I don't. Instead I push gently through the crowd of my family and approach my girlfriend, my darling, darling Amy.

"Emma—" Jaquelina calls from behind.

Annie shushes her. "Let her go to her."

I touch Amy's face lightly, horror at her weakness piercing through me. This is my Amy? This is the beautiful, strong girl who's always been there for me, who saved my life many times from the terrors of her own world? This weak, pale girl with sad, vacant eyes?

"Amy..." Her skin is colder than usual.

The poor thing struggles to acknowledge me. "Emma..."

"Oh, Amy, don't worry baby, don't you worry," I whisper, sliding my arms under her back with some difficulty. "We'll get you safe." With heavy strain on my arms and back, I heave her to my feet and take a few cautious steps.

Amy's dead weight is almost too much for me, but I manage to balance her somewhat in my arms and I carry her like a baby, like my baby, a few steps. Then I fall again and find I cannot rise; I'm too weak to carry her. I hold her hand to my face and sob desperately.

Then I feel a loving hand on my shoulder; Jaquelina kneels beside me and reaches for Amy's hand. Terror flashes through Amy's eyes, but Jaquelina shushes her like she were her own.

"No, no, don't worry, darling, we won't hurt you." Amy looks to me desperately, and I let out a quick breath and smile as best I can.

"They won't hurt you, love."

Amy relaxes and her eyes roll back in her head. Her eyelids fall closed and her face relaxes. I dive for her hand. "Amy? Amy? *Amy? Oh, God!*" I scream into the sky, desperate tears pouring from my eyes. I can't believe this. I can't believe this is how it ends, after all we've been through, after all we've fought for and given our lives for—this is our ending?

"Shhh," Jaquelina coos, putting her hand on my cheek and pulling me into her arms. "Shhh, shhh, shhh, shhh." She rocks me back and forth as I sob uncontrollably, letting all the tears, all the pain of my past, all the anger and spite, all of it, out of my spirit.

"Ohhh," I moan. She strokes my hair.

"There, there, Emma, get it out. Get it all out." She pulls me to my feet and Kristina helps support me as I shake violently, barely able to stand. Robert bends down and gently picks up Amy. Jaquelina and Kristina help me as I take a few shaky steps and begin to stumble across the lawn and Robert carries Amy carefully—if I didn't know better, I'd say almost lovingly—through the cemetery and up the hill.

Hell must be freezing. They finally believe me.

When we get home, I race for the bathroom and barely make it to the toilet before the acidic bile is retching out of my mouth. My stomach and esophagus convulse severely and I can hardly breathe as the violent puking takes over my body. When I finish, I notice Jill sitting next to me, her hand on my back. Her is hair frazzled and her skin dirty. Robert is in the doorway, holding Amy. I stand with some difficulty and help him lay her gently on the bathmat.

"I'm going to get something for her," he whispers, kissing me. "Don't you worry."

I nod. Her blood shines bright red in the light shed by the sconces on the wall. Instinctively, I put my hand to the area, and the blood smears all over my fingers. It's warm with Amy's life, the little warmth her spirit provides her. And it won't stop pouring from the wound.

"Oh God oh no please no God no…" I can't breathe and can't think. My hand yanks forcefully on the end of the toilet paper and at least three feet fly off the roll. I wipe off her neck, then press the stuff onto the wound, willing the bleeding to stop

"Emma—" Jill says, trying to figure out how to help. I ignore her. I need to get this flow stopped. That's all I care about. Soon the toilet paper is red through and through, and I have to reach for another piece. "Oh, my God," I whisper. Will she die? What if she already has? I'm so terrified. My love. My dear, sweet Amy. I'm willing to sit with her all night, watching, praying. Praying that she'll be all right. Praying I'll get to see her, laugh with her, and kiss her again.

Two more balls of toilet paper sail off the roll and turn bright red before Robert re-enters with a damp cloth.

"Here, love," he says, handing it to me. Sniveling, I place it over Amy's bite and hold it on, applying as much pressure as I can without hurting her. When I finally manage to get the flow under control, Robert kneels by me and takes the rag, placing another over my neck and slowly wiping the drying blood from my skin. I cringe in pain but do not pull away.

"That was her then? Madam Noctis?" he whispers. I nod.

"She got both of us this time."

He's silent for a moment. "How about the living room?" I nod hopelessly and he picks her up again. I flip the light switch and Jill and I follow them out.

The couch is soft, cozy, a welcome relief after all I've been through. Robert lays Amy on the couch, with me, the upper half of her body resting gracefully in my arms. Jill sits at the other end, Amy's feet resting in her lap. Robert pushes my hair out of my face and kisses my forehead as Jaquelina brings in a glass of water.

Desperation surges through me as I stare at Amy's pale, unmoving face. She's lost so much blood. What can I do? I can cut myself, perhaps slit my wrist and drip the blood into her mouth.

But if I do restore enough to her stream, I'll probably bleed to death before I can stop my own flow. And I can't do that to her. I can't return her to her awful existence by killing myself, the one true light in her world. Since a nonfatal cut would never be enough to restore her, I have no choice but to hold onto her sweet body and pray with all my heart and soul.

I lean my head on her chest and tightly close my eyes. This can't be happening. It can't be true. This was how it's all going to end? This is the answer to my desperate question and frantic praying? No. No. Never. I'm going to break down. Why does it have to happen like this? *Why?*

"Amy…" I whisper. "Oh, Amy, please wake up, baby…"

She doesn't even twitch. I moan in despair and lean down to lay a gentle kiss upon her beautiful lips. They are as cold as ice; I kiss them tenderly yet forcefully, as if willing my life to flow through the connection and into her. I don't pull back for a long time, not wanting our lips to ever separate. I feel that the moment they do, I'll lose her forever.

"It-it's all my fault!" I sob. Jill looks up.

"What?"

"If I hadn't started that fight with her, if I hadn't gone out looking for her…if I hadn't been attacked, forcing Amy to reveal herself to Madam Noctis—"

"Hold on, hold on!" Jill cuts in. "None of this is your fault, Emma! Stop blaming yourself, right now!"

"But—"

"No. It is *not* your fault, Emma. Amy would have revealed herself anyway when she saved Annie. None of this is your fault, so don't bring yourself more grief than you already have! Otherwise your heart will explode!"

I stare at Amy's beautiful face, so pale, so sad.

"I don't want her to die," I whimper. "She can't die. She can't."

Jill scoots closer to me and takes my hand. "There, Emma, there."

"I love her…I love her so much."

"Oh, I know. Dear God, I know."

"That night…that night we…you know…made love," I struggle to say, "was one of the most amazing, beautiful nights of my life. Just to feel her…feel her so close to me that we were almost one…oh God, Jill, it's just that…she's the most amazing, beautiful woman I have ever met."

Jill nods me on.

"She is so amazing and kind, Jill; she gives me care I had never before known, and, no matter how bad I feel, she talks to me and holds me and somehow soothes my spirit. No problem is too trivial for her, and…and…oh!" I start weeping. Jill puts her arm around my back.

"She doesn't deserve this! She deserves a long, happy life! With a lover, and a daughter, and a great career, and a big house with flowers and big windows to let the sunlight in—" I can hardly control myself now. "—to let it shine in on her beautiful face and—and—make her happy!"

Jill sits with me for a long time, trying her best to comfort me. But nothing she does works; the only thing that soothes me is the lamentation that is slowly melting the great wall of pain I've bore for nearly a year, eventually running my emotions out and leaving my sleepy. At some point, Jaquelina comes in and turns the lights way down before retreating to the family room. Without even realizing it, I fall into a soft doze with Amy in my arms and Jill holding onto me, giving me support through her presence.

I was sitting on Aunt Maggie's couch, flipping through the channels on the muted TV. Jill was leaning on me, hugging my arm. The listings were so bad tonight. Dumb shows, dumb ads, dumb movies. So much for quality television.

The phone let out its shrill squeal. Kristina got up from the dining table and Jill and I listened as she picked it up in the kitchen.

"Hello, Hayes residence…no, no, this is her niece, Kristina Levesque…yes, uh-huh, Celina is my mother…"

Jill and I whipped around and Annie looked up from her term paper. Natasha, who was knitting in the recliner in the corner of the living room, got up and approached the kitchen hesitantly. Aunt Maggie emerged from the downstairs bathroom. Kristina was leaning against the counter, her legs crossed. She frowned as she listened intently to the voice on the phone, then her eyes widened and the receiver slipped from her hand. We could faintly hear the person on the other line calling out.

"Ma'am! Ma'am! Are you still there?"

Like a robot, Kristina reached for the dangling phone and put it back to her ear. "Y-yes, I'm here…yes…yes…yes…okay, hang on." Kristina turned the phone over to Aunt Maggie, who was listening in the corner of the dining room. She traded places with Aunt Maggie and buried her head in her hands.

"Hello?…Yes, this is she…what is it?…Oh, no. Oh, oh, oh no." Aunt Maggie took a shaky breath and I saw Kristina's shoulders spasm in a sob. "Yes? Yes. Yes. No. No. Uh-huh. I have the number. Okay. Thank you. Bye." Aunt Maggie placed the receiver back in its stand and turned a fragile face to Natasha.

"Margaret?"

Aunt Maggie voiced what the rest of us had figured out. "She's gone." Then her thin mask broke and Natasha caught her as she fell, heartbroken, to the floor. Aunt Maggie's breakdown caused Kristina to release herself, too, and Jill put her face in her arms and heaved a few isolated sobs. Annie had a look of deep grief in her eyes, the one you might see on a person who has been grieving over a lost loved one for a few weeks. I sat, frozen with shock. The blanket of reality didn't fall over me until an hour later when I was holding Jill in bed as she wept. Then, out of nowhere, it dawned on me that my mother really was gone. That, for the first time in my life, this world was revolving without her *breath. And I couldn't believe it was still turning. Jill and I shared deep grief well into the night.*

The next morning I couldn't look at Natasha's Bible, which sits, with a few other relevant books, between bookends on my nightstand. I couldn't look at crosses or even the Star of David. I couldn't think about religion anymore, and suddenly it seemed religious icons were everywhere—on billboards, in bookstores, at home, in the mall, at the park, even in the car. My soul was sheared and all my faith had vanished in that one sleepless night. The funeral was scheduled for Thursday, but I was sure Thursday would never come. Time had suddenly begun to move so slowly. I felt myself falling quickly, slipping into a state of conscious unconsciousness, and I didn't try to stop it. The world was fading, becoming a nightmare. And I honestly didn't care.

Chapter Forty-Two

Emma

As the night goes on, a new dread overtakes me.

Sunrise.

There is no time to get Amy back to her grave. We won't be able to dig it up in time. We have a basement that is mostly surrounded by soil; will it be sufficient? I decide it's my only option, so I carry her down two flights of stairs to the cold basement bathroom that I hate so much.

Fear tugs at my heart as the seconds tick by. I'm terrified she's dead already. Since her heart doesn't beat, I can't take a pulse. All I can do is stay with her and hope for the better.

Hope for what? I think bitterly. *If she isn't gone, she may stay like this for a really long time.* What am I to do? I cry at the very thought. I don't want to know. I don't want to think about it. All I want is to have my girlfriend back.

And, after a long night of uncertainty, the hope comes to me. After I've calmed down, the desperation has melted to stomach-turning fear, and my senses have started functioning normally, I begin to notice the unusual warmth around Amy's body, and the second I feel it, I know she's still with me. I'm so relieved, I could cry out, but terror still plagues my heart. I bury my face in her hair and pray, even though I don't believe in God.

As the minutes drag on, each one more terrifying than the next, the mingled hope and fear seem to magnify. I have never felt so emotional in my life, not even when Mama died. I stay next to her, holding her and praying for her, all night.

Eventually, Jill comes down and tells me the sky is starting to lighten. She stayed up all night for me, in case I needed help. When I expressed my concerns about the sun and told her I was going into the basement, she agreed to stay upstairs and watch the sky for me.

"Ohhhh…" I put my face in my hands; I feel like I'm going to puke. Jill places her hand on my shoulder.

"It's all right, Emma. I'm sure that no matter what happens, you and Amy will

never be separated. I'm, sure that no matter what happens to her body, Amy will be fine. It will be all right. It will be all right. Do you want me to continue to watch the sky?"

I nod; she hurries back upstairs. And a moment later, the warmth around Amy stops flowing.

My heart races. My blood pressure might have broken a scale. Is she gone? I'm sure she is, but I can't admit it to myself. I can't bring myself to face the truth. I cling to her, unwilling—no, *unable*—to set her down. This is how I held her while she still lived. I don't ever want to let that go.

I poke my head out the door; the stairwell glows with the pink of the sunrise. More tears fall over my face; I pull Amy back into my arms and kiss her again. I must stay there for fifteen to twenty minutes, holding someone I'm sure has died.

But as I stroke her hair gently, praying to that nonexistent God that she's still alive, I feel her twitch a little. My heart stops, and I stare intently at her face. She lies, silent and motionless, for another few minutes, then her eyelids flutter and open.

Her beautiful, glowing green eyes. Staring right at my face and quickly filling with recognition and love.

"Amy!" I pull her up into a tight embrace. "I thought I'd lost you!"

We lie together, talking and kissing, and all I can think about is how happy I am to have her back, to have never lost her, in fact—until she asks about the time. Then the reality of our situation come crashing back to me and I groan as my head spins. Fearfully, I explain our dilemma as gently as possible.

"Take me out there," she says, after a moment of silence.

"What? But Amy—"

"Please, Emma." A look of mingled sadness and joy overtakes her face. "Please."

My lip trembles. How can I take her out there where the sun might burn her to death? How can I do that to the girl I love?

"Please. Do it. For me."

"What if—what if—the sun burns you?"

"I'll take that chance."

I bite my lip and frown in fear. What if she still has a chance? I don't want to destroy that chance by taking her out into the sun.

Stop, a voice in my mind commands. *You know she hasn't got a chance. And by the sound of it, she knows it, too. Why deny her final wish for such an impossible hope?*

It's painfully difficult. I almost can't do it. I begin to go numb. I can't imagine seeing her burn, her beautiful body turning to ash at the mercy of the sun.

"Emma," she sighs. "Emma, it—it won't happen, my dear."

But still I worry.

"Please," she whispers. "Please."

"If you do burn," I begin tentatively, hiccupping breaths at the end, "will a blanket stop it?"

She stares into my eyes, then slowly nods. "Yeah. As long as it doesn't let any sun through." Gradually, weakly, I lift her off the floor and carry her upstairs and out the front door, into the front yard, stopping only to retrieve the heavy comforter from the closet under the basement stairs.

Just in case.

The sky is astounding, like an artist's palette spilled across a pool of water. As soon as we pass through the door and her eyes light upon the many vivid colors splashed across the clouds, Amy utters a little cry and I pull her body into mine and squeeze my eyes shut to force out lingering tears. The air is painfully still; not even a tiny breeze graces us with its cool breath. Amy's incredibly heavy, and I finally stumble to a rest in the grass by the edge of the gravel. I kneel gently and set her on the cool grass, then lie down and slip my arms around her body, under her arms, and my legs around hers.

Amy clutches my hand and pulls it to her lips, giving my fingers kisses that leave a sweet dampness in their wake. "Wow." Her voice is growing weaker, her body trembling with pain, with death. "I'd forgotten how beautiful it is. I-I've only seen the first few light blue stripes in the east. Never this."

I wrap my arms around her and bury my face in her shirt. She kisses my head and I look up into her eyes, wanting to ask her the question that's been burning inside me for a while now but afraid of her reaction.

She reads it in my face. "What is it?"

I take a deep breath, force myself to say the words. "I want you to…I want you to bite me."

Her eyes widen in astonishment. "What? Why?"

"Because." I let out a sigh, remembering Madam Noctis's poisonous bite. "I've been bitten three times, and it's always been horrible. But you said it can be painless, wonderful even, and—and you told me once that because you love me so much biting me would probably be the most wonderful thing, and I want to give that gift to you."

She glances at the ground, thinking for a few moments. Finally she looks back to me. "Then come closer."

I oblige eagerly, leaning my head in a little more so her mouth is on my neck. She inhales deeply, kisses my throat a couple times, and then…

The pain of her bite is small, bittersweet, not unlike the pain I felt when she first entered my body only a few nights ago. What now feels like an eternity.

Her tongue, warm, hot even, tickles across my skin and when she takes her first suck, waves of excitement pour throughout, awakening nerves from my neck to the very tips of my toes—and *everywhere* in between. By the second suck, I already feel the way I did when she was making love to me—intense, eager, even a little ravenous. Every muscle inside me tightens and I feel my body almost convulse as she takes a final sip and then kisses the bite once, twice, three times.

"Wow," I manage, practically lost for words. "That was…wow. Just…" I don't finish my sentence; instead I kiss her, and the blood on her lips is bitter, but I don't care.

"You were right, Emma," she whispers. "I weakened myself without hope. I became too weak to remember life, to remember my spirit; I never really believed I could go to heaven, or whatever beauty is out there. But you gave me hope again. You reminded me to believe in myself."

I reach up and wipe away my tears, streaking them across the sides of my eyes.

"Emma!" She's staring joyfully at her hands, which are reflecting the brilliant hues of the sunrise. "I'm not burning! I'm not burning, Emma, look!" I realize then that the sun has come over the horizon, its rays shining brilliantly on a beautiful face that hasn't seen them in an eternity.

"Oh, God, Amy." My hand grips hers lightly like she's my lifeline.

"Emma," she sighs, "I can't just die here. I can't just leave you like this. Dying in your arms and making you return me to my grave…I can't do that to you." Her body is trembling in my arms. I can see that every second the strain to stay alive is harder and harder on her.

I shut my eyes tightly. No. I can't do this. I'm not strong enough. This can't happen. But when I open my mouth to speak, I voice my true reply to the hardest decision I'll ever have to make.

"No," I whimper. "No. Don't do that to yourself. The best gift you can give me is the one you have deserved all along: to be free." I feel myself choke up. I'm losing her.

"Emma." She stares at me with those soulful green eyes. "I know this will be difficult for you to believe, but you must understand that I will never, ever leave you, not even for a second. I will always be by your side. Promise me that whatever you do, you'll remember that and be happy."

I stop breathing. Making the promise would mean letting her go. It would mean that I would be accepting the fact that she's moving on. But isn't that what I want? Isn't that what we both want? And she isn't moving on from me. Just her life as a vampire. I nod. "I promise." She's still for a long time, not even daring to breathe. Tears fall out of her eyes and onto my chest. It's a long time before she speaks. "I promise, Amy."

"Thank God." And the next thing I know, she's kissing me. Her lips are so soft, so tender. "I love you, Emma. I'll love you forever. Nothing will ever change it."

I rub her back. "And I'll love you forever, Amy. I will. You mean everything to me. You gave me my first kiss. My first love." I weep into her shoulder. She runs her hand through my hair, sending warmth through my scalp.

"Emma…" she whispers. "Emma, listen. Keep everything that will remind you I'm still with you. Take my corset too. Keep it forever."

"O-okay." I heave a heavy sob and kiss her for what I know will be the final time.

She smiles sadly and utters her last words. "I love you, Emma. I love you so, s-s-so much."

"I love you too, darling." The tears are falling like a sad rain. "I love you too."

She continues to smile, her eyes casting a warm glow into mine. It surges through my blood and pours into my soul.

Then slowly, sadly but blissfully, her eyes close for the final time. The smile, the warmth, and the love remain frozen on her face. A warm breeze seems to come out of nowhere and blows my hair back and tickles and kisses my face.

"Amy…" I whisper. "Amy, Amy…" I shake her a little, but she doesn't even twitch. "Oh, Amy…Amy…" She is…is she really?…my lover, my friend…my Amy…is she really…dead?

I look to the sunrise; a front a few miles up is rapidly shaping and reshaping the clouds as they blow across the sky. The heavens are transforming, perhaps welcoming her arrival. The arrival of the most beautiful woman in the world. Her body lies in my arms, finally given the rest it has always deserved.

"Oh, Amy…" I breathe, squeezing her hand. I feel the truth begin to seep slowly through my skin.

She's gone.

Amy

There are no dreams. Just blackness. Long, drawn-out blackness. I float in it, live it, breathe it, knowing it will never end.

Yet it does, slowly fading into the shapes and colors of an unfamiliar room and a pale redheaded girl whose face is stained with a mixture of dried dirt, blood, and tears.

"Oh, Amy," she breathes. Fresh tears fill her deep cerulean eyes. "I thought I'd lost you."

I try to move my arms, but I'm too weak. I lie there as her tears began to fall down her face, creating rivers through the dirt. "Emma," I whisper. It's all I can manage at first. I want to lift my hand to her pained face, but it's like it's a sandbag. "Emma."

"Amy, uh-I—" She lets her mouth stay open, making those tiny vocal noises people use when they're lost for words.

My body feels so heavy. I can't remember anything that happened after Emma saved me from her parents...except pain.

"What happened?" I ask.

"I killed her."

"Who?"

"Madam Noctis. I wrapped garlic around her ankle, and when she let you go, I put it around her neck. We fought, and I got the stake that killed Jason and Elizabeth—it was lying nearby—and shoved it through her heart. She—she's gone, Amy. She will never hurt you again."

I smile. I don't even care. All that seems to matter is the moment. I'm with Emma. She's with me.

Then I spot her neck. The two bite marks are freshened near her collarbone. "She bit you!" I gasp weakly.

She cocks her head slightly. "Yeah. She was sucking my blood when I killed her."

"You killed her? Through all that miserable pain?"

She shrugs. "I guess."

I shake my head in amazement. "You are so strong, Emma." She's the strongest person I've ever known. I would never have been able to kill Madam Noctis while she was feeding on me.

Her pearly-white teeth show in the beautiful grin of relief and joy that brightens her face, and before I know it, her lips are against mine, and we're once again locked in the familiar embrace that nearly makes us one.

"Happy birthday, Amy," she whispers between kisses.

Happy birthday? Is it my thirty-eighth birthday already? Time has begun to move so fast for me.

"What time is it?" I ask her as we part. Fear falls over her face.

"The sun's coming up," she tells me. "I don't know what to do. I moved you into our basement. But...I don't know if it will be good enough."

I still can't move my arms. The fatigue is weighing on my body like bags of wet cement. "Take me out there," I whisper.

"What? But Amy—"

"Please, Emma." I don't know exactly what happened to me after Madam Noctis. But I know I'm not going to make it. I don't have enough blood inside me—and I don't have enough energy to replace it. There's no way I could get a transfusion—the hospital would know immediately something's abnormal about me—it wouldn't work, and besides, I don't want it to. I want to see the sun one last time, even if it does hurt me. But somehow I know that won't happen. "Please."

Her lip trembles. I feel a wave of sadness rush over my chest. How can I possibly tell her I'm dying, this time for real?

"Please," I plead. "Do it. For me."

"What if—what if—the sun burns you?"

"I'll take that chance."

She still hesitates, so I prod her a little more. "Emma. Emma, it—it won't happen, my dear. Please. *Please.*"

"If you do burn," I begin tentatively, hiccupping breaths at the end, "will a blanket stop it?"

I nod. "Yeah. As long as it doesn't let any sun through."

She bites her lip, then stands, slowly and with prolonged effort. My poor baby—obviously so exhausted. She carries me out of the bathroom, up the steps, through the living room, and out the front door.

Emma finally collapses with me on front lawn and puts her arms around me, wraps her legs with mine. I pull her hand to my mouth and kiss each of her warm fingers. She pulls me in closer and buries her face in my shirt.

My eyes bulge at the vibrant shades of orange and pink sprayed across the clouds. The sunrise has always been extraordinary, but today, it is magical. "Wow," I say. "I'd forgotten how beautiful it is. I-I've only seen the first few light blue stripes in the east. Never this." I feel her start crying again, kiss her head, and shift my eyes from the sky to her as she looks up. I see the great mix of joy, pain, love, confusion, and anger that lies just beyond those two blue orbs. It makes me want to cry. We inch closer to each other, and I notice a trace of deep longing in her eyes.

"What is it?" I ask her.

"I want you to…I want you to bite me."

Shock fires through my nerves. "What? Why?"

"Because." She sighs. "I've been bitten three times, and it's always been horrible. But you said it can be painless, wonderful even, and"—she takes a deep breath—"and you told me once that because you love me so much biting me would probably be the most wonderful thing, and I want to give that gift to you."

It occurs to me that if I bite her, I'll die with some of her blood in my body. And I'll have a tiny part of her with me for all eternity. My eyes cast to the ground, and I think about her soul. A few sucks will barely get anything, it'll go back to her immediately...and I'm much too weak, much too far from life, to lose control with her. A few sucks is all I'll be able to manage.

"Then come closer," I whisper. She moves as close as she possibly can, and I put my lips to her neck, right under her ear. The heat radiating from her skin and the deep pulsing from her carotid artery make the blood pound through my lips. I move to a safer spot, an area that won't bring much pain or much blood. I take a deep breath, rub her back rhythmically, and, with the care of a surgeon, slip my teeth into her neck.

Tiny droplets of blood flow from her skin and settle onto my lips, running into my mouth and teasing the tip of my tongue with an enticing taste of sweetness laced with life and love—love for me. The astonishing taste fills my body with lust and arousal, and I become hyperaware of her breasts against me. I suck once, twice...she gasps with pleasure and wraps her legs tightly around mine. A strength rises from deep inside. This is real. Happiness is real, and I am strong enough to overcome this hell, to find heaven—and I don't have to die to do it, because I already have. Five months ago.

After the third suck, I withdraw, kissing the bite with tender affection. Emma pulls away a little and strokes my hair out of my face.

"Wow," she whispers. "That was...wow. Just..." Our lips meet; if she minds the taste of blood on mine, she says nothing. Her lips stroke mine with a forceful love that warms my heart and opens my soul. The tears come. They spill from my eyes as I kiss her back compassionately—I have never loved anyone so much in my life.

"You were right," I whispered to her. "I weakened myself without hope. I became too weak to remember life, to remember my spirit; I never really believed I could go to Heaven, or whatever beauty is out there. But you gave me hope again. You reminded me to believe in myself."

As she reaches up to wipe tears from her eyes, the golden orb pokes over the horizon. My face twists in a terrified cringe as I wait for the fire to start, to burn away my flesh until I'm nothing but a faint silhouette against the early morning light.

But it never comes. I slowly open my eyes and gaze into my hands, so white they're a blank canvas for the bright colors penetrating the air.

"Emma!" I gasp ecstatically. "I'm not burning! I'm not burning, Emma, look!" The light reflects off my ski, turning it a bright orangey-pink, but there's no smoke, no blackening, no searing pain. Just the caress of the cool April air. I gaze into the sun, the magical ball of light I haven't seen in what seems like an eternity. I can do it. Any moment now, I can let go. And, though the struggle to stay alive is becoming more and more difficult, I hesitate.

"Emma, I can't just die here. I can't just leave you like this. Dying in your arms and making you return me to my grave…I can't do that to you." My whole body is clenching in tremendous pain with the effort of hanging on for her. It feels like I'm gripping the edge of a cliff now, my fingers sliding off the rough, unforgiving rocks. If I stop trying right, now, just let myself free…it'll all be over. And yet I cling. For her.

She squeezes her eyes shut, then opens them again. Her voice holds a waver. "No," she whimpers. "No. Don't do that to yourself. The best gift you can give me is the one you have deserved all along: to be free." She chokes on the last words. It's obviously the toughest decision she's ever had to make.

"Emma." I gaze intently into her beautiful blue eyes. The eyes that have seen and endured so much pain, so much agony. "I know this will be difficult for you to believe, but you must understand that I will never, ever leave you, not even for a second. I will always be by your side. Promise me that whatever you do, you'll remember that and be happy."

She's still for a long time, not even daring to breathe. Tears fall out of her eyes and onto my chest. It's a long time before she speaks. "I promise."

"Thank God." I lean in gently and kiss her soft, pink lips. "I love you, Emma. I'll love you forever. Nothing will ever change it."

"And I'll love you forever, Amy. I will. You mean everything to me. You gave me my first kiss. My first love." She kisses me and cries into my shoulder. I manage to bring my hand up and run it through her soft red hair.

"Emma…" I whisper. "Emma, listen. Keep everything that will remind you I'm still with you. Take my corset too. Keep it forever."

"O-okay." She lets out a sob and kisses me one last time, her amazing lips caressing mine with a devotion only love can bring. Tears create rivers on my face and I can barely get out my very last words to her.

"I love you, Emma. I love you so, so much."

"I love you, too, darling. I love you too."

The sun shines bright orange in the colorful sky, its beams welcoming me to what I have yearned for since the beginning of time. The lovely colors of Heaven. My freedom.

Emma's lips gently touch my cheek, and I use the last of my strength to squeeze her hand. My eyes close for the final time, and my body is gone.

Chapter Forty-Three

Amy

No one would be expected to forgive them. Why should she? They're murderers, destroyers of life. They leech on people's everlasting spirits so they can have it for five minutes. No one should be expected to forgive them.

And yet I do. As I waft through the sky, a misty form appears before me and I recognize the face instantly.

"Amy."

I cringe away in fear. "Don't touch me!"

She shakes her head, smiles slightly. "No, Amy. I'm not her. I'm Victoria." Her face is beautiful, warm rather than icy. Her long blonde hair flows behind her as she opens her creamy-peach arms to me. I stare at her for a moment, caught between offering myself to the woman who's stolen everything I ever had and backing away like I believe she, Victoria, was at fault.

"I'm not going to hurt you, Amy."

I shake my head like I'm denying an accusation. "I understand. You have no reason to believe I won't hurt you." She puts

her arms down and sighs, then begins to move away, giving me one last smile.

No fangs.

"Wait."

"Yes?"

"Come back." I start towards her, we meet halfway, and I wrap my arms around her before she even offers a hand.

"I knew *her*. *She* was a monster. But I don't know you, except that I know your pain is probably even greater than mine." *I got raped, killed, and tortured too. But I never had to kill my loved ones.* Lying in her arms is terrifying for me, but I force myself to stay and keep speaking. "I wish I could have gotten to know you."

I feel her lips move next to my ear. "But I know you, Amy. I watched you all that time—I loved what I saw," she whispers. "I love you. I've loved you since the day I first saw you, when Madam Noctis came after you. It was terrible to see myself do all those dreadful things to you. I'm so, so sorry. You poor thing. I feel so guilty. I don't expect you to ever forgive me…"

"There's nothing *to* forgive—it wasn't your fault, Victoria. It was hers. And she wasn't you. You two haven't been the same since that demon separated you from your body and you lost control."

She snivels. "I should never have said yes."

I sigh jadedly. "Honestly, Victoria…given your circumstances, I think I probably would have done the exact same thing."

"I just had no idea that I had a side of me that was that…that…*evil.*"

"No one ever thinks that. Even after they become it."

"Do you think it's true? That in heaven there's no pain, no fear?"

I shrug. "I dunno. Maybe."

She smiles again. "You're the first woman I ever loved," she says. "I've wanted you for so long. I always watched you, wishing she would stop, wishing she wouldn't destroy your opinion of me." She sighs. "Thanks, Amy. For, you know…everything." And she's gone as quickly as she arrived.

She was in love with me. It all made sense—because I was her type. It made sense that her body craved mine and her soul loved me.

Poor Victoria. I don't know how I would ever be able to tolerate watching myself harm someone I love, night after night…

I tuck my legs into my chest and rest my cheek on my knees. I'm not going without my Emma. We're doing this together, I'm staying on earth and protecting her for the rest of her life, every moment—waking and sleeping. Until she's ready to join me, I'm there with her. I'm protecting her. I'm waiting for her.

Emma

We're moving to Laramie. No ifs, ands, or buts about it. We're not even waiting for the end of the school year. After everything, Robert and Jaquelina looked into what must be every city on the continent, and Laramie is the only one with no record of vampire attacks. With such a close call, they want to get us as far away from it all as possible. We have a nice new house there; it's an A-frame, with cathedral ceilings, a gorgeous view of the city, and a huge basement. Robert and Jaquelina say we're getting pool, air hockey, and ping-pong tables and they're gonna fix it up real nice.

But the only thing I ever knew Laramie for was the murder of someone different. Someone like me. I guess I can't be too paranoid, because its not like people are standing there with axe blades, just waiting for me to arrive. But still the notion instilled fear in my heart, if only for a moment.

The Mayflower we got is huge. I stand in the front yard, arms crossed tightly over my chest, watching as the fat mover with a chain hanging off his waist and the nearly skeletal one with the torn-up washed-out jeans haul the couch up the ramp. As I twist the tiny gold band on my finger, the last connection I have to Amy, the past few weeks play through my mind for about the fiftieth time that morning.

The night after Amy's death, I stayed in my room all evening, and then snuck back in from Jill's room and stayed up all night, waiting for Amy to arrive, just like always.

But she never did.

I didn't go to school the day after Amy's death, a bleak and rainy Wednesday. The sky was dark and a steady stream of rain poured from the sky. It was probably a good thing; Salt Lake City always needs rain. But I didn't feel good about it at all, because it brought my spirits lower when I thought I couldn't feel any more goddamn sickened.

Gone. Amy was gone. I'd never talk to her, never kiss her, never touch her again.

Robert and Jaquelina came into my bedroom at around one. They sat on my bed, where I was lazily playing PacMan. I'm so good at it I don't have to think about it; my mind was on nothing and no one but my one true love.

Neither one of them spoke for a few minutes.

"Emma?" Jaquelina finally began cautiously.

I looked up at them with my sad, angry face.

"Emma…" Jaquelina placed her hand over mine. "Emma…" She sighed and fell silent.

"You really loved her, didn't you?" Robert said softly, patting my leg. I nodded, holding back imminent tears.

"Emma…we're so, so sorry," Jaquelina whispered.

"So why did you try to kill her?"

"Because we were foolish," Robert confessed. "We had no proof that she was the one harming you, and we didn't listen when you tried to show us. We understand that, had we understood in time, we may have been able to help you protect Amy. You shouldn't have had to do all of that on your own. It's too heavy a burden for someone your age to be carrying."

"How do you know all that?"

"Your sisters talked to us."

"Did they? *They* believed me. *They* tried to help us through everything." I lost the game despite my skill and closed the computer screen to look them in the eyes. "Why couldn't you?"

Jaquelina sighed again.

"How did you even find out about the coven?"

"Darling," Robert whispered. "That's a long, sad story."

"Fine. Could you just leave me alone, please?"

"All right." Jaquelina patted my hand. She pulled her hair up absently as she stood and my eyes caught the two tiny scars on the side of her neck, right behind her left ear.

That night, as I lay in bed, trying futilely to sleep, I turned on the light and opened the top drawer of my bedside table and pulled out the pictures of Amy and me Jill had taken. There we were, the two of us, sitting in my closet. Our inside arms around each other's shoulders, our outside arms holding hands between our laps. Her beautiful blue-black hair shining in the closet light as it fell and curved gracefully around her breasts; her green eyes glowing with the fiery passion we'd felt for each other. I traced her full red lips with my index finger and move my own lips over each other, remembering how wonderful hers had felt on mine. *Oh, Amy.*

I looked at the next one, which was of her laying a gentle kiss upon my cheek. Tears fill my eyes. I remembered that kiss. I remembered it so well.

Her hugs, her kisses, her caresses…every display of love she gave me, from her gentle pats to her passionate strokes between my legs and inside my body, had passed so much energy to me, so much adoration, so much love…I remembered holding her, stroking her, feeling her soft, warm skin…how I missed her.

I love you, Emma. Her beautiful voice, an angel's echo, rang though my mind. *I love you so much.*

I buried my face in my pillow and wept.

Returning her to her grave was so difficult for me, I almost couldn't do it. But Amy had wanted me to be the one to return her, and no matter how much it killed me, I did it for her, the need to honor one of her last wishes overpowering my pain. We did it around noon on the day she died. I spent the entire morning crying, her lifeless body in my arms, until finally Jill came out and laid a hand on my shoulder.

"You have to let her go, sweetheart."

And so my sisters helped me carry her down and stayed outside the cemetery to give me a moment alone before I let her go.

With great difficulty, I carried her through the graveyard to the beautiful marble headstone that read *Amy Leanne Wyle, April 1, 1970, March 25, 1986.* Graceful engravings of doves and ribbons decorate both sides of it; that small poem lay just below her name and the dates. I kneeled in front of it and stared into her beautiful white face. Her body had changed a little; some of the blood had drained from her lips, turning them rosy-pink. I sat there for ten minutes, unable to make the move that I so deeply dreaded.

But it had to be done. Finally, after sitting with her body and crying silently for the better part of fifteen minutes and placing two copies of the pictures Jill took of us in her breast, I placed her against the stone and leaned in to give her lips a final kiss good-bye.

They were as soft and tender as they'd always been; the only difference was that, without a spirit to provide warm energy, they were colder with death than ever before. And they didn't kiss me back. Rivers of tears ran down my cheeks as I moved my lips over them passionately, almost willing her to return to life and give back my symbol of love. But she didn't, and I pulled away reluctantly, our lips the last parts the separate.

And, with a solemn evanescence, her body was gone and in its place was nothing but air.

I put my forehead in my knees and broke down.

About ten hours after we buried her, as I was getting ready for what I knew would be a painful, sleepless night, I discovered her little Emma doll in the corner of my closet. Had she left it one night? Why hadn't she noticed? My first instinct was to dig up her grave and give it back to her body, but then I realized how ludicrous that idea was and that she had her ring. Instead, I sewed Velcro on both dolls' hands and placed them together, tiny cloth hand in tiny cloth hand, on my pillow. I'm hoping that eventually they'll begin to serve as a reminder that Amy is still with me. But for the time being I just hold them in my arms each night as I cry myself to sleep.

Madam Noctis is dead. I still shock at the fact that I killed the woman that killed my girlfriend and tried to kill me. She put Amy through such pain, such misery, all those years, and I killed her. Despite what she told me the morning of her death, I sometimes wonder if Amy would have been sad that she had never done it. If she'd think that she was unable, that she was too weak.

I know better, and by the time she died, she'd overcome that self-doubt. She said it was because of the strength I gave to her.

I really don't know what happened to everyone else. Robert and Jaquelina managed to kill two of them, a man and a woman, but I'm unsure how many others there are. I wonder if there are vampires all over the world, taking life, devouring souls.

Those thoughts plaguing my mind, along with those of the permanent absence of my Amy, the other side of my bed cold and empty, I bitterly wept myself into a stunned half-sleep.

Our last day at Clear Creek Central was also the last day before spring break. And everyone went *nuts*. I must have looked like a thundercloud in a sea of suns, but I couldn't help it. In one year, I'd lost the two most important people in the world to me. My spirit was broken. My sisters tried to cheer me up, but it rarely worked. It seemed hopeless. I'd never feel better.

We were doing a watercolor unit in painting. Mrs. Larson was trying to demonstrate salting techniques to the class on April 12, but no one listened. A blonde girl, Anna, could not stop singing a parody of "Stayin' Alive" and Tesa lost control after the demo, laughing like she was on gas and almost knocking me over by mistake as I went to dump my water in the sink. Others seemed to be catching Tesa and Anna's cheer, but all it did was annoy me. How could people be so happy? Is this how I had been before mother got sick? And how come they got to be so happy when I was trying futilely to recover from the death of my very first lover?

"Emma," Mrs. Larson called as I headed for the door when the bell rang, signaling the end of the day.

"Mm?"

"Do you have a first wave bus?"

I shook my head. "Third wave."

"Then come here, honey. I want to talk to you." She pulled one of the stools off the tables and sat. I followed her lead and took down another one.

"Emma, what's going on?" she asked, the lines around her eyebrows darkening as concern covered her face. "You've seemed very unhappy recently, and…and I just think you need to talk to someone. You don't have to tell me, but I'd like you to get your feelings out."

I sighed. We were moving, and I'd never see Mrs. Larson again. No more secrets. "Jill used to speak a lot more than she does."

"I believe it."

"But, like I said at the beginning, something awful happened to us last summer and…we've had a lot of trouble getting over it."

"What is it?"

I took a deep breath. She would be the first non-relative I told, next to Amy. "Our mother died."

"Oh—!"

"Of breast cancer. After four years of hopeless treatment. We all sort of expected it, but...but...I don't know. We moved out here from Maine last fall, because our father was granted custody. He and Mom divorced when I was really young and he's lived out here since. He never called us or even wrote."

"Oh, Emma..." Her face twisted in sympathy. "I'm so, so sorry."

I nodded. "Also..." I stopped. What was I thinking? Telling Mrs. Larson about Mama was one thing, but was I really going to tell her about *Amy?* But I felt a need to. I felt like, if I told someone I trusted but didn't live with, I might feel a little better. Who knew? Maybe she'd give me some good advice.

"What, Emma?"

I wondered if it would be a mistake to just come out to her. Maybe I should make sure she supports me first? But I trusted her, more so than any other adult right now, and I took a shaky breath and fingered my wedding ring. "Well, last month, my...my...my girlfriend died too."

A look of horror gripped Mrs. Larson's face. "Oh, darling..."

I shook my head, squeezing reluctant tears from my eyes. "It was her time. She was trapped in a reality she didn't deserve, and she was really unhappy, and I know a peaceful death was what she deserved. I know it's selfish of me to cry like this, because she was really hurting, but...but..." The tears began to flow more easily.

"It's not selfish," Mrs. Larson said. "It's not selfish!" she insisted as my wails grew louder. She took me in her arms and rocked me back and forth while I let all the pain out.

"She was...she was...she understood me like no one else ever had. I mean, she was so sweet, and I loved her so much, and she was my first love, and..." I can't even finish. Mrs. Larson held me close to her and rubbed my back rhythmically, trying her hardest to soothe me.

"Emma," she whispered, looking into my eyes. "When I was a bit younger than you, I lost a lover too."

My eyes widened. "Really?"

"Yeah. It was sudden and really difficult. One day she was there and the next...she was gone."

"She? You mean..."

"Yes, Emma. I am."

I heaved a heavy sigh, the shock of Mrs. Larson's revelation taking some of the sobs out of me. I had known she was a lot like me, that she understood me like no other teacher of mine ever had, but I had had no idea we shared something as intimate as sexual identity.

"Emma," she whispered after a moment. "That drawing in your sketchbook, the one of the girl with the long dark hair…was that her?"

I nodded, wiping a final tear away.

"She was beautiful. She looked a lot like my girlfriend did."

"I'm going to miss you, Mrs. Larson."

"I'll miss you too. You were one of my best students. You weren't difficult and you cared about me when others didn't. I really appreciate that."

"Can I write to you?"

"Of course, love. My email is on the school's website."

I finally stood and sighed. Time to leave yet another person I love. "Thank you, Mrs. Larson," I said as I put my stool up.

"Anytime, honey."

"You were the best teacher here." *The only one who really seemed to get me. The only one I felt spiritually connected to.*

She smiled sadly, stepped forward and hugged me. I wished the moment didn't have to end, because in her arms I felt safe, protected from the horrible world. Just like I was in Mama's arms.

"Bye, Emma," she bid softly.

"Bye, Mrs. Larson. I'll never forget you."

As I turned to leave, I caught sight of her nametag that I'd never really examined. *Kelly Larson. Teacher.* And as I walked out the door, I realized suddenly why that picture of Amy's old girlfriend had looked so familiar to me.

The next morning, the Saturday after Amy died, I took a heart-shaped iron ornament to her grave and pushed it into the soil. I kissed the headstone, sat against it, and closed my eyes. The body of my sweetheart was right below me; this was as close as I could possibly get to her now.

Why couldn't we have been together?

"Hello," a deep voice greeted. I jumped and looked up; a tall young man, probably in his early thirties, stood over me, a tiny angel ornament in hand.

"Oh, hi," I returned, quickly wiping my tears and standing. The man set the little iron angel on the base of Amy's grave and turned to look at me. He was striking; mildly pale skin, big, bright green eyes, and pointy facial features. A mat of straight black hair hung, a few inches long, around his ears and eyes, shimmering navy blue in the sunlight. And, despite my homosexuality, I felt a tug of attraction to him. He looked an awful lot like a male version of Amy…perhaps that was why?

"Do you have a connection to Amy?" he asked.

"Y-yes," I stuttered.

He laughed. "She was my older sister. We had a lot of fun together and were really close." He sighed. "She passed away when I was only nine years old."

A shock spread through me. Was this…could it be?…

"*Nathan?*" I asked incredulously, without thinking.

"Nathan Wyle," he replied, holding out his hand. "That's my name. Don't wear it out." He gave a lighthearted laugh that made my heart soar.

"I'm Emma. Emma Levesque." I shook his hand and dropped mine. He gave me a twisted smile and turned back to the grave.

"She wasn't really dead, was she?"

"What?"

"She wasn't really dead. She was still alive."

"Well, not exactly—I mean—"

"She was undead. A vampire. Right?"

My jaw dropped. "How did you—I mean, how do you—"

He stood, exhaling audibly. "I know they're out there. And I know you know because you're too young to know her from her life."

"Have you known all along?"

"Since college. In our junior year, my wife, Sara—she was just my girlfriend then—suddenly got very pale and weak. We lived together, so I watched over her the first day. By mid-afternoon, she was complaining of bad neck pain, so I took her to a doctor. They found a bite right behind her ear. They said it looked like it came from large dog, but she hadn't been bitten by one. After a few more tests, the doctors sent us home, saying painkillers would probably do the trick. Later that night, when I got home from the drugstore, I found her in our bed—and something was lying on top of her.

When I walked in, it looked up and saw me—" He shuddered. "It was horrible; I could see her blood dripping from his teeth in the hall light. He ran and didn't come back. But I remembered my sister, and her sudden and inexplicable death. Her sickness was so remarkably similar to Sara's. And I had suspected ever since. And then…" He lowered his face to mine and speaks in a soft voice. "I saw her."

"I know. She told me."

"Did she? I was visiting old family friends from this neighborhood, and when I was getting in the car to leave, I saw her. Staring at me with those green eyes of hers. The moon was full, and I knew I saw her. Her eyes were inhumanly bright, and her skin was too pale, but I knew it was her standing there, looking just as she did when she was sixteen. I knew those eyes and I knew that hair. For a few seconds I thought I was hallucinating. Or crazy. But then I remembered Sara, and…that was that."

"She was a vampire," I told him. "But she also wasn't."

"What?"

"Amy was different from the other vampires because she still had her soul in her heart. It's a complicated story, but the point is that she didn't need blood and she hated killing people. She was just like a human, except that the only thing she needed to take in was water."

Hope brightened his face. "Can I ever see her?"

Oh, God. Why does this have to happen now, so close to the end of her life? If it were just a month earlier…

"She died a few days ago, Nathan. She was bitten again, and she—bled to death." I was choking up.

His face fell into a look of absolute suffering, and I felt the dam holding in my emotions break. I started crying.

"It's better this way," I insisted. "She's not suffering anymore."

Nathan bent on one knee. "Did you know her well?"

"We were together all winter," I replied. "She was…"

"Your girlfriend."

I nodded, sobbing now. "I—I—I loved her, Nathan."

He patted my knee knowingly. "She was an incredibly lovable girl."

I sighed, trying to catch control, but it took a few minutes. "L-listen, Nathan," I finally managed, "don't worry about Amy's life as a vampire. She was a wonderful girl, and she was very happy before she died. We were both happier once we found each other. I was really sad when we met because my mother died. But she made it...she made my life better."

"That sounds like Amy," Nathan laughed.

"How is...the rest of the family?" I asked hesitantly.

He shook his head. "Our mother died recently."

My head snapped up at this.

"Yeah. After Amy's death, she became manic-depressive, and one day I guess her body just couldn't take it anymore. Her heart gave out two years ago. She was in her early sixties, lived a good life, I guess. The two of them were so close. I guess they're together again. After all these years." He stood. "I really need to get home. Sara's gonna want me to help her with Amanda and Jacob." He grinned at me. "Our children."

My heart swelled as I hear the word *children*. Amy had a niece and a nephew. My eyes fell in grief as I imagine what an amazing aunt she would have been to those kids...and what an amazing mother she would have been to her own.

"I—I should go, too." I stood up and brushed off my backside.

"Nice to meet you, Emma." He shook my hand again.

"You too."

I sat on my balcony, writing the story Amy had inspired. It was coming along well, but how on earth could I end it on a happy note? I wanted my books to have happy endings, but this was basically autobiographically based, and I didn't feel a spark of happiness in the ending Amy and I had. So maybe Amy is finally free. Maybe that's what's right. I certainly know that, even though it hurts, it's what I wanted for her too.

But how on earth could it be happy, how on earth could it be right, if we weren't together?

I looked out into the front yard, where Amy had died in my arms only a week before. A tear fell onto my keyboard, and I wiped it off with the bottom edge of my shirt. I miss her so much. She'd promised me she'd be with me always, but for some reason, I felt more alone than ever. I touched my lips, desperate for her kiss. The kiss that was lost to me forever.

That wasn't fair. I'd promised Amy I'd be happy, and I was not. I knew I needed to make friends, knew she'd wanted me to. But I just couldn't find the strength within me.

I gazed into the sunset, something that both of us adored, and wondered if she was sitting next to me. The colors were so brilliant. It was like it was when Amy had died, only on opposite side of the sky. Many times, we'd sat together on that very bench and talked, hugged, and kissed. I wanted her so badly; it was so hard to bear. I heard the door open and shut, saw a shock of red hair out of the corner of my eye. "Hi Jill."

She laughed. "How did you know it was me?"

"Cosmic twin sister."

She grinned, put her hand over mine.

"Do you remember that idiot who spoke out against gays on TV the other night?" I asked. "What an intolerant boob."

"Oh yeah. He was pretty bad, huh?"

"Yeah."

"There's so much intolerance in the world, Emma. Did you ever notice how the vast majority of cruelty in the world is a result of the intolerance in people like him?"

I remembered thinking about vampires being an analogy to human evil, sigh heavily. The world is so screwed up.

"Jill…"

"Yes?"

I tell her about the analogy, and about what Amy had told me about evil taking your soul.

"Wow. Evil as a result of hatred as a result of bias. So many connections! You know, the evil vampires set upon us is horrible, but…not much worse than, say, the Holocaust."

The Holocaust. One of the most horrifying events in history. Nearly everyone who didn't fit the description of "perfection" was heartlessly slaughtered…Jews, Muslims, handicaps, most anyone of a different race, homosexuals…homosexuals.

"Gays were killed in the Holocaust. Both Amy and I would have been killed. And for what? For loving each other. For daring to care so deeply about each other we'd give up our souls. There's nothing wrong with us. I'm a Jew, so I'm 'doubly guilty'…"

"Oh, God, Emma, I know. And you're such an amazing person. You're going to do something amazing for the world. The fact that you're Jewish and a lesbian mean nothing to your true value. It's too bad Hitler couldn't see that."

I shrugged. Another thought had slipped into my mind. Since that horror is so easily represented by vampires, that horror had kind of killed Amy anyway, even though the Holocaust had been forty years before her time...

"What happened to Amy, exactly?" Jill asked.

I sighed. "Her body is dead. Really. Dead. Her soul has moved on."

"Ah."

"I think our relationship saved her soul from the hell of her body. It's like I saved
her or something."

"You said that Amy said evil consumes your soul, right?"

"So?"

"But you saved her soul? After she was turned?"

"Yeah." My eyes widened with realization. Evil was after Amy's soul for twenty years, but in only five months I had been able to save her from it.

"So...are you saying that if evil takes your soul, love will save it?"

Jill smiled. "Just a thought, honey."

My God. It's just as Amy said. *I believe that love is the strongest force in the universe, Emma. I believe it conquers everything.*

"She isn't gone, you know," Jill said.

"I know."

"I know you know. But I don't think you *know*. I don't think you feel it, believe it in your heart."

I shrugged.

"You need to believe that, Emma. You need to believe that the girl you love is still with you."

"You mean 'loved'."

"No, I mean love. So her body has died. Does that mean you don't love her anymore?"

"I....I guess not—"

"And she loves you too. She hasn't left you."

I'm out of words. Jill places her hand on my leg. "True love is too strong for earthly limitations, Emma. True love lasts as long as you feel it. That could be forever. She's always with you, Emma. *Always.*" She squeezes my knee.

I hold in a sob. A tear escapes my eye and I wipe it away angrily.

She hugs me gently. "Let them fall."

On our last night in Salt Lake, I lay in bed with my Emma and Amy dolls in my arms, staring at my clockless lampless bedside table and all the boxes piled in my room, no more than dark shapes in the little light pouring through the crack in my bedroom door.

We're still together, I kept thinking to myself. *We're still together. We're still together.*

And I still don't believe that.

It was another one of those flying dreams, I thought at first. It was also one of those dreams where you figure out you're dreaming, but you can't force it to end. Lucid dreams, I think they're called. I was soaring above the bright orange clouds, the cool air blowing over my face. The gleaming pink waters of Great Salt Lake twinkled below, just visible beyond the giant cloud. I closed my eyes and smiled, enjoying it.

"Emma!" My eyes shot open. It couldn't be!

"*Amy!*" I threw myself into her arms in a fit of tears. "Amy! *Amy!*"

"Shhh, shhhh." I felt the familiar tickle in my scalp as she runs her fingers through my hair. "Shhh, Emma, it's all right. It's all right."

I felt hiccups escape my chest as I let the tears fall. She stroked my hair, rubbed my back, rocked me back and forth. Intense feeling flew through every nerve in my body. Love, misery, joy. I was overcome, lying in her arms and never wanting that moment to end. Never. I never wanted to let her go. I didn't want to lose her again.

"Oh, Emma," she whispered, kissing the top of my head. "It's all right, dear. I'm here for you, lovely. I'm here for you."

I looked up into her face. It was her, it was my Amy, but she was different; her skin was still pale, though now a bit darker than mine, her cheeks were rosy, her lips a dark shade of pink rather than off-red, and I realized this was what she must have looked like in life. She gave a smile that made my heart flutter; her beautiful white teeth caught the sunlight, but her fangs were gone now. She was still Amy, but she'd lost her haunting perfection; now her appearance was inviting, comforting, like that of a human. She was less like a vampire. More like a woman. I buried my face in her chest, inhaling her tantalizing scent. "I missed you so much!"

"Sweet baby. I know the truth can be hard to understand or to accept at first." I felt her chest heave in a small giggle. "Believe me, I know. But it's all right, because you freed me. You saved me from the horror of a lonely, everlasting existence as one of the Undead. You encouraged me to stand up to Madam Noctis and to fight for what I had, although I only had two things to fight for."

"What things?" I whispered, although I already knew the answer.

She ran her hand over my hair. "The only two things that could possibly mean more to me than anything else. The only two things that were worth risking everything for. One was my soul. The other was you."

I squeezed her even more tightly.

"And you also gave me the strength to believe in myself and to let my body die peacefully. If you hadn't been there for me, if I had been alone like I was before I met you, the weakness that had taken over me would have caused me to die cold and miserable. But thanks to you"—she kissed my cheek—"I died happy. You saved me from that weakness. You saved my life."

"Oh, Amy," I whispered.

"Yes?"

"When I killed Madam Noctis, I thought that vampires, you know, might be kind of a literal manifestation of the evil humans carry out."

"That's an interesting thought."

I released a heavy sigh. "How many are there? How many more must I kill?"

She let out a hopeless-sounding giggle. "I'm afraid that you'll never be able to get rid of vampires. They're everywhere, all over the world. Your idea about them being nothing worse than the dark side of humans is good, you know, and I'm afraid that as long as there are humans to feed their race, there will be vampires. As long as there's cruelty in people's hearts, there will be vampires out there to thrive on it. That's just the way it goes, darling."

"But…they steal people's souls."

"Well so does our dark side. If we let it."

"I'd never let it."

"I know you wouldn't."

We were silent for a moment, and the cool breeze blew my flowing dress around the skirt of hers. Then a thought struck me and I looked into her spirited green eyes.

"Please take me with you."

"Oh, baby, I can't."

"Why not?"

"You have so much going for you. You have a life ahead of you. You have talent, you passion, potential, and you're going to go so far. If I took you now, I'd be robbing you of all that!"

"But…" I snivel. "But…"

"I know my body isn't with you anymore, Emma. But I still am. I know it's hard for you, but I need you to push on. When I died in 1985, the truth was hard for me to accept. It was so hard that I thought I'd never adjust to the bitter life I was given. Remember how I wanted to commit suicide, because I thought there was no better way out? But I didn't, because something told me to keep trying, that I could to it. And what happened because of that?"

The clouds encircled us lightly, colored the brilliant hues the sun painted them with. "I-I—what?"

She smiled, her eyes welling with tears. "I found you." And she leaned in and put her lips to mine tenderly, lovingly, her soft black hair tickling my cheek. Her love coursed through my body and soul, giving me a feeling of warmth and rebirth. She lifted my chin. "Can you do that for me? Can you live?"

After letting a tear slide down my cheek, I nodded. She smiled. "...and when you and I are together up here, we'll come back, live the life we've always wanted. Together."

"We're leaving in twenty minutes, girls."

It's now or never. I take the bouquet of roses—Amy's favorite flower—into my hands and hurry down the long gravel driveway, the driveway I've walked down so many times, to the park, to the bus stop, to save Amy's life…the driveway I'll now never see again. Every battle scene, every place Amy and I cuddled, snuggled, kissed, touched…I'm leaving it all behind.

But I'd still have my bed. The bed in which Amy and I did the biggest, most impacting and divine thing we'd ever done, the bed in which we let each other in, slowly became one, one soul, one entity, one being…it's with me still, just as she always will be.

I wanted to plant the flowers, but I won't be around to care for them. So I'm bringing them in a vase instead. They'll last a few days, but better to bloom and die than to never live.

The cemetery is peaceful, the sun shining brightly on the headstones and glittering on the glass sculptures on the newest ones. Amy's stone stands tall and proud, and I place the flowers on the base next to Nathan's angel. The sunlight in the graveyard seems to give the place a feeling of hope, a small piece of heaven shining on a place that harbors evil.

The headstone is cool against my lips, and I walk away slowly, not wanting to look away. "I'll come back, my love," I whisper. "I'll come back as soon as I can. I promise, Amy. I promise."

And so I turn, face the iron entrance and the virgin yellow of the midmorning sun, ready to face my new life. With Amy by my side.

MEET THE AUTHOR

SARAH NATALIA LEE

Sarah Natalia Lee was born in a dusty old town in Idaho. She began writing at the age of seven, creating original children's stories even though she could barely spell. She continued writing until she finished Saving Amy, her first full-length novel. She plans to write inspiring, meaningful novels until the end of her life.

Sarah's writing is inspired by many things: music, art, writing, movies, even the scenery around her home. Anything that speaks to her has the potential to influence a story. The rest she acquires from her own experiences and her feeling that a certain issue needs to be addressed in a book. Saving Amy was inspired by a performance of Dracula, and much of its tone was inspired by Fallen, debut album of the rock band Evanescence.

She has one pet: a black-and-white English setter she describes as "spunky, affectionate, intelligent and stupid at the same time...likes to sleep all day and explode energy after dinner." An avid artist, Sarah plans to teach at a middle- or high-school level after earning her bachelor's in art education. She also hopes to pursue a personal career as an artist, working in the mediums of drawing, painting, glass, beads, and jewelry.

Printed in the United States
120035LV00008B/140/P